EXPERIMENTAL HEART

PIECES

BOOK 2

SHANNON PEMRICK

Pieces
Experimental Heart | Book Two

Cover Illustration by Jackson Tjota
Cover Typography by Amalia Chitulescu
Editing by Sandra Nguyen and Cody Anne Arko-Omori

ISBN 978-0-9912213-7-0 (paperback)
ISBN 978-0-9912213-6-3 (hardcover)
ISBN 978-0-9912213-8-7 (e-book)

To Sammie
For your unwaivering support, inspiration and dedication to seeing this story come to life.

And

To my friends, Joe, Frank, Kathryn, and Taryn
Your support, help, and silly ideas, shaped the path of this series more than you'll ever know.

BOOKS BY SHANNON PEMRICK

EXPERIMENTAL HEART
Destiny
Pieces
Secrets
Exposed
Surrendered
Reborn

ORACLE'S PATH
Prophecy of Convergence

Prophecy Tested
Prophecy Chosen

LOOKING FOR GROUP
Spellbinding His Ranger
Protecting His Priestess
Summoning Their Elementalist

My gaze remained on the wall as I stared hopelessly. Rylan had been dragged away some time ago and I refused to sleep until he returned. He would be the last for the night, the soldiers were that predictable, but that wasn't my reason for remaining awake. I was responsible for the torture he endured. I would remain awake until he came back.

I glanced at the cell door when boots stomped down the hall. Moments later, two soldiers showed up with a white-haired, tan-skinned man in their arms. He hung limply, and I worried Rylan hadn't done so well this time around.

The soldiers threw him into the cell carelessly and slammed the door. The moment they left, Rylan got to his feet and sat down next to Ryoko—his state a ruse to throw off his torturers. I had no doubts he'd used his ice abilities to keep himself safer. Knowing he was fine, I closed my eyes, allowing unconsciousness to follow—and the memories.

CHAPTER 1

He's my son."

Dalatrend bustled with life, even at this late hour. Streetlamps lit up every street of the four quadrants, and spotlights illuminated the fortress at the far end of the city belonging to our *ruler*, Zarda. Cats fought in the alleys, people shouted, and cars roared and honked in the sleepless night. My violet hair moved with the slight breeze, and the full moon's light bathed my light skin in a silver sheen as I stared out from my perch on top of our house. The battle from earlier, while seemingly unknown by the rest of the city's occupants, weighed heavy on my mind.

Even though we had won, the battle took a toll on our supplies and numbers. Two things we couldn't afford to be so careless with.

I turned away from the city when a door leading back into the house opened. A young man, appearing not much older than I, maybe his early thirties, with tan skin, short black and red hair, and black facial hair, walked out onto the roof and looked around. His sapphire eyes rested on me and then he shook his head. "Of all the places you could be, Eira, you chose to be up here again?"

I crossed my arms. "Yes, Raikidan, I am up here. Getting away allows me to think. Today has been a bit stressful."

He held up his hands. "No need to get testy."

My jaw clenched. He was right. That snap was uncalled for. "Do you need something from me, or are you a lost puppy looking for home?"

"I'm not a lost puppy…" he muttered. "I came up here to see if we could talk."

My brow rose. "About?"

"Ryder."

I resisted sighing. Ever since I had dropped the bombshell about Ryder's connection to me after the battle, I had avoided Raikidan because of the questions I'd receive. He'd make it out to be a bigger issue than it really was.

I shrugged. "I guess. I don't see what needs to be talked about. He's my son. Nothing crazy there."

Raikidan crossed his arms. "You claim you don't want to be close to anyone, especially males, and then you say you have a son, but it's no big deal?"

"What part of 'we're tank-born' don't you get?" I asked. "I didn't choose to have him, but that doesn't deny who he is."

He held up his hands. "All right, all right. I guess I can go with that. So who's his father, then?" I shifted my gaze away from him. "Eira?"

"It's…" I sighed. "It's Rylan…"

"Wait, what?"

I looked him in the eye. "Rylan is his father."

"Yeah, I got that part, but I don't know. I'm just really confused. I thought you said Rylan and you are only friends. You said you had no, and still don't have any, attraction to him in the least."

"And you would be correct. There isn't anything between me and Rylan. We are only friends." Raikidan's brow rose in question and I exhaled slowly in irritation. "Ryder wasn't Rylan's or my choice. He was Zarda's. Zarda figured using my DNA and Rylan's DNA was a good idea, so he made it so. That's how it goes with us. What Zarda wants, damn everyone to hell if he doesn't get it."

"So why you two?"

"Because of the bond. Even though Zarda scrapped the project, he still had great interest in its potential. He believed the bond has special DNA properties even though none of it could be proven. So he ordered the geneticists to combine Rylan's and my DNA, with the demand the only alteration made was life longevity attempts. Zarda assumed with the types of DNA he was combining, Ryder wouldn't need much more alteration."

"All right. I think I get, it but why is he so young? I thought you said you guys don't come out of your tanks unless you're around seventeen."

I sat down and nodded. "That's true, but there was a problem."

Raikidan walked over and sat down next to me. "What kind of problem?"

"Ryder stopped developing, and the longer they kept him in there in hopes it would resume, the faster his life force faded. Not wanting to lose him, they took him out. He didn't grow past the age of ten."

"So was it the alteration that messed things up or the accelerated growth?"

I shook my head. "They didn't accelerate his growth. They didn't want to risk it since Rylan and I hadn't had that kind of treatment. They feared the acceleration might kill him."

"I see." There was something off about the tone in his voice. Like he was piecing something together that wasn't a part of this conversation. "So when you found out about Ryder, how did that affect you guys?"

"Well…" I thought for a moment to figure out how to word myself. It wasn't something I wanted to say, but he would keep pestering me until I did. "Rylan… Rylan thought he could use Ryder as a tool to get me to care for him. He figured if we had something to connect with, together, then I might change my mind."

Raikidan snorted. "Even I know that wouldn't work."

I laughed. "Well, you're a little smarter than him, because he tried it and it pissed me off enough where I wouldn't even look at him for five months."

"Ouch. A little harsh, don't you think?"

I snorted. "Hardly. I had been fed up with him not listening to me in the first place. And the fact that he thought he could use a child as a tool disgusted me. I couldn't stomach looking at him. But harsh or not, the treatment got Rylan to understand I didn't see him that way. My refusal to acknowledge him at all showed him the depth of my rejection. I didn't want to crush him as bad as I did, but it was the only way he'd give up. It was the only way I knew I could get him to stop."

"So what is Ryder's opinion on the matter?"

"He… he doesn't know."

Raikidan's brow rose. "What do you mean, he doesn't know?"

"I mean, he doesn't know Rylan is his father. Or, as far as I know he doesn't. I decided it would be best not to tell him."

"How does Rylan feel about this?"

"He hates it. He fought with me for a long time over it. He still thinks I made the wrong choice. He thinks I'm being selfish."

"But you don't think you are?"

I shook my head. "I thought it would only make the situation worse. With Ryder's developmental issues, he's got a mind that's stuck between a child and a grown man. If Ryder knew the truth about his lineage, it would only confuse him. He would struggle to understand why Rylan and I weren't together. I wouldn't do that to him because it wouldn't be fair. No matter how much Rylan wanted Ryder to know, at that time, I knew it wouldn't be right. Now that time has passed I just wait for him to ask. I figure that's the best way to tell him because by then he'll be ready to know."

Raikidan went quiet. Discomfort fell over me. The silenced didn't feel right. I stood to leave, given our conversation was over, but Raikidan grabbed my hand and pulled me back down.

"You want to talk about something else?" I asked. "Because there's nothing more to say about this current topic."

Raikidan looked at me, but still didn't speak. His expression wasn't readable, making it hard for me to figure out what was up. Then suddenly, he reached up and stroked my cheek with the back of his finger. My eyes grew wide and my breath caught with his sudden, bold behavior. He leaned closer to me.

I pulled away. "What are you doing?"

He attempted to move closer again and lightly touched my chin. "I still want that kiss."

I pushed him back by his face. "I just get done telling you I have a kid and you want a kiss from me? What is with you? Most would want nothing to do with me after that, regardless of the fact my son is tank-born."

He pulled my hand off his face. "I just want to know what it feels like. It doesn't matter that you told me you have a son or that you rejected Rylan, his father. It's not like this is supposed to mean anything. It's just a kiss. I want to know what it feels like."

I scoffed and rose to my feet. "I told you, find a hooker to kiss. I won't do it."

"Why do you have such a problem with this? It's just a kiss."

"You don't get it, Raikidan. A kiss is never just a kiss. It's supposed to mean something. That's the point of a kiss. Depending on the emotion placed into it makes it different every time."

"I don't understand. You're just pressing your lips against someone else's."

"Obviously you don't get it! There are different types of kisses. There's one for each emotion you place into it." I peered out at the city, my arms crossed.

"Eira, what are you not telling me?"

So much, you have no idea. My chest swam with all manner of negative emotions the longer my mind remained on this topic. *A kiss can be a lie too...* I let out a quiet breath and walked over to the door. "Stop trying to get a kiss out of me, Raikidan. It's not going to feel the way you think it will, and I don't want to be a part of it. Keep your mouth away from mine."

I shut the door behind me and headed for a different place to be alone. If I didn't, I wouldn't be able to stay calm, and I didn't want to lose it over such a topic.

❦

It was dark—more than dark. It was black. I couldn't see anything. I couldn't hear anything. I looked around frantically, but I was alone. There was no doubt about it. The empty feeling that loneliness brought, crept all over my body. I didn't like it. I didn't like being alone. Then I heard it. It was quiet at first, but it became louder.

"Eira." My eyes darted around, searching for the person calling to me. "Eira."

The voice was masculine. I knew this voice, but I couldn't remember whom it belonged to. I didn't like that. I wanted to put a name, a face even, to the voice.

"Eira." I ran for it. I needed to find the source. I needed to feel like I wasn't alone. "Eira."

I spun around. The voice came from behind me now. Or maybe I had gone the wrong way.

"Laz." I liked how the voice said this name. I liked how it rolled off his tongue. I wanted him to say my name like that all the time. "Laz."

I stopped dead and cranked my neck. The voice's direction changed, confusing me. Where was it coming from?

"Laz. Laz. Laz." I held my head. It was coming from all directions. "Laz!"

I fell to my knees and screamed. "Someone help me! Please, help me. I don't want to be alone anymore…"

"Laz…"

The grip on my head tightened and the feeling of loneliness gripped tighter. Then a new feminine voice spoke—one I recognized. She had no face—no name. She was the darkness inside me.

"You cannot find it. Loneliness is your only destiny."

I punched the black ground. I wanted it all to go away. I wanted to be free of this place.

"Please… someone… anyone… save me…"

CHAPTER 2

The clouds gathered at a rapid pace. Dark and sinister, they signified a bad storm was heading our way. It would put a damper on our assignment, but I wouldn't think of that now. Right now I had to focus on the task at hand, and that was pretending to hold a conversation with a comrade of mine at this large café while trying to overhear any important information.

The information seeking wasn't great, and my conversation skills were even worse. I didn't know this comrade well, which was a common problem for me with most of the team since I rarely ever saw them, but he was patient. I remembered his name was Kent and he had a cat. I blinked slowly in realization that in the hour we had been talking, that was all I could remember about him. Had I not been paying attention, or did I really not find this information interesting enough to remember?

Kent continued to smile at me as I thought of something to tell him. I hadn't come up with much in the past hour, and I felt sorry for him. I had forced him to talk so much, but as I observed at him, I could tell he didn't mind.

He glanced over to a corner of the café. "Tell me about your friend."

I glanced over to see whom he was talking about and suppressed a sigh. Raikidan sat, arms crossed, at a corner table. He glared at me, although to most people he would have looked emotionless. I realized I was getting really good at reading him.

He's still pissed at me. He didn't want to wear the black hair dye. I figured he would have liked it more since it was closer to one of his natural hair colors.

"The hell I'm okay with this, Eira!" he said. *"This stuff stinks and I can still smell it long after it's washed out."*

"Well, you're just going to have to deal with it, Rai. This is how we do things. You offered to help, and now you're stuck doing it our way. I warned you, but you still insisted on helping. Now quit being a baby and finish getting ready. I laid clothes out for you on your bed."

I didn't care, though. I was still angry with him, so he could be pissy all he wanted.

"This is stupid. You should be shedding blood, not hiding in plain sight and failing at getting information that isn't there."

I rounded on him. "Shedding blood solves nothing! Nothing good comes of it. I learned that long ago. It just creates more problems!"

I had stormed out of the bathroom and slammed the door after that the argument, and we hadn't spoken to each other since. I had driven us to this café in silence, and we had parted the same way.

I shrugged. "Nothing really to say. He's quiet mostly."

"No wonder the simulator paired you two up," he teased.

I sighed and stirred my tea. "The simulator pairs you up for battle. That's it."

"Uh-oh, sounds like the two of you are fighting."

I grunted. "Something like that."

"Tell me about it."

I shook my head. "It's not important."

"It must be if you have to fight over it."

I chuckled. "No, really, it's not. It's over something really stupid."

"Like what?"

"Hair color."

His brow rose. "Hair color?"

I played with my teaspoon. "Yeah, I told you it was stupid."

He chuckled as he shook his head. "I don't know. It had to be important to someone for it to have caused a fight so bad neither of you will talk to each other."

I sucked air through my teeth. "It's my fault really. I'm not good at talking."

As I had been sitting here I had honestly started to think this. Had I been more willing to hear Raikidan out on the matter than to brush off his concern, we may have come to a better understanding.

He waved me off. "I doubt it's solely you. Sure, you struggle with something most people would think comes as second nature, but you're not bad at conveying your points. Blunt, yes, but sometimes that's what we need."

I played with my tea some more. "Yeah, but only sometimes."

"We should probably leave." I glanced up at him, brow lifted. "We're not going to find anything out. I've been on these assignments for over a month and haven't learned a thing. Either there really isn't anything new going on or these soldiers have learned to keep their mouths shut."

I sighed and stood. "I guess you're right."

Kent followed the motion and the two of us left after disposing of our dishes. We parted ways when we made it to my car, and I sat on the hood to wait for Raikidan to finally come out. I was surprised by how long I had to wait. I expected him to come out almost immediately, showing how much he didn't want to be on this assignment. I waited for him to reach the car before I went to the driver side.

"What, no complaints about my lateness?"

I ignored him and unlocked the car. Once I was situated in my seat, I made sure my foot was on the clutch and started her up. Raikidan slid into the passenger seat, and I shifted my car into gear, cruising down the road without a care. We had some time to kill, and I didn't need to be scolded by a child for abandoning my assignment too soon.

I glanced at Raikidan. He had been trying to talk to me, his lips moving, but nothing came out. I focused back on the road, content to continue to ignore him. *Looks like I still have it.* My mentor, Shyden, taught me the trick. It allowed us to concentrate better on tasks that didn't require us to be aware of our surroundings. It also made it easier to live in the city and put up with people.

The city streets passed by as I took turns aimlessly. I didn't worry about getting lost. If I had to, I'd use the built-in map Argus installed to get back.

I glanced down at my hand when something warm touched it, to find Raikidan's hand enveloping mine. I let go of the stick, smacking his hand away. "Do you mind not trying to hold my hand? Thanks."

"You aren't listening to me."

"I don't have to if I don't want to."

"I've been trying to tell you to make a turn to go somewhere. Did you even hear a single word I said?"

"No."

He let out a heavy breath. "Just take this turn up here."

"Why should I?"

"Because I want you to."

"You don't know where you're going."

"I have someone giving me directions."

"Well, you can tell Seda to save her energy. I'm not taking the turn."

Raikidan grabbed my hand again. "Take the damn turn."

I smacked him away. "I don't take orders! Especially not ones from you."

He latched onto the steering wheel and yanked it. The car swerved into another street. People shouted at the recklessness, but I was too pissed to pay much attention to them.

"What the hell is your problem?" I barked as I righted the car.

"If you had just listened to me in the first place, I wouldn't have had to do it."

"There are rules you have to follow. Do you realize what you could have done if I hadn't kept control of the wheel?"

Raikidan's brow rose. "Rules?"

I couldn't believe him. "Do you not pay attention to how I drive? All these rules I follow are to keep us and others outside safe. You can't just take a turn at will at any speed. You have to worry about civilians walking around on the sidewalks, and you have to worry about oncoming traffic, not to mention if the street is a one-way or not."

"What would happen if you didn't follow these rules?"

"You'd cause an accident, and I don't know about you since you're a dragon, but for me, I'd get seriously hurt."

"But you're—"

"I'm what? Invincible because I'm some freakish superhuman experiment? No, it's not like that, Raikidan! I bleed. My bones break. You should know this, given you saw it first hand back at the West

Tribe. Dragons may not be so fragile, but just because I'm a soldier doesn't mean I'm not human. Ryoko hits like a damn train. A train could kill me. An accident could kill me if it was bad enough. It could kill someone else!"

Raikidan looked away. "I'm sorry. I didn't know."

I snorted. "Course you didn't. You just assume you know everything in a place that is foreign to you."

I shifted down a gear and stopped at the end of the street. I had no idea where I was now thanks to Raikidan, and all he had done was make me go down one street. I had to collect my thoughts and think.

"Take a right," Raikidan instructed, his voice quiet.

"Why is this, whatever it is, so important?"

"Because it is, so just go right."

I sighed and took it. I might as well since I had no idea where I was. If I was lucky, I'd get to a place I recognized, and I wouldn't have to listen to him again. Raikidan continued to tell me where to turn, and even after I figured out where we were, I kept listening, though I wasn't sure why. It was like I had to know where the end result was. As if I needed to know what he was thinking of.

"Pull up here."

I pursed my lips in confusion as I pulled into a side parking space. "The park? You wanted to bring me here?"

"Yeah."

I titled my head at him. "Why?"

"Well, if you had been listening to me earlier instead of ignoring me, you would have heard me trying to apologize to you for earlier."

"Oh…" I turned the car off and climbed out of my car. Raikidan slipped out as well and jerked his head to beckon me to follow. I complied and followed him.

The sky was much darker now, and the trees over us swayed in the wind. My black dyed hair whipped around my face as it was caught up in the gusts of wind. "So why are we here?"

Raikidan shoved his hands in his pockets. "You were relaxed when we were here last. I figured since you were mad at me still, coming here might make you feel better."

"You were mad at me too."

"I was mad because you were mad." I chuckled and shook my head. His brow rose. "What?"

"I was mad because you were mad."

"Please tell me you're joking."

I shrugged. "Well, I was mad on my own too, but mainly because you were."

He grunted. "So I could have been sitting with you instead of by myself this whole time?"

I leaned against the rail of the bridge and watched the river slowly run by. "I suppose, but then again, you were glaring at me the whole time, so maybe not."

He blinked. "How did you—"

"I'm getting better at reading you. To someone else, you may look normal or expressionless, but me, I see the real look, and you appeared pretty pissed, so there was no way I was going to let you be near me."

He shook his head. "I should have figured as much. You're so perceptive it was only a matter of time before you were capable of doing that."

The wind ruffled my dress. It made me feel even more uncomfortable. I couldn't believe Ryoko had managed to get me into this stupid thing. It was the other reason I had been in such a foul mood.

"You look nice," he said.

"I look stupid."

"No you don't. That dress looks nice on you."

"I hate it."

"Why?"

I fussed with the stupid dress again. "Because it's too feminine."

Raikidan's brow rose. "You don't want to feel feminine?"

"No. It makes me feel weak and like I can't do anything on my own."

"There's nothing wrong with that."

"Yes, there is. Everything is wrong with that."

"Why?"

"Because I'm human. Being feminine makes you eye candy. It makes you a fuck buddy, and then your use is up."

He tilted his head. "Is that why you hate men?"

My hands clutched. "I hate people."

"Talk to me about it."

"No."

He touched my elbow. "Why not?"

I jerked away. "Because I don't want to."

"Eira."

"It's not important."

"If it bothers you, then it is."

I glared at him. "Why do you even care?"

He blinked. I could tell my comment had hurt him, but I didn't care. "Why? Because I do. Now tell me."

"Just drop it, Raikidan."

He braced his arms on either side of me. "Tell me what bothers you."

I tried to push him away. "Don't get this close to me."

He leaned in closer until his breath hit my lips. My mouth dried. "Are you afraid?"

"I don't fear."

"You're lying."

My eyes narrowed. "I'm not."

"I can smell it. It's masked well, but it's still there. So tell me, what are you afraid of?"

I shoved him away and stormed off. *I don't fear anything.*

"Eira, come back." He followed close behind. "Eira."

"I thought you wanted me to feel better?"

"I do. I just didn't think you'd freak out at my compliment. You know, it's hard to compliment you. You're always finding some reason to throw them back at me."

"I don't deserve compliments."

He let out a deep aggravated breath. "Why do you talk like this? I've never met anyone who was ever this harsh to himself."

Refusing to engage in this topic any longer, I clamped my mouth shut and sat down in the grass, looking out across the lake. The sky made me uneasy.

Raikidan sat down next to me and scratched his head. "Thanks… for, uh, dying my hair black."

"Don't mention it. I figured you'd like it better."

"I do. It feels a little more natural to me."

I looked at him, his words stirring a question within me. "Raikidan."

"Yeah?"

"Out of curiosity, if you had the chance to choose to be either a red dragon or a black dragon, what would you choose?"

He gazed up at the sky. "Well, if you had asked me that around the time we had met, I would have told you I wanted to be a black dragon. But now I'm not so sure I would change to be either."

My brow rose. "How come?"

"Being around you and the others made me realize if I chose either, I wouldn't be the same. I wouldn't be Raikidan. I'd be someone else. I don't want to be someone else."

My gaze fell away. "I see."

"Why would you change, Eira?"

My brow quirked up. "What?"

"You told me once you would change if you had the chance. Why? I see nothing wrong with who you are."

My hand curled, the dark feelings returning. "Course you don't. No one does. No one will…"

"I don't understand."

"I'm not me when I'm undercover, and I'm not me when I'm not. No one knows the real me."

He tried to look me in the eye. "I want to."

I averted my gaze to avoid his. "No, you don't. She's not worth knowing."

He wrapped his arms around me and pulled me back into his hard chest. I fought the red flush that attempted to emerge. He was making me feel weird again.

"Don't say that," he murmured in my ear. "I want to know."

Before I could press the argument further, a drop of water splashed onto my face. My eyes fluttered and another one hit me. I suppressed a smile when Raikidan grumbled something that sounded to be in his tongue.

"We should go," I said. "We don't want to be caught up in this rain while driving. It looks like it's going to be a bad storm."

He sighed and let me go. "Fine."

I rose to my feet gracefully and led him to the car. I sent a silent prayer of thanks to the gods for their timing. It couldn't have been better. Just as I turned the key in the ignition, the sky opened up and poured down on us. I sighed. *Maybe I sent that prayer too soon.*

CHAPTER 3

I jogged up the stairs of the basement. For the past few days a rare tropical storm had sat on top of Dalatrend and caused quite the trouble. Missions had been put on hold and work was nonexistent due to flooding. Thankfully, the storm finally broke several hours ago.

When the clouds dispersed and the low sun cast orange rays over the city, I had gone to check the sewer systems to see if they were going to be usable. During heavy rains like this past one, the rain filled the water plant quickly and forced it into the run-off locations. The sewers were one of those locations, causing issues for the rebellion at times.

I looked at the dead rabbit in my hands. The sewers had flooded like I thought, but not enough where the run-off tunnels couldn't drain the extra water and keep walking paths cleared. One run-off tunnel in particular had been the full objective of my search below the city.

A young woman with long brown hair, sun-kissed skin, and dog-like ears where nu-human ones would be, greeted me with a warm smile as I opened the door—her golden eyes twinkling with the warmth of her personality.

"Oh, hey, Ryoko," I greeted.

"Hey to you, too." Her brow then rose in question when she noticed the furry bundle of flesh in my hands. "You couldn't have grabbed one of those special meal packages you brought with you from your outside city excursion to eat?"

I shrugged. "The spell doesn't protect the food indefinitely, so I loaded what I had left into the kitchen." I looked at her with playful accusation. "Someone then proceeded to eat it all."

Her eyes narrowed. "I did not eat all of it, and you know it."

I chuckled. "Yeah, sure. You keep saying that, Miss Hole-for-a-Stomach."

"Laz, stop teasing me!" She then stomped over to the couch and sat down.

I noticed she had my Library book in her hands, but I didn't mind. It'd be good for her to expand her horizons.

I placed the rabbit down on the bar and pulled out a cutting board before skinning it. I glanced at Raikidan when his presence filled the kitchen. He watched me with curiosity and I waited for his questions. I knew him well enough now to know they'd come.

Raikidan leaned on the bar next to me. "Where did you get this?"

"It doesn't matter," I said.

The truth was I didn't want to tell him because I'd look like a hypocrite even though that wasn't my intent. I had checked a particular run-off tunnel because of its convenient location to the forest next to the west side of the city walls. It made for a good escape route, but it was also well guarded, like many of the other run-off tunnels due to their escape potential. They used to be barred off, but we rebels removed them so often the military gave up and posted sentries to check them at certain times of the day.

The rabbit was only an extra prize. It had bounded into the open just as I was about to head back to the house. I couldn't pass up the opportunity.

"You left, didn't you?" he whispered in my ear.

"I went to the forest." It wasn't a complete lie.

Raikidan looked at me as if he didn't believe me, but he remained quiet and I went back to carving the rabbit. My stomach begged for relief, and although I would have preferred to finish carving the animal before I ate, I chose to give in to its needs. Slicing off a piece of the hindquarter, I stuffed it into my mouth. Noticing the hunger in Raikidan's eye, I cut out a chunk and handed it to him.

His brow rose. "You sure?"

I nodded. "Yeah, why not?"

He grinned and took the meat. He popped it into his mouth and swallowed it without chewing. This impressed me. I would have thought a chunk of meat that size would have gotten stuck in his throat.

Ryoko scrunched her nose. "That's disgusting. How can you eat raw meat? That's just not right."

I snorted. "Your kin do it."

"They're full wogron. They don't look human like me. It's a little different."

Raikidan grunted. "Hardly. Besides, there's nothing wrong with eating meat raw."

Her face scrunched. "It's disgusting!"

I grinned, making her blink in confusion. I cradled the head with one hand and carefully carved out the eye. I looked up at her, my grin still intact, and popped the eye into my mouth. Her face contorted with disgust. I was sure she was trying not to gag.

"That was the most disgusting thing I've ever seen you do!"

Raikidan nudged me and pointed to the rabbit. "Can I have the other one?"

"Are you serious?" Ryoko screeched.

"Eyes are rich in protein," Raikidan said. He looked at me again and tilted his head.

"Sure." I shifted the rabbit's head and carved the remaining eye out. I handed it off to him and he took it gratefully. Glancing at Ryoko, he tossed the eye into his mouth and swallowed.

"By the goddess, I'm going to be sick." Ryoko tossed the book down on the couch and bolted to the bathroom.

Raikidan and I lost ourselves in laughter. Looking down at the carcass, I carved out some more meat and ate. Every now and then, I'd offer some to Raikidan, who would scarf it down as if he were starving. I watched in amazement. *Where is it all going?* Shaking my head, I went back to carving the rabbit. I needed to get it all done before the sun went down.

I sat in the middle of my bed with photographs strewn about me.

In my hand, I carefully held an old photograph. In it were two people, one of them being me.

I wore a typical assassin military uniform before they had been modified and improved. Hard, but flexible, dark red and black metal protected my chest and neck—my stomach and a small patch above my chest the only parts of me left exposed. Thick, strong cloth covered a spot on both of my sides where the chest armor met. A wide belt wrapped around my waist and held my chest armor together.

Metal pauldrons protected my shoulders and forearm guards covered my wrists. Black gauntlets covered my hands and half of my arm under my forearm guard. I wore black pants on my legs, and fitted to my feet were knee-high plated dark red and black metal boots. My hair was held up by my hairclip like I normally wore it, and my daggers were strapped to my arms and thighs. In my hands I held my assassin mask, and on my hips rested a gemmed dagger I hadn't seen in a long time.

A woman with an athletic build, long, aqua-colored hair and bright green eyes stood next to me in the photograph. A purple cloth was wrapped around her forehead, and a beautiful crystal hung from one ear. The uniform she wore was the style the assassin uniforms were changed to look like in the future at the time of this picture. The only difference was that hers had more bulletproof material due to how often she saw direct combat. A dagger also rested against her hip but the gemming was far different than the one I carried.

The woman had her arm around my shoulder, and the two of us were smiling. I couldn't help but smile as I studied the image. Seeing her did that to me. I was glad I hadn't forgotten her face.

"That picture must be important if you're staring at it this intently."

I nearly jumped at Raikidan's voice. After the two of us had finished off the rabbit, he had gone off to do something on his own while I cleaned the usable parts of the rabbit for later use. Shortly after, Ryoko gave me a photo album, and after some thought, I decided it couldn't hurt to fill it with photographs I wasn't worried others would see.

"How long have you been there?" I asked.

"Long enough to know you've been staring at this one photo for some time instead of going on to the next one."

"I didn't hear you come in."

He smirked. "I'm good like that."

I grunted and went back to gazing at the photograph. I glanced at Raikidan when I began bouncing on the bed, and watched him climb over to me, careful not to damage any of my photographs. Again, I hadn't heard him move. "How do you do that?"

"Do what?" he asked.

"Move without even the slightest of sounds."

Raikidan shrugged. "I thought I was making plenty of noise. Maybe your hearing is going." I snorted and looked at the photograph again. "She's pretty."

I nodded. "Yeah, she is."

"Who is she?" he asked.

"General Amara. My general," I said.

"You're smiling in this."

"She had a way of doing that to me."

"I can tell you were close with her."

I nodded slowly. "She… was one of my favorite people…" I smiled and then began laughing when a memory came to me. This caught Raikidan by surprise. "Sorry. I just remembered when she pulled a prank on my mentor, Shyden, because she didn't approve of his methods when I failed an assassin test. It wasn't a horrible prank, but it did mess with his pride enough for him to learn his lesson."

Raikidan smiled. "Don't be sorry. I like it when you laugh."

My cheeks warmed, as did my neck and chest, and I focused my photograph so he wouldn't see. Others have said that before to me, but never had it made me react like that. *Why am I acting so oddly to what he said?*

Raikidan picked up a photograph. "How old is this picture?"

I took a look. Pictured was a young girl, no older than eight, with light skin, black hair, and bright blue eyes, with me kneeling next to her. "That was shortly after I joined the rebellion."

"Genesis hasn't aged at all…"

"Well, yeah. I told you she was the first successful nu-human experiment."

"I know, but what I'm saying, is that she hasn't grown up into an adult in all this time that has passed. Why?"

I shrugged. "We don't know. Besides nu-human, we're not even sure what she is, because there's no way she's only nu-human."

"Do any of you have any guesses?"

"Argus proposed she may be demigod."

Raikidan tilted his head. "Would that be possible?"

"Sure, if the humans who made her used DNA from a god. We may not know what a demigod's limitations would be, but it'd be safe to assume if they weren't immortal like their god parent, they'd at least live for a long time."

Raikidan rubbed his chin. "What god would offer their DNA?"

I shook my head. "The only one I could think of would be Nazir. The type of god he is, it would make sense, along with her necromancy abilities, since he's the god of death."

"Do you believe this is how she was made?"

I shrugged. "I'm not really sure. There isn't enough evidence to prove or disprove the theory for me."

He nodded. "Understandable." He then picked up another photograph and raised an eyebrow. "What is Argus holding?"

I looked at the tan and muscular man with green eyes, slicked-back brown hair and manicured beard. Around his neck and arms hung a large snake with white and light brown coloring. "Oh, that's Argus' pet. She's a python with a rare queen bee pattern. Gave that to him as a gift shortly after defecting from the military."

"A pet? What's that?"

"A type of companion. The most common pets we humans have are dogs and cats."

He shook his head. "You humans are weird."

"In human lore, dragons were said to sometimes capture humans to keep as pets, especially young maidens who could sing."

"But that's a human. They can at least hold conversation."

"The stories never said anything about keeping humans to talk to. If it was a maiden who could sing, she'd be forced to sing whenever told."

"And if it wasn't a maiden?"

I shrugged. "It was never said. The lore only spoke about dragons and maidens."

Raikidan shook his head. "You humans come up with weird stories."

I laughed and then grinned before pointing to the snake. "Shift into that. We'll pull something on Ryoko."

His brow rose in question, but his curiosity got the better of him and he studied the creature before transforming. Once in his long, scaled form, I heaved him over my shoulders and grinned. "Hey, Ryoko, come in here a minute!"

I listened as someone ran from the living room and burst through my door. Ryoko's cheery face switched to sheer horror when she laid eyes on Raikidan. A scream erupted from her mouth. "Snake! Ew! Laz why would you do that to me? You know I hate snakes. They're so gross!"

She ran out of the room and slammed the door behind her. I burst out in a fit of laughter and Raikidan shifted back, also laughing. "Did that seriously happen?"

I nodded. "She has an irrational fear of snakes. She was not happy when I gave Argus his pet."

My laughter was short lived when hot breath touched my lips. I froze up, my cheeks and body warming by the second. I stared at Raikidan, but he didn't stare back—his eyes too unfocused. "R–Raikidan, w–what are you doing?"

His eyes fluttered and then he pulled away quickly. Before I knew it, I was alone on my bed and he sat on the windowsill, staring at the floor. Confused wouldn't come close to how I was feeling at the moment. One moment he was about to try for a kiss again, and then the next he was trying to stay as far away as possible.

Finally finding the strength, I scooted to the foot of my bed. "Rai?"

He continued to stare at the floor. "Sorry."

"I'd rather an explanation than an apology."

"I'd rather not."

I snorted. "You try to kiss me, when I chewed you out the other night telling you to never try to get one from me again, and then, before you try, you back off. You expect me to not want an explanation?"

He sighed. "It's… complicated…"

"Try me."

He peered up at me and held my gaze. When I didn't give in, he sighed again. "It's a dragon thing." I waited for more. I wasn't going to settle for that. He sucked in a tight breath. He knew I was going to be stubborn. "You shared your food with me."

I raised an eyebrow in question. "Okay?"

He scratched his head. "Dragons only share food with family or their mates, and I know for a fact you're not family. Your offer… it… it's confusing my instincts." He rested his forehead in his hand. "It's clouding my judgment."

"We've shared drinks before," I said. "And we ate together at the shaman village and that restaurant. You never acted like this for either occasion."

"Drinks are different. Liquid is a readily available resource and commonly shared, so it doesn't have any pull. Food, on the other hand, isn't readily available. Most dragons would rather fight over scraps than go hungry. We can also work together to hunt more game and split it evenly among those who participated in the hunt.

"The time at the village and restaurant were different because of how the food was laid out, and how we were sitting and acting. It was more like we'd hunted together and feasted as comrades, making it okay. This time though…"

"Was more intimate," I finished.

He nodded. "You made the hunt and allowed me to be close when you offered me part of your meal. Only family or a mate would ever do that."

I nodded. "Then I won't do that again."

Raikidan looked up at me. "What?"

I moved back to my original spot on my bed and picked up another bone. "If I had known it was going to cause a problem, I wouldn't have done it. I won't do it again in the future."

"Eira, I don't want you to be upset."

My brow rose at him. "Who said I'm upset? You're the one who's getting all worked up over this. I'm just avoiding another problem before it starts."

"Oh… well… thanks."

I nodded and looked down at my photographs. Silence fell over us as I filed through more photographs. Then, Raikidan spoke. "Can I ask you something?"

"Yeah, sure, what's up?"

"How is it that you humans can keep pets?" he asked. "Most dragons by nature scare things, no matter which form they take. Humans and human-like creatures are the only things that don't fear us in forms other than our natural ones." He smirked. "Though there are some who are fearless, regardless."

I snickered. "I would suspect it has to do with the fact that dragons use draconic power and humans don't. This resource is unique to dragons, and is raw and powerful, as I experienced firsthand when trying to take control of your fire. This resource is so foreign, creatures are afraid of it when they sense it. Humans, on the other hand, rely on Lumaraeon's energy, hence elementalists and shamans. This power is much more recognizable to creatures and are less likely to be afraid of something it understands."

"But then why aren't humans and human-like creatures afraid of us?"

"We lack the natural instinct to sense draconic power. Unless they teach themselves, they will never be able to sense your type of power."

His brow rose. "Really?"

I nodded. "I actually had to train myself to sense it, but it took time and it's still not easy for me to sense, unless I put some effort into it. Had I not known about draconic power because of our stories, I doubt I would be able to sense it now."

"That explains how you know about it and have your theory. I'm impressed. The theory is well thought out, and I'm struggling to think of any other possibility it could be."

I smiled. "Thanks."

"So, what other things do your stories tell?"

"Different things, really. Possible legends you might have or possible things you guys can or can't do. They're all different, depending on who's telling them."

"Tell me a legend your stories claim to know," he said, interested in this topic.

I looked up at the ceiling and thought for a moment. "I was told of a legend that sounds completely absurd. It talks about a dragon and a human becoming mates and having a child whose power is incredible and unmatched by many others. It was thought, depending on how that child was raised, it could do great things for Lumaraeon or destroy it."

Raikidan snorted. "That's definitely a legend, and it's a stupid one at that."

His comment intrigued me. "Go on."

"Nothing else much to say. A child like that coming into Lumaraeon is impossible. Dragons and humans aren't compatible. There is no way a child like that could exist."

"It could exist if it were like us."

"It's unnatural." He blinked and then snapped his gaze on me. "Eira, I'm sorry. I didn't mean—"

I waved him off. "Don't worry about it. It's okay. I know my existence is unnatural. I know I wouldn't exist if it weren't for someone creating me artificially. I've come to terms with that. We all do at some point in our lives."

"You shouldn't have to."

"There's only so long you can run from the truth. It always catches up to you in the end."

Raikidan opened his mouth to speak, but someone knocked on my door and then opened it. A tall young man with tan skin, white hair and goatee and heterochromic blue and gold eyes poked his head into the room.

"Hey, Rylan, what's up?" I asked.

"We have an assignment. Genesis is about to brief us."

I nodded and piled my photographs together to be put away later. Raikidan and I then followed him into the living room to find out what was going down.

4
CHAPTER

My breath came steady and quiet as I peered around the wall of my hiding spot while the others moved into position. According to our intel, this outpost had information worth stealing. So that's what we were here to do, except I wasn't one of the people going in for once. At first I thought it strange for Genesis to assign me to lookout duty, but it made sense after she explained that only those in our house would be completing the assignment, and of those, Rylan and I were going to be the look outs.

I held my bow tightly in my hand. This was the main reason I had been okay with taking this position. After Genesis had briefed us, she gave us time to prepare, and this had fallen out of my closet. I had forgotten about it, and decided to try to research all I could on it since Tla'lli had told me it'd help me one day. That was when I discovered the symbols on the bow had not only meaning, but purpose.

The symbols allowed the user to use spiritual energy as a projectile in place of an arrow. The impact from such fast-moving energy would incapacitate the target by shutting it down. It wasn't lethal, making it the perfect alternative to using arrows in this situation. Unfortunately, I hadn't had a lot of time to practice. Until I did, I'd be unable to utilize the ability well, as I'd use up a lot of spiritual energy per shot.

And thanks to my shaman training, I was going to need some of it to function.

"We're all in position," Ryoko said through the communicator.

"I'm also in position," Rylan rang in.

"Okay, good," I said. "Everyone hold tight while Rylan and I clear this place out."

"Right," Ryoko said.

Keeping low, I slunk out of my hiding place and searched for soldiers who would get in the way. When I found one, I aimed my bow and drew back the string. But before I could muster up the spiritual energy needed, my head started to hurt.

The wind, no more than a gentle breeze, was a welcome relief to the midsummer heat as I strolled through the forest. I walked the familiar path as I had so many times during the past years. But this time was different. This time I hadn't tread this path for some time.

"Not now," I muttered. Bad time for my mind to start acting up, not that it was ever a good time.

Del'karo walked beside me. He was grinning ear to ear, and I doubted anything could wipe the smile off his face. Not even Maka'shi and her foul attitude. His smile brought one to my face. I was the reason he was so happy. I was glad I was able to make him so proud.

I took a deep breath and forced myself to focus before mustering up the energy needed to take down the soldier. But before I could do anything he twitched and then stumbled. I grumbled when he fell to the ground and I noticed the dart sticking out of his neck. Noting he was out, I searched for another soldier and found a female taking a break. I aimed my bow, but like with the first soldier, this one slumped over; a sleep dart sticking out of her neck.

Damn you, Rylan. His gun gave him a serious advantage over me. I knew I shouldn't be annoyed; this was what he was good at after all, but I didn't particularly like being showed up. I decided to move to another location. We were too close to each other to effectively take out these soldiers.

I stopped dead in the middle of my relocating when I caught the sound of someone walking nearby. Readying my bow, I pinpointed the source of the footprints and sought them out. I drew my bow-string back when I located the soldier on patrol and mustered up the spiritual energy needed to disable him. When a white-ish green light formed into the shape of an arrow, I let it fly. The man stopped dead in his tracks and then fell to the ground almost immediately. I stared with surprise. He had gone down quicker than the ones affected by Rylan's sleep darts.

Shaking myself of my state, I jumped down and checked to make sure he wasn't actually dead. The book may say it couldn't be lethal because it used spiritual energy, but I wanted to make sure. With me as inexperienced as I was, and our orders not kill anyone on this assignment if it wasn't necessary, I needed to be sure. I pressed my fingers against the soldier's throat and let out a relieved breath when I felt his pulse. Content knowing he was alive, I went back to sneaking around and taking down all soldiers who crossed my path.

I leaned against a wall and breathed with effort after taking out my sixth soldier. *I'm spent.* I wanted to help out more but I needed my energy in case of an emergency. And I couldn't lie to myself, I was pretty sure I had already over done it.

"Rylan, I'm out of ammo," I called in.

"It's okay," he replied. "We're all in the clear now. Save your energy."

"So we're free to head in?" Blaze called in.

"Yes. We'll keep an eye out for stragglers and alert you to any danger out here."

"And be cautious inside," I advised. "We don't know how many soldiers will be in there."

"Don't worry about that, Laz," Ryoko said. "We have Raikidan with us. He'll keep us safe." She snickered. "Unless you'd rather him watch your back."

I went to retort out a reply but snickered instead when she yelped.

"Focus, Ryoko," Raikidan muttered.

"Fine, fine, let's get going," she said grudgingly.

I took a collective breath and headed for higher ground to be able to act as a good lookout. When I found it, I made myself comfortable and kept my eyes peeled. Everything was quiet, even the communicators. It was too quiet.

I held my bow at the ready when I heard a noise and then relaxed when nothing appeared. I was getting paranoid now. *Hurry up, guys.* I knew it was best not to rush, as it could cause an issue, but this silence was too abnormal, and I was growing more paranoid by the moment.

My blood ran cold when a siren blared and the compound lit up.

"They were expecting this! They trapped a room," Ryoko screamed.

I swore under my breath and readied my bow. "Get out of there, now. No information is worth lives."

"We'll keep things clear out here as best as we can," Rylan added.

"Right," Ryoko replied.

I kept my breath steady as I waited for the soldiers. It was only a matter of time before they'd swarm the building. Spiritual energy welled up inside me when one came into sight and I released the arrow. The solder crashed to the ground, and I didn't waste any time aiming another spirit arrow at another soldier who came into view.

I breathed heavily as my energy drained. I wouldn't be able to do many more of these. Thank the gods, Rylan was on top of his game. I watched as several soldiers fell to the ground in succession, taken down by sleep darts.

"You're pathetic," the malicious voice in my head insulted.

Just then, Ryoko and the others sprinted out of the building. More soldiers than Rylan and I could handle swarmed in to intercept, but the others were ready and took them down. When the others took off for the planned exit, I left my perch and set a fast pace to catch up.

I threw out a quick spiritual arrow at a soldier that crossed my path and stumbled right after. *Not good.* Righting myself, I continued on but my pace was far slower. I really shouldn't have done that.

"Idiot."

I gasped when I was jumped from behind, but before the soldier could engage me, someone plowed into him and knocked him out.

My brow rose. "Raikidan?"

He grabbed me by the wrist. "No time for questions. Let's go."

"Don't trust him."

He yanked me forward, but I struggled to keep up. "Raikidan, just go ahead of me. I expended too much energy. I can sneak out at a slower pace than you."

"No, we're getting out of here together." He turned around and scooped me up into his arms and then continued on so quickly that I was momentarily stunned.

"Raikidan, I'm a liability to you," I finally said. "It's my fault for being in this state."

"I'm not going to tell you again."

I stared at him. *Is this him being stubborn or something else?*

"Don't trust him."

Raikidan put me down suddenly and took out a soldier running around the corner. I hadn't even heard the guy. *My lack of spiritual energy must be messing with my senses.*

"You're pathetic."

I swung my bow behind me when movement caught the corner of my eye and I nailed a soldier in the face. The solidness of the bow knocked the soldier out, and Raikidan chuckled. "I'll have to make sure I don't piss you off when you're carrying that."

I grinned. "I doubt that will stop you."

Raikidan scooped me up again. "You're right. Now let's go."

I let out a strained breath. I didn't like that he was carrying me, and I really was slowing him down. But it was obvious he wasn't going to listen to me, so I kept quiet; knowing full well I'd attract unwanted attention if I didn't.

I bit my lip when Raikidan stopped running and kept close to the wall of a building. Just beyond was the hole in the fence to get out of here, but I could hear soldiers as well. They had found our way out and as I listened, it became apparent they were also aware of our presence. My heart began to pound as they approached. We needed to think of something fast.

I took a deep breath when I knew what I had to do. It was risky and stupid, but if it got us out of here then I needed to do it. Getting Raikidan's attention I indicated I need him to put me down. He was reluctant but relented when I continued to insist.

Peering around the corner, I took a head count before readying my bow and I filled my body with spiritual energy. But Raikidan stopped me. He shook his head to indicate he didn't approve of my choice and I shook my head back to show him this had to be done. He scowled with disapproval, but we didn't have time to argue like this. I built my energy up again, and when it was ready, I moved from our hiding spot and shot an arrow at one of the three soldiers.

My target fell to the ground, shocking his comrades, allowing me to take another one out. I nearly fell to my knees as my energy drained from me, but I refused to give into my fatigue. There was one more soldier needing to be dealt with. He turned around and aimed his gun when he spotted me. But before confrontation happened, his body twitched, and a mostly hidden dart was seen sticking out of his shoulder before he fell. *Sleep dart?*

I gasped when someone landed on the ground behind me and readied my heavy bow to swing it, but relaxed when I realized it was Rylan. "You shouldn't do that."

"You shouldn't push yourself so much," he countered. "But we can argue later. I waited until you two got here so I knew everyone was out. We need to get moving before we're caught."

I nodded and went to head for the exit but stumbled. Raikidan caught me and helped me walk to the fence and I didn't fight him this time. Once all three of us were through, Raikidan picked me up again and Rylan motioned for us to follow him. My eyes grew heavy as we ran but I fought the urge to sleep. I couldn't do that until we were safe.

"Laz, are you okay?" Ryoko asked when we caught up with them.

"She over did it," Raikidan said for me. "Like always."

"Not always," I muttered.

"Are you going to be okay?" Ryoko asked, not allowing an argument to transpire.

"Yeah, I'll be fine," I said. "I just used up too much energy. It'll come back soon. But we have more important things to worry about right now. We need to split up into pairs and shake these guys. Ryoko and Rylan will go one way, Blaze and Argus another, and Raikidan and I will go our own way."

Argus nodded. "Sounds like a good idea."

"Good, let's get too it then," I said.

The others nodded and broke off into their pairs and disappeared into the city. Raikidan chose a direction and set a quick pace through several back alleys. The sirens of the compound blared in the distance, pushing us further and further. My energy came back to me slowly. When I felt I had enough to be able to at least run for a little while on my own, I grabbed Raikidan's attention and had him hide us in an alley.

"What gives?" he asked. "We can't afford to stop."

"I need to run on my own now," I said.

"You don't have the energy and we don't have the time to argue about this."

"I have enough energy to run now. Besides, you can't carry me the whole time. It'll raise too much suspicion if someone sees us."

He let out an exasperated sigh. "All right. I won't take the time to argue this, but if you stumble even once, I'm carrying you, you got that?"

I chuckled and slipped down the alley. "Sure."

"Laz," Seda messaged telepathically. *"Head for the park."*

My brow furrowed. *"Why?"*

"There will be a psychic waiting for you. He will cloak you so you can seek shelter there and lower your threat level."

"What does he look like?"

"Trust me, you'll know when you see him. He's not exactly the most... subtle person."

I chuckled and Raikidan glanced at me. "What's so funny?"

"Something Seda just told me," I admitted. "We'll see how interesting things get in a moment."

His brow rose. "Huh?"

I smirked. "We're heading for the park. Follow me."

"You're not making any sense."

I chuckled some more and led him to the park. When we made it to the end of an alley directly in front of the park, I crouched down low and peeked out to look around. It was unusually quiet, but since I could still hear the compound warning sirens in the distance, I was sure people were staying off the streets so they wouldn't get into trouble.

I wondered if it would be a good idea to head across the street but then thought better of it. For all I knew people were looking out the windows of these buildings. I couldn't take any chances.

I ducked backed into the alley when the sound of people talking somewhere down the street caught my ear, but then chose to peer out again when I realized they were laughing. A man and a woman rounded a street corner, the man's arm hanging over the woman's shoulder, and I couldn't stop my brow from rising.

They were a bit of an odd couple. The woman, who was borderline young enough looking to be called a girl, was dressed in designer clothes and accessories many of the rich citizens in Quadrant Four indulged in wearing, where the man could only be described as a punk. Dark clothes with spikes, chains, dyed and spiked hair, he exuded the definition of stereotype. The only thing off about his look was the blindfold over his eyes. *It can't be.* They were the only two on street, so it was possible he was the psychic who was supposed to help us, but I found it hard to believe. I ducked back into the alley as they headed our way and waited for them to pass.

Just as the pair walked in front of the entrance to the alley, the psychic turned his head our way and smiled. *"I'm cloaking you. You have thirty seconds to get across the street. The soldiers aren't too far away."*

He really was the psychic Seda had told me about. This surprised me.

"What are you smiling at?" the psychic's companion asked.

He looked at her and continued to smile. "Just an alley cat stalking a rat."

"A rat?" she shrieked.

"Don't worry. I'm confident the cat will take care of it."

The woman breathed with relief.

"Twenty two seconds, Eira. Better get your cute little ass moving."

I snorted and then grabbed Raikidan by the hand before dashing across the street.

"Are those sirens still blaring?" the woman asked the psychic.

"Looks like it," the psychic replied. "You aren't scared are you?"

"I just don't want to get into trouble for walking down the street or anything," she admitted.

He bent closer to her. "I'll keep you safe, but if you really want to get off the street, we can go back to my place."

"No rodents?" she asked.

"No rodents." He chuckled. "Can't be so sure on snakes, though."

I rolled my eyes. He really wasn't subtle.

"Eira, where are we going?" Raikidan asked, pulling my attention away from the psychic and his companion.

"Farther into the park," I said.

"Why?" he asked. "How is it going to help us get out of this mess?"

"Well, I thought it would be a good way for us to play up my amnesia alibi," I said.

"How so?"

I held up my bow. "By using this as a prop. We are supposed to be from a village, after all, and I'd rather have the job of hunter than tailor or stay-at-home wife."

He nodded. "Not a bad idea. When did you come up with it?"

"Just now."

His brow quirked up. "Seriously?"

I found a secluded spot by a tree to sit down by. "Well, Seda is the one who told us to come this way, without any other plan, so I wasn't sure what to do. But having to carry this heavy thing around and seeing that psychic blend in by… well, not blending in, I thought about how we could use both to our advantage. This is what I came up with."

Raikidan sat down next to me. "Is that bow really that heavy?"

"Lie," the malevolent voice in my head hissed.

"When I'm at full strength no, but I'm so low on energy right now that it is. I also converted most of what energy I do have to endurance, and not strength, so that attributes to the heaviness. And even if I was at full strength, because of its size, it is difficult to carry the way I have to in order to move around. As useful as honing this technique is, I don't think I'll be using it again."

"Do you think you could make something smaller?" he asked.

I shrugged. "If I could unlock the secret on how this was made, then maybe, but I don't think I'll find that easily. Finding out how to use this one was tough enough."

He nodded and then shifted his focus elsewhere when soldiers entered the park, shouting and running about. It was time to put on our act.

"Are you sure I'm doing this right?" I asked Raikidan.

He chuckled. "Of course I'm sure. You're picking it back up real quick. Your skill level is already half of what it used to be."

"Was I really that good?"

He grinned. "One of the best."

I smiled and then looked away when two soldiers approached. They had weapons drawn but their posture wasn't aggressive so I chose not to act defensively. Instead I was going to mess with Raikidan.

I turned my gaze back onto him. "I told you we should have gone home."

He gave me an unamused look before looking back at the soldiers. "We can explain why we're here."

One of the soldiers, a ranking officer, stared us down. "You have a lot to explain. First, what are you doing here with such a weapon?"

"Trying to get her to remember how to use it," Raikidan explained.

"It's part of her recovery process. We have no arrows, so we're of no danger to anyone."

"Recovery process?"

The subordinate soldier leaned closer to the officer and kept his voice low. "She's the amnesia woman who works for the shop owner, Zane, and the club owner, Azriel."

The officer nodded. "Very well. Either of you two care to explain why you're still here? Can you not hear the warning sirens?"

"You outrank him. Teach him a lesson for his attitude."

Raikidan nodded. "We don't live close by and since we walked here, I thought it was best if we stayed put. We didn't want to cause any of you more trouble than needed."

The officer watched us suspiciously and I worried he wouldn't buy our story. Raikidan was being diplomatic, which honestly shocked me given how he usually acted around soldiers, and he made our story sound convincing to me, but with the odds stacked against us it may not be enough to clear us.

"Don't you dare start groveling!"

I gave the officer my best innocent look I could muster and it seemed to help because he nodded. "Get these two some passes and send them home."

He walked away without another word, leaving the other soldier to deal with us. He was far friendlier. "Please follow me. I have to get you some passes to give you passage through the city."

"Can't we just go home?" I asked.

"If you didn't have that bow with you, yes," he admitted. "But since you've already spoken to us about its presence we'll need to write something up in case. We don't want another squad on patrol giving you trouble."

I nodded and the two of us followed the soldier to the entrance of the park. We waited as he filled out two passes and I thanked him before the two of us went on our way.

The two of us were quiet for several blocks until Raikidan determined we were in the clear. "How are you feeling?"

"Don't tell him."

I shrugged. "Okay, I guess."

"Anything I can do to help?"

"Stay away from him."

I shook my head. "There's an advanced healing ability that allows one person to transfer spiritual energy to another to help with their low spiritual store, but I don't know it, nor do I know how to teach it to someone. Just means I'm going to have to recover it slowly,"

"How long will that take?"

I shrugged. "Couple hours. A day. I've never depleted my spiritual energy this bad before, so I don't know."

"You shouldn't have pushed yourself so hard."

"Don't let him scold you. He's not your father."

I shrugged again. "I did what needed to be done."

He shook his head. "You're insane."

I smirked. "You say that like it's a bad thing."

My smile faded when Xye caressed the back of my shoulder with the back of his finger.

I sighed and pulled away. "Xye, don't do that."

"Why not?"

I fixed him with a hard stare. "You know why."

He frowned. "Laz, just give me a chance."

"I told you I'm not interested."

"Why not? I care about you. You know I do. You know I'd never hurt you. Why can't you give me a chance?"

"Xye..." I looked away. "I can't. I can't see you as more than a friend."

Raikidan chuckled. "With you, it's hard to tell." He then held out his hand. "Let me carry your bow."

"I got it."

"Eira, let me help."

"You don't need help," the voice said.

"Raikidan, it's fine."

He stopped walking. "Hop on my back then. I'll carry you."

"Don't be pathetic," the voice said.

"I don't need to be carried."

"I either carry the bow or you. Your choice."

I snorted. "I'm choosing neither."

He grinned and then grabbed me by the waist. "Then I'll choose."

I tried not to laugh as he hauled me over his shoulder. "Rai, stop!"

"Nope, I'm choosing and I'm going to carry you."

"Not like this!"

"Then how?"

My face burned when I realized I had just partially agreed to this. "Carry me on your back or something like a civilized intellectual being. Not in a way that a caveman would."

Raikidan grinned. "So in my arms?"

I lifted up the bow as best I could. "I will hit you."

He chuckled and put me down before crouching. "Hop on my back then."

I let out a defeated breath and complied. When I was securely situated on his back, Raikidan stood and continued on. "Better?"

"You're pathetic," the voice insulted.

"No," I muttered. I then rested my head on his shoulder when fatigue flooded over me. "Maybe… thank you."

He chuckled. "You should learn to lean on others when you need it."

I kept running. It's what I knew best. It's what I knew that kept everybody safe. I wouldn't stop. I couldn't stop. Not for me. Not for anyone else. This was the only way for me to live now. Never again would I live alongside others. Never again would I hurt another. Never again would I let my guard down even for a second. Never again would I let someone in. Never again would I allow someone to hurt me.

"The way I do things is fine."

"Eira, you can lean on me when you need to," he said. I eyed him suspiciously and he glanced at me. "Trust me, and ask for my help when you need it."

"You can't trust him."

I let my bow slide down my hand a little and then pointed the tip at his throat. "Don't get weird and sappy on me."

"I'm being genuine, Eira. Trust me more."

I looked away. "Let's get home so I can rest."

He sighed and continued on, leaving me to think on whether I could actually start trusting him or not. A part of me wanted to. It wanted to be able to rely on someone again. The other part, it knew better. It had learned from the past.

5
CHAPTER

I glanced up from where I was reading and watched the boys. The three of them were spread out across the living room, tossing a football around. None of us could convince them to go outside or down stairs to play, and with the limited seating in the kitchen, I had to read standing up.

I could read in my room, but today I didn't want to seclude myself. Raikidan, on the other hand, wasn't the least bit thrilled by the idea of possibly being hit by the leather ball, and chose to hide.

Keeping my eye on them, I went back to reading, though it was more like learning than anything. I hadn't been able to find anything more on dragons like I had hoped I would. And although I couldn't admit it to Raikidan, I was curious about his kind. Everything he had told me about them piqued my interest more and more, even though I knew I should ignore all that.

Sadly, I had been unable to find anything, so I settled with brushing up on the Elvish language for no real reason at all.

Air rushed past me as Argus dove for the football. I wanted to roll my eyes and sigh. I couldn't see how they got enjoyment from throwing a ball around, especially if they ended up getting hurt in some way while doing so. It was like each ounce of pain made it that much more fun to do.

I glanced up as Raikidan walked past me and made his way into the kitchen. He came back out, an apple in hand, and headed for my bedroom again, but he didn't go that far. Instead he stopped when he was in front of me and turned to face me. "I don't understand why you're insisting on standing and reading when there are plenty of places to sit in safer locations from your friends' strange choice of fun."

I rolled my eyes at him. "Maybe I enjoy standing and reading."

He grasped the book and took it from me. "Maybe you should choose a more normal activity."

I stomped my foot. "Raikidan, give that back!"

He chuckled. "Why should I? Maybe I want to read now."

I reached for the book, but he pushed me back and placed one hand on the wall beside me, partially boxing me in, while holding my book just out of my reach with his other hand. "Raikidan…"

"Can't you learn—"

"Watch out!" Blaze exclaimed.

Raikidan's body crashed into mine and my eyes widened in shock. His lips were warm and soft as they touched mine and my cheeks and ears burned. His eyes were as wide as mine as I was forced to stare into them.

"Oh, shit…" Argus stated as he moved away. "I didn't mean to crash into you guys."

"Did you make them kiss?" Blaze asked, too interested in the idea.

Raikidan, now free of Argus' weight, slowly pulled away. I wasn't sure if I was supposed to feel angry or embarrassed. In the end I chose the first emotion. Regaining some composure and the ability to move, I grabbed Raikidan by the shirt and threw him to the side. I let my angry gaze rest on Blaze.

"Shit. You might want to start running, Blaze," Rylan advised.

Blaze looked to him with a perplex expression. "Why me?"

"Either because of your comment or, more realistically, she knows you were the one who threw the ball," Rylan said.

"How would she know I did it?"

"You're the one who yelled out and you're the one at the exact angle Argus would need to be at to run into Raikidan!" I seethed. I yanked out a dagger from its sheath and spun it in my fingers.

Blaze backed up a little. "Now, now, Eira. Let's not get rash. It was an accident. I swear it!"

"I don't give a damn!"

"Eira, it's not that bad. It was just a small kiss. No harm to it." I snarled and he backed up more. "You can't seriously tell me you didn't like it even a little."

"I'm going to cut you into pieces while you're still alive. Then I'll feed you piece by piece to the crows."

Blaze gulped and bolted to the staircase of the front door. Not wasting any time following him that way, I jumped over the couch and slipped through the open window. As I propelled myself over the railing of the small balcony, I watched Blaze bolt out the front door and hang a right to avoid running into me. Once my feet hit the ground, I was running after him. I'd make him regret this.

I slammed the front door shut and stormed up the stairs. I had almost caught Blaze, but he managed to escape and then disappear into a huge crowd of people. I tried to find him by his scent, but there were too many mingling smells to find him.

Once I reached the top step, I was met with several pairs of eyes. No one spoke to me, but since I didn't have blood on me, they more than likely assumed I hadn't caught Blaze. Raikidan glanced up at me from where he sat at the bar but lowered his gaze back down to focus on his bowl of cereal. I averted my eyes from him as well. At least we were on the same page of awkwardness, but that didn't make me feel better. It actually made me feel worse. I didn't want this feeling. I didn't like it. I wasn't even sure if it was a real feeling, or just me being unsure about how to react to such a situation.

I headed to my room and slammed the door shut. I needed to be alone. I couldn't be around anyone who would be a risk of asking unwanted questions or be around Raikidan. I needed to calm down first before I could be around him again.

I jumped onto my bed and snuggled into my pillows. They were so soft and comfortable I couldn't resist. Snuggling into them always made me feel a little better. I growled when the front door opened and closed. If I hadn't been so comfortable, I would have thundered out there and tried to go after Blaze a second time.

"Don't worry, Blaze. Laz is in her room," Rylan informed him.

"All right good," he said. "If she's comfortable, she won't come out and chase me again."

"And here I thought you liked women chasing you," Ryoko teased.

"That's a different kind of chase," Blaze said, his tone dry. "Eira's chase was the crazy-killer chase that I definitely hate."

Ryoko laughed at him. "Serves you right, though. You should have been more careful. And you should have been smarter about choosing your words."

"Whatever." He brushed off her words without a moment's hesitation. "So, Raikidan, how does it feel to be the only guy to ever kiss her?"

The only reply he received was the barstool screeching as Raikidan pushed back and a ceramic bowl lifting off the granite counter. The door to the roof opened and slammed shut soon after, and Raikidan stomped up the stairs. At least I wasn't the only one who didn't want to deal with Blaze or want the topic to continue.

I sighed and buried my face deeper into the pillows. *Day, will you just end, please? I want to not have to deal with these strange feelings anymore. I don't want to remember this happened.*

I knew I'd remember. No matter how much I wanted to forget, I would never be able to. Although what had happened shocked me, I was also shaken by the rush of feelings that came with it. I didn't like any of them, and all I wanted was for them to go away. I groaned.

Just go away already and let me be the lonely, emotionless freak I am!

It was dark, damp, and hard to see where I was walking, but I followed him. He wanted to show me something. He told me to follow him, so I was.

"Raikidan, where are we going?" I asked.

He cranked his neck to look at me. Even in the darkness, I could tell he was giving me his famous cocky grin. "I told you, you'll see when we get there. Now keep following me."

I groaned. "I can barely see where I'm walking in this stupid cave. How do I know you're not lost?"

He chuckled. "Because you trust me, and you trust me to know where I'm going."

I smiled. I did trust him. He gently tugged me closer with the light grip he had on my wrist, and I didn't fight him as he led me through the tunnel.

The more we walked, the lighter the tunnel became, allowing me to make out the smoothness of the carved stone and Raikidan's face, creased with determination. His grip was strong but tender and almost felt protective. My heart skipped a beat but I didn't understand why.

The tunnel became even brighter, and I noticed a light ahead of us. Raikidan flashed a grin my way and quickened his pace but I struggled to keep up. Whatever that light was, it was what he had been wanting to show me this whole time. It was the reason I had been following him so blindly.

He turned and faced me just before we walked into the light. He smirked and let his grip on my wrist loosen until he held my hand. He grasped my other and pulled me into the light. The light was bright, and I had to close my eyes to protect them.

"Open your eyes," he encouraged. I hesitated. I didn't want to be blinded. "It's all right. Open them."

Slowly I did as he instructed. I stared in awe at the sight before me. I stood on a ledge at the lip of the cave that overlooked the most amazing landscape I had ever seen. But what made it the most beautiful was the sunset. Its red and orange rays blanketed the sky and turned the clouds pink.

"What do you think?" he whispered in my ear.

I turned to look at him. "You brought me here to see this?" He grinned and I gaze out across the landscape once more. "It's beautiful."

He chuckled. "Just like you."

I spun around to look at him and my eyes widened when his hand cupped my chin and his lips claimed mine. Soft, warm, and inviting, my body warmed from the contact and I could find no part of me that wanted to push him away. I kissed him back.

Suddenly, his lips parted into a grin and then a sharp pain shot through my back. Blood rushed into my throat, and my body became stiff and unresponsive.

Raikidan chuckled. "You're such a fool."

I swallowed some blood. "W—why? Why… would you—"

"Why would you trust me? What type of fool trusts a dragon?"

I watched him pull away from me, and I watch helplessly as my body fell and hit the ground with a sickening thud. I couldn't move. I couldn't feel.

He chuckled again. "Any attempt to get up will be futile. While you were so distracted with the trivial scenery, I stole your dagger, which is now in your back."

I gulped. "Why?"

"Why not?" He snickered. "I have no attachments to you or your friends. I'm sick of helping you without getting anything in return. Zarda was right to want to throw you away. You really are a worthless failure."

The sound of ripping clothing enveloped my ears, and his breath become stronger and deeper. I watched as his dragon body wrapped around me in the tiny space. He looked me in the eye. I saw no sadness—no regret. I could only see my reflection and the hurt and betrayal that reflected in my eyes. Then, in a blink of an eye, he took to the skies. He didn't look back. He didn't speak in his tongue—just left me to die.

I was alone with a great emptiness aching in my chest as the sun became a mere sliver. I wanted to yell—to scream out in frustration. But worst of all, I wanted to cry.

The coldness of the stone floor seeped into my skin and my blood trickled out of my back and mouth. With the sun now gone, it would be only a matter of time before I'd be dead. I really was a fool. How could I have been so stupid to believe he could be one of us? That I could trust him? Where did I go wrong?

All I had ever wanted was to have my freedom. All I wanted was to be able to live a normal life like everyone else. Why did he have to do this? He had the choice to let me die before. He had the choice to not offer to help. He could have left whenever he wanted if he no longer wished to help. What did he gain from doing this to me?

Slow, steady footsteps approached me. My eyes darted about, but the darkness prevented me from seeing anything. "Such a shame."

The voice belonged to a woman. Her voice was as smooth as silk, but I could taste the venom on the tip of her tongue. I knew who this woman was.

"You thought you could trust him? I thought you learned that men weren't to be trusted. I thought you were smart enough to learn from the past."

I spat out some blood. "Have you come here to mock me?"

"Did you honestly think you could have your greatest desire?" she hissed as she walked around me—her warmth teasing my cold skin. "Are you that much of a fool to think we can have such a heaven?"

I saw a small ember spark in the darkness that soon became a flame. The woman held it close to her face, illuminating her features. She was me, but she also wasn't. Her eyes were cold and filled with hatred and mistrust. But most of all, they were filled with pain.

"Did you really think he could give us what we wanted? Did you honestly think life would allow us to have that?" She spat on the ground. "We were not made to be happy. We were made to kill. We cannot be happy. We cannot feel. We cannot be like everyone else. There is no one we can trust. We are no more than tools, and once our use is over, we are worthless. No one wants us and no amount of hoping will ever change that."

"You're... *lying*," I breathed.

"I am? Then why is it that you're dying on the ground? Why is it that when you placed your trust in someone who appeared to care, he turned around and hurt you without hesitation, just like before? You can't trust anyone. You can't live with anyone."

"I want... I want to live," I managed—my life slipping away with every breath.

She laughed. It was a cold, dry laugh. "You want to live? Well, let me spell it out for you. We can't. Our heart may beat so we can live, but all we can do is survive. There is no life for us. We have no future."

"Then... what's the point... of living?"

She snorted. "I don't know. You tell me. You're the one who wishes to live. You're the one who finds irrational reasons to keep going. You're the one throwing your trust into the hands of others who can't be trusted. You tell me, what's the point when all we've experienced is pain?"

I couldn't reply. I had no strength to. My eyes closed and my life faded. She spoke again, her words hitting me before the darkness took me.

"You can't trust him. He will only hurt you."

$$6$$

CHAPTER

(RYOKO)

I tied my boots and looked myself over in the mirror before heading out of my room. I couldn't stop thinking about what had happened between Raikidan and Laz yesterday. She had gotten angry and nearly went psycho-killer on Blaze, but I knew that was her way of covering up her embarrassment.

Raikidan, on the other hand, had grown quiet. He sat at the bar and ate while he lost himself in his thoughts. But it was the look on his face that had given him away. I knew that expression, and I knew there was something between the two that neither was willing to admit, the gods only knew why. I had a plan to get to the bottom of this, and since today was my turn to go get groceries, I couldn't see better timing to implement it.

Raikidan sat on the couch reading, and Laz was nowhere to be seen. I guessed her to be in her room. She hadn't been in the greatest mood this morning so I suspected she thought it be best to stay away from everyone until she felt better. I personally thought she should be doing the opposite, but no way would I get her to listen to that opinion.

"I'm going shopping for food," I said to Raikidan. "Can you come with me to help?"

He looked at me with a raised brow and then stood. "Sure?"

I smiled. "Thanks."

I led the way down to the garage and headed for my favorite SUV. Hopping in, I grabbed the keys in the console and started the vehicle up. The moment Raikidan shut his door, I threw the car into drive and zipped through the garage.

The ride to the store was quiet. I had thought up this idea and ran it through my head over and over to make sure I knew what to do, but now that I was doing it, I wasn't so sure. I didn't need to mess this up and ruin everything.

"So, why'd you ask me to come with you?" Raikidan asked. "Rylan was free."

I chuckled. "What, am I not allowed to ask for your help or something?"

"No, it's not that. I just know he would have been more than happy to go with you."

I shrugged. "I wanted to ask you this time."

He grinned. "You're trying to get him riled up, are you?"

I did my best not to become embarrassed from the not-so-far-off accusation. "No, of course not."

"He likes you, so it'll work. Quite well, actually."

I shook my head. "No he doesn't. I've known him long enough to know how he reacts to someone he likes. It's obvious for every party around him. He just sees me as a friend."

Raikidan snorted. "Then tell me, if it's not because of him, why did you ask me? You don't ask me to do many things with you."

"So I'm not allowed to at all?" I teased. He was too smart to buy my act and I liked it. *Well, here goes nothing.* "How do you feel about Laz?"

He eyed me cautiously. "She's nice. When she's not having one of her moments, that is."

I giggled. He would say it that way. "That's it?"

"Ryoko, what are you trying to get at?"

I took a deep breath. "Do you like her?"

He sighed. "Don't start with this conversation."

I pulled into a parking space. "Oh we are going to have this conversation."

"There's nothing to talk about."

I climbed out of the vehicle. "I beg to differ."

"Ryoko, drop it."

I walked close to him as we entered the supermarket and nudged him several times. "C'mon, I see how you act around her. And I saw that look when then the two of you had that accidental kiss. You liked it."

His movements became stiffer and he tried to grab a cart and ignore me, but I spotted the slight tint in his cheeks. My nose also alerted me to the chemical change in his body. I was right.

I continued to nudge him. "Admit it. You want another. You want to get to know her on a more personal level."

"Ryoko, I don't, now stop it."

I grinned. I wasn't going to give up. "You can't lie to me, Rai."

He let out a strong aggravated breath as I stopped to pick out some produce and lowered his voice. "I'm not human."

My brow furrowed and I looked at him funny. "What?"

He glanced around carefully and continued to keep his voice low. "I'm a dragon."

I dropped the potato in my hand and stared at him. "Y–you're a what? That's not possible." He held my gaze instead of replying, and I struggled to comprehend this. "But you're—"

"We're not extinct."

I shook my head and then started laughing. "Don't even try to pull that one on me. You're trying to distract me."

Raikidan continued to stare at me and then, something happened with his eyes. It was slow, but they shifted from a normal human-like eye to a more lizard-like one. But this wasn't like any lizard or snake eye I'd seen before, and I'd seen them all. As much as I wanted to believe this was a trick, I knew it wasn't. This was something different. This was…

"You're telling the truth…" I murmured when his eyes suddenly changed back. I then yanked him away from the cart and into an empty isle. "Show me again."

His brow twisted. "What?"

"Do that eye trick again."

"Um, okay…"

He bent closer to me and his eyes changed once more. My body tingled and I felt bubbly. This was so amazing. I couldn't believe dragons were still alive. And Laz knew this whole time! *I can't believe she was keeping this from us—from me! Me of all people. You think you know a person…*

I thought about this a bit more. This would explain a lot about her actions with Raikidan. Even if she were attracted to him, she wouldn't see a way of it working. But my plans weren't dashed, not in the slightest.

"So, can I see what you look like?" I asked.

His eyes changed back and he headed for the abandoned cart. "No."

"Oh, c'mon. I'm sure Laz has seen. Why not me?"

"I said no, Ryoko."

I huffed. "Fine, back to what we were talking about before then."

He let out a tight breath. "There's nothing to talk about. We're not the same species."

"Okay, so what?" I challenged. A perplexed expression crossed Raikidan's face. "I'm a halfling and the person I'm created from was a child of a true interspecies relationship. It works."

He shook his head as he placed some carrots in a bag. "It's not that simple with us."

"Whoever said it was? C'mon, admit that you like her."

He chuckled and pushed the cart on. "You're so lucky you're not a dragon. Your mother would have eaten you."

I laughed and grabbed a watermelon before we left the produce area. "I'm pretty sure if I had real nu-human parents they'd have dropped me off at an orphanage or shipped me off to a boarding school."

I went back to nudging him as we went down the bread isle. "Stop trying to change the subject on me. Just admit you liked that kiss and you like her." Raikidan didn't respond but I saw the redness in his cheeks appearing again. "See, see, thinking about it gets you all flustered."

He sighed and I waited but what came out of his mouth disappointed me. "Let's finish shopping."

I huffed. "Fine, but if you want to finally admit how you feel and want some help in the right direction, come see me."

He shook his head and kept on walking. I followed, but I was working on plans to get these two to stop being so stupid, and a way to convince Raikidan to show me his dragon form. I was very interested in that too.

7
CHAPTER
(EIRA)

The air smelled sweet, of spring flowers and the fresh scent of the lake. The sound of its lapping waves on the sandy shore enveloped my ears. A small girl with violet hair crouched on the shore, crying. She didn't notice my presence, or the water washing over her bare feet. She looked so miserable, as if she were lost and scared.

Then a feminine, caring voice called out. I couldn't make out what she said, but the girl could. She wiped the tears away with her arms and jumped to her feet with a smile. She ran toward the voice and I watched her.

Some ways off, two figures stood close together. I couldn't make out their features, but I could tell one was male and the other female, the source of the voice.

"I'm coming!" the little girl called.

She ran as fast as her little legs could carry her. But, although she ran farther away from the lake, she didn't get any closer to the two figures. The little girl didn't notice, though. She continued to run, regardless.

As she ran, she grew older until she became a young teenager. Although stronger and faster than she had been before, she still gained no more ground. Suddenly, the male figure turned and started to walk away. The woman who had stood next to him reached out, but didn't stop him.

"Wait, don't leave!" the girl cried out. "I'm coming! Please, wait for me."

The male figure didn't seem to hear, or stop to listen. He kept walking until he disappeared into the darkness of the surrounding woods. The woman who remained held out her hand and called again to the young girl.

The girl tried to pick up her pace to gain more ground, to no avail. As she ran, she grew older once again. Now she was a mature young woman, and I recognized her. I blinked to make sure my eyes weren't deceiving me.

When I opened them, I was no longer watching the woman. I was running as she had been. I was running toward the woman who was calling. The young woman was me.

"Eira," the woman called again.

"I'm coming!" I ran as fast as I could, but I knew I wasn't going anywhere. I couldn't understand why. Then the woman started to fade. I reached my hand out. "No, don't go!"

The woman continued to fade away. Suddenly finding the power to close the distance, I lunged for her outstretched hand, but I was too late. As I made it to her, she disappeared, as did everything around me.

I picked myself up off the ground and looked around frantically in the darkness. "Mom? Mom! Mom, come back! Dad? Dad, are you there?" My head whipped around more. "Anybody?"

No answer. Emptiness crept into my heart and squeeze so tight it hurt to breathe. "I don't want to be alone..."

Just then, a pair of strong, warm, masculine arms wrapped around me protectively. I smiled and rested my hands on his arms. I wasn't alone. But who was with me?

"You're not alone." The voice was deep and almost came out as a growl. "I'm here for you."

My eyes snapped open and I sat up—my breath heavy. I did not like that dream at all.

"Eira, you okay?" I glanced over at Raikidan, who was standing next to my bed and had his hands positioned as if he had been about to grab me. "I came over to check on you because you were having a nightmare."

I took a deep breath and then slipped off my bed. "I'm fine, just go back to bed."

"But what about you?" he asked.

"I said I'm fine," I growled as I left the room.

I headed straight for the bathroom and shut the door behind me. Turning on the sink faucet, I dipped my hands under the running water and splashed it onto my face. Taking a few shaky breaths, I leaned on the counter and stared at my reflection to collect myself, but my mind was abuzz.

"Laz, are you okay?" Seda messaged. *"I noticed how upset you were."*
"I'm fine."

"Okay," she replied. *"If you need someone to talk to, you know I am here."*
"Yeah, thanks."

I hung my head for a moment, and when I looked up again, I was taken aback by the red and black haired woman with piercing golden eyes over my shoulder in the reflection. I whipped around, but found no one in the room with me. Looking back at the mirror, I saw only myself reflected. Something was up. That woman I saw was the same one who had startled me before, after that mission weeks ago, no doubt about it. It wasn't every day you saw a person with feathery wings. *Who is that woman?*

I shook my head and cut the water flow. *I'm crazy.* I was the only one in here. I stared at my reflection. *I look pathetic.* I snorted. *Such an understatement.* So much turmoil over such... trivial feelings...

I roared with anger and smashed my fist into the mirror.

Seda gasped. *"Laz."*

The bathroom door flew open and Raikidan rushed in. "Eira, are you all right?"

"Get out," I muttered.

"But—"

"Please. Just... just leave me alone," I begged in a hushed voice.

"Okay..."

He left and I stared at my broken reflection. It was a good look for me. The mirror showed most of who I really was for once.

A defeated breath escaped my lips. *"Seda, why am I such a screw up?"*

"Do not say that," she said. *"You are not a screw up. Not even close."*

"Yes I am. I can't save people and I can't connect with people. I can't do any-thing right..."

"That is not true. You do a lot of things correctly."

"Why does life have to be so unfair, Seda?"

"Laz, you know I cannot see dreams. What did you dream about that has you so upset?"

I hesitated. *"My parents... Me being alone. Everything I love and hate. Everything I want but can't ever have..."*

"Laz—"

"I'm sorry, Seda, I shouldn't be bothering you with my problems. I'll replace the mirror tomorrow. Good night."

I took in my reflection one last time and then turned off the bathroom light before heading back to bed. Raikidan sat on the windowsill, but I didn't pay him any mind. I just lay down on my bed and waited for unconsciousness to take me.

CHAPTER 8

I squeezed my eyes tighter to block out the light of the morning sun. I didn't want to wake up, but truthfully, I didn't want to sleep. Somewhere in between sounded like a nice idea.

I snuggled deeper into my bed and tightened my grip on my sheets. At least I thought I was snuggling into my bed until it moved slowly up and down… like a body would while breathing. This concerned me, so I opened my eyes. My breath caught when I found myself curled up on a muscular chest covered by a white tank top, which my hand was securely grasping.

"About time you woke up," a smooth, husky voice joked.

My cheeks flushed and my body warmed. I immediately let go and bolted up. Raikidan watched me as he lay where he was with his arms behind his head, as if nothing strange was going on.

"You really are cuddly when you sleep," he said.

I let out a slow, annoyed breath. I wasn't planning on yelling, but I wasn't able to stop it. "I told you to stay off my bed!"

"Eira—"

"Why can't you just listen to me for once?"

"Eira, please—"

"Why do you insist—"

Raikidan sat up and placed his hand over my mouth. "Will you shut up and let me explain?" I glared at him but nodded. He let go of my mouth and lay back down. "After you fell back asleep last night, you had another nightmare. You were muttering and shaking, which turned into thrashing sometimes. I thought it'd be a good idea to wake you. I figured you'd want that, so I came over here, but as I reached you, you calmed down.

"I turned to head back to my sleeping place when you reached out and grabbed my arm. You had a strong hold on me, and I didn't want to risk hurting you by trying to pry you off, so I just laid here next to you. I figured you'd let go after a while, but instead you curled up to me and stayed there until you woke up."

I relaxed. I had jumped to conclusions. He hadn't ignored what I had said, at least not intentionally. Besides the nightmare I had woken up to, I didn't remember having any more, though I was sure I didn't want to.

I looked down at my lap. "Sorry."

"Don't worry about it. If I were you, I would have reacted the exact same way you did. It would seem as if I wasn't listening."

I glanced up at him with apprehension, but I was put to ease at the sight of his cocky smile.

I looked away and noticed a small vase with a bright flower arrangement. Picking the vase up, I examined the various flowers and then pulled it close to inhale all the different scents.

"Honeysuckle, snapdragons, and a single rose." I sighed contently from the mixture of pleasant smells. "Not the most elegant arrangement, but not the worst either."

"So you like them?" Raikidan asked.

I smiled. "Yes, thank you. But where did you get it?"

He avoided my gaze. "I did it myself."

So it was him. When he gave me the forget-me-nots, I suspected he might have grabbed them from my greenhouse, but could never find any evidence in my large patch. Now I knew. No way he could get these kinds of flowers in this healthy of a variety in the middle of the night. "You little thief. Those flowers in my greenhouse aren't just for anyone to pick."

He frowned. "Sorry. After last night I thought you could use something to make you smile."

I chuckled. "Relax, I'm teasing you. I appreciate the thought and effort."

"I remembered you telling Valene you liked honeysuckle a lot so I made sure to put some in the vase. They are your favorite flower and best possible choice, right?"

I grinned slyly at him and then turned to put the vase back down. "One of the best choices at least."

Raikidan sighed with slight aggravation and I giggled. Once I was sure the vase was safe, I lay down next to him, making sure I left a decent amount of space between us, and made myself comfortable. "You're not going to leave my bed, are you?"

He glanced at me from the corner of his eye. "Nah, I'm good."

I chuckled. "When will you ever listen to me?"

He looked up toward his forehead as if he were thinking, and then focused back on me. "Probably never."

I scoffed. "Figures. Do you find enjoyment in tormenting me?"

He chuckled. "I don't torment you. Annoy, yes. Torment, not so much."

"Right, so that would be a yes."

He laughed. "Only because you make it so easy."

I crossed my arms with a huff, and Raikidan chuckled. "What?"

"You're cute when you do that." A flush rushed into my cheeks and I looked away. Raikidan rolled on his side, closing the distance between the two of us. "Eira…" I pushed him back by his chest. "Eira, it's not a bad thing."

"He's lying to you."

"Don't say things like that."

"Why not? It's true."

"He's doesn't mean it."

"I don't want to hear things like that…"

My breath caught when Raikidan grabbed me by the shoulders and straddled me. He looked me in the eye and my chest tightened. "Just because you don't want to hear it doesn't make it untrue. I'm trying to compliment you."

"Get off me." I struggled, but he didn't move. "Raikidan, seriously, get off me."

He still didn't move. My body tightened up, and I struggled more. "Seriously, Raikidan!"

Raikidan's brow furrowed, but he didn't move. Breathing became harder. I needed to get him off. Wiggling and struggling against his grip, I managed to get my leg free and kick him off. He fell off the bed with a *thud*, but I didn't care.

I pulled myself up into a sitting position and hugged my legs close to my body while I buried my face into my knees, counting down from one hundred. I couldn't believe I had been in that position—how similar it felt to that first time.

"Eira? Eira, I'm sorry!"

I ignored him. I couldn't acknowledge him when so much was swirling around inside me and he was the cause. In that moment, I had experienced fear again—experienced pain from the past. In that split second, I had been reminded why I was always alone.

The street was quiet and only a few lights illuminated the dark street. I sat on the rooftop and monitoring the house across the road, aware of the single heartbeat inside picked up on my communicator. That heartbeat was my target.

After recovering from the situation Raikidan had put me in this morning, I had gone out and bought a new mirror to replace the one I had broken in the bathroom. My mood hadn't been good while I was out, and it soured more as I installed the new mirror, as I had been forced to remember why I had broken the reflective glass in the first place.

When Genesis had come to me with an assassination assignment, I jumped on it. I knew it wouldn't make my mood better, but it would distract me, even for a little while. The first target had been easy, and when I called in to tell Genesis of my completion of the assignment, she had offered up another one. I didn't see the harm in accepting it, as I was already out in the field, and here I was. I suspected this would also be an easy job.

My target was male, unlike the last one, and a skilled weapons creator. Muramasa was the name he went by. No one was ever sure if it was his real name or not, but that didn't matter much to me. I had seen his work many times and had never been disappointed by what he could create.

I didn't like the idea of killing such a talented man, but the Council had tried to sway him to our side, including resorting to bribery. However, he proved far too loyal to Zarda, and ultimately needed to be eliminated from the equation. He was too much of a threat to be allowed to live.

The man may have had money, but he lived modestly, having a small house in Quadrant Three, with no top-of-the-line security, and living under an alias, keeping him low on the radar. Had it not been for our moles, we may have never found him.

Noting the coast clear and the heartbeat still in the same location in the house, I slipped into the shadows and made my way to the other side of the street. Muramasa may not have had security systems or guards, but he was a weapons maker, so he would be undoubtedly capable of defending himself. This forced me to be extra careful as I made it to the side of his house and searched for a way in.

Finding a cracked open window, I slid it open more and slipped into the building. The house was still and all the lights had been turned off. My target was upstairs, and if my scanner was correct, he would be asleep, making my job easy. Taking my time, I made my way through the house without a sound. I was aware of the weapons strewn about, as if a possible break-in never even crossed this man's mind, and I was also aware it was the only mess to be found in any room. His cleaning habits were by far the strangest I'd seen.

Making my way upstairs, I was aware of every sound I made as I followed my heartbeat sensor. It led me to a large bedroom, but I became suspicious when it told me my target was lying in the bed. The way the bed was bunched up and how little it moved from someone breathing—*Trap!* I spun around and narrowly missed the knife slashing at me.

My assailant was a tall, burly man with pale skin and almond-shaped crimson eyes. He carried a dao sword in one hand and a combat knife in the other. This man meant business. My assailant also happened to be my intended target. I should have known this couldn't go as easily as hoped.

"Did you not think I was expecting this?" Muramasa hissed. "Did you not think I couldn't see you hiding in the shadows waiting to take me by surprise?"

"Kill him."

He slashed at me again, but I was quick and drew my favorite dagger and deflected the blow. Using my quick wit, I transformed it into a single sai and used it to disarm his hand with the combat knife when he came at me again.

The weapons maker grinned with amusement before swinging his dao sword. "Impressive weapon you have there. I'll enjoy learning all about it once I pry it from your corpse."

"Rip out his tongue first."

I snickered. Muramasa had refined swordsman skill, but I was better. "Afraid I can't allow that to happen."

Splitting my sai into two and then transforming one into a kukuri, I went on the offensive. The weapons maker defended himself well—too well. It wasn't until I had swung at him several times with my kukuri did I realize he was toying with me.

Muramasa smirked. "You can't beat me that way. Let me show you how it's done."

He turned the tables quickly and threw out an onslaught that was hard for me to defend against. I couldn't even get in enough time to try to switch the shape of my weapons. This wasn't going well at all.

I attempted to use objects around me to slow his assault down, but nothing fazed him. His blade struck my arm and I gritted my teeth as pain rushed through it. *This isn't good…* I couldn't believe I was being beaten so badly. At this rate he'd actually kill me.

"Desire to kill. Crave blood."

The weapons maker swung his dao sword and missed. He also over-extended his swing, throwing himself off balance. *There!* I wasn't going to miss this perfect opportunity. Swinging my kukuri down, I chopped into his arm and the man screamed in pain. He dropped his dao sword and held on to his arm with his uninjured hand. Without missing a beat, I thrust my sai at his chest, but he ducked instead of side stepping, and my weapon plunged into his throat—blood splattering everywhere.

The malevolent voice in my head laughed gleefully. *"Beautiful."*

Muramasa choked, his eyes rolling to the back of his head before he slumped over. I withdrew my blade from the corpse, taking several breaths as my heart pounded in my ears. That had been too close a call. He may be a weapons maker, but I hadn't expected him to be a weapons master as well. Maybe I had lost my edge—too out of practice for these types of situations.

"Your desire to kill is too weak."

Wiping his blood on my pants, I returned the weapon to its natural shape and sheathed it. I took a long calming breath and then examined my wound. It wasn't bad, but I'd have to make sure I took care of it when I returned home.

I then went about looking at all his wares to see if there was anything worth taking while I called Genesis.

"Oh good, I was beginning to worry," she said when she picked up.

"He knew I was coming," I informed "But after a quick scuffle I disposed of him. Nothing major."

I knew it wasn't good to lie to her, but I didn't think it important for her to know I actually almost screwed up this assignment.

"Good. I have another assignment, since you're out."

I picked up an interesting-looking knife. "Well this guy has some nice stuff I could grab instead…"

"Council already has someone coming by to make it look like a burglary gone wrong," Genesis said.

"Nice, so the choice was already made for me, and the assignment offer was out of formality, then."

"Eira."

I exhaled. "Yeah, I'll take it. Plenty of nighttime hours left anyway, so I might as well. Someone will have to retrieve a bloody weapon though. My target managed to draw a little blood."

"I'll make sure whomever they send will remove any traces of your activity. In the meantime I'll have Aurora relay information on your next target."

She cut the line and I sighed as I put the knife down and left the house to reduce any risk of being caught by a neighbor.

I dragged my feet as I made it to my room. I was sticky with sweat and blood and smelled even worse, but I didn't want to shower. I just wanted to sleep. I could handle two or three assassination missions, but five was far too much for one night.

I flopped down on my bed with a groan. Sleep was now the only thing on my mind. Not a shower. Not a change of clothes. Sleep. I sighed contentedly as I snuggled my face into my pillows.

"You lied to me."

I blinked. I thought I was the only one in my room. Then again, I hadn't bothered to look around. Slowly I sat up and turned around. Raikidan sat on the windowsill with his arms crossed. He didn't look happy in the least.

"What are you talking about?"

"You lied to me." My brow furrowed. I had no idea what he was going on about. "I tried talking to the others. They weren't willing to speak, but their reluctance helped me piece everything together."

I stood. "What the hell are you talking about? You're not making any sense."

"How old are you really?"

My brow rose. "How old am I? I told you, twenty-seven."

Raikidan advanced, his shoulders tight and grabbed my wrist. "You're lying! Tell me the truth."

I tried to struggle away. "What is your problem?"

"Who are you?" I was getting so confused. "I'm only going to ask you one more time. What is your real age?"

I ripped my arm free and shoved him. "I told you! I'm twenty-seven."

"Liar! I know you're lying. The inconsistencies of time, of all the events that have happened in your life don't match up! You said you were in your tank for seventeen years. You said your son took ten years to come out of his tank, and that was after you were out of yours. You had enough time in the military to gain the rank of commander. You had time to run and learn the ways of the shaman.

"That doesn't all happen in twenty-seven years. Your friends helped me put it all together. I had been suspicious before, but they were reluctant to talk about anything that told of a time frame. They mentioned getting the truth from you and wouldn't tell me what they meant. They told me I needed to see you about that."

I glared at him. I didn't like where this was going. "Leave."

"No. Tell me what is going on. How old are you?"

"I said leave."

"You will tell me."

"You really want to know that badly? Fine!" I threw my hands out. "I'm eighty-four. Happy?"

"I'm being serious here, Eira. How old are you really?"

"I am being serious. You wanted the truth, so here it is."

His brow furrowed. "Why didn't you tell me this before, when we first met?"

I placed my hands on my hips. "I don't know, Raikidan. Maybe because I didn't know you? Maybe because I didn't trust you? Maybe because you wouldn't have believed me?"

"I would have believed you."

"Oh, would you really? I'm human. Do I look eighty-four? Do I look that old?" He didn't reply. "Didn't think so. You would have thought I was lying if I had told you the truth."

"Then why didn't you tell me later when you knew I would?"

"Because it was too late, that's why! I was too deep into the lie. How was I supposed to tell you? 'Hey, Raikidan, nice day today. Oh, by the way, I lied to you about my age. I'm actually eighty-four years old. I figured I'd clear that up between us.' Yeah, that would go over great during morning breakfast."

Raikidan remained quiet, clearly soaking in the truth of my words.

"Not that it matters." I turned away. "In the end it never matters. Now get out of my room."

"Tell me your real name."

"My name is Eira."

"No, it's not."

Muscle twitched in my neck. "Have you not heard others call me by that name?"

"I have, but those closest to you call you by another name. You've told others to call you by this name. Laz isn't a short version for your shaman name. Your friends didn't know you were a shaman until you came back, but they called you by that name regardless. Now, what is your real name?"

"Get out of my room."

"What is your real name?"

"I said get out!"

"Not until you tell me the truth."

"My name is Eira, and that is all there is to it. Now get out of my room."

"Is your name Lazmira? Is it that name on that box? Is it?"

I rounded on him. "I told you to get the hell out of my room! Now go and don't come back in. I'm done dealing with you. I don't want you around me, so do us both a favor and leave. I don't want to see your damn face anymore. Now get out!"

Raikidan glared at me but didn't argue. He spun on his heels and slammed the door behind him as he stormed out. I threw myself onto my bed and sighed. I wasn't going to be able to sleep now. I was too angry.

I hate him. I hoped he would leave for good. I hoped I wouldn't have to see him ever again.

9
CHAPTER

My boots clomped on the basement stairs as I ran up. My plan was good—perfect even. Or it would be if I had control over everything. Sadly, I didn't, and there were two players who didn't like playing by my set of rules. Still, I was determined to have them play right, even if my methods had to go into the crazy and weird zone.

I opened the door, and as luck would have it, Raikidan was passing by. By the sound of it, Laz was also in the living room. *Perfect.* I knew the two were having a spat, and they weren't talking at the moment, but that didn't change how they felt about each other. The argument would blow over and things would go back to normal. And I was going to push it along—and farther. So wherever Raikidan was going, was going to have to wait.

I grabbed him by the wrist. "Come with me."

"But why?" he asked.

"Just 'cause."

"Where are they going?" Rylan asked.

"I have no idea," Laz replied.

I grinned. She may be mad at him, but I was sure I caught a hint of annoyance in her voice. She didn't like that I was taking Raikidan away. *Good.*

"Ryoko, what are you up to?" Raikidan asked as I dragged him through the basement.

I didn't say anything. Instead, I pulled him into the garage, where I had moved around some vehicles so there was a good open space. I let him go and turned around to face him. "This should be enough room right?"

"Excuse me?"

"I want to see your dragon shape. This should be enough room right?"

He shook his head and turned back toward the stairs. "We've been over this, Ryoko."

I grabbed him by the wrist again and yanked him back. "Oh, no you don't." Pushing him onto a car hood, I pinned him there with my body. "You're going to show me this dragon form of yours."

Raikidan stared at me for a moment. "Get off me." I grinned and grabbed onto his shirt. His brow furrowed. "What are you doing?"

"All you have to do is shift once. Else your clothes come off."

"You really think that's going to work?"

I yanked his shirt up. "Only one way to find out."

He tried to fight me but I was too determined to fail. After a brief struggle, his shirt found the floor. Raikidan glared at me, but I wasn't going to lose this time. I wasn't some prude trying to bluff him. I'd strip him past his skivvies if I had to.

Just then, someone walked into the garage. I glanced over my shoulder and found Laz staring at us. I grinned. *Perfect.* This was going to be fun.

"What the hell is going on here?" she demanded.

Raikidan held up his hands. "It's not what it looks like."

It really wasn't, but Laz didn't know that, and I wasn't going to let Raikidan spoil this. I giggled. "Got a problem with this?"

"No, of course not," she responded, though her eyes said otherwise.

"Then why are you down here?" I asked.

"Why are you?" she said, clearly agitated.

Good. It's working. "Just having a little fun is all. Wanna to join in?" I grinned. "Or would you rather climb up on him and take my place?"

Her face turned bright red. "Ryoko!"

I snickered. "Oh, so you do then."

She snorted. "Hardly."

"Hey, don't I have a say in all this?" Raikidan asked.

"Stay out of this, Raikidan," Laz and I said in unison.

He held up his hands and muttered, "That's kind of hard with Ryoko on top of me."

I half laughed, but he was silent after that. I focused back on Laz— her emotions were definitely getting the best of her. *Jealous much, Laz?* I continued to push. "Well if you've got a problem with what's going on, just say so, Laz."

She crossed her arms. "I don't. I just think you should get off him. He clearly doesn't want you there."

I grinned. "He's a big boy. If he's unwilling, he could push me away. What's it to you anyway?"

She ground her teeth and then spun on her heels. "Whatever, I'm out of here."

I watched her storm off before climbing off Raikidan. That was fun. I grinned at Raikidan. "Told you she likes you."

Raikidan didn't respond. Instead, he stared after Laz.

I giggled. "You see it too. I can tell. You want her just as much as she wants you."

He slipped off the hood of the car and put his shirt back on. "No, I don't, now knock it off, Ryoko. And stop trying to force me to shift."

He stormed off as well. I couldn't stop grinning. They were both too stubborn for their own good, but they weren't the only ones.

CHAPTER 10

(EIRA)

My room was quiet. There was no loud beat of his heart—no soft growling snores from his throat—no warmth from his body—no annoying questions. It had been like this for days now. When I had told Raikidan to leave, he did. He hadn't left the house, but he hadn't tried to come back into my room. I had thought to talk to him yesterday, to attempt to clear things up, but it was made clear to me he didn't want that.

My mood sucked. Everyone avoided me as much as possible, and I stayed in my room when I could. Loneliness encased my heart, but I didn't care. I was used to it. It was my fault anyway. I pushed myself away—pushed them away. I pushed the most against the ones who tried the most. *I pushed him away…*

"You don't need them."

Pushing him away was for the best. I knew it was.

"You don't need anyone."

I huffed and slid off my bed. I couldn't be in here anymore. I couldn't get over the fight. I couldn't get over the emotions that had raged through me when I found him and Ryoko doing the-gods-only-know-what in the garage yesterday.

I needed to force this pent up aggression out. I needed to feel better. Changing my clothes, I stormed downstairs and worked my body. I pushed it to its limit—pushed past its limit. The walls were scorched and my body ached, but I wouldn't stop. I couldn't stop. I couldn't find the strength to stop. I was so angry.

Strong male hands grabbed my arms. "You need to stop."

I sighed and tried to struggle away, but I was too exhausted to fight too much. "Rylan, let me go and leave me be."

"I'll let go when you agree to give it a rest," he said.

"Yeah, seriously, Laz, you need to stop before you kill yourself." I looked at Ryoko. She leaned on the railing of the stairs—concern flashing through her eyes.

"Leave me alone, guys."

"Tell us what's bothering you," Rylan said.

"It'll make you feel better," Ryoko added.

"I don't know…"

"You can tell us," Rylan insisted.

"I don't know!" I ripped my arms out of his grip and stormed over to the closest wall. I placed my hand on the vertical surface and stared at it.

"Tell us."

"Don't hold it in."

"You can trust us. You know that."

"You don't need to bottle it all up. We're here for you."

Turning around, I slid down to the ground and stared hopelessly at the floor. "I don't know…"

"Are you sure?" Ryoko asked.

I nodded. "I thought I knew… but now I don't…"

The room grew silent. I didn't look up to see if they had left. I knew they were still here, though I didn't know why. There was nothing they could do. I blinked in confusion as Rylan, in his wolf form, wriggled himself under my arms and laid half his body on my lap. It wasn't long after that Ryoko curled up against me with my other arm around her shoulders. I didn't understand. They had avoided helping me all this time, and only now they were choosing to comfort me in a way only they could.

I pulled them closer and rested my chin on Ryoko's head. It didn't matter. I needed to feel better. I needed to feel better fast so I could do what I was supposed to do. Protect them. I was to be their armor and could only be that if I wasn't damaged.

"Thanks, guys…" I murmured.

"Come back and keep us safe," Ryoko murmured.

"We need you," Rylan said.

I nodded but didn't speak. I had too much on my mind.

I took each step quietly and carefully. I couldn't find him in his room or anywhere else in the house, so the roof was the last place to check. I hoped I wasn't too late and he hadn't decided to leave for good.

Pushing the door open, I peered around it and looked for him. A small smile crept onto my face when I found Raikidan sitting on the ledge of the roof. *I still have a chance.*

I came to a halt when I was several feet away—doubt crawling inside me. I didn't want him to brush off my words. I blinked. What was I going to say? I had known when I was walking up the stairs, but now I was drawing a blank.

Raikidan, noticing my presence, turned around. I swallowed and scratched my arm. It was too late to leave now, and I still wasn't sure how to place my words. "Um… hey."

"Hey."

An awkward silence enveloped us. *This is pointless… It's not going to happen. I can't find the words…*

I turned to leave. "I'll leave you alone."

"You wanted to say something." I stopped dead. "What did you want to say?"

"I… I…" I chewed my lip. "I was just going to apologize… for the way I acted. I should have been calmer and used the moment to clear things up instead of perpetuating the terrible lie." I chewed my lip. "I don't even know why I lied to begin with. It's not like it would have caused any issues for you to know my true age or anything."

I stiffened when his arms wrapped around my waist and stifled the shiver his hot breath on my neck brought up. "Apology accepted."

"You accepted it so easily."

"Because I should be the one apologizing. It was my fault you were upset. I should have approached the subject better and shouldn't have pushed you so far."

"So we're both sorry?"

He tightened his grip quickly and then loosened it. "Yes. So can I now come back to your room? I don't like it in that other room. It's quiet and I didn't like not being able to hear you sleep to help me sleep." I looked at him funny and he hesitated. "I, uh, I—I guess what I'm trying to say is… I missed being around you."

I fought a small blush. He had disliked the situation as much as I had and for the same reason. I wasn't sure if that was what embarrassed me so much, or if it was that fact that he was so okay with admitting it out loud. I managed to push it away when I realized how close I was starting to get to Raikidan. It wasn't supposed to be like this. I wasn't supposed to get irritated when Ryoko wanted to hang around him without anyone else around. I wasn't supposed to desire him to be around all the time, or miss him when he was gone. *He's not supposed to miss me…*

"No, I like having my room to myself," I lied, pushing him away.

"Oh, c'mon." He grabbed my wrist gently and pulled me closer. "You can't say you didn't miss having me around."

I drove away the wave of awkward embarrassment that threatened to surface and pushed him away again. "Not for a second."

"Fine, be that way. But can I at least sleep in the same room as you again?"

"No."

"All right, thanks!" He bolted past me and slammed the door behind him.

"Raikidan!" Yanking the door open, I chased after him. When I reached the living room, I attempted to turn toward my room, but I slipped on the wooden floor. Catching my balance, I ran to my bedroom, only for the door to slam in my face. I jiggled the handle and banged on the door, but it didn't open.

"Raikidan, open this door." I pounded on the door again, to no avail. Grumbling, I headed back up the stairs.

"Looks like they're back to normal," Zane commented.

"Good. I didn't like angry Eira and mopey Raikidan," Blaze said.

I chuckled. Reaching the ledge of the roof, I climbed down the fire escape as quietly as I could. Grinning, I swung through the window. Raikidan wasn't looking in my direction. He was focused on holding the door.

"Can't get rid of me that easily," I said.

He spun around. "How—"

I pointed to the window and he grunted. He strolled toward me, and I met him halfway. Raikidan kept his gaze on me as I passed him and grabbed the doorknob. As I opened it, he lunged and I grinned. Swinging the door open and ducking under him, I pushed him out.

Raikidan caught himself and grabbed the doorframe as I threw the door closed. He groaned in pain when the door slammed into his hand, and I cringed and cursed quietly. I hadn't meant to hurt him.

Raikidan twisted his hand around to grasp the door and forced his way back in. "You're not kicking me out this time."

"Like hell I'm not," I grunted out as I tried to push the door closed. "I'm keeping my room to myself."

"Don't be selfish." He pushed with effort and forced me back.

I stumbled and was unable to catch myself. I hit the ground hard. "Ow…"

My bedroom door slammed into the wall and then slammed shut from the force. I gasped when Raikidan fell. He landed on me but immediately propped himself up so he was hovering. My cheeks flushed several shades and my heart thundered in my ears as the two of us stared each other in the eye. Like all other times when I made eye contact with him, I was snared into those sapphire pools. But this time, the staring had an effect on my body. I held my hands close to my chest as a warm sensation flooded over me, making me feel awkward and self-conscious.

Then suddenly, he jumped to his feet. Not taking my freedom for granted, I stood as well and put some distance between us. The distance gave me the time to get myself back to its normal, comfortable state.

Raikidan scratched the back of his head. "So, are you really eighty-four years old?"

Thankful he was trying to diffuse the tension with an unrelated topic, I sat down on my bed and nodded. "Yep."

He sat down next to me. "You don't look it."

"You don't look two centuries old either."

"Yeah, but I'm a dragon."

"And I'm a war experiment and nu-human."

He chuckled. "Fine, you win. But is it common for you guys to live this long?"

I nodded. "The average nu-human can manage four centuries. As for experiments, we're not completely sure, although some of the Council members are running up in the three-century range, and as you know, Genesis is well beyond those numbers. It's believed though, that our enhancements extend our lives."

"Why don't you know?"

"Well, not enough of us have died off from natural causes to get a concrete average."

Raikidan nodded. "All right, I think I get it. But why didn't you tell me your real age in the first place?"

"I already told you, I stupidly thought you wouldn't have believed me, so I made up the lie and eventually it became far too late to fix it."

He nudged me. "You should have told me. I would have believed you if you had explained it."

"I don't like talking, and let's be honest. Our communication skills with each other could use some work."

He chuckled. "Good point. So how does the aging process work for you nu-humans?"

"Well, it's a lot like elves, except the first part of our lives. We age at a standard human pace until we hit adulthood, which would be around twenty, give or take a few years depending on the individual. Once we hit adulthood, the aging process in our bodies slows significantly, only ever showing signs every ten or so years. Sometimes it even takes longer for signs of aging to show. There are, of course, some who don't age as gracefully and look older than they are."

"Interesting," he mused. "It's similar to dragons, except our aging process slows a bit earlier. Could you give me a breakdown on how you lived your life?"

"Sure. As you know, I spent seventeen years in a tank growing. I spent forty more years serving under Zarda. For five years we spent our time fighting back. At the end of those five years, I left and ran for another five years. This is when I met the shamans. I spent twelve years with them and then had to leave. I spent five more years running, and that's when you found me."

"You didn't find me?"

I snorted. "I was too busy dying to find you."

Raikidan chuckled. "True. So give me a breakdown of everyone else's ages."

"Well, it's a given that Genesis is the oldest. She's older than any known nu-human living today. Zane is the second oldest here. He's getting to be around two and a half centuries now, maybe a little older. Argus and Seda are next with being around two hundred and forty, give or take a year or so. They were designed, created, and released from their tanks in the same years."

Raikidan held up a hand. "Wait, I thought you said war experiments like you didn't happen until after Blaze was designed. How could Seda have been created so much sooner than you?"

I rubbed the back of my head. "About that… I lied, but not because I wanted to fool you. The truth is a touchy subject for most, and the average civilian doesn't even know. The reason being, Zarda did experimentation in secret before he was our leader. It's why the council members are so old, and how Rylan's design is so much more perfect than previous experiments. It took over two hundred years for him to get to Rylan's design."

"Do I want to know why he did it in secret?" Raikidan asked. I shook my head. "All right, so Seda was a secret experiment then?"

"Well, no. The thing about psychics… they're always an accident. No one knows how to unlock the secret of making their power. It just happens. It's always been that way since humans have existed."

"So it doesn't matter if they're tank-born or not?"

I shook my head. "Only half of the psychics in the military are tank-born. When a psychic is born outside the tank, they are found by other psychics and taken away to be trained."

"So they have no hope of living a life like everyone else born outside tank creation?"

I nodded. "They're cursed, just as we are."

"Keep telling me about everyone's ages."

"Blaze is next, being only a year or two younger than Argus and Seda. I met Argus, Blaze, and my uncle around the same time after my release. They had already been out of the military by that point and working at the shop."

"How long had they been out?"

I shrugged. "I'm not sure. My mother never told me since she was so bitter about it and I never thought to ask the guys."

"She wasn't able to leave?"

I shook my head slowly. "Zane was released early from duty due to a serious injury. It's why he doesn't help us with the fighting."

"He has that limp."

I nodded. "He was released when we had our previous leader. He was much kinder than Zarda, much, much kinder. Argus and Blaze requested a release to give Zane a hand since they had known each other all their lives. Unfortunately, by the time my mother and aunt would have been allowed to leave, Zarda was in control and he wouldn't allow it. My mother always resented Zane's luck."

Raikidan titled his head. "Why didn't she leave like you had?"

My expression sobered. "Because she didn't want to leave me behind."

Raikidan lowered his gaze. "I see."

"Rylan is the same age as me but was released a half year before me." I needed to change the subject before he started asking too many questions. "Then Ryoko ties everything up by being the youngest. She's a year younger than me."

"All right, now tell me, how do you know how long you were running?"

I shrugged. "The solstice."

"The solstice? Like the summer and winter solstice?"

I nodded. "During the summer solstice, my fire is at its strongest, and during the winter solstice, my fire is at its weakest."

"And the equinox?"

I shrugged. "I'm not affected by the spring or autumn equinox."

"Interesting…" he mused. "Any particular reason?"

I shrugged again. "Shva'sika said something about it having to do with my main element and my opposite. My main element being fire means the summer solstice heightens my abilities as long as it's happening. But because one of fire's opposites is water, as well as its sub-element of ice, and my most logical opposite element thanks to my mother, the winter solstice does the opposite to my abilities. Both equinoxes are related to earth and air, and have neutral effects on fire, thus having neutral effects on my ability during the equinox."

"Interesting, but makes some sense, I guess."

"I guess you're not affected?"

Raikidan shook his head. "I've never felt any different during any seasonal change."

"Too bad. You might like the extra power the solstice gives."

"Maybe, but I'd also hate the lack of power for the opposite solstice."

I snickered. "You're a lot smarter than you look. Most would want what I feel. They'd want the extra power for one day without any thought to the negative later on."

Raikidan shoved me. "I do have a brain. As hard as you find that to believe."

I smirked. "I'm not fully convinced, but you've proven to me enough you have more than I once thought."

Raikidan pushed me again. "Just because I piss you off a lot doesn't mean I don't have a brain."

"Oh, it doesn't?"

"I like getting on your nerves."

"Sure you do. That's why you begged to come back in here after telling me you missed being around me."

Raikidan bumped my chin with his fist. "I said I like to get on your nerves, not your bad side and be banned from being around you." I chuckled and shook my head as I stood to head for my dresser. "Where are you going?"

"We have work tonight," I reminded him. "And there is a dress code."

Raikidan grumbled. "Do we have to? I hate that place, and I hate having to pry men off you. It's a pain in my ass."

I gave him a long stern look. "And you think I enjoy it?"

"You don't show that you mind."

I snorted. "This is me we're talking about. If it were up to me, I'd work the bar and kill anyone who tried to touch me."

Raikidan chuckled. "If you didn't choose to hide who you were, you could."

"If I chose to reveal who I really was, we'd have more problems than horny drunk men looking for some ass to grab."

Raikidan snorted and headed for the door. Just as he made it there, he stopped and glanced back at me. He looked as if he wanted to say something, but decided against it and left for me to change alone.

I smiled when the door closed. At least he was being decent and not making a fuss about leaving while I changed—this time. I eyed at the walking death traps called shoes and the skimpy clothes called a uniform. When Rylan had first given them to me, I thought he had stopped at Midnight, though I knew I shouldn't have since I had seen the waitresses wearing them prior to me becoming an employee. Upon putting them on the first time, I found the short-shorts uncomfortable, and the cropped shirt made my breasts look huge, not that Ryoko wouldn't say my breasts were huge even without the shirt accentuating them. I personally would disagree, especially in comparison to her, but she never listened.

I had hoped Azriel would have made an exception for me and given me something a bit more appropriate. Sighing, I reluctantly changed into my work clothes. I hoped it would go smoothly for once.

CHAPTER 11

My eyes closed and then opened slowly, and my lips curved into a deeper, more seductive grin. Zo continued to ramble on about some stupid war tale with him in it as I leaned on his table and listened. I forced myself to laugh or show great interest at the appropriate times, even though none of it was funny or interesting.

I had hoped for a decent night, but that desire had been dashed immediately when Raikidan and I walked inside. Zo was already here and, along with his table mates, had been causing a problem.

"Good. You're here," Azriel greeted. "I need you to take care of a specific table."

"Sure, which one?" I shouldn't have agreed before knowing.

"The one Zo is sitting at," he informed me.

"No!" I shook my head and threw out my hands. "We agreed the first day I came to work I wouldn't have to deal with him."

"I know, I know, but I really need you to do this," Azriel begged. "The men have been harassing the other waitresses, and now the waitresses are refusing to serve them."

"Well, of course they're getting harassed. Zo is their ringleader."

"But that's the thing. He's not doing it," Azriel had defended. "He's acting completely out of character. The others have reported his actions as anxious. It's like he's waiting for something and couldn't care less about the women around

him. Please do this for me, Laz. I can't afford to lose a single customer right now. Zarda has been taxing us too much. I'll pay you extra when I have the money."

And here I was. I hadn't been harassed by the other soldiers, but Zo had been all too inclined to bother me. I wasn't blind, nor was I stupid, and as much as I hated that Argus and Ryoko were right, I couldn't deny the truth. Zo was anxious because he has been looking for me. I couldn't see why his focus was always on me. I wasn't anything special.

Zo held up his mug. "You wouldn't mind topping me off, would you, Sweetcheeks?"

I smiled. "Sure thing, Zo."

As I left with his glass in hand, I tuned my ears into listening to the others at the table.

"Zo, can we talk to the woman now?" one of them asked.

"Yeah, can't you share?" another one voiced.

"You three don't know how to handle a woman," Zo said.

"The hell we don't," the last soldier defended.

"You scared off the last four that came to this table tonight," Zo spat. "I'm not going to allow you three to scare her off."

"Hey, we have needs," that last soldier replied again. "It's not our fault they can't handle us."

Zo snorted. "And this is why you can't be trusted around women. You don't know how to handle them. They're fragile."

Fragile, right. He obviously didn't know all women. Sure, there were women who were fragile, but there were many others who could hold their own, and not all those women were soldiers. I filled Zo's glass and headed back to the table.

"I don't see why she's so special to you," the first soldier muttered. "You've never cared so much for a woman in your life."

Zo shook his head. "Those other women weren't like this one. Eira is different. She's… something else."

I wanted to gag. I wasn't sure what was worse, Zo actually finding interest in me, or the fact he was trying to compare me to the whores he had been with in the past.

"Here you go, Zo." He took the glass gratefully and toasted me before gulping it down. "You boys need anything?"

The three soldiers glanced at each other and then pushed their mugs toward me with grins plastered to their faces. Picking up the glasses skillfully, I turned to head back to the bar and bumped into someone.

"Oops, sorry," I mumbled. "I really should watch where I'm going."

"Don't be sorry. It was my fault for walking up on you." I froze. I knew that voice. Slowly I looked up. The young man I had been accosted by the first time I'd been back here since my return stood in front of me with a sly grin on his face. "Hey, baby."

"Great, it's you."

I pushed past him, but he grabbed me by the elbow. "Hey, don't be like that."

I ripped my elbow away. "Get lost."

He grabbed me again and pulled me close. "You owe me a dance."

"No, I don't."

"You're right." I felt his grin on my ear. "You owe me a little more than just a dance."

"I owe you nothing."

"Listen, you—"

His presence left suddenly, and my curiosity forced me to spin around. I suppressed a smile at the sight of Raikidan holding the soldier by the back of his head. "She told you to leave her alone."

"Let me go, you bastard, and mind your own business, or else," the soldier barked.

"I don't think you're in a position to make threats, Anders," Zo said.

Anders narrowed his eyes. "General, shouldn't you be taking my side?"

"You shouldn't be harassing her."

Anders snorted. "What's with you lately? You've never had a problem sharing in the past."

I was starting to feel uncomfortable. I didn't like the direction this conversation had taken.

"It's time for you to leave," Raikidan growled at Anders.

"Over my dead body. I'll leave when I get what I want."

Raikidan grinned. "That can be arranged."

"The dead part," I added.

"Stay out of this, Eira," Raikidan warned.

"Like hell I—" I stopped when a woman screeched. Whipping around, I found one of the other waitresses being manhandled by a drunk soldier. My eyes narrowed into slits, and I slammed the three glasses down on the table, making all five men around me jump. I stalked over to a nearby table and stole a glass from a patron.

"Hey!" he protested.

"I'll get you another one," I promised.

Making my way over to the waitress in distress, I changed my stride into a seductive sashay. The drunken soldier turned his gaze on me and grinned. "Well, looky here. It must be my lucky day."

"Hey there," I cooed. "Why not let her go and spend your time with someone better?"

The soldier's grip left the waitress, who was all too happy to sidle away from him. With a grin, I stepped closer to the soldier, but just as he went to grab for me, I tipped the glass of beer over his head. The soldier froze, his eyes wide, and his buddies at the table laughed, but I wasn't done yet. Grabbing him by the front of his shirt, I pulled him from his seat and smashed the glass down on his head.

The soldier hit the ground with a *thud* and was out cold. The other soldiers at the table stopped laughing and froze. I looked around the room and realized everyone was looking at me. Even the DJ had stopped playing his music. I didn't care much about what they thought of my actions. I just wished they would stop staring. My actions weren't that surprising; at least, I didn't think so.

Resting my hand on the young waitress' back, I ushered her toward the bar. As I did, the music resumed and the club went back to their business.

"Thank you, Eira," the woman breathed with relief.

"Don't mention it," I replied. "It felt good to actually hit one of them and get away with it."

She laughed. "I wish I had the same courage as you, but I guess that's what happens when you live outside the city most of your life."

"You have to learn to survive. If you don't have the courage to face your fears out there, you'll never make it."

Azriel had agreed to use my immigration story as a cover and had told it several times until he knew all the workers had heard and understood it. Those who had known me before had agreed to go with it, and those who didn't, believed it quite easily.

I addressed the olive-tan-skinned man with a dual set of ears as we reached the bar, "Az, I think an early break is in order for her."

Azriel nodded in agreement. "Sounds good to me too. Bethlana, go take a break. You can still have your regular one later tonight."

"Thank you, Azriel." She smiled kindly and headed for the back room. I ducked under the bar to grab four glasses.

"I can't believe you, Laz!" Azriel shouted when she was gone. "What were you thinking? Were you even thinking at all?"

"Chill out, Az," I told him as I began pouring ale into the glasses. "It's not like I killed him."

"You knocked him out!"

"Your point? It wasn't like anyone else was giving her a hand."

Azriel sighed. "Laz, you can't be hitting people like that. You're a waitress."

"And this is a club. A regular club where people come to dance, hook up, and get drunk off their asses. This is not your brother's strip club. I'm not going to sit around and let them manhandle us anymore. I don't care if you're having issues with money. We shouldn't have to put up with it, and if you don't like it, I'll quit and go back to working for Zane."

"No, don't do that," he begged. "I need you here."

"Then choose. Me putting these unruly patrons in their place or you losing me since no one else wants to come up with a better solution."

He let out an exasperated breath. "Just don't get out of hand, okay?"

With a triumphant smile, I walked around the bar with four drinks on a round serving tray. "I won't do anything that would reveal who I really am or get your place closed down. I promise."

"That's not what I'm worried about," Azriel muttered as I walked off.

I should have asked him to clarify, but I had work to do. Stepping over the knocked-out soldier before two bouncers could haul him away, I placed a glass in front of the man I had stolen the beer from, and sauntered back over to Zo's table.

Raikidan was no longer at the table, but then again, neither was that Anders guy, which led me to believe Raikidan was taking care of him. Placing the glasses down on the table with a smile, I pushed them toward the three soldiers. "Anything else I can do for you boys?"

The three looked at each other and then me. They shook their heads and drank their ale. I glanced to Zo and raised an eyebrow.

Zo chuckled. "You've gone and scared them, Sweetcheeks."

I laughed. "Oh c'mon, be serious, Zo."

"I am serious."

My eyes squinted as a smirk slipped up the side of my face. "And you call yourselves soldiers."

"You knocked a soldier out," one soldier muttered. "Female civilian or not, if you're crazy enough to do what you did, you're not someone to mess with."

I laughed. "You seem unaffected, Zo."

He grinned and leaned closer to me. "I prefer a strong, independent woman like you."

I refrained from retching. That had to be his most blatant pass at me yet.

A strong hand touched my back. "You forgot stubborn, too."

I laughed. "You say it like being stubborn is a bad thing there, tiger."

"Bad? No. Annoying? Yes," Raikidan teased with a grin.

I grunted. "Like you're any better. What are you doing over here anyway?"

"Azriel wanted to talk to you again."

I sighed. "Great. What does he want to yell at me about now?"

"I don't think he's mad."

"Yeah, I highly doubt that. He was pretty angry when I was over there last."

Raikidan moved his hand to my shoulder. "C'mon, you'll be fine."

"Yeah, sure," I muttered as I turned away from the table with him.

Raikidan wrapped his arm around my shoulder and guided me away. I noticed him look back and shoot off a glare.

One of the soldiers chuckled. "Looks like Zo has a little more competition than we thought."

With a grin, I reached up and rested my hand on Raikidan's hanging arm. Raikidan looked down at me and smirked.

Another soldier chuckled. "Looks like he's doing a better job than you, Zo. How does that make you feel?"

Raikidan glanced back and grinned more. I refrained from laughing when I heard a glass break.

"Oh, looks like he doesn't like this one bit." the last soldier taunted. "I'm starting to like this. I might want to stick around more often to see how this will play out in the end."

I snickered when the soldier yelped in pain.

"You enjoy their misery," Raikidan observed.

"You don't?"

"Not as much as you. Although I am finding that general's anger most entertaining." I opened my mouth to say something but he continued. "I also don't particularly care for the way he treats you. Whether you mind or not, I'm not going to tolerate it, and I will be stepping in."

My cheeks warmed a bit. He didn't need to act this way, but I couldn't find the strength to tell him to ignore his protective nature, or find a part of me that didn't like how he was acting. In the past that would have unsettled me, but right now I embraced it. "I don't want his attention on me, so no close contact, and I will agree to this."

Raikidan grinned. "Can't promise anything if that general starts to get grabby."

I grimaced. "Satria forbid he does."

Raikidan laughed. "Do you mind if I ask something a little odd? I've been meaning to get an answer from you for a while, but never figured out the best way to ask."

"Lay it on me."

"What's with Azriel's ears?"

I laughed. "You were better off asking it like that sooner. Azriel and his brother have two sets of ears as an attempt to give nu-humans better hearing."

Raikidan's brow rose. "He has a brother?" I nodded. "He isn't gay too, is he?"

I laughed. "Hell no. Andariel is as straight as you can get."

"Good. Dealing with one gay man is enough for me."

I snickered. "Not all gay men are like Azriel. Most act like everyone else and give people their space. Azriel is… how should I put it…"

"Dominant?" Raikidan finished.

I nodded. "That would be a good word for it. You've probably met a few gay men and never realized it."

"All right, now back to this ear thing. Why doesn't everyone have ears like them? Did it not work?"

I shook my head. "The theory was correct, but the outcome wasn't. They theorized a second set of ears would allow more sound to be picked up, but by the time Azriel and Andariel were let out, the second set of ears they had only grew to the length of a half-elf's instead of the standard nu-human length and the result they wanted didn't happen. They hear the same as I do, it's just split between the two ears."

"So if you covered one set of their ears, what would happen?" Raikidan asked.

"They'd hear half as well," I explained. "So in the end, it's still an advantage, since if you covered my ears, my hearing would be cut by more than half."

"But that's the only advantage," Raikidan mused.

I nodded. "Yes, and that's why Zarda decided there was no need to change our basic design. That one advantage wasn't enough to change the formula to make nu-humans, so he had their design scrapped."

He opened his mouth to say something, but Azriel's voice interrupted him. "Good. You're here."

I sighed. "Yeah, I am. What do you want to yell at me about?"

Azriel gave me a quizzical look. "Yell at you? Who in their right mind told you that I wanted to do that?"

"Told you," Raikidan said.

I blinked. "Then why do you want me over here?"

"Adrian went home early. Said something about his little girl being sick and her good-for-nothing mother not being able to do jack shit. Or something like that, so I need you to work the bar."

I grinned. "I thought you'd never ask. But who is going to take my tables?"

"Cassandra came in. She'll be taking the tables."

I laughed. "Those poor souls."

Standing at an abnormal height of six feet seven inches and made entirely of muscle, with an attitude to match, Cassandra was as scary as civilians came, and she put most tank-borns to shame. I was surprised the blonde hadn't scared any customers off by now. Or Azriel hadn't given her a bouncer position.

Maneuvering around the bar, I gazed at Azriel expectantly. "So what do I do first?"

He smirked. "The first thing you do is teach Raikidan how to do this."

In confusion, I looked over at Raikidan, who also appeared puzzled. "Um, what?"

"I need more bartenders now," Azriel said. "Remember how a few quit last week?"

I had completely forgotten all about that. They had been pissed by the recent soldiers' behavior and tight money situation, preventing them from picking up extra hours.

"When he's not bouncing, he can tend the bar. That should make up for any time you work and he can't come in as a bouncer."

"All right. Raikidan, get over here." He made his way around the bar and stood next to me. Azriel disappeared soon after, leaving the two of us alone. "I guess I'll teach you the different drinks since you'll need to know them by name before you can make them."

He nodded and listened as I went about explaining everything to him.

CHAPTER 12

My violet hair whipped around me as I spoke with a comrade. We were out doing an information exchange, and it was going well. Even though Ryoko and I had little information ourselves, these two women had an endless collection to share.

"Zarda finally got his hands on Astoria," one said.

Ryoko gasped. "No way! That elven city's defenses are ridiculously tough."

"Not all that surprising if you think about it," I countered. "Zarda has been slowly cutting off their resources, while hammering away at their defense. They were bound to crumble eventually."

"But you have to admit, the fight they put up was a good one," the other woman said.

I nodded in agreement.

"And from what we gathered, he's going for Ravenward next," she said.

I chuckled. "I wish him all the luck with that."

The first woman shook her head. "Why even get sarcastic about it? Everyone knows that elven city doesn't have any defenses. They'll be obliterated in seconds."

I snorted. "You obviously know nothing about them. The city and the forest are one entity, and those in control of the city, as well as those protecting it, are all earth elementalists. That city is protected, it's just not as obvious."

The woman rolled her eyes. "I still doubt they're capable of fighting off an army of this city's caliber."

Conversation ended at the sound of two approaching motorcycles. The four of us watched as two men parked their motorcycles and climbed off them.

"Wow..." the second women breathed. "I wish my housemates were that hot. You two are so lucky."

"You have to admit it, Laz, they do look good." Ryoko sounded a little hungry, and to be honest, I couldn't blame her.

I couldn't feel the way she did, but I could approve of how the boys looked. Both were decked out in leather and hid their eyes behind reflective sunglasses with colored lenses, and they had also chosen to keep their hair their natural colors, though it appeared Raikidan had worked some gel into his hair, as it stood in a way that it appeared as though he had spread the gel on his hand and quickly ran it through his hair.

I had to admit to myself, and only myself, I liked this look on him. I liked it a lot. I lowered my sunglasses to show my approval.

Ryoko giggled. "I am right. You do like him."

I scoffed and rolled my eyes as I put my sunglasses back over my eyes. "You're still wrong. I just approve of what he's wearing."

"I'll take either of them if you won't," one of the women said, a clear hunger in her eye.

I noticed Ryoko tense, and grinned. "Don't like him, huh?"

Ryoko blushed three shades of red and went to open her mouth to protest, but was unable to as the boys made it to us.

Rylan grinned and ran his finger along Ryoko's hair. "Blue looks nice on you."

Ryoko smiled. "Thanks."

I was tempted to shake my head. She was trying hard not to show her feelings. I didn't understand. Then again, I didn't understand those feelings in general.

I gazed up at Raikidan when he leaned on my motorcycle. "What, no compliments?"

Raikidan grunted. "Why would I give you one? You throw them back at me."

I laughed. "There's that brain again."

He leaned closer. "You know it's not nice to say things like that."

"I never said I was nice," I said as I pushed him away by his chest.

He grinned but didn't get to say more.

"Hey!" a man cried out behind him. "We need our keys."

Rylan and Raikidan reached into their pockets and pulled out a set of keys. They tossed them to the two men standing by the motorcycles, who caught them with ease.

"Let's go, ladies," the other called.

The two women sighed and headed toward the two men but not before giving both Rylan and Raikidan seductive looks. "Bye, boys."

Raikidan, clueless as ever, didn't understand, and Rylan rolled his eyes, apparently unimpressed. "Let's head back to the house."

Ryoko threw a fist into the air. "Yes, please! My back is killing me today."

Agreeing with them, I turned to climb onto my bike, but was stopped by Raikidan grabbing my cropped jacket. "What gives?"

"I'm driving," he said.

"Like hell you are. I don't ride passenger on motorcycles."

"Well, you will this time." He pulled me back and climbed onto the motorcycle. "Now get on."

I crossed my arms in defiance. "No."

"Stop being a baby, Laz, and get on," Ryoko teased. "It's not going to kill you."

"I don't ride passenger."

"Fine, then you can walk home," Rylan stated as he climbed onto Ryoko's motorcycle. Everyone stared at him. "What?"

"I can't believe you actually suggested that," Ryoko breathed. "You never say stuff like that."

Rylan shrugged. "If she's going to act like a child, then let her. We'll treat her in the same respect. Besides, I'm not going to sit around here while Laz behaves this way. I want to get out of these stupid clothes."

"I think you look nice…" Ryoko murmured as she climbed on the motorcycle behind him.

Rylan's face tinted with a small flush, and it grew as she wrapped her arms around him. He fumbled with the keys in the ignition but recovered and started the motorcycle.

Grumbling, I climbed on the motorcycle behind Raikidan and wrapped my arms loosely around him. Raikidan didn't say anything as he started up the motorcycle and kicked it into gear. My grip tightened as we took off down the road quickly. He was as crazy as me when it came to driving, but my grip loosened once I became accustomed to it.

"Why do you hate this so much?" he asked.

"Because."

"That's not a reason."

"I just do."

"You have a real reason. What is it?"

I sighed. "When you learn to rely on only yourself, it's hard to go back to relying on others. It makes you feel weak."

"This makes you feel weak?"

I nodded. "In a car, I still have some control, even if it's only where I sit. On a bike, however, I have to rely on you completely to get me somewhere. I'm not in control of something as simple as getting from point A to point B."

"Having the chance to rely on someone else is nice," he told me. "Makes you feel less alone."

I grunted. "I thought you liked being alone."

"I choose to be alone because there is no one I can rely on. There is no one around I can trust."

Instead of replying, I looked at him and ran his words through my mind over and over. I tightened my grip around his waist and rested my head on his back. A small ounce of shock rippled though his body, but he didn't voice a protest.

"You look nice," I murmured.

A chuckle rumbled through his chest. "What is with you all of a sudden?"

I gnashed my teeth, fighting a tightening sensation in my chest. I wasn't sure why, but the way he said that, kind of hurt.

He turned his head to look at me, but I avoided his gaze. Raikidan focused back on the road and then rested his hand on top of mine, making me tense. I could feel the definition of his abs as he held my hands against his body. His skin was warm, which was a nice contrast to the cool wind around us.

Just as suddenly as he had grasped my hands, he let go and placed his hand back on the handlebar. I gazed at him. He glanced back at me with a small grin.

"I meant what I said," I said.

"You only like it because I'm shirtless."

"I'd be lying if I said you were wrong." His brow twisted and I laughed. "I'm kidding."

"Don't make me kick you off this thing."

I tightened my grip and rested my head on his back again. "You wouldn't be that mean."

"You're right." He chuckled. "I'd throw you into the arms of your favorite general we just passed."

My eyes widened. "We what?"

"Yeah, he looked pretty shocked to see us. I hope you can come up with a good excuse the next time you see him face-to-face."

I groaned. "I knew I should have dyed my hair."

"I like that you didn't. You look better with your hair this color."

A flush rushed through my cheeks. "I think I looked better with red hair."

"You did look good that way. And with black hair as well, but I can't call you Butterfly unless you keep it this color."

"Then maybe I'll dye my hair red when I get home and make sure it's a permanent."

"I wouldn't do that," Raikidan said. "At the club I saw Zo doing that thing you call flirting, with a woman with red hair, and he was being more aggressive with her than he is with you."

I groaned again. "When will my hellish torture end?"

"When you say it's okay for me to kill him."

I blinked. "Why do you want to kill him so bad? It's not like he's after you or something."

"His actions are upsetting you, though. That's reason enough for me."

My face burned again. "Um, well… thanks… but I don't need to be protected or anything. I do fine on my own."

"Doing fine shouldn't be good enough. You shouldn't be settling for anything less than perfect."

"Why would I do that when I'm not perfect myself?"

Raikidan didn't respond, caught off guard by my words, even though

I didn't think he should have been. I was nowhere near perfect, and I never once expected anything to be perfect. Nothing could truly be perfect, so why try to force the impossible?

"Eira…"

"Yeah?"

"You… you look nice today. Your clothes match… your personality."

I smiled despite myself. "Thanks."

Shock rippled through Raikidan's body. I didn't blame him. It had been the first time I had accepted one of his compliments.

"Eira."

I chuckled. "Yes?"

"I think you're a little more perfect than you realize."

I shook my head. "No, you're wrong, Raikidan. I'm far from that."

Raikidan shook his head and focused on driving. He wasn't going to agree with me, but no one else did, either. No one else could see me the way I did. I didn't have low self-esteem. I just knew how to handle the truth a little bit better than most.

Ryoko tossed her jacket on the floor and plopped face down on the couch with a moan. I pitied her. She didn't deserve it. It wasn't like she asked a large chest, but then again she didn't strive to go out and get them reduced, either.

"Ryoko, why don't I give you a massage?" I offered.

She tilted her head and looked up at me. "Really? That would be amazing."

"I'll go get the table, then."

Opening the door to the utility closet, I pulled out a long table and headed back to the living room. Ryoko climbed off the couch and onto the table while I entered my room and came back out with a small bottle of oil. Applying a thin coating of oil to my hands, I rubbed my hands over her back. A content sigh escaped her lips.

With knots everywhere, easing her pain proved no easy task. It was typical for our bodies to tense up from the stress we put them under, but Ryoko had gotten the short end of the stick. No matter how much you worked with her, it would come back sooner than anyone wanted. I figured it had to do with her design, but I couldn't be sure.

"How do you feel now?" I asked her after cracking her back for the fifth time.

"Much better," she mumbled sleepily.

I snickered. "Maybe you should go sleep in your room?"

Ryoko shook her head. "Too relaxed and comfy."

I laughed and nudged her. She groaned, but after a few more pushes, she finally rolled off and dragged herself to her room. With a shake of my head and a small chuckle, I put the massage table away. Bottle of oil in hand, I headed to my room to change. It was only sunset, so sleep was out of the question for now, but I figured I'd get comfortable anyway.

As I hung up my jacket, my door closed. Poking my head out of my closet, I looked at Raikidan to find him leaning against the door with his arms crossed and staring at the floor with a furrowed brow. He appeared deep in thought, but I needed him to leave.

"I need to change," I said. "Come back in a little bit."

"Can I ask you something first?" He didn't look up as he spoke.

"Um, sure?" I couldn't think of anything that would make him want to ask me questions now.

"What is this massage thing you gave Ryoko? I've never seen anything like it or seen anything make someone so relaxed by touch alone."

I leaned against the frame of my closet. "Well, it's a type of relaxing technique humans use to unwind our bodies. By touching major muscle groups, joints, and pressure points, we're able to relieve built up stress from the body. It also helps with realigning any joints that have moved out of place."

"Interesting…" He drummed his fingers on his bicep. "Are humans the only ones who do this?"

I shook my head. "Elves use the technique too."

He nodded and went quiet. He didn't leave, which made me wonder if he had something else to say. I waited, but he remained silent. "Do you want one?"

He looked up and blinked. "What?"

I held up the bottle of oil. "Do you want a massage?"

He swallowed hard. "Does it hurt?"

"Sometimes, but I'll be gentle."

He nodded. "All right, I'll give it a try."

"Take your vest off and lay face down on the bed," I instructed.

Raikidan complied. While he lay down on the bed, I coated my hands with the oil and then walked around the bed. Once he was comfortable, I climbed onto my bed and straddled him and he tensed.

"Relax," I murmured.

"Do you have to sit on me?" he grumbled.

"It's easiest to do it this way," I explained. "The bed isn't as stiff as the massage board, and your body shape is much different than Ryoko's, so to make it most comfortable for you and for me, I have to do it this way."

Raikidan grumbled to himself in what sounded to be his tongue, causing me to giggle. His complaining turned into soft grunts and sighs as I worked on his back. I held back a smile as I watched him enjoy his pampering, far more than he thought he would.

I slipped off him when I was done, and he turned his head to look at me. "That's it?"

I nearly laughed. He definitely had enjoyed it more than he thought he would. "Turn over so I can get your chest."

He eyed me warily. "Do I have to?"

"Well, no, but you seem to want more, and your back is pretty much done, so your front is all that's left. It'll be good for you, too. Your back was incredibly tight, so I can only assume the rest of you is as well. It's probably due to the shifting and the fact you've never received any treatment like this before. But ultimately, the choice is yours."

His brow furrowed as he thought over his options. I didn't care what his choice was either way. I made the offer for only Satria knows what reason, and even if it would put me in an awkward position, I had to honor it.

Raikidan rolled onto his back and eyed me cautiously. He was acting strange about this. *Must be some weird dragon thing.* Whatever the reason was, his choice was clear.

Applying a little more oil to my hands, I moved from where I sat and straddled him. He continued to eye me as I settled myself. I could feel how tense he was as I began to work. He wasn't the only one feeling tense about the situation. Sitting on him like this made me feel rather awkward, but I did my best to appear calm as I rubbed my hands across his chest. I focused on keeping my touch gentle to ensure he remained comfortable, but also firm to make sure no knot went undetected.

As I worked, his body temperature was rose, which I found quite strange. It rose more as I migrated to his abs. I looked up through my lashes, and found him watching me intently. *He's nervous.*

"You need to relax," I said in a soft tone. "I can't heal your muscles if you're tense."

"You're not healing them."

"In a sense I am. It may not be fancy like shaman healing or different like your fire healing—which is quite interesting, I might add—but it does heal the muscles and joints. It loosens them so they're no longer stressed and at the risk of tearing or being involved in some other injury."

"I don't think I can stop being tense."

"You weren't tense while I was working on your back."

"I couldn't see exactly what you were doing."

"Then close your eyes." Raikidan's brow furrowed and I laughed. "All right, that sounded a little weirder than I had wanted. If you close your eyes, you can't see what I'm doing, and if seeing what I'm doing is making you nervous, then don't watch."

Raikidan grunted and stared up at the ceiling. He didn't close his eyes like I instructed, but it was enough for me to feel his body relax more. As I worked, I caught him looking at me from time to time, but as I did, he'd look away. I shook my head each time. *He's so strange.*

Feeling like I had done enough on his chest and abs, my hands migrated to his bicep. This interested him, as he didn't look away when I caught him watching. As I glided my hands over his muscles, I couldn't believe how defined they were.

When I was sure both his arms were done, I slid my fingers gently across his collarbone, looking for any small knots that might have formed around there. I assumed I'd find a few from his shapeshifting. Even though he had never had this done to him before, it amazed me how many knots I had found. His shapeshifting had to be a major factor in that. Sure, he claimed to rarely ever shapeshift before meeting me, but staying in his natural dragon form couldn't create this many knots. Not with the way he moved in that form at least.

I froze when Raikidan suddenly sat up. My cheeks burned as my arms hung loose around his neck, and my breathing nearly stopped as his hands touched my back and his breath touched my lips.

"I—I guess you're done," I managed as I slid off his lap.

Grabbing the bottle of oil, I made a hasty retreat to my closet and busied myself. The temperature of my body rose at an alarming rate and my flustered state sunk in deeper. *All he had to do was say he had enough. Why couldn't he have done it that way?*

The fire escape creaked, announcing Raikidan's departure, and at the same time, my body calmed down. I hated what he did to me. I hated that I reacted in ways that made me uncomfortable. But most of all, I hated that I didn't know how to stop it from continuing and going down a path I knew I should not tread.

CHAPTER 13

My breath came slow and calm as I lay on my bed and meditated. I could barely hear Raikidan's slow breath as he read from my library book. So lost in my meditation, I almost missed hearing my door creak open.

"Laz?" I didn't open my eyes to Ryoko's quiet feminine voice. "Laz?"

"She's meditating," Raikidan said in a hushed tone.

"Strange way to meditate."

"I can hear you, you know," I muttered.

"Oh, sorry," she said.

With a quiet sigh I sat up. "What did you need me for?"

She held up a small book. "I told you I'd loan it to you after I was done reading it. I finished it a while ago and just remembered about it."

The book sailed through the air and I caught it. "Uh, thanks. I'll get to it when I feel like it."

She nodded with a smile and then left without another word. Once the door clicked shut, I glanced at the book's cover and then leaned over to my nightstand. Opening the top drawer, I placed it in there. After shutting it, I lay back down to go back to my meditation.

"How come you're not reading it?" Raikidan asked.

"Because I want to meditate."

"But you've been waiting a long time to read it, haven't you?"

"I've been waiting a long time for Ryoko to loan it to me. I said nothing about reading."

His brow ticked up. "So you don't want to read it?"

"No."

"Why not?"

"I don't know what it's about."

"I don't understand."

I sighed and stared at the ceiling. "I can't read. Happy?"

"Why would I be happy about that? What's so special about you not being able to read?"

I sat up and studied him for a moment before looking down at my hands in my lap. "It's expected of humans to learn how to read, write, and speak. If there are one of these that you can't do, it's thought that something is wrong with you."

Raikidan closed his book and came over to sit on the bed near me. "So why can't you read?"

I shrugged. "It was hard enough for me to learn how to speak."

"You couldn't speak?" I shook my head. "For how long?"

"About five years," I admitted.

This bit of knowledge interested him greatly. "That's not normal?"

I shook my head. "Natural-born humans start to talk between their first and second year. All experiments are supposed to come out of their tanks with a full vocabulary and ability to communicate it. I had the vocabulary; only I couldn't say any of it. And when they tried to teach me to read and write, I couldn't picture the words. I didn't understand how words were made by letters and how those letters worked with how we spoke, especially when some words looked nothing like what we said."

"If you couldn't speak, how did you communicate with others?"

"Body language."

"That worked well for you?" he asked, clearly surprised.

I nodded. "It was enough to communicate what I wanted or needed."

"Well, then if you don't need to read or write to function, what's the big deal?"

"Why aren't you surprised by any of this?" I asked. "Why aren't you surprised that I couldn't speak for a long time?"

Raikidan shrugged. "Dragons can't speak for the first five or so years of their lives. It didn't occur to me to think it was abnormal."

I snorted. "I'm not a dragon."

"Point taken, but you still haven't told me why it's a big enough deal for you to get upset over admitting it."

I pulled my legs up to my chest and rested my chin on them. "I was seen as a freak by my own kind. No tank-born outside of my company wanted to be around me. They thought there was something wrong with me, and imperfections were to be avoided at all cost. Then, after I learned to speak, they continued to avoid me because they were afraid of me. It didn't matter what I did or said. They still saw me as some sort of freak."

"Eira, is this why you don't talk to anyone?"

I nodded. "Why say anything when it's pointless? Words only hurt in some way in the end."

Raikidan rested his hand on my shoulder. It was warm and his grip was soft. I leaned my head and rested it on his hand. I didn't understand what was with me lately. I'd been more willing to talk to Raikidan when he wanted to, and now I was seeking some sort of comfort from him.

My plans to keep him at a distance were starting to crumble, and I didn't know why. I had never had this much trouble keeping someone away. *That's not true and you know it, Eira…*

"Eira—" He stopped at the sound of thundering footsteps. They were everywhere. Some were heading downstairs while others were heading to the roof. One in particular headed to my door.

The door swung open and Ryoko barged in. I slid to the edge of the bed. "What's wrong, Ryoko?"

"We're needed immediately." She was trying to stay as calm as possible. "Raynn's team screwed up a mission, and now we have to get them out of there. They've already lost seven members."

I swore under my breath and launched myself off my bed. Raikidan was close behind me as I made my way into the living room. Before I could say anything, two communicators flew through the air at me. Catching them both, I tossed Raikidan his and then secured mine on my head.

Argus thundered up the stairs from the basement and tossed Raikidan and me a carbine and a pistol each. He then threw us a small satchel of spare ammunition faster than we could get ready.

Seda spoke with urgency before anyone was finished getting ready.

"You must leave now. Aurora will send you the coordinates through your communicators. Two other teams will also be joining you along with some others from our team. You will all have to meet and jump in immediately. There will not be time to discuss tactics."

"That bad, huh?" I said.

She nodded. "This assignment required stealth, which is not what happened. Now there is a large army on the defensive."

"Raynn's team was a bad choice if they wanted stealth," Rylan muttered as he loaded his rifle. "They enjoy making a commotion too much."

"I agree. Now you must go."

Everyone was rushing up the stairs before she could repeat herself. The urgency of this mission was enough to pump our adrenaline and make us move without question.

I played with my communicator's signal as I jumped from our rooftop to the next one over. "Aurora, do you have those coordinates for us?"

"I sure do, babe," she replied. "I'm sending them over to all of you right now, as well as the frequency you'll want to set your communicators to."

"Thanks," I replied as I read them.

As I had figured, we were heading for Quadrant Two. The Council had been doing a lot of assignments there lately for unknown reasons.

I set a quick pace toward the battlefield, and before I knew it, the smell of the battle hit my nose before I could see it. It smelled of fire and burning bodies.

Bullets flew through the air and soldiers fell to the ground all around on both sides of the battlefield.

"Take them all out! Don't let a single one live!"

My heart pounded in my ears as we scaled the rooftops. My eyes darted all around as my scanner picked up movement in all directions. I held my gun at the ready. I couldn't be sure if these figures were friend or foe, and with Raikidan becoming tenser by the second beside me, I was having a hard time thinking straight.

As we closed the distance on the battlefield, many of the figures on the scanner came into view. They were other rebels. I couldn't believe the numbers. I had figured maybe twenty would show up, but I was getting a reading of fifty or more. The realization of how dire the situation really was had now begun sinking in.

"We need a team to pick up the right flank. It's under the heaviest fire," a male voice rang through the communicators.

"Team Three will take it," I said.

"Very well. Satria go with you."

Landing on the ground, Ryoko took the lead as our shield. Rylan stayed on the rooftop and went about finding a suitable location while keeping an eye on us. Bullets rained down on us before we were even able to reach the thick of the battle.

"Rylan, if you see any tanks, let Ryoko know," I ordered.

"Will do," he replied.

I unloaded magazine after magazine on the opposing military, but it did nothing to their numbers. I flinched when bullets graze my arms and face, but I kept on fighting. Slowly, more members swarmed in, adding to our small team, but even the added numbers didn't help our odds of prevailing.

Fire blasted out from one of the alleys. Men and woman screamed in pain, and ran as their flesh burned. Raynn's obnoxious laughter echoed through the street. *Figures it'd be him.* I forced my way up and flanked Raynn.

He glanced back at me and grinned. "Still playing with toys, I see, Eira."

I snorted and took out three more soldiers. "At least now I know why you fail so miserably at simple assignments. Are you sure you were born with a brain?"

Raynn growled and pulled the trigger of his flamethrower. "At least I can take—"

A large blast of fire shot past us, taking out a mass of soldiers, and I chuckled. "What were you going to say, Raynn? I was too distracted watching Raikidan show you up."

"Stupid bitch," Raynn muttered.

"Insult her again and you'll be my next target," Raikidan threatened as he flanked Raynn's other side. He pushed past Raynn and moved closer to me. "So are you going to stop playing around, or am I going to have to do your work for you?"

I snorted and slung my carbine over my back. "Never challenge me."

Rushing forward, I spat out two small embers into my hands and formed two massive flames that consumed them both. Mustering up as much power as I could, I tossed the flames into the swarm of soldiers. Many jumped out of the way, but those who weren't fast enough became my unfortunate victims.

Raynn muttered insults at my supposed weak display, but I wasn't done yet. As the flames around me burned, I felt their heat and pulled their inviting warmth closer to my chest. The flames responded, and I forced them to submit to my control. Moving them, I merged them into a giant flame and spun it around me, creating a circular wall. Filling my body with more energy, I forced the wall out in one large wave that covered the width of the street.

Soldiers attempted to flee, but to no avail. They weren't fast enough to avoid my flame and cried out in pain, falling to the ground in seconds as the intensity of the heat torched their very essence. The fire only died when the heat of the borrowed flames died in my chest. My breath came in small, ragged bursts, but I wasn't finished. There was still more fighting to be done.

I turned and grinned at Raynn. "You were saying?"

Raynn glared at me instead of speaking, and I gladly soaked in his humiliation.

"Not bad, Butterfly," Raikidan mused as he made his way over to me. "Although I thought you could do better."

I snorted. "I'd like to see you do better."

Raikidan opened his mouth to respond, but loud shots that caused my heart to skip rang through my ears. I gazed around in bewilderment as a building began to collapse. Raikidan grabbed onto me and pushed me into a small alley as a building came crashing down on us. Raikidan held me close protectively—our breath coming short as adrenaline coursed through us.

"We need to fall back!"

"No. We fight to our dying breath. That is Zarda's order."

"General, be reasonable."

"We are to fight to the end. We will not let them have this area. That is an order!"

"They've brought in tanks. I'm counting seven in total on our side," Rylan called in. "And it looks like there are more on the way. Ryoko won't be able to stop all of these."

Pulling away from Raikidan, I peered around the corner of the building. Rylan hadn't been joking. Tanks were pulling in at a rapid pace, and were shooting out rounds after rounds at any enemy target they could find. Ryoko rushed at a tank and did her best to dispose of it, and I tossed a grenade in hopes it would give her a hand, but it did little to help our situation.

"Assassins, fall back."

"Commander, don't you dare."

"I will not lose any more to your stubborn pride, General. A good leader would know when to fall back and regroup. Our past general knew that, and it's best you learn that fast or you'll be eaten alive."

"You will listen to my order!"

"I do not answer to you."

This was going from bad to worse. There was only one thing left to do. "Fall back!"

"Commander, are you crazy?" someone cried.

"It's best to retreat to live another day than to die for nothing," I replied. "A true fighter uses the wisdom of their better judgment to guide them. You must pick and choose your battles, and this battle is lost."

"I outrank you," Raynn sneered. "And I order for everyone to keep fighting. The more we take out now, the better chance we have of finishing this war in the future."

"And I rank as high, Raynn," another officer called through. "And I side with Commander Eira. Her judgment has never led us astray, unlike yours, Raynn. Team Five will fall back immediately."

"Agreed," another officer stated. "Raynn's judgment is the whole reason we are in this situation in the first place. I can't afford to lose any more members to his fuckup. Team Two will fall back as well."

"Let's go," I told Raikidan as I ran from the safety of the alley.

Ryoko closed the gap between us quickly, and Blaze and Argus flanked us soon after. Another building collapsed as a tank shot out more destructive rounds. Rylan jumped off the building as it fell.

"You okay?" Ryoko asked him.

He nodded and gasped for breath. I had to admit that was too close of a call. The tanks continued their assault, forcing us to continue our retreat. Raynn, being the coward he was, fell in line with us, and his team was soon to follow his lead.

A tank shot for us and missed, but the shrapnel was a different story.

Raikidan shot out a blast of fire, creating a small shield, but it wasn't big enough to help those in front or behind us. Another tank shot at us and missed, its fire coming up short.

"Fall back! Everyone fall back! This area is lost."

A man fell to the ground as they retreated, screaming out in pain. "Someone help me! Please!"

I stopped dead when a male voice cried out in pain. I turned and watched in horror as one of Raynn's teammates dragged himself across the ground, his leg trailing lamely behind him and blood pooling everywhere. It wasn't hard to imagine what happened.

I stopped retreating to turn at his plea. He was dragging himself in a desperate attempt to flee.

"Please, don't leave me behind!"

"Watch my back."

"Commander, are you crazy?"

"Watch my back!"

I tried to move closer to the man, but a strong hand gripped my shoulder.

"Leave him," Raynn ordered. "He's a dead man."

I yanked my shoulder out of his grip. "How dare you call yourself a leader? Team, watch my back!"

I sprinted toward the man without a second's hesitation, with Raikidan and Rylan close behind. Mocha screeched in protest, which left me confused until rockets flew past us. Rylan chucked a grenade and a few smoke bombs, giving us a small window of cover. Reaching the man, I crouched and hoisted him onto my back.

"Why… why didn't you leave me… behind?" the man managed.

"We entered this battle together, and now we leave together. Dead or alive," I told him. "I never leave a comrade behind, even if it kills me."

"Thank you. Thank you for coming back for me."

He chuckled. "Thank… you."

"What's your name?"

"Zen… Zenmar."

"Well, Zenmar, don't thank me. It's what a real team does. We look out for each other."

He chuckled again, but it cut short. I glanced back at him in worry. His eyes were closed and his breath was shallow. He had passed out, and his life was fading fast. I needed to get him out of here and treated immediately.

The heat of Raikidan's flames bore down on my back as I carried Zenmar. Ryoko dropped the rocket launcher once she emptied the small clip and rushed over to help me. Argus and Blaze shot out blindly through the smoke and fire barrier. All of us were going to make it out together, or die trying.

"You're welcome."

I paced, agitation raging within me. I hated waiting. Zane and the boys were downstairs with Azriel in our hidden infirmary, trying their best to keep Zenmar's vitals from falling, while we waited for Azriel to come upstairs with the news of Zenmar's condition.

"Will you stop that pacing?" Raynn barked. "It's irritating the hell out of me!"

I rounded on him. "I wouldn't be pacing if you hadn't put us in this situation!"

"Don't blame me for this. I had nothing to do with this."

"Oh, really? It's because of your bad leadership that your team fucked up a simple assignment. It's because of your shitty leadership three other teams had to be dragged into your mess to clean it up. It's because of you there were unnecessary deaths and a man dying down in my infirmary below us!"

"No one told you to save him. I told you to leave him behind. You had your chance to avoid this burden."

I had Raynn by the throat and pinned to the wall within seconds. "How dare you stand here and say such a thing? How dare you have no loyalties to those who put their lives on the line beside you? You have no right to call yourself a man, let alone a general. It should be you in his place. You should have been the one left behind to die!"

Raynn didn't respond, not that he could. He fought to breathe, and he fought to get me to let him go. I may be weaker than him on a normal day, my anger more than made up for it now.

"Laz, let him go," Rylan insisted. "This isn't going to solve anything."

I continued to squeeze Raynn's throat instead of listening. "You have no loyalty in your body."

A firm grip pulled me away from Raynn.

"Stop, Eira," Raikidan said. "Killing him won't solve anything. Besides, he isn't worth your time."

Raynn slid to the floor and coughed. I growled and went back to pacing. *What is taking Azriel so long?* My comrades moved to other areas of the room to avoid my anxiety. I could tell many wanted to tell me to stop moving, but they were too afraid to say anything. I wanted to be able to calm down, but couldn't.

I halted when the sound of footsteps came down the hall. I waited patiently as Azriel made it around the corner. He was cleaning his hands with a small white rag, and his face was devoid of its usual cheerful light. He stopped moving when he made it into the living room, but he didn't utter a sound. He only stared at the floor.

"Well?" I asked.

His eyes rose slowly to meet mine. "He's stable, but…"

"But?" Ryoko leaned over the couch. "What's the but?"

Azriel worked his jaw. "We have to amputate his leg."

The room grew still.

"Are you sure, Az?" I asked.

He gave a sorrowful sigh. "If there were any other way, you know I'd do it. Whatever hit him took off his foot and tore everything else up to the middle of his thigh. There's no saving it past there."

I slammed my fist into the wall. "Son of a bitch!"

"We can either take off what's gone or we can take it off completely," Azriel said. "The call is yours, Laz."

"No, it's my call," Raynn said.

"Like hell it is!" I snapped. "You gave up your right when you chose to abandon him. Az, save what you can. In the meantime, Ryoko, I want you to get on the horn with Aurora and see what kind of prosthetics you can find on the black market."

"The black market? Are you sure?" Ryoko asked. "That could take some time."

I nodded. "It may take longer, but it won't leave a paper trail, keeping this a secret from the military."

Ryoko nodded. "All right, what are you going to do in the meantime?"

I sucked air through my teeth. "Figure out a good physical therapy regimen for him. He's going to need to learn how to use the new leg after he's healed up if he has any hope of returning back to the field."

"And what about us?" One of Raynn's teammates questioned.

"Everyone else who doesn't live here, or isn't directly helping Zenmar, leave," I ordered.

No one protested and the room emptied, leaving what part of my team that wasn't downstairs alone, except for one woman who remained sitting the couch. As Zenmar's girlfriend, she wouldn't move from that spot until she'd be allowed to see him.

With a quiet sigh, I entered my room and slammed it behind me. Rummaging through my dresser, I found a small metal octagonal object and grabbed it. Sitting down on my bed, I pressed the top of the object and watched as a hologram appeared. I lifted my finger and went to work.

My door opened without a knock and I figured it was Raikidan, but as I looked up, I was surprised to see Zenmar's girlfriend. "Commander?"

"Yes?" I asked.

"Will Zenmar ever be able to fight again?" she asked, her voice low.

I focused back on my planner. "I don't know. I hope, with a good therapy plan, he'll be as close to normal again as possible."

"But you can't be sure."

I sighed and looked her in the eye. "Look, I'm not going to lie to you. I don't know what's going to happen to Zenmar. Even with a successful surgery, great healing, and therapy, he may never be able to walk without some sort of crutch. Only time will tell what will happen."

She smiled. "Thank you."

"For what?"

"For being honest. Most would lie or sugarcoat the situation, but you came outright and said what has to be said."

I worked with my planner again. "I see no reason to lie. If I lied, it would get your hopes up, and if it didn't turn out the way you expected, you'd be hurt worse than if I had told the truth. The truth may hurt, but in the end it doesn't hurt as bad."

"Only someone who had been lied to could say such wise words," she commented. "No one has ever mentioned you being hurt by someone, Commander."

"Nor will they ever," I said. "I do not discuss my personal life with others. It's pointless and wastes time."

"I think you do it to protect yourself." I glanced up at her as she left.

"Zenmar always said he wanted to be a part of your team, and I now can see why. You're a great commander, and those who are privileged to serve under you are very lucky."

I wanted to say something in reply to her words. I really did, but nothing came to mind. Instead, I thought of something else. "You may stay here as long as needed. You can have one of the spare rooms or stay with Zenmar in the infirmary. It's up to you."

She smiled and left. She squeaked when she ran into Raikidan. "Oops, sorry."

Raikidan only nodded and moved aside to allow her to pass. He shut the door behind him when he finally entered my room. "She didn't react like the other women I run into."

"That's because she's Zenmar's girlfriend," I said.

"Girlfriend. That's that test-phase term, right, like boyfriend?"

I nodded and moved objects around on the hologram. "Yes."

He came over and sat down on the bed. "Would you explain to me why you humans have this test phase?"

My brow furrowed. "Well, I'm not sure how else you'd find out if you're compatible with someone in that way if you don't date."

"So you just guess and try it out?"

I nodded. "Yeah, that's all we can do. Humans base their choices off of a few factors, like sexual attraction, common interests, life goals, and even emotional connection. If enough factors match, then we see if it'll work. If it doesn't, then we go our separate ways."

Raikidan studied me for a moment. "You mentioned emotional connection just now. Is your difficulty with emotions why you chose to be alone?"

I focused on my planner. "Leave me out of this."

His eyes softened as he spoke as if he were trying to connect with me on a personal level. "I'm being serious here."

"And so am I. My personal life isn't going to be dragged into this. My reasons are my own."

"Is it because you don't want someone that close, or is it because you don't think you can feel anything close enough to that connection?"

My lip curled. "How about we go with both so you can shut up? I have work to do here and I don't want to talk about it, so drop it!"

Raikidan held up his hands. "All right, all right. What are you working on?"

I looked at my device. "It's a training planner. I can use images to set up a regimen for Zenmar to help him get back up in the saddle, so to speak. Once I'm done, I can send it to Aurora to take a look at and for her to store it away until Zenmar is ready to use it."

"He's not your teammate and yet you're doing this for him. Why?"

"Who else will show him loyalty? Raynn doesn't know the meaning of it. He only thinks of himself. Zenmar didn't deserve what he got. He shouldn't be the one down there having his leg removed. It's not fair to him. If Raynn wasn't such an arrogant, self-preserving prick, then this wouldn't have happened. People wouldn't have died without a reason."

"Why are you so different, Eira? Why do you show so much loyalty to others when they can't?"

I shrugged. "What is there to life when you have no loyalty?" Raikidan watched me and waited until I sighed. "My loyalty is rooted deep. It's not something I can ignore. If anything, it's the only good quality I have going for me anymore."

Raikidan slid off the bed. "You should see yourself better. You have quite a few good qualities you enjoy overlooking."

I snorted as he shifted to his dragon shape. "Right, and I can sprout wings and fly."

He'll learn in time. They all do in the end.

CHAPTER 14

Asigh escaped my lips as I opened my eyes. *I give up.* Sleep was not on my side tonight. I had tossed and turned all night, and now I wasn't the least bit tired. Sitting up, I rubbed my eyes. I tilted my head when I saw Raikidan.

He was fidgeting and growling as he slept. *A nightmare?* It was possible. I had never seen him have a nightmare before, but no one was immune to them. I held on to my blankets as tight as I could when Raikidan thrashed suddenly. I exhaled and released my grip as he calmed down, but grabbed onto them again when his thrashing came back, and this time it lasted longer than the last. He smacked his head into my bed and then into the wall. This repeated several times before he calmed down.

His thrashing concerned me. Not only would it wake the whole house, but he could hurt himself. I slid off my bed and inched closer to him. I needed to wake him up before his thrashing became worse.

"Raikidan? Raikidan, wake up." I rested my hand on his nose. His scales were warm and I was glad he didn't jolt awake. "Raikidan, wake up."

Raikidan moved his head and I figured I had stirred him, so I pulled my hand away. My heart stopped when he began thrashing again and came at me. Before I could even blink, I was on my back and pinned down by his giant claws. His teeth were bared and a long growl escaped his throat. To add to the problem, his eyes weren't open. *Is this some sort of screwed up sleepwalking?* I tried to wiggle free, but he was too heavy.

"Raikidan, wake up!"

Finally managing to pull my arm free, I reached up. *I need to wake him up somehow.* Resting my hand on his nose, I hoped for the best. Raikidan didn't stop growling, nor did his grip loosen, but his thrashing stopped.

"Raikidan, wake up." I was glad the pressure he put on me was light enough to allow me to breathe. "Raikidan, please, wake up."

Raikidan pulled his head away and growled again. I was at a loss on what to do. He couldn't hear me, and I was too weak to get him off me. My eyes widened and my breath caught as Raikidan shifted forms and wrapped his hands tightly around my neck. His eyes were open now, but they were empty. He was still asleep. I grabbed his wrists in an attempt to loosen his grip.

"Rai… wake… up… p…please…"

I couldn't even wiggle away. He was sitting on top of me. Why wasn't he waking up? I let go of one of his wrists and reached out to him. My hand lightly grazed his arm in the process. I had to try this one last way. I could feel my life slipping away as he hindered my ability to breathe.

"Rai…ki…dan…"

My hands shook as I reached for his face. My reach fell short. My fingertips could only graze his cheek lightly, but I wasn't about to give up as long as I still had an ounce of breath in me.

"Rai…ki…dan… please…"

I continued to reach for him, and my fingertips grazed his cheek again. Raikidan froze and a flicker of hope flared in my chest. I grazed his cheek one more time.

"Rai…ki…dan… wake… up…"

Raikidan blinked and let go suddenly. I gasped and my back arched as air flooded into my lungs. Raikidan jumped to his feet and backed away, allowing me to roll onto my side and cough. I pulled myself up on my knees and took as many deep breaths as I could to ease the pain in my lungs.

"E–Eira… I'm… I'm sorry… I–I didn't mean to…"

I pulled myself to my feet and faced him. He stepped back a little as I did so. "Raikidan… come back here."

He shook his head and stepped back again. "I almost killed you."

I stepped closer, and he mirrored my movement by stepping back. I let out an exasperated breath. "Raikidan, come here."

"No." He turned to leave through the window, but I rushed over to him and grabbed his hand. Raikidan froze for a moment and then turned to look at me. I smiled and pulled him back toward my bed. Raikidan, bewildered by my actions, complied without a fuss.

As I sat down on my bed, I scooted over to make room for him and pulled him over to me. He was reluctant at first, but after a few good tugs, he climbed onto my bed. Reclining back against my pillows, I made myself comfortable and forced Raikidan to rest his head on my lap.

"You shouldn't be doing this," he said. "I almost killed you.

I hushed him. "You were having a nightmare. It wasn't your fault if your body reacted to it. It was my fault for getting too close."

"You were only trying to help. You didn't need to get hurt because of me. I shouldn't be near you."

"Will you shut up and relax? It was an accident."

"Yeah, an accident that could have killed you."

"I'm alive, though, and that's what matters. Now listen to me and relax."

"You're going to have bruises on your neck!"

I tugged his ear. "Raikidan, shut up."

He sighed and lay still. I smiled when he started to relax as I stroked his head lightly with the back of my fingers. I felt bad for him. I knew he hadn't meant to do what he had done, and I was grateful for his remorse for almost killing me, but he didn't need to beat himself up over it.

I tilted my head. I wasn't sure why I had done this. I hadn't made a conscious choice to do so. Though, I honestly couldn't find a single part of me that minded. I couldn't find a part of me that wanted to hate him for what he had done. I only found a part of me that was starting to enjoy the situation—enjoying being this close to him.

I frowned. That was concerning. I shouldn't be enjoying this. I shouldn't want any of this. I sighed. But I did and I wasn't stupid. I knew what was going on. I was beginning to care far more than I should. I knew what trouble those feelings brought, and it was why I buried them away long ago and pretended they had never existed.

Beyond that, Raikidan and I were extremely different species. This wasn't a matter of a pairing between and elf and human or a dwarf and elf. Dragons and humans didn't mix, and that kind of relationship would fall apart quickly. *I know that all too well…*

It didn't matter how my dumb heart felt. My mind was smarter and I was going to push that all away. It was for the best.

I looked down at Raikidan when a strange noise escaped his lips. His eyes were hooded and his lips turned up into a half smile. The sound was similar to a growl, but it was also different. Like a strange purr. The sound was so odd and new, I wasn't sure what to make of it. I wasn't sure if it was a good sound or not, so I stopped stroking his head.

The sound stopped soon after, so I figured I had made the right choice. I watched Raikidan's eyes flutter, as if he had been in some sort of trance, and then went back to resting at half-closed. My eyes grew heavy all of a sudden and I didn't fight the sleep that beckoned. After this night, I needed it. I'd worry about the condition of my neck tomorrow.

Raikidan said something, but I was already far too gone to hear it beyond muffled gibberish.

15
CHAPTER

I sat on the edge of my bed with my feet soaking in water. It felt nice, and although a bath would have been preferable, I wasn't going to get that thanks to Ryoko. She had managed to hop in before me, and after an hour, she still wasn't out. I didn't understand how her skin didn't stay shriveled up.

I suppose it's not a completely bad thing. Had I taken a real bath, I would have had to apply cover-up on my neck again. My throat had bruised and swelled by the time I woke up. Seda had come in unannounced, which had confused me at first since she never did that, but once she handed me the small canister of cover-up and an ice pack, it was made clear. It would figure the incident last night hadn't escaped her eye. She had also shown me how bad the bruise looked.

Raikidan had stayed quiet while she had been in here and refused to look at either of us. I knew he was still upset with himself for what he had done, and I wished he'd stop. Seda had assured me she knew it was an accident and she had attempted to console him, but he didn't want any of it. He had only been willing to look at me once I had finished covering up the bruise, and even then it was rare.

Raikidan's refusal to look at me ended when his curiosity about my feet soaking took over, although he had yet to ask any questions.

"All right, I'm done trying to figure it out on my own," he finally said. "What the hell are you doing?"

I giggled. "I was starting to worry you had been replaced with a robot who couldn't ask questions."

Raikidan snorted. "I don't know what a robot is, but I'm not about to ask. I just want to know what you're doing."

"I'm soaking my feet."

His lips spread into a thin line. "Why?"

"To make them feel better."

"They hurt?"

I nodded. "A little, but it's normal."

Raikidan titled his head. "How is that normal?"

"I've beaten my body up. It's been bruised, bloodied, and broken. It now hates me for what I've done to it and aches sometimes. I would soak my whole body in a bath, but Ryoko is using that right now." Raikidan's lip curled. My brow rose. "What?"

"How can you talk so calmly about something like that?"

I let out a tight breath. "I know it's hard for you to understand, but you really need to, Raikidan. Fighting is a part of my life. It's all I know."

"I can't! How can you humans act so careless about women?"

My lips pressed tight together. I took in a sharp breath, trying to word myself so he'd understand. "It's not carelessness. At least, not in this situation. Yes, there are plenty of people out there who see women as disposable—to be used for their own gratification. There are people who think the same of men. But as a whole, we just don't see a difference between the sexes. So, one shouldn't get preferential treatment just because they were born a certain sex. Dragons and humans are different, Raikidan. I advise you to accept this. You need learn to live with this reality; like I have."

Raikidan leaned back against the frame of the window, conflict raging in his eyes.

My gaze fell to my soaking feet. "I make light of my situation because there is no changing it. What has happened in my life is unchangeable and what will happen is set in stone. My situation is ironic because I'm supposed to be weak because I'm a woman. It's ironic because I can take out entire armies on my own with the right motivation and no one would ever believe me. It's ironic because I am feared for my fierceness in battle and yet struggle to obtain basic respect as a living being. So why not be so calm about my body's pain? Why not make a joke out of my injuries? Why wallow in self-pity when it does nothing?"

Raikidan stared at me instead of replying. *Whether he likes it or not, this is our reality. And he can't change that.*

I went back to caring for my feet. I was in dire need of a foot massage, but because I didn't trust anyone near my feet, my own hands would have to do.

"Here, let me help you," he offered, strolling over.

"I can do it myself."

"It's the least I could do for the massage you gave me."

"I said I can do it myself."

He grabbed my foot anyway. I glared at him and tried to yank it away, to no avail.

"Let go," I ordered.

"I'm not going to hurt you."

I pursed my lips. "Who said anything about hurting me?"

"Human feet are delicate compared with a dragon's. It'd only be natural for you to not want me to touch them."

"I don't like anyone touching my feet." I attempted to take my foot back again, but his grip was as firm as it had been before.

He began rubbing my feet. "I promise I won't hurt you."

I glared at him but didn't say more. I wasn't going to get my foot free, and if I struggled while he did this, I would end up getting hurt.

My gaze softened as he treated my foot. It did feel nice, much better than if I had done it myself. I watched him as he worked—his brow furrowed with deep concentration. *He really does want to do this, but why?*

It didn't make any sense. Even thinking he was trying to use it as an apology, it was a little strange. I guess it didn't matter, though. I relaxed on my arms as I let him work. He was keeping his promise, and it did feel good.

Raikidan placed my foot down on the bed when he was finished and reached for my other one that was still in the warm water, but I pulled it away. I could tolerate him touching one foot because I had no say, but to willingly give him the other, I wasn't fond of the idea, regardless of how nice the massage was.

"Eira…"

I sighed and gave him my foot. With a triumphant grin, he grasped my foot and worked. A content exhale escaped my lips as he worked the stress out. When I decided he had done enough, I pulled my foot back suddenly, a big mistake on my part. Raikidan, unstable due to the way he knelt on the edge of the bed, fell on me. I froze as I stared him in the eye. *Why me?* Raikidan appeared shocked as well as he braced himself over me.

A loud knock at my door pulled me out of my frozen state, and I kicked Raikidan to the floor. He hit his head against the wall as the door opened and Ryoko peered around it.

She looked at Raikidan with a furrowed brow. "Are you okay?"

He rubbed the back of his head. "Yeah, I just tripped over Eira's stupid bucket."

"Maybe you should watch where you're stepping," I shot at him. I was so glad he had chosen to lie to Ryoko, but that didn't mean I was going to go easy on him.

"Maybe you shouldn't do weird things like soaking your feet," he said.

I went to open my mouth, but Ryoko interjected. "I don't want to be the starter of some weird quarrel, so I'm going to tell you what I came here for. Arnia is here for you, Laz, and she has a present for you."

"Oh, goodie." I spun my index finger in the air. "I love surprises."

Ryoko laughed. "Don't lie. Everyone knows you hate them."

I slid off the bed and stepped over Raikidan. "You're right, but I might as well see what she has for me. Hopefully, it'll be good."

"I hope so. She's refusing to tell us until you come out."

I chuckled and entered the living room. A tall woman with ivory skin, long blonde hair with red tips, and green eyes lounged on the back of the couch. She wore standard military attire and a large backpack rested on the floor under her feet.

"Hey, Arnia," I greeted.

"There you are!" she exclaimed in greeting. "I thought you ran away again."

I laughed. "No, not this time. I figured I'd stick around a little longer."

"You'd better not run away again," Ryoko muttered. The two of us laughed at her.

"So what brings you here, Arnia?" I asked.

She picked the backpack up off the floor and opened it. "I brought you those files you wanted, along with a few other things."

Ryoko squealed with delight as Arnia pulled out a handful of dog tags. "Azriel didn't forget!"

Arnia laughed as she handed them over. "Jay was going to give them to Azriel, but since I was coming over here, he handed them off to me."

Ryoko handed Rylan, Argus, and Zane their dog tags and realized that was all of them. "Um, where are Laz's tags?"

Arnia pursed her lips and then rummaged through her pack until she finally found the missing tags. She handed them over to me, but I refused. "I already have a number burned into my skull. I don't need pieces of metal also reminding me where I came from."

Arnia looked at me sadly, as if she was some scolded child.

"They're not that bad," Ryoko insisted.

"I said no!"

Ryoko flinched and dropped the subject. Arnia, understanding my dislike for the tags, tossed them back in the backpack. I had a feeling she had left my tags out of the initial handful on purpose. It wasn't a secret to anyone I hated physical reminders of my military past.

When Arnia glanced up, she looked past me. "I think your friend there is a little confused."

I looked back at Raikidan, who stood in the doorway of my room. "What's wrong, Rai?"

"You said something about a number burned into your skull just now. You also said it at the club. What are you talking about?"

Everyone diverted their attention elsewhere in the room. This wasn't a comfortable topic for any of us, but it wasn't something we could avoid now.

I turned and faced Zane. "Do you mind showing him?"

"Only if you don't call me bald," he teased.

I laughed and nodded. "Fine, fine."

Zane removed his bandana and turned around, revealing a vertical string of numbers. I watched as Raikidan found major interest in what he was seeing. Zane was the only one in this house comfortable with showing his numbers.

Raikidan turned his gaze to me. "Numbers?"

"Have you not seen the back of Zo's head?" I questioned. "I know he has some hair, but it's shaved enough where you can see his."

"I don't usually pay attention to him when he's around," he said. "So why numbers?"

"We're given numbers and not names when we're first designed since they don't want to waste time naming experiments that aren't going to make it."

"Okay, why put numbers on your head?"

"The numbers are used to track us. It's also a type of obedience torture where they shave our heads to show our number," Arnia told him. "Not many experiments like their number shown. It shows that we're only a creation. If we don't misbehave, we get to keep our heads covered and our numbers hidden, though lately it's been more of a tactic used on women since the men have chosen to keep their hair shorter than in the past."

"I see," he mused.

"Right, so what else do you have for me?" I asked Arnia.

Arnia rummaged through the bag and pulled out a folder filled with a few papers. "The papers you asked for are on the top. There are seven of them. The rest is some other stuff you'll want to see."

I took the folder and opened it. The top seven papers were of the experiments I wanted to know about. Relying on muscle memory, I analyzed the strange symbols scribbled on each sheet. There was nothing strange about their DNA—just strength enhancements. I had hoped there would be something significant about them. Sighing, I tossed them on the floor and peeked at the papers that were left. My brow furrowed as I flipped through them.

"I figured you'd want to see these," Arnia said.

"What are you looking at, Laz?" Ryoko asked.

"Our files," I stated. "And they're untampered."

"That's impossible," Rylan voiced. "I made sure they were tampered with."

I handed a sheet of paper over to Ryoko and then one to Rylan. "See for yourself."

They both looked the papers over.

"Where did these come from?" Rylan asked.

"They were in the computer system," Arnia explained. "There were two files on you and Ryoko. The tampered ones and the untampered ones. I don't know where the second file came from."

"I'd like to know where you found my file," I said.

Ryoko's brow rose. "Say what?"

I held up my sheet of paper. "Last I remember, we destroyed my file before we left."

Rylan's eyes narrowed. "Something weird is going on here. I was with Jasmine when she destroyed your file and made sure Aurora did a double check. There is no way that paper should exist."

"Well, it does, as do the rest of us in this house," I said as I tossed papers on the floor. It wasn't only us in the house either. Everyone who had escaped had a file.

"Am I in there?" Genesis asked.

"Doubt it," I said, not bothering to pick any up to have someone check. "They lost your file shortly after you were designed, remember?"

Her shoulders slumped. "I guess you're right."

"So what are we going to do about these files?" Argus asked as we gazed upon the papers.

Snapping my hand up near my mouth in a blink of an eye, I exhaled an ember and forced it into a flame as I brought my hand down. I tossed the flame on the papers and watched them burn. No one questioned me. We'd clean the scorch mark on the floor later, and if we couldn't get rid of it, we'd make up an excuse for its existence or cover it up with something.

"Did you destroy the digital versions?" I asked Arnia.

She nodded. "I had Ezhno hack the system and do a run-through when I was done."

I nodded. "Good."

"Oh." She pulled out another folder from the bag. "I found this too, and you're not going to like it."

I took the folder and opened it. My eyes widened. "By the goddess…"

"These experiments haven't been let out of the fortress yet. I've seen them from time to time inside, and it's not good," Arnia said.

Ryoko looked at me. "What are you two not sharing?"

"They're using my DNA…" I whispered in disbelief as I flipped through the papers. They were the same, every single one of them. A sense of dread fell over me. This was not good.

"But there's something different about them," Rylan said as he joined me by my side and took a look. He was one of the few I would ever allow to see these. I didn't share my DNA information. I didn't like thinking about what I was. "These, whatever they are, aren't exact copies. They're different. Even though they share the exact DNA as Laz, they're engineered differently. Their attributes are much more… lethal."

"Why?" Blaze questioned. "What's so special about Eira? No offense."

Rylan and I exchanged a glance. I shook my head, and he nodded in understanding. No one was to know unless I said so.

"Um… a better question is why are they being made and why are our files suddenly popping back up?" Ryoko understood why we were avoiding his question, and I appreciated her sticking her neck out to change the focus.

Arnia shrugged. "Not sure, but they're gone now."

"Or are they?" Everyone focused on me. I was getting a bad feeling about all of this. Something wasn't right.

"What are you talking about?" Blaze questioned.

I threw the files in my hand into the fire I had made on the floor and watched them burn. "Jasmine told me something once. It was so long ago I forgot until now. She told me there was a secret place where files were stored and only certain people had clearance to access this place."

"Are you saying there might be a computer backing up the files we destroy?" Arnia asked.

Without answering, I threw the basement door open and rushed down the stairs. I needed to figure this out, and there was only one place to find my answer.

CHAPTER 16

The giant metal doors creaked open as I moved them with everything I had. These doors were made specifically to require more than one person to open them, unless you were Ryoko, so this task was quite difficult on my own. The others had yet to catch up with me, but their whereabouts weren't my main concern.

People stared as I dashed across the room. Aurora stared in surprise when I appeared at her computer station. "Hey there, babe. What—"

"No time," I interrupted. "Give me the computer."

She squeaked when I nudged her roughly out of her chair and took over. "You know, you don't have to be pushy."

I ignored her and typed away on the keys. I had no idea what I was doing, but I knew what I had to do. After a few moments of failing to make any progress, I sighed with defeat and looked at her. "I need you to help me hack the fortress' computer system. I need to find something."

"Oh, well, why didn't you say so? That's easy."

I blinked in stunned silence as she took over the keyboard and hacked into the system within seconds. I chuckled. "Did I ever tell you, you're the best?"

She laughed. "Yes, but it doesn't hurt to hear it again. Now tell me what is going on. I've never seen you so frustrated before."

I worked my jaw as I moved objects around on the screen with my fingers. "Arnia came by with files."

"Okay, what's so frustrating about it? Were they not what you were expecting?"

Before I had a chance to say anything, someone spoke for me. "I found things… that shouldn't exist anymore."

Aurora swiveled her body. "Hey there, Arnia."

I glanced up at Arnia as she placed her hand on my shoulder and the other on the computer station. She was panting. "You know, you're really hard to keep up with when you have your mind focused on something." I chuckled and continued to search. "Find anything yet?" I shook my head. "I told you I—"

I touched a file and my information came up. "You were saying?"

"Impossible…" she breathed. "I swear I destroyed it when I found it earlier."

"I know." I pulled up more files that should no longer exist. "And I swear Aurora made sure it was gone the first time it was deleted. Isn't that right, Aurora?"

"What the hell is going on?" Aurora demanded.

"Eira thinks there's a computer backing up the files," Arnia explained.

"You can't be serious," Aurora laughed. "That computer is only a myth. I've searched for it myself."

"It's hidden. It takes a lot to find it and even more to get into it," I said.

She scrutinized me. "You can't seriously believe it exists."

"Jasmine told me it was there and I have never doubted her in the past, so I'm not about to start to now."

"Then tell me, did she tell you how to find it?"

I sighed and sat back in my seat. "Yes and no. She told me a riddle, but it didn't make any sense and now I've forgotten most of it."

"What do you remember?" Arnia asked.

"A door that's not really a door but holds the key to the hidden door…" I mumbled.

Aurora snorted. "That's helpful."

"At least I remembered something!" I shouted.

She flinched. "Okay, okay, sorry…"

"Well, let's figure out what the door is." I peered up at Ezhno, who now leaned over the top of my chair.

He was a handsome young man with an athletic build, short black hair, lavender eyes, and olive skin. He had a cup in his hands, and from the smell of it, I assumed it was filled with coffee. I didn't mind him being here. Ezhno wasn't actually bad, unlike the main portion of Raynn's team. He was quite nice, really, and hated cheating. It was a shame he was forced to take orders from Raynn.

"Well, if you have any bright ideas, I'd love to hear them," I told him.

He pointed to the computer. "We should look at the screen and see if we can find anything out of place."

Sitting up in my chair, the four of us stared at the screen. I chuckled when heavy boots clomped on the cement floor as the wearer jumped up and down. "What's wrong, Ryoko?"

"I can't see!" she complained. "I wanna help look too."

I chuckled. "Ryoko, I'd love for you to help, but there isn't any more room. You'll just have to sit this out like everyone else."

She huffed and kicked a metal box. "Fine…"

"Don't get down, Ryoko. This means you'll be needed for something more important later," Rylan encouraged.

"Yeah, it's not like they're going to find something," Blaze said. "They're—"

"Hey, what's that?" Arnia asked.

"You were saying?" Ryoko muttered.

"What's what?" Aurora asked.

Arnia pointed to a small distorted file. "That."

"Looks like corrupted data to me," Ezhno mused.

"I don't know…" Aurora reached and touched the screen.

The file that Ezhno thought was corrupt reacted and the screen changed.

My brow furrowed. "What's going on?"

"I don't think that was a corrupt file," Arnia mumbled.

"Aurora, you're a genius," Ezhno said.

Aurora blushed but didn't say anything. My gaze dragged from one side of the large screen to the other. There were all sorts of symbols and numbers running across the screen. "Does anyone know what these strings, of whatever, are saying?"

"No," Ezhno and Aurora replied in unison.

Arnia and I looked at them. Aurora's face was red as a tomato, and

Ezhno was scratching the back of his neck. I shook my head and went back to focusing on the computer. I didn't want to know.

"If I had to guess, though, it's what you've been looking for," Ezhno stated, recovering from his strange situation.

"The door that wasn't really a door is this?" Arnia asked.

Aurora clapped her hands together. "I get it!"

I shook my head. "Good, 'cause I don't."

"The door that's not really a door… It's a passageway," she told me. "They can look like doors, but they're actually not."

"Then what does the key mean?" Arnia asked.

"A passage can sometimes be referenced as a key," Ezhno stated. "It leads to the real door, and in order to get to the door, you have to go through the passage, just like you can't open a locked door without its key."

Arnia crossed her arms "So will this lead us to th—"

The screen went black and a small box popped up.

"It wants a password," Aurora murmured. She pushed me out of my seat and took her computer back. "Ezhno, I'm going to share this with your station. We're going to need to work on this fast before we're booted from the system."

"Why would you get booted?" Arnia asked.

"We can only be in the system so long before we're shut out," Ezhno explained. "If we're in too long, we'll be caught and then it's all over, so the security system was set up to kick us out after a certain amount of time."

Arnia nodded with understanding.

"Laz, you wouldn't happen to know any clues on the password, would you?" Aurora asked as Ezhno headed back to his station.

I shook my head. "That's all I remembered. I know she told me you had to have special clearance to get to the actual room where this computer is stored, but I don't recall the part of the riddle about a password."

Aurora nodded and began typing away. A small image of Ezhno appeared on the screen as she worked and I watched them work together. I knew this was hard, but I wished they'd figure it out faster. This was too important to take our time with.

Aurora sighed and leaned back in her chair. "I give up. I can't figure it out."

Ezhno let out a tight breath as well. "I'm with you. This thing is locked down too tight."

I did my best to control my anger. I needed to get into this. I needed to know what was going on.

"Sorry, Eira," Arnia said. "I know you wanted to get whatever was in here, but it doesn't look like it's going to happen. It's too bad we can't talk to Jasmine."

A light bulb lit in my head. "Maybe I can."

"What?" Arnia tilted her head in confusion.

"That's right!" Ryoko exclaimed. "Laz is a shaman now. Maybe you can ask her."

I nodded and dropped down in my meditative pose.

"That looked like it hurt," Blaze commented.

"I doubt she felt it," Rylan replied.

Ryoko shushed them and I smiled. I needed as little distraction as possible. I slowed my breathing, my heartbeat following, and felt for the thin line that separated the living plane from the spiritual one. I prayed I could find it. I didn't have much training in this. My blood ran cold when I found it and could feel my soul being pulled from my body. My body's natural instinct to fight back kicked in, but I forced it away. I needed to do this. I just wished I had been more willing to learn how to in the past.

I opened my eyes and gazed around once my body and spirit separated. The room I was in was now cold and gray. The people around me moved slowly as if time moved faster here. I climbed up to my feet and searched for Jasmine.

A female voice chuckled. "Behind you."

I spun around and my heart stopped at the sight of the pale skinned, lithe woman with long black hair and single blue streak. "Jasmine…"

Her lavender eyes danced with amusement behind her thin-rimmed glasses. "It's good to see you again. Unfortunately we don't have time to catch up." Her hips swayed as she approached. "Take this."

She grabbed my hand and placed something light and soft into it. When she pulled away I peered at the strange orange and red feather in my hand. I opened my mouth to speak, but she spoke first.

"He will be reborn."

My brow furrowed. "What?"

"I'm sorry, we really don't have the time for me to say much more."

"But how is this supposed to help me?" I asked. "This is too important to put a time limit on. I need your help, Jasmine!"

She smiled and began to fade. "All of you are smart. You'll figure it out quickly."

My chest hurt. Seeing her go hurt me more than I thought it would.

"One last thing, my darling niece," her disembodied voice said. "Listen to your heart. It may have been placed in a cage, but that doesn't mean it can't be trusted."

What? Before I had a chance to think on it more, my soul's need to continue to live sucked me back into my body.

I took a deep breath of fresh air. Because there was no need to breathe on the spiritual plane, an untrained body stopped breathing the longer they stayed there. The more a shaman trained to go to and from the spiritual plane, the easier it was for them to train their body, but due to some of my issues, that kind of training wasn't something I had at the moment.

"Hey, you okay?" Arnia inquired.

I nodded and relished every breath I was breathing in, even though it was polluted.

"So did you talk to her?" Ryoko asked.

I nodded. "Yes, but she wasn't as helpful as I would have liked."

"What did she say?" Arnia asked.

"He will be reborn," I replied.

Ryoko threw her hands in the air. "Like that's any help. Why couldn't she have told you something that made sense?"

I opened my hands. "She also gave me this."

Ryoko peered over my shoulder. "A feather?"

"Strange-looking feather if you ask me," Arnia said.

"It's unique to say the least," Ezhno said. "But what does it mean?"

I stared at the long feather. The colors started out a dark red at the base that then lightened in a gradient fashion to the orange-yellow tip.

Raikidan stretched out his hand. "May I see it?"

"Sure." I handed it over and watched him inspect it carefully.

"Not something you'd find out in the woods, that's for sure," he said. "It looks like a feather that would come from a creature of legend."

My brow furrowed. *Something of legend?* What type of creature was feathered and thought to be a myth? "Phoenix…"

Aurora blinked. "What?"

I pushed past Arnia and took the computer from Aurora. Staring down at the keys, I began to type out the password. The feather was one part of the key. Jasmine's words were the other. I hit the Enter key once I typed the last letter.

Aurora gasped as the computer read it and accepted my entry. "You did it…"

"What was is it?" Ezhno asked.

"Phoenix Reborn," I murmured.

Arnia tilted her head as files started to scatter across the screen. "That's weird. Weren't you sometimes referred to as *Phoenix*?"

I nodded. "Yes, but this isn't about me. Jasmine referenced 'he', meaning whatever these files are linked to, they're about a man."

Aurora pressed files as they appeared and opened them. "It looks like they're backups to every experiment made or, at least, experiments that had files."

"But what's the point to it?" Ezhno mumbled. "Why have backups?

"I don't know, babe, but we're about to find out," Aurora said as she went about messing with the files.

I noticed a red flashing object on the screen and pointed to it. "What's that?"

Aurora tilted her head and touched the flashing file. The screen flashed and the files began to move around the screen. In the center of the files an outline of a man appeared.

"Is that who I think it is?" Rylan asked darkly.

"Zarda," I growled.

It was only an outline, so his face wasn't defined, but I recognized him regardless. Anger boiled up in my chest.

"Why is he in here?" Ryoko grumbled. "What does he—what are those files doing?"

I watched in stunned silence as the files of experiments became larger to show a photograph of them and then shrank as the large image of Zarda absorbed it. A computer's voice read off the experiment's name each time and stated they had been compatible.

"Compatible? What are they compatible with?" Ezhno questioned.

I snarled when I realized what this was. My anger boiled higher and my mind began losing its grip on reality. I stepped away from everyone. I couldn't believe he was doing this. *It isn't right.*

I cringed when my hand pierced metal. I had let myself go for a split second and had punched a metal crate. I yanked my hand free, bringing severed and active wires with me.

I stared down at my hand in shock. Not only had I lost control of myself, but I had done the one thing I had always strived to not allow to happen. My hand had warped, stuck in an in-between phase of metamorphosis with a larger and bonier appearance than my normal hand. My finger joints were more defined than they should have been, and my nails were slightly longer and sharper. My skin's texture had changed in areas, appearing almost scaly. I enclosed my transformed hand in my normal one protectively. I didn't want anyone to see.

"Laz?" Rylan asked in a hushed tone as he came over. "Are you all right?"

"I'm fine," I lied.

He placed a hand on my shoulder and kept his voice low. "Laz, what's wrong?"

"It's nothing."

"It's something. I can feel the bond's tug. I haven't felt it tug like this in a long time. Tell me what's going on." Sighing, I opened my hand to show him. He grunted. "That would be why it's tugging. Can you change it back?"

I shook my head. "I'm trying, but it's not responding in the least."

"You're probably still too worked up," he said. "Here, give me your hand."

I did as I was told and placed my hand on top of his. Rylan enclosed his hand over mine and rested his head on my temple. My eyes grew heavy as the will of the bond forced me to obey.

"All right, you're all set," Rylan murmured.

I opened my eyes and looked at my now-normal hand. I let out a slow breath. "Thanks, Ry."

He backed away and pushed my head lightly. "Sure thing."

I smiled a little and then frowned when I remembered there was business to be done. "Aurora!"

She turned in her seat. "Babe?"

"Put this on the screen for everyone to see, now."

"You sure?"

"Just do it."

She nodded and typed a few keys. I turned around to take a look at the larger screens as she connected her computer to them. People stared up at the screens and began to murmur amongst themselves.

"What's going on, Laz?" Rylan demanded.

"Zarda is taking our DNA and putting it into himself," I stated grimly. The whole room went quiet and hundreds of eyes fell on me, but I stared up at the screen.

"You have to be kidding! That's impossible," someone shouted.

"Obviously you're blind if you don't believe her." I turned my gaze up at Nioush as he stood on a tall stack of metal crates. His actions were confusing. *Don't think too hard. I just can see the truth before these idiots can.*

I grunted and focused back at the screen.

Ryoko gasped when her file popped up but then let out a relieved breath when the computer spoke.

Experiment two nine eight seven seven zero five, incompatible.

"Obviously it's not going as he planned," Blaze commented. Blaze's file came up and the computer spoke.

Experiment two four six one six eight one, compatible.

"Not cool!"

"Sucks to be you," Argus teased.

"But why Blaze?" Arnia asked. "Nothing special about his design."

"Hey!" Blaze said. "I am special."

Ryoko's eyes squinted. "Yeah, in Blaze Land."

Everyone laughed but me. I understood their desire to lighten the mood about the situation, but this was much too serious to joke about. "All right, ladies, settle down."

Rylan growled as his file appeared.

Experiment two nine four six four eight eight, compatible.

I swallowed. That wasn't good. The room went quiet as my file appeared next. I pleaded to the gods it wouldn't make it in.

Experiment two nine seven zero three five eight, incompatible.

I sighed with relief, but it was short lived when Raynn's irritating chuckle graced my ears. "How does it feel to be useless, Eira?" Raynn's file popped up just then.

Experiment two one seven eight nine one one, rejected.

"I don't know. How does it feel, Raynn?" I jeered.

Raynn growled and his anger only worsened as my team laughed at him. Mocha, who was standing on a stack of metal crates near Nioush, let out a quiet breath when her file came up incompatible. I watched as several psychic files, including Seda's and Nioush's, were tried, but read out to be incompatible.

"He's an idiot," Nioush muttered. "He'd never be able to get our power to work with his weak body."

"We can't keep watching these files be added to Zarda!" someone yelled. "We have to do something."

"But what can we do?" someone asked.

"Call the Council," I ordered. "It's time for an overdue meeting."

We stood together in a large, strange room. It appeared bottomless and dark, with nine platforms hovering within. Seven of the platforms held a small handful of each team's members selected for this meeting, and another one, one that was much higher up, held the Council. The last platform was the largest and was located in the center of the room between the Council's platform and the teams' platforms. On the walls of the room were several screens, which showed the team members in the simulation room who couldn't fit into the Council Chamber.

A tall, light-skinned man, with shoulder-length white hair and crystal eyes, walked to the edge of the Council's platform. "We are all assembled as requested. Three of each team's officers will step forth, and we shall discuss the matter at hand."

Ryoko, Rylan, and I exchanged a glance before we stepped forward on the platform where a new one was beginning to materialize. Once we were on the new platform, it began to move toward the center platform. Raynn, with Mocha and Chameleon, came up next to us.

"Hey, don't move," Argus whispered. "You can't go with them. You have to stay here with us."

I rolled my eyes. Of course Raikidan would try to leave his spot. I had even told him not to do anything unless he had been specifically directed to.

No one moved from the small platforms as they reached the center. We knew better. I gazed up at the Council to take in the situation. Each Council member was accompanied by a psychic except, of course, the two Council members who were psychics themselves.

Nioush was up there with Adina, the first successful shapeshifter experiment, and next to them stood Seda and Genesis. The man who had started the meeting, Elkron, was the first elementalist experiment. To his right, stood Hanama, the first anthropomorphic experiment, and next to her stood Enrée, a male Battle Psychic, and his twin sister, Akama, a Seer, the first two psychic experiments. Lastly, Eldenar, the first war experiment stood next to them.

"State names and ranks," Enrée and Akama stated in unison.

The three of us listened as each team listed off their names and ranks until it was our turn. Ryoko was the first to speak. "Ryoko Dreadmore, lieutenant."

"Rylan Nytefall, captain."

Then it was my turn. "Eira Rysrin, commander."

"Now state the business of this meeting," Adina ordered.

All eyes turned to me. I figured it'd be this way. I was the one who had figured it out and called the meeting, after all. Jumping over the rail of the platform, I landed on the center platform and made my way to the center. I looked up at them and spoke. "Council, we need to speed up our efforts on this war. We need to find an end to it faster."

The Council chuckled.

"We are doing what we can, Commander," Elkron stated. "We are proceeding as fast as we can with minimal casualties."

"It's not good enough!" I snapped. Losing my temper with them wasn't going to help me, but they needed to see the reality of the situation. It was always a fight to get them to listen. It was the reason I hated listening to them.

Elkron exhaled a slow breath to keep himself calm. "I suppose you have a reason for feeling so strongly about this?"

I nodded. "Zarda is using our DNA to enhance himself. He's mixing our DNA with his to make himself stronger."

Enrée snickered. "Did you hit your head while you were gone, Commander? What you are claiming is impossible."

I grunted and held up my hand, a mix of electrical and psychic energy pulsing around me. *Such a strange room…* Moving my fingers in a typing motion, the space where my fingers touched lit up as if I were typing on a keyboard. A large screen appeared in the room, and several of the Council members gasped at the sight.

"You were saying?" I sneered.

Enrée swallowed but didn't reply.

"How is this possible?" Adina asked. "How can he be able to do something so unnatural?"

"I'm not sure," I admitted. "But it is happening and it is a problem."

"How do we know this is not a trick?" Hanama questioned. "How do we know this is not a plot to get us to focus our attention on something other than the true threat?"

"Because this was locked up in the secret computer everyone thought was a myth," I informed.

The Council members looked at each other before Hanama spoke again. "We need more proof."

I ground my teeth together. This was why I hated talking to them. Nothing was ever good enough to convince them to ever take action.

"Proof and reasoning," Akama clarified. "What reason would Zarda have to combine his DNA with ours?"

"Power," Rylan said. Everyone focused on him. "It's no secret Zarda is power hungry. Why wouldn't he want to try this? The more power he has, the less he needs us, the more Lumaraeon will fear him, and the more likely he'll rule whatever he wants. Why not do it?"

The Council shared more glances. I hated their private conversations. It was annoying.

"We still need more proof," Eldenar told us.

I clenched my fists together. This was infuriating.

"Aiden said something." I spun around at Raikidan's voice. I did my best not to yell at him. He wasn't supposed to speak. Only officers were to address the Council unless spoken to otherwise.

"The outsider does not listen to our rules," Elkron said. "Commander, you had best have a good reason for him to speak out of place."

I nodded. "Raikidan has an incredible memory and valuable information. He may not have an officer rank, but I still value his words."

"Very well," Elkron stated. "Raikidan, explain yourself."

"Now you can go join them," Argus whispered to him.

Raikidan stepped forward and a small platform appeared. We waited for him to be carried up over to us. Once the platform reached the larger platform Rylan and Ryoko were standing on, Raikidan climbed onto it but then jumped down to join me.

"Weeks ago Aiden told us Zarda was rarely seen. He rarely ever left his sleeping quarters," Raikidan informed them.

Rylan hit his fist into his open palm. "That's right!" Everyone's attention changed to him. "We all assumed his actions were because of an execution that was going to take place, but what if this procedure makes him weak for a period of time? That would explain his lack of communication with others. He wouldn't want others to be aware of the weakened state and risk be attacked."

"You are sure this is the information you heard?" Hanama asked.

I nodded. "I was there when Aiden told us. Our initial assumptions were wrong."

"I was there to hear it as well," Seda piped in.

The Council spoke amongst themselves telepathically before Elkron spoke. "We believe you."

A relieved breath escaped my lips.

"But I still do not understand why he would do it," Akama remarked. "It is understandable he wants power, but to put his body through such methods? Where is the logic in it?"

"Whoever said Zarda was logical?" Disguising my fire breath, I formed fire into my hands and shot it out in several directions. At the same time I willed it to morph into objects that described past events. "These fires play events that show what Zarda has done. He has killed innocent people. He has designed tools of war that are so dangerous he has to put us on a leash to control or risk being killed himself. He has schemed, lied, and murdered, all for power. Now, if any of you can tell me where he has made a logical decision, please, feel free."

The Council members spoke amongst themselves, leaving the room silent for several moments. When they were done, they all faced us and Genesis climbed onto the railing. She was the only Council member who had yet to speak, so I was intrigued by what she had to say.

"It has been decided," she stated calmly. "These facts are too great to ignore. Even at the risk of increased casualty rates, we must take a less cautious approach to this war and finish what Zarda started decades ago.

"Although we cannot stop him from using DNA that is stored in the labs, we can destroy these files permanently so he cannot re-create any more of those who are already alive. Technicians have their orders, and all teams are now dismissed."

I grabbed Raikidan by the arm and made a steady pace toward Ryoko and Rylan. "You owe me for covering your ass."

Raikidan snorted. "I don't see what the big deal is about me speaking out."

"The Council likes order, and anyone who speaks out of term is being disorderly," I said. "If anyone could speak when they wanted, nothing would get done. That is why only three officers per team are allowed to face the Council and only the highest-ranking officer is allowed to stand on the platform to address them directly. But I'm glad you had something useful to say."

"So no thank-you?"

I narrowed my eyes. "You have no idea how much trouble I could have gotten into if you hadn't had something worthwhile to say. If you couldn't back up what you said, my argument could have been thrown out and they would have dismissed us without hearing another word."

His gaze fell. "Sorry."

"Thank you for having a good memory," I said quietly. "No one would have remembered that bit of information, and it won us the argument."

Raikidan placed his hand on my back and leaned closer to me. "If you wanted to thank me, you could have done it without trying to put me down first."

"Would you have accepted the praise otherwise?"

Raikidan mulled this over. "I guess not."

"There you go." I picked up my pace and jumped up onto the platform where Ryoko and Rylan were waiting. "Let's go home."

The book flipped another page as I relaxed on my bed. I was in need of something to enlighten my brain, and watching TV with the others in the living room didn't interest me. I glanced up when my door opened and Raikidan entered. "Didn't want to watch TV anymore?"

He shook his head and sat down on the windowsill. "Whatever they're watching, it's boring."

"What was in it?" I asked.

"A lot of explosions and some guy trying to rescue a dumb female who got herself caught by walking into a building." I laughed and he tilted his head. "What?"

"That's an action movie," I said. "It's supposed to be entertaining and exciting."

He snorted. "Well, it's not. I don't understand how they're enjoying it."

I shrugged and looked back down at my book. "It's just something they like."

"What are you reading?"

"Nothing, really. I haven't found anything that's kept my attention for very long. I'm wondering if I should sleep."

"It is late for you. You normally fall asleep sooner."

"It's a little creepy that you know that."

Raikidan shrugged. "Not really. I'm in here all the time."

I chuckled and placed the book on my nightstand. "True. Well, I hope you don't have any plans to stay up late to chat because sleep is sounding really nice right now. Today was a long day."

"Eira, why do you hate your number?" he asked suddenly.

I curled up to my pillows. "I'm created, not born."

"So?"

I grunted. "So you wouldn't understand. You were born. Someone chose to have you out of love and compassion, and you get to choose how to live because of it. I was created for a specific purpose, not out of love or compassion, but out of greed and power, and once that purpose ends, my existence means nothing. I don't get a choice."

I closed my eyes when Raikidan didn't respond. I figured it was safe to assume he wasn't going to press the matter, but I was mistaken. My eyes flew open when he lay next to me and rest his hand on my shoulder. "What do you think you're doing?"

"Talk to me about it," he said.

I yanked my shoulder free and rolled over to put some space between us. "Why should I?"

"If it upsets you, you should." He scooted again. "It would make you feel better."

"I'm not going to talk about it."

"Why not?"

"Because it doesn't matter."

"Why doesn't it matter?"

"Because I don't matter!" Raikidan pulled back at my loud outburst but didn't take long to return to his previous position. "My purpose will end at the end of this stupid fighting. I won't matter after that. I was created to kill, and with this war's end, I am nothing."

"How do you do it, then? How do you find a reason to keep going?"

"I don't. I just…" I sighed. "I don't have the will to end it…"

Raikidan's grip tightened, but I didn't think much of it. Instead, I yanked my shoulder away from him and curled up more. His reaction was normal. My existence, on the other hand, was not. I sighed and closed my eyes. A part of me wished I had the will, the power, even. Misery wasn't a friend I willingly chose.

"I like your number…" he whispered. "It's complicated, like you."

I cranked my neck to look at him. "That has to be the most ridiculous reason I have ever heard."

He grinned. "Ridiculous but true. I like complicated things. They're interesting."

I snorted. "So now I'm a thing?"

"Eira…" he growled. "Don't twist my words."

"I will if I want to." I childishly stuck my tongue out at him.

"That's it," he said as he grabbed my sides.

I bit my lip and twitched. "Oh, don't do that."

He chuckled and grabbed my skin multiple times in an attempt to tickle me some more as he sat on me. Unable to control my twitching or hold in my laugher any longer, I squirmed and laughed uncontrollably.

"Raikidan, stop!" I begged. "Please!"

"Not until I see tears."

"But I… I can't produce… tears…" I managed.

"Everyone can produce tears. You can too."

I shook my head and continued laughing. My abs hurt and his tickling was relentless. My laughter became contagious as Raikidan began laughing as well.

I gasped for air. "I... I can't... please... stop. I... I can't... breathe!"

Raikidan stopped as I asked and tried to get his laughter under control. "Feel better?"

Freeing my legs from him, I pushed him away with my feet. "You're an ass."

He chuckled and pushed my feet away. "Do you feel better?"

I smiled. "Yes, no thanks to you."

He smirked and slid off my bed. "Good. Now remember this. Your life is controlled by no one but you. What your purpose is, is determined by you. Now go to bed."

I smiled when his back was turned and curled up. *Thank you, Raikidan.*

CHAPTER 17

A light breeze filled the living room as it flowed through the open window. I stretched my shoulders and then went back to relaxing on the couch as my Library book read to me. Ryoko lounged next to me, and Raikidan did the same on my other side, although I could tell he was tempted to read along with me. Rylan and Argus sat at the far end of the couch, closest to the kitchen, working over some schematics, while Zane read a newspaper in the kitchen.

My attention snapped up from my book when a door slammed and we heard feminine feet stomping down the hall. I watched Seda storm through the living room and into the kitchen. She was muttering to herself, and slammed closed every drawer she opened.

"What are you looking for, Seda?" I asked.

"A knife," she muttered.

"Why do you need a knife?" Ryoko asked.

"So I can legally kill a certain dick hole on the other side of the house. He won't shut up, no matter how many times I tell him to."

Ryoko and I exchanged glances. This was definitely not like her. Not only was she speaking like a normal person, but she was swearing, and not hiding the fact she wanted to kill Blaze for some reason or another.

"Seda," I said.

Seda looked up and realized everyone was staring at her. She closed another drawer and sighed. Zane stood and patted the stool for her to sit down on. Seda complied without a fuss.

Seda was quiet for a long time. "Well? Is anyone going to ask or not?"

"I didn't think a question was needed, but fine," I stated. "What the hell is up with you?"

In all honestly, I knew the answer to my question, due to my history with her, but everyone else needed to hear the answer.

"Not the most tactful way of stating it," Rylan muttered.

"Or the nicest," Argus said.

"Hey, no comments from the peanut gallery over there," I warned.

The two shut up and waited.

"Clarify your question, please," Seda requested.

"Why are you acting so normal now?" I said. "Why aren't you speaking as if you have no emotions?"

Seda sucked air through her teeth. "Because I have to force myself to speak like that."

"Why?" Ryoko asked.

Seda crossed her arms on the bar and rested her chin on her arms. "Because it's part of the oath."

"What oath?" Rylan asked.

"Psychics are supposed to remain detached from everything," Seda explained. "We're supposed to portray ourselves in a way where others won't want to get too close. We're forced to take an oath vowing we'll do this. In my case I make myself appear emotionless."

"That's stupid," Ryoko said.

She sat up a little. "Excuse me?"

"You're human. What's the point of being detached? It's not like it's going to kill someone if you act normal."

"We see everything," Seda explained. "We see thoughts, wishes, and dreams. We can see the future and look into the past. If we're close to anyone, it's feared we'll give away something vital and disrupt the balance."

I snorted. "I'm with Ryoko. So you have abilities that give you unfettered access to other minds. You still have a right, just like every other human, to feel and act as though you do have them. To expect otherwise is asinine. Besides, your brother doesn't listen to that oath."

Seda grunted. "Battle Psychics never listen. They do as they please."

"Then maybe you should do the same," I said.

She cocked her head. "What do you mean?"

Putting my book down on the couch, I stood and made my way over to her. "You're going to do what you want, and not care how some psychic council, or whatever they are, tells you how to live. Now let's start with changing up your look and cutting your hair."

Seda grabbed her hair protectively. "I–I don't know… I've always had my hair long."

"All the more reason to do it," I said, dragged her out of the kitchen. "It's not like it won't grow back if you don't like it."

Ryoko jumped to her feet. "You'll need my help!"

I nodded and pulled Seda into the bathroom and sat her down on the sink counter. Ryoko came in, scissors in hand, and shut the door behind her.

"I don't know if I can do this…" Seda admitted quietly. "It doesn't feel right."

"The Battle Psychics do it, so why not you?" Ryoko said.

"But they're braver than us Seers," Seda said. "No one can control them."

I chuckled. "Then follow their lead. Don't push away your courage. You have it… in everything else but this. You can do it. Trust me."

She smiled. "I've told you some of my deepest secrets. I trust you."

I nodded and then went about discussing with Ryoko the haircut we would choose. Unfortunately we were struggling to find something that would work with her veil.

"Well, I do have a different one," Seda said in a quiet voice.

"Yeah?" Ryoko said. "You sound a bit nervous to admit that."

Seda wrung her hands together and smiled meekly. "Psychic training comes in 3 levels, and once I made it to level two, I went from this veil to another one. I went back to this one when I joined the rebellion because it fit the look I was using."

"What does it look like?" Ryoko asked.

Seda projected an image of a leather blindfold with a golden hexagram painted in the center and four leather straps that, I assumed, connected at the back of her head.

Ryoko gasped. "That's so nice! I know exactly what we can do if you wear that one!"

My brow rose. "Really? Just goes to show I'm only good at cutting hair for guys."

She giggled. "Yeah, let me go get some paper so I can draw it out."

Ryoko dashed out of the room and closed the door behind her. As the minutes passed, I noticed a change in Seda.

"I sense you're a lot calmer now," I said.

Seda nodded. "I'm getting used to the idea of you giving me a makeover. I think it's Ryoko's enthusiasm that's winning me over."

I chuckled. "She's got that effect. You do understand this means you have to remove your veil while she's cutting your hair."

She nodded. "I know. I'm working up the courage to deal with that."

The door opened and Ryoko strolled in with some paper rolled up in one of her hands and a pencil in the other. Seda scooted over on the sink to give Ryoko room, and our little Brute-class friend began sketching. When she was done, she proudly showed it to us. I bit my lip so I wouldn't laugh, but Seda wasn't able to keep herself from giggling as we looked at the crude drawing.

"Don't laugh!" Ryoko whined. "I'm not good at drawing."

"I'm sorry," Seda said. "I'm just not sure if that's supposed to be a nose or a mouth."

"I think it's an ear," I said.

The two of us cracked up, and Ryoko huffed. "Okay, my drawing skills really suck, but I got the hair right and that's all that matters."

I shook my head and stole a piece of paper and the pencil from her. "I got a rough idea, but we need more to go with to understand exactly what you're going for."

I began sketching and Ryoko gave me some advice when I didn't get a certain part correct. I revealed the drawing to them both when I had finished.

Ryoko crossed her arms and huffed. "Sure, show me up with your artsy-fartsy skills."

I snickered. "Well you can style hair, whereas I can't really."

"Fine, I'll take a consolation prize. But you're still too gifted when it comes to all that."

"I've had a lot of time to practice."

"Whatever. What do you think Seda? Laz's drawing is pretty close to what I'll want to do."

Seda smiled. "I think it'll work. And if it doesn't, like Laz said, it'll grow back."

"That's the spirit!" Ryoko beamed.

"I should get you some new clothes to wear," I said. "Might as well not be idle while Ryoko gives you the haircut, and you can't go around wearing spandex like you have been ever since I've known you. Even I know that's not a great fashion choice. I don't even know how you come up with so many clothing choices with just spandex."

Seda laughed. "You'd be surprised what you can do when you're desperate to keep your distance. I do have some *normal* clothes tucked away, but not much. You can go through them to see if they'll work or not. Genesis also knows where I store my other veil."

I nodded and headed for the door, but stopped when Ryoko asked Seda to remove her veil so her hair could be cut. Seda bit her lip and hesitated.

"Seda, it's going to be okay," I encouraged.

Ryoko's brow ticked up, but she remained quiet while Seda worked out her internal conflict. Finally, Seda reached up and untied her veil.

Head tipped down toward her lap, her long hair covered the front of her face, until she found the courage to look up. Her face appeared normal until you hit her bright blue eyes. Her pupils weren't circular. Instead, they were the shape of a parabolic spiral. Around the corners of her eyes were heavily defined veins that shot out to the sides of her face.

Seda's eyes flicked to me and then to Ryoko apprehensively. Ryoko's eyes widened, causing Seda's fear to seep out in waves. I understood her fear, but I knew Ryoko well enough to know the fear wasn't going to be needed in this situation.

Ryoko sidled closer to Seda. "May I?"

Seda nodded. Ryoko lifted her fingers to Seda's face and lightly traced the veins by her eyes. Seda relaxed when she realized Ryoko was simply curious, rather than afraid or disgusted.

"This is really neat," Ryoko breathed.

"Told you so," I muttered to Seda.

Ryoko stopped touching Seda's face and looked at me. "You knew about this?"

I nodded. "She showed me a long time ago."

Ryoko focused back on Seda. "Could you explain this all to me?"

Seda sighed, gaze lowering to her lap. "The human body struggles to handle the power psychics. Because of this, it distorts our eyes because our power is concentrated in the brain."

"All right, I get that," Ryoko said. "But why do you hide it?"

"It's another requirement, but for good reason," Seda said. "Most people don't react the way Laz or you reacted. Most become frightened or disgusted, so it was agreed by all to hide our eyes. It made it easier for us to live and fit in, because, even though we stick out with our eye covers, we don't stick out in a bad way like we would if we didn't wear them."

"So you were hesitant to show me because you thought I'd judge you?" Ryoko inquired.

"Yes… and no." Seda licked her lips. "I've always been afraid of being judged poorly for it, and it's hard to guess how one person will react over another. I know you're not judgmental, except there was still a chance you'd freak out. But there's also a bigger meaning behind removing our eye covers, one that we all adapted over time that I hold very close. We don't take our eye coverings off unless we really trust someone, see them as family, or want to be intimate with them."

Ryoko placed her hands on her hips. "Well, I'm sorry to have to say this, Seda, but even though I'm attracted to women too, I don't feel anything for you, so I'm going to have to remain friends."

Seda placed her hand on her chest, exaggerating several blinks. "You're breaking my heart, Ryoko."

The three of us laughed. I was glad Seda was okay with this now. She needed to be allowed to have a normal life for once.

"And here I thought psychics wore eye coverings because they were blind," Ryoko said. "I was way off."

"No, I can definitely see, but most people think that, so don't worry. We just use our power to see past our chosen eye covers. That's why you've never seen me walk into anything."

"That's cool. So do you mind if I ask you something?" Ryoko asked.

"Sure, what is it?"

"Please don't be offended by what I'm about to ask." Ryoko scratched her head. "I know you're speaking normally and all, but your voice is still really hollow, and, now that I think of it, I've never met any other psychic with a hollow voice. What's up with that?"

Seda laughed. "That's just how my voice is. No further explanation than that."

Ryoko hugged her. "All right. Thanks for not being upset over that. Now let's get your hair chopped and looking great."

I left the room and went about searching for clothes for her. Genesis helped me track down all the clothes Seda owned, along with the blindfold, and I was impressed by what Seda did have in the terms of "normal" clothes. Even with my limited fashion skills, I managed to pull out a dark-blue sleeveless shirt with an extremely low cowl neck and hood, a white tube top to wear underneath in case the low cowl was too low, blue denim pants, knee-high black boots, and a black choker with a D-ring around her neck.

Genesis held up a v-neck shirt and some sort of strappy… harness? I wasn't sure what it was. "What about this instead?"

My brow lifted. "What exactly is that thing?"

"I think she called it a cage bra. She used to wear it a lot in the past, before we moved in with everyone when the resistance grew in strength. It's either paired with another style bra or worn by itself. Gives it some tasteful sex appeal… I think. I'm not good with that part. I just know it looked good on her."

I cocked my head. "When did she start dressing the way she does now?"

Genesis pressed her lips together. "When we moved. When it was just the two of us, as long as we weren't going anywhere, she never went to the extremes she has these past few decades."

That explained the collection of clothes.

"I told her I didn't like it, but she insisted following the oath with so many others around."

I smiled. "Well, now she has us to argue with. And we all know mine and Ryoko's stubbornness could win their own wars."

The tiny girl's eyes squinted as she smiled. "Thank you. Seeing you do this, even if it pushes on Seda's comfort zone, makes me so happy."

I patted her on the head. "It's what she deserves."

I chose to stick with my outfit choice. Something told me, it would be best to allow Seda to choose the extra sexy look on her own terms, when she was less stressed and more comfortable with this change in her life.

Clothes and blindfold in hand, I entered the bathroom just as Ryoko was finishing up. I waited patiently, and when Ryoko was officially done, she stepped back and let me have a look. Seda's blonde hair was now just above her shoulders in the front and the back had been trimmed short enough she could gel it to vary up the look from time to time. To the right side of her face, she had a small long section of hair to help frame her face while bangs swept over the other side.

I nodded with approval and handed Seda her new outfit. She changed and then clutched her amethyst pendant tightly before turning around to take in the new her.

"I look…" She trailed off.

"Nice?" I finished.

"Amazing?" Ryoko corrected.

Seda turned and looked at us with a smile, tears brimming her eyes. "Yes. Thank you, both of you. I feel… like I can be a real person now."

Ryoko smiled. "I'm glad. Can I ask, what's the meaning of the hexagram symbol? You had it on your old veil, this new one, and it's on your necklace."

"The hexagram is a symbol of protection." Ryoko switched her gaze to me curiously as I spoke. "The star represents the elements and spirit of Lumaraeon, and the circle around it encases them protectively."

"Wow, that's really neat. So the shamans and psychics see it the same way, then."

I nodded. "We see each point as an element, and in the center you find spirit. All elements are connected and protected within the same circle. The illusion of differences is just that. An illusion."

Ryoko's eyes were filled with awe and wonder, though I didn't see what had been so special about my words. Seda cleared her throat and Ryoko snapped back to reality. "We need to show everyone your new look!"

"Wait, wha—"

Ryoko didn't let her finish. The bathroom door was thrown opened and Seda was being dragged out before I could realize what was going on. I followed the pair into the living room.

"Ta-da!" Ryoko exclaimed as she pushed Seda closer to the boys.

Seda nearly fell on her face from the force. The four men in the room stared. Seda played with her fingers and shuffled her feet, struggling to look at them. And the longer they stared, the more nervous she became.

"Well, someone say something," Ryoko said.

"I'm trying to think of something to say," Argus said. "You… you look great, Seda. You really do."

The small rose tint that flashed across Seda's cheeks didn't escape Ryoko's or my eyes. *Bingo.* That just cleared up a lot of speculation I had, and now that I knew, I would be more than willing to help Ryoko nudge someone in the right direction.

"I think Argus summed it up for all of us," Zane said.

Ryoko clapped her hands together suddenly, and everyone looked at her. "I just thought of something! I'll be right back."

She dashed down the hall and disappeared around the corner. Everyone waited in silence for her to return. When she came back around the corner, she didn't appear to have anything with her.

"Ryoko!" I exclaimed when she grabbed Seda's mouth and started messing with her center lip ring.

"I know what I'm doing."

"I don't care! You don't grab people's faces and yank on their piercings."

Ryoko ignored me and backed away when she was done. Seda rubbed her mouth. In the spot where her center ring had been was now a small titanium labret spike. I cocked my head to the side. It looked nice, but that didn't excuse Ryoko for her actions.

"You know, you could have asked," Seda muttered. "That hurt a lot."

"What did she do?" Rylan asked.

Seda turned to show them. Rylan and Argus blinked.

"Ryoko, where did you get that stud?" Argus asked.

"Your room," she replied.

Seda gasped. "Ryoko!"

I smacked my forehead. "Seriously, Ryoko? You went into his room and stole a lip stud?

Ryoko shrugged. "Yeah. He doesn't use it, so why not?"

I buried my face into my hand. "You can't take things from other people's rooms without permission. You should know that. And how did you know it was in there, or where it even was? Honestly, I feel like I'm scolding a five-year-old."

Ryoko huffed in offense at my words.

Seda looked at Argus. "Sorry. If you want it back, you can have it. I don't want to take anything that doesn't belong to me."

Argus waved her off. "It's fine. You can keep it. Ryoko is right. I don't use that one anymore. I prefer this curved one. Besides, it looks better on you than it does on me."

Seda's face flushed again at his compliment. "All right, thanks."

I wanted to laugh. Seda really was showing us her normal side. I never thought I'd see the day where I'd see her embarrassed, let alone twice in an hour.

"Blaze!" I shouted. "Get your ass out here."

Ryoko's brow rose. "What are you doing?"

"You'll see," I said. "Blaze!"

Blaze ran around the corner of the hall. "What do you—whoa… who's the cute blonde?"

"What, you don't recognize Seda?" I teased.

Ryoko giggled quietly. "I know we gave her new clothes and all, but c'mon, Blaze."

Blaze's brow furrowed with confusion. "What are you two talking about? I know this chick is about as freakishly tall as Seda, but she looks a whole lot better than Seda."

Seda nearly bared her teeth. "Six feet is not freakishly tall, you ass!"

He shook his head. "What the hell am I missing here?"

I grinned. "We gave her a haircut, like I'm about to do with you."

"Like hell you are!"

He back peddled, but I grabbed him by his jacket before he could get far. "You're getting this long-ass hair of yours chopped off, whether you like it or not."

Blaze struggled to get out of my grip. "Chicks dig my mane. Now let go."

He slipped out of his jacket, but before he could make it anywhere, Ryoko grabbed onto him and hauled him into the bathroom. I closed the door behind me and covered the mirror with a towel before grabbing a spray bottle from the closet. The guys laughed in the living room over Blaze's unfortunate situation. Ryoko held Blaze down on the toilet as I filled the spray bottle with water. For what I had planned, I was going to need it.

Suddenly, Blaze tried to make a break for it, throwing Ryoko off guard, and he bolted to his feet. I gasped when he knocked the bottle out of my hand, his force causing it to crack open. All three of us gasped as water splashed all over me.

Blaze froze, more afraid of how I was going to react to the water than trying to make his escape. "E–Eira, I'm sorry. I didn't mean to…"

I sucked in a tight breath and then slammed my palm into his forehead. "You moron!"

Blaze yelped and held his forehead as he stumbled back. Ryoko grabbed onto him and forced him back down on the toilet. I picked up the scissors and snipped the air.

"Please don't," he begged.

"You're going to regret not listening to Seda when she asked you to pick a different mental topic," I threatened. "And you're going to pay for spilling water all over me."

He whimpered and froze as I removed his hat and bandana and began cutting off his hair. "Please, Eira…"

"Don't be such a baby, and take your punishment like a man."

"I promise, I won't do it anymore," he said. "I don't want to have to shave my head after all this."

I continued to cut his hair. "You're lying. You'll never change how you think, and you get your kicks from torturing Seda the way you do."

"I look horrible without hair!"

Ryoko snickered. "Well, maybe this will finally teach you to be considerate of resident psychics when you let your mind go wild."

"Why should I?" He glowered at her. "I have a right to think as I please. It's not my fault she has freak abilities."

I cut a large chunk of hair. "Oops."

Blaze whimpered, but got the hint and shut his mouth. I continued to cut his hair until it was to my liking, and then rummaged in the closet for some hair gel. Once gelled up, I opened the bathroom door and Ryoko shoved him out into the hallway. The house grew still.

"Go ahead and continue laughing," Blaze grumbled.

"Um, I'm not sure I can, because you actually look good," Argus said.

Blaze's brow furrowed. "What are you talking about?"

"Didn't they show you what you looked like when they were done?"

Blaze shook his head and walked back into the bathroom to check. I leaned against the hallway wall and waited. He returned a few moments later, focusing his gaze on me. "You didn't butcher it."

I chuckled. "I never said I was going to. You just assumed I would."

Raikidan snickered. "Psychological torture. You really are cruel, Eira."

Blaze looked at me with a stupid expression. "I don't get it."

"That's because you're a clueless idiot," I said as I walked into the kitchen.

The boys all laughed at that. I leaned against the bar and bit into an apple. Today was good. I got to torture Blaze, and Seda was now going to be able to be normal.

Ryoko leaned next to me. "You wanna go for a walk?"

I shrugged. "Sure. Why not?"

"You boys wanna come?" Ryoko asked.

"Sure," Rylan replied.

Raikidan nodded.

"I'll pass," Argus said. "I should finish working on these plans."

"All work and no fun," Ryoko teased.

Argus shrugged. "I enjoy it, so it is fun."

Ryoko shook her head. "Whatever, crazy man."

I headed for my room. "I'm going to change real quick. I'm not walking around the city in wet clothes."

Ryoko nodded. "Okay, don't take too long. We'll wait for you outside."

I rummaged through my dresser and found a good pair of denim pants and a white tank top. After changing into them quickly, I sifted through my closet and found a cropped black and red jacket. Shrugging it on, I headed for the front door to meet up with the others.

The day was warm and the walk had been nice. Ryoko gabbed on and on about random things, and I just listened. I didn't know anything about half the things she spoke about, but, luckily, Rylan did, and he was able to hold a conversation with her. They were lucky they had so much in common. I remembered Zane would complain from time to time that he couldn't find someone to be with because no one shared anything in common with him.

Thinking about it and looking at these two made me wonder what was so great about finding someone. Why was it so important to everyone? Wasn't it better to be alone than to be hurt over and over again trying?

"Here." I looked at Raikidan when he handed me a bottle of water. "You look thirsty."

"Oh, um, thanks." I took the bottle and gratefully took a swig. I took another when I realized how refreshing it was. "Where did you get this?"

Raikidan jerked his head in some direction. "I bought it."

I chuckled. "Where do you get all this money?"

"What, do you really expect me to hand over everything to you when we get paid?"

I smiled. "I suppose not. Well, thanks again for the water. It was… thoughtful."

Raikidan opened his mouth, but Ryoko called out to us before he could speak. "Hey, guys, you might want to come over here and look at this."

Curious, I made my way over to where Ryoko and Rylan were standing. Ryoko pointed to strange symbols carved into the brick wall of the building. Raising an eyebrow, I took a closer look at them.

"Recognize those symbols?" Rylan remarked.

I nodded. "I sure do, but they're not making any real words."

"Do you think there are more located around here?" Ryoko asked.

"I was wondering the same myself," Rylan remarked as he pulled out a crumpled piece of paper and a broken pencil from his pocket. "I'll write these down, and if we find anything else, we can figure out if they're related in some way."

I nodded. "We should split up to cover more ground. We'll meet at the park in an hour. Sound fair?"

Ryoko and Rylan agreed and ran off. Rylan turned on his heels and came back to give me a strip of paper. He also broke a piece off from his pencil before he went to catch up with Ryoko.

Raikidan moved closer to me. "What's going on?"

"To be honest, I'm not sure, but if you see anything that looks similar to these symbols carved or written anywhere, tell me, okay?"

He nodded and then followed as I took off. I searched around, taking several turns down alleys. The more I looked, the more I started to feel something was wrong. These symbols were important. They had an important message, and it was urgent to find the rest, which was going to be hard. The sun was setting and in an hour it would almost be nightfall. Once darkness hit, it would be impossible to find any if they were out there.

"Eira, right here," Raikidan called.

I turned around but didn't see him. "Where are you?"

He poked his head around a corner to a small alley I had overlooked. "I think I found something here."

I rushed over to him and took a look. He was right. There were a few symbols carved into the wall. There were only five in total, but it was better than nothing. Quickly sharpening the broken pencil with my dagger, I wrote the symbols down in the same exact way I saw them.

"All right, I got them," I told him. "Let's keep checking the rest of the main alley and then head to the park to meet up with the others. If we're lucky, we'll find some more on the way."

Raikidan nodded and followed me. We searched high and low in the rest of the alley but didn't find anything and were even less lucky on our way to the park. Once we got there, we sat down on a bench to wait but I became increasingly agitated as time passed and I couldn't explain why.

"Calm down," Raikidan whispered. "You're getting yourself worked up."

"I can't help it," I admitted. "I'm getting a really bad feeling, and the longer we wait, the worse it gets. I can't get it to go away."

"Why are you getting this feeling?" he asked me.

I looked down at the piece of paper. "Because of these. The more I read them and see how much we're missing, the more I realize how rushed they were carved and how important it was for whoever wrote it to put it in cryptic fragments."

"You told me you couldn't read."

I nodded. "That's true. I did say that. I can't read common. But I can read these. These symbols are an equivalent to common to me. While we were in the military, we chose to design something I could read and write with ease, instead of forcing the impossible on me.

"You see, I can understand pictures. I understand what they mean when you put them together, so it was decided that a symbolic language would be made up for me and for only select people to learn. It was up to me to decide what each symbol would be and what it would mean." I looked at him. "In the end, the rebels adapted this when I left the military to be used as a type of secret code to allow messages to be passed around without the military finding out."

Raikidan took the paper from me. "So you're saying this message is from a rebel?"

I nodded. "It's the only explanation, and if that's the case, then this is really important."

Raikidan nodded and gazed over the paper some more. "So why pictures?"

I shrugged. "I think it's because I can imagine images better than I can actual words. Shva'sika tried to teach me how to read and write in Elvish, but I struggled and only know half of the language, if that. I don't think it's possible for me to read or write properly."

"It might only take more time for you," Raikidan encouraged. "Maybe you just need an extra push."

I grunted. "I need something, all right."

Raikidan laughed at me, and soon after I was joining in. I didn't know how he did it, but Raikidan knew how to keep me calm in the simplest ways.

"Thanks, Rai."

Raikidan tilted his head. "For what?"

"For knowing how to distract me long enough to calm me down even if it wasn't your full intention."

Raikidan placed his hand on my shoulder and opened his mouth to speak, but our attention was drawn elsewhere when quick footsteps headed our way.

"Find anything?" I asked Rylan when he stopped in front of us.

He nodded. "A few more. They were only a few symbols long, but it's better than nothing. You guys?"

I held up my paper. "We found one. I would have loved to find more, but it's better than nothing."

Rylan nodded and glanced around. "Where's Ryoko?"

I shrugged. "I figured she was with you, but I guess you two separated?"

He nodded. "We were together for most of the time, but when the alley we were in split, we thought it would be best to separate. I would have figured she'd beat me here."

"I'm here!" Ryoko cried out. She stopped when she got to us and leaned on her knees to catch her breath.

"You okay?" I asked.

She nodded. "Yeah. I just ran into some soldiers, that's all."

I noticed the ounce of alarm rush through Rylan's eyes. "They didn't harass you, did they?"

She shook her head. "They thought I was lost, so I pretended they were right, and they helped me get to a main road. I was a lot farther away than when we had started searching, so I had to run to get here."

I shook my head and chuckled. "That would be your luck."

She laughed. "Yeah, especially when it was shortly after Rylan and I split. But I did find something important while I was running that you're going to want to look at before we get to the house."

She handed me her strip of paper and I looked at it. I froze when I read two words she had scribbled on here. "Arnia and Jaybird…"

Rylan cleared off the coffee table, and I placed the pieces of paper down on it. We had to decipher this as quickly as we could. With the help of Ryoko and Rylan, we started to piece everything together. We analyzed the way each symbol had been spaced and how they had been written. I rubbed my temples when we came to a standstill. We had only a few words put together, and we had letters to spare.

"What words do you have so far?" Zane asked.

"*Help, found*, and *find*," I told him.

"We also have their names," Rylan added. "But right now that doesn't do us much good. Seda, you're sure we found all the pieces of this message?"

Seda nodded. "Yes. I even did a second scan to be sure."

I examined the remaining symbols and mused over the words we had. "Help. Found. Find." My gaze slid to a small group of symbols and something clicked in my head. I placed symbols together to form words as I spoke. "Help. We have been found out. Find us."

"By Satria…" Ryoko breathed.

"Shit!" I jumped to my feet, nearly knocking over the coffee table. "This is bad. This is very bad. Seda, I need a communicator."

"Laz, stay calm," Rylan advised. "We need to keep our heads on so we can get this fixed."

"I can't stay calm!" I yelled. "This is really bad!"

"We know. Having anyone found out is bad," Ryoko remarked.

"No, you don't understand." I grabbed my forehead in distress. "Arnia and Jaybird are unaltered twins!"

The room was silent. It didn't even sound as if anyone was breathing. I started to pace in agitation.

"Can someone fill me in on what I'm missing?" Raikidan asked.

Ryoko drummed her fingers on crossed arms. "How much do you know about twins?"

"Not much, honestly."

She nodded. "There are two types of twins in Lumaraeon. Unaltered twins and altered twins. Altered twins are experimental. They are our attempt at creating twins at will, but it's very rare they make it through the tank growing phase, and even rarer for them to last long outside the tank after growing. They're not stable enough.

"Unaltered twins exist naturally and through experimentation. Essentially they're a chance occurrence, and while they're not as rare as altered twins, they're still rare in comparison to the rest of the population. In the case of tank-born twins, they manifest within hours of being placed into a tank to be grown after the DNA creation process is done. In those who are born naturally, the cells for identical twins split and grow into two separate people in the same womb. Fraternal twins are two separate cells of different DNA that end up growing in the womb together.

"Most unaltered twins are psychics. It's believed the process of sharing a natural or false womb is what creates the physic bond between the two children. But there is a type of twins who do not have psychic abilities, but do have special properties.

These twins appear no different in a setting like this than you or me, as they have no distinguishing physical characteristic that can separate them. What sets them apart is what is known as a *life-force share*. The two twins can feel each other's presence, no matter the distance between them, and can share their life force, such as a time when one is gravely ill or hurt, allowing them to stay alive when others would have perished.

"Some believe this is a type of psychic bond that wasn't able to manifest into true psychic ability. Whatever the case, this life force bond is not always helpful. Unfortunately, because they share a life force, if one is to die by unnatural causes, the other dies as well."

"So basically, if one of them is killed by the military, we lose them both," Raikidan clarified.

Ryoko nodded. "Exactly. While the term unaltered twin would encompass all twins that weren't purposely made, the term is typically only used by the military to refer to these special twins, as their bond has an effect while in service, whereas on the outside it wouldn't. Those who are not military, or are not in a military situation, generally just use the word twins."

Raikidan looked at me. "Then Eira's agitation is justified."

"Yes," Ryoko replied. "But what I don't understand is how you know, Laz. Twins never tell because of the risk. That information isn't even put on file because the scientists don't want it to come back and harm the twins at some point."

I chewed on the tip of my nail as I paced. "Arnia told me. She thought it was necessary for me to know, just in case, since she's a mole."

"It's good that she did," Seda remarked as she came into the living room. "Sorry it took so long to give you this. I was hoping to locate either of them telepathically, but I wasn't successful. Sorry."

"It's fine. At least you tried." I took the communicator from her and put it on. I switched the setting and tried to find Arnia's communicator signal. When I couldn't find it, I searched for Jaybird's signal. My hope sank every second I couldn't find it. Finally, I gave up and changed the signal once more. "Aurora."

"Yeah, babe, whatcha need?" she asked.

"Alpha red-nine."

The sound of her keys typing stopped. "W—what? Who's in trouble?"

"Arnia and Jaybird. We need to find them now. I can't pick up either of their communicators' signals. I need you to find them."

"I'll get right on it. I'll also get another team to give you a hand and bring more from our team into the loop. This should buy us some time while I find either signal. It's going to take a while."

"Fine, whatever," I replied quickly as I ran down the stairs. "Tell the teams to meet us on the rooftops near Ninth and Main. We'll need to figure out a plan."

"All right. I'll contact you when I have something. Try to contact them again when you meet up." She cut the line before I could reply.

I rushed downstairs and the others followed. Quickly preparing ourselves, we ran back up the stairs and were met by Seda and Genesis. Seda spoke to us as everyone took the communicators from her hand. "I've already informed the Council of the situation. All available psychics are looking for them as best as they can. Twins are hard to locate telepathically as the bond they share creates a barrier that psychics have a hard time crossing. The Council has also reassigned all active assignments into lookouts. You'll have more looking out than you realize, so keep your communicators on at all times. I'll contact you if I find anything."

I nodded and bolted up the stairs to the roof. Without making sure the others were following, I jumped to the next rooftop. Clearing the jump with ease, I kept going and jumped to the next available rooftop. I picked up speed as I went. I thought I could hear shouting, but I was too focused on going forward to try to find out if anyone was really yelling or not. It could have been just about anything. It was a city after all.

I glanced to my right when nails hitting the gravel-covered roofs and heavy panting came up behind me. A wolf with a carbine grasped in his jaws ran up next to me. Thanks to the lack of chains and dark fur color, I knew it was Raikidan and not Rylan.

Raikidan shifted back to his nu-human shape quickly, far faster than I would have expected. I wondered if he had been practicing and that was all it took to make the shifting process take less time.

"You need to slow down," he panted. "The others are falling behind."

"They'll catch up. They know where we're meeting the others.

"We can't keep up. You're designed to run fast. They aren't. I'm not."

"You're keeping up fine."

"You have no idea how much energy I'm expending right now," he growled. "You need to save yours."

"I'm fine. You fall back with the others."

"I'm not leaving your side."

"Then use all your energy. It's up to you."

"You'd actually do that? You'd let me use up all of my energy so I could run with you?"

I gave him a long stern look. "It's your choice to keep up with me. I'm not making you, so if you want to waste your energy keeping up with me, then so be it. I'm not going to stop you. You'll just regret it later."

"So much for working as a team," he muttered as he slowed his pace.

I rolled my eyes and kept running. This had nothing to do with being a team. The truth was, I couldn't actually get myself to slow down. I had so much adrenaline pumping through my veins, I couldn't do anything more than run fast.

"Eira, please," Raikidan begged as he caught up with me again. "Please, slow down."

"I can't," I admitted.

"Please."

"You don't get it, Raikidan. I physically can't stop myself. I can't get my body to slow down in the least. I have no control over it."

Raikidan grinned. My brow creased. *What's with the—* "Catch!"

He tossed his carbine to me and I yelped when my feet lifted off the ground involuntarily. I held Raikidan's carbine tightly against the length of my body as he held me in his arms. The way I was holding the weapon, I looked like a civilian who had been given a gun for the first time in her life to hold. *Eira you're pathetic.* I wasn't sure what was bothering me more, the fact I was being carried or the fact Raikidan was doing this on purpose.

He cleared the next jump and skidded to a halt. He panted hard and stared down at me. A large grin was plastered on his face. "There, now you've stopped."

"Put me down!"

He chuckled and let me stand on my own. "I'll take my gun back now."

I tossed him his gun and crossed my arms, turning my gaze away from him. "Thanks for helping me."

He messed with my bangs. "You're welcome."

I swatted his hand away.

Raikidan smirked before looking around. "This is where we're supposed to meet everyone?"

I nodded as I sat down on the ledge of the roof. "Yep. This is Ninth and Main."

He sat down next to me. "Well, it's a good thing I decided to do what you hate most."

I laughed and shoved him. "Just don't do it again, you hear?"

He shoved me back with a chuckle. "Sure, sure. You look nice by the way."

I looked down at my clothes. "I look average at least." Raikidan snorted, tempting me to laugh at him. He really didn't like it when I didn't accept his compliments. "At least it's not feminine looking."

Raikidan gave me a skeptical look. "You don't know what feminine is, do you?"

My brow rose. "Huh?"

"I may not be human, but you do look feminine in this. It's a less fragile and… girlie—I think that's how you humans describe it—and more of an 'I can kick your ass' sort of feminine, but feminine nonetheless."

I snorted. "I'm not the least bit feminine."

"You're female. No matter what you do, it will be feminine in some way."

I rolled my eyes. "Whatever."

Raikidan eyed me, but I didn't pay him any mind. He was wrong. No part of me was feminine. *To be feminine is to be alluring… exquisitely beautiful… Something I'm not…*

"That's not true, Chickadee. That's not true at all."

Muscles all across my body tightened. *Tannek?*

Ryoko and Rylan landed on the roof suddenly, and Raikidan put some space between us. I was thrown off by his sudden coldness. It wasn't the first time he'd done it, he tended to do it when others were around, but I still found it strange… and a bit irritating. He would only be friendly if he didn't think anyone was paying attention.

I'm not much different though… I was a lot friendlier with him when it was only us two. I held in a sigh. Our relationship really wasn't going the way it was supposed to. He just made it hard to keep some distance between us.

"Looks like we're the only ones here," Rylan said.

I nodded. "Looks like it."

"Not anymore," Blaze said as he and Argus landed on the roof. "And can I say, Eira, you need to learn how to run slower."

"It's not like you all weren't going to catch up," I muttered.

"Looks like our help is here," Rylan observed as he peered into the distance.

I looked up to spy dark figures running across rooftops toward us. "You didn't think we'd leave ya hangin', did ya?" a deep voice boomed.

Standing up, I swiveled my head. I recognized that voice. *But where…* Just then, a large hand reached up and grabbed the edge of the roof in front of me and a man with umber skin pulled himself up onto the building. He was tall and muscular and had his hair cut high and tight. He wore tan khakis and a red men's tank. His eyes were hidden behind black shades, and what appeared to be suspenders attached to his pants were actually bandoliers.

I walked closer to the man. "Couldn't be normal and get on the roof like everyone else, eh, Xantar? Been a long time."

"Too long there, kid." Xantar balled up his hand into a fist and bumped the flat part of his arm against mine as a type of altered high-five. "It'll be fun working with ya again. Too bad it's on shitty terms."

I nodded in agreement and then frowned when that familiar chuckle I despised so much graced my ears.

"I don't see how you find working with little Eira fun, Xantar," Raynn mocked as he landed on the roof near us. "But then again your team is filled with oddball defects."

"Look who's talking," Ryoko jeered.

Raynn snorted and crossed his arms. His team filed in on the rooftop behind him just as I noticed my communicator flashing. Unhooking it from my belt loop, I placed it on my head. The visor snapped over my eyes and connected the two signals.

"H–hello?" a quiet, scared voice said.

CHAPTER 18

I couldn't believe my ears. "Arnia?"

"E–Eira, is that you?" she asked.

"Yes, it's me."

She started to sob. "T–thank the goddess. I–I thought I'd never reach anyone."

"Arnia, calm down. It's going to be all right. Where are you?"

"I–I don't know." She continued to sob. "J–Jay t–told me to hide, so I ran and ran until I found someplace to hide."

"Arnia, listen to me. I need you to stay calm and describe things around you."

"I–I—" She gasped. "They're coming. I have to go."

"Arnia, no!" The line went silent. "Arnia? Arnia! Dammit!"

I tossed my communicator on the ground in frustration. I froze when it began levitating in the air. When it hovered at eye level a band of psychics came into my field of vision.

I nodded in greeting at the two who led them. "Akama, Enrée."

"I think you dropped something," Akama said, a teasing smile on her lips.

"Why are you here?" I asked.

"We're here to help," she informed. "The rest of the Council may not understand what it's like to leave the safety of their living quarters, but we psychics do. We know what you go through from day to day, and we're here to give you a hand in the field instead of staying tucked in our beds, where it's safe."

My eyebrow lifted. "All of you?"

"Seers and Battle Psychics alike," Enrée stated.

"We thought we'd follow Seda's lead," Akama said with a smirk.

"Seda?" I wasn't about to hide that I was confused. Seda wasn't even—

"It's not polite to spy, Akama." I whirled around to see Seda touching down on the rooftop behind us.

"I like your haircut, Seda," Akama said. "It's very fitting."

Seda didn't reply to Akama's compliment. Instead, she used her abilities to take my communicator, which Akama was now holding, and handed it off to me. "Keep that with you. I told Aurora of your brief contact with Arnia. She's triangulating the signal as we speak."

I secured the communicator to my head. "I'll make sure I don't miss her call."

"So, Commander, what are your orders?" Seda asked.

Raynn grunted. "Why are you asking her? You should be asking someone of higher rank."

Xantar snorted. "Like you? Last I remember, you were the reason we lost over seventeen members to a simple assignment. Why would anyone entrust you with this important mission?"

Raynn growled. "Watch what you say, Recruit."

"That's Corporal to you, you motherless cur," Xantar barked.

"Enough," Enrée said. "Or I'll throw you both over the edge of this building and make sure you can't brace for the impact."

Xantar backed down, but Raynn wasn't going to be as submissive.

"I wouldn't mind seeing him go over," I remarked slyly. "I'd throw him over myself if needed."

"Shut it, C—"

Enrée flicked his hand and Raynn flew across the rooftop. He crashed on the gravel and groaned in pain. "Now, Commander, we're wasting time."

I nodded. "Yes. Everyone will split up into four groups. Two groups are to look for Jaybird while the other two will search for Arnia. Once found, one group is going to have to act as a distraction long enough for the other group to get them out of sight."

"Where will we bring them once found?" a rebel asked.

"To our house," I replied. "It's a low-key-enough location where the military won't raid right off in a search for them. It will buy us enough time to figure out how to get them somewhere safe."

"Where will we know where to search?" someone asked.

I pointed to the Temple far off in the distance. "Raikidan and I will make our way over to the top of the Temple. That will give us a clear view of most of the city. If we're lucky, we'll be able to catch movement from either of them. Any questions?"

"What signal should we connect to, to know location updates?" someone else voiced.

"We'll choose Aurora's for now. I'll be relaying information to her anyway, so it'd be best to save time." I looked at Raikidan. "Ready?"

Raikidan nodded. "Of course."

"You all have your assignments. Now go." I took off before I had the last part of my orders out of my mouth.

Raikidan tossed his gun to me, and as we reached the edge of the roof, he shifted into a large steppe eagle. Making sure his gun was secured on my back, I cleared the gap between the two buildings and continued on, picking up my pace steadily as I went. Eventually the buildings became taller, and I was forced to climb them.

Raikidan enjoyed himself by taunting me. He favored flying low and grabbing at my hair before flying out of swatting range.

"Stupid dragon…" I muttered.

I blinked as the Temple came into perfect view. I hadn't realized how fast I had been running. Ninth and Main was close to the Temple, but for the average free runner, it still would have taken some precious time.

Forcing a lot of energy into my next jump, I reached for the temple walls. As I soared through the air, my shoes disappeared from my feet. I would need the extra grip if I was to scale this tall building in a reasonable time. As I climbed, Raikidan took the liberty of flying around the Temple to gain altitude and to point out my slowness.

Ryoko's voice rang through my communicator. "I wish you could see how you run and climb. You look so swift and acrobatic but still able to put a strong look to it."

I grunted. "Shouldn't you be heading off somewhere to search, instead of watching me?"

"Well, a lot of us figured watching you was more productive than watching mud-brained men fight over who was leading who to what and to where," Ryoko replied.

I laughed. "Well, tell the mud brains to shut it and get a move on before I come back there and kill them all."

Ryoko began laughing. "That shut them up real fast."

"Good. Now get moving."

"Okay, okay, okay. You don't have to be so pushy. It's not like us being delayed is going to harm anything. We can't successfully search for either Arnia or Jay without further instruction from you or Aurora, and the more energy we spend aimlessly searching, the less energy we have to help when we're finally needed."

"You need to stop using your brain when you're supposed to so you don't sound smart at random."

"Bitch…" she muttered before cutting the line.

I chuckled and continued on.

"Laz."

I groaned. *"What, Seda?"*

"You need to move faster. Raikidan is getting really impatient and his thoughts are vexing me."

I gnashed my teeth. *"Well, do me a favor and tell him to shut up, because, unlike him, I can't fly, so I'm going as fast as I can."*

I swatted at Raikidan as he swooped at me. Obviously, he didn't like my response. "Go to hell, Raikidan! I'm going as fast as I can."

I was about to lose it. His impatience was downright irritating. I was at a disadvantage here and he didn't care. I sighed with relief when the wall changed to the curved roof and then yelped when a pair of strong hands grabbed the back of my jacket and hauled me up farther onto the domed roof.

I yanked myself away and glared at Raikidan. "I can do it myself!"

Raikidan pulled away. "Okay, okay. You don't need to bite my head off. I'm just trying to help."

"And I'm still mad at you, so don't touch me!" I snapped as I walked up the rest of the incline.

"Why are you mad? I just wanted you to move faster since I figured this was an urgent mission."

I whirled on him. "I'd like to see you try scaling a wall with nothing more than your hands and feet! Oh, wait, you can't. And I can't fly, so I'm forced to struggle my way up while you take the easy route and have time to think that I'm too slow."

Raikidan flinched. "Sorry. If you had asked, I'd have flown you up here somehow."

I snorted and turned away. "I'd rather chew off my own arm than ask that."

"Don't you think that was a little harsh?" Seda asked.

"No."

She sighed but didn't say anything. I didn't pay it any mind. She wouldn't understand. She enjoyed flying when she could. I, on the other hand, did not enjoy the concept one bit.

Steadying myself as I crouched down, I scanned the city. Searching up here was a long shot, but hopefully we'd manage to pick something odd up.

"So how are we going to do this?" Raikidan asked as he crouched next to me.

It was obvious my annoyance with him had affected him little. "The fastest way to locate Jay would be to heat sense. As long as he's moving outside, we should be able to spot him at this height."

"What about Arnia?"

"If she's hiding, it'd be inside a building. I doubt we're going to find her this way, unless, of course, you're able to heat sense through walls."

Raikidan snorted. "I have limits too, you know."

"That's what I thought."

Taking a deep breath and exhaling slowly, I willed the heat in my chest to fill my eyes. My sight distorted and I scanned the city. There were hundreds of people still walking about this late, making my job harder, but I had expected as much.

Raikidan pointed in the direction of Quadrant Three. "I see two of the groups over there."

I pointed toward the direction of Quadrant Two. "The other two are over there. They're spread out well. I just hope one of them is close enough to intercept."

"We have to find this guy first," Raikidan reminded me.

"I know that," I muttered.

I continued to scan the city. Movement caught my eye and I leaned forward. A single person streaked through the back alleys of Sector Eight. Soon after, a mob followed suit. Sliding closer to the edge of the roof, I peered harder. I wanted to be sure it wasn't a gang chasing a poor civilian.

"That looks to be him." As I continued to move, I switched my communicator to Aurora's signal so she could figure out the coordinates.

"Oh, good!" Aurora exclaimed. "I thought I'd have to wait for you to answer my call in. I was able to get a rough idea of where Arnia is. The signal was cut before I could pinpoint her exactly."

"It'll be good enough," I replied. "It's better than what we have now, and if we can manage it, we can spread ourselves thin to cover more ground."

"All right, she's somewhere in Quadrant Two. At one point it looked to be on the border of Sectors Four and Five, but I couldn't get a second reading to confirm it. It looks like our team is in the same area, so I'll let them know," she informed me.

"Sounds good. Raikidan and I will join them. Before you do, though, I need you to figure out the coordinates of this video clip I'm shooting. It's Jay, and I believe he's in Sector Eight. The other teams will need to get there ASAP to help him."

I could hear Aurora typing on her keyboard. "I'm receiving the feed now. I'll hand it over to Raynn's team and pray they won't mess it up."

"I was hoping you'd be able to get another team to help us," I muttered.

"Sorry, they were the only ones available. If it weren't for the Council, I wouldn't have been able to get half of them, and as you can see, even with a Council order, Nioush chose not to help. As much of an ass as he is, he would have been a powerful asset."

"As much as I hate to agree with you, you're right. I'm glad Seda isn't like him."

Aurora laughed. "I think we'd be down one psychic if she were."

I chuckled and cut the connection. I slid to the edge and Raikidan grasped the back of my vest. I turned my head and glared at him. "Let go."

"I don't want you to fall."

I slipped out of his grip to move closer to the edge. "I don't need your help. I can take care of myself."

"But—"

He didn't get a chance to continue. Once I reached the ledge, I jumped.

"Eira!" Raikidan shouted.

Gravity pulled me down like a lead weight. The wind whipped around me and deadened my hearing. Twisting my body, I faced the wall and searched for a place to push off from. Finding the right nook, I grabbed hold and then pushed off with my feet. Using my momentum to my advantage, I converted the vertical movement to a horizontal one. I twisted my body again as I came close to the building I was aiming for.

Positioning myself correctly, I rolled on the roof and pushed myself to a standing position. I looked back up at Raikidan as I came to a stop and I gave him a smug snort before continuing on, hiding my limp as best as I could. I hadn't landed as well as I had planned, thanks to the guns on my back, but I wasn't going to let that stop me. I could take care of myself. I'd done it all my life. I wasn't about to stop now.

Large wings flapped above me as I ran. Looking up, I spotted Raikidan following at a distance. As long as he didn't complain to Seda about my supposed slowness, I'd be fine.

"I'll take my gun back." I almost jumped. I hadn't expected him to shift, let alone attempt to run beside me.

My lip curled. "What, tired of flying, or am I still too slow for you?"

Raikidan let out a tight breath. "Just give me my gun. I'll be out of your hair after."

Pulling the gun off my back, I tossed it at him—my pace picking up instantly. *Wow, I had no idea it affected me that much.*

"Let me take your gun. It'll let you move faster."

"It'll slow you down more."

He shrugged. "I don't care. If I have to use up all my energy to keep up with you, I will."

I snorted. "I'll carry it myself."

"You don't have to do everything alone!"

"I don't need anyone's help," I muttered. "I can take care of myself like I have in the past."

Raikidan stopped running. "Are you saying I should have left you to die? I should have turned a blind eye to your condition?"

"It would have made my life a whole lot simpler if you had..." I murmured as I slowed down my pace. "...and yours too..."

Raikidan grabbed my shoulders, forcing me to stop. "I'm not okay with that answer. I'm not okay with you not allowing me to help."

I pushed him away. "Why do you even care? I'm a human, not a dragon. I mean nothing to you."

"That's not—"

"I mean nothing to everyone… I came back to help the others and get Zarda off my back, that's all. There's no help for me…"

"I want to help."

"It's too late!" I bared my teeth. "Where were you when I needed help twenty years ago? Where were you when I needed help ten years ago? Where were you?"

He didn't answer.

"That's right. You weren't there for me, just like everyone else. I had to do it all on my own! I had no one to rely on then, and I need no one to rely on now. When this is over, I'm out of everyone's hair and on my own like before. You might as well accept that."

I ran off before he could say anything. Hopefully, he'd get the hint this time. He was better off not making a connection and I was better off alone. That's how it was meant to be.

Holding on to the wall, I peered into the large window of a warehouse, only to sigh when I found nothing. There wasn't even a heartbeat reading from the communicator. Ryoko looked up at me hopefully, and I shook my head. Her ears drooped.

We had been searching for over an hour now and we still hadn't found a trace of Arnia. Raynn's group had lost Jaybird, putting them back to square one, except, this time, they weren't going to get help from Raikidan or me.

Ryoko greeted Rylan and Raikidan as they walked around the corner of the warehouse. "No luck for you two either?"

Rylan shook his head. "No. I'm starting to think she's moved from this area."

Raikidan glanced at me briefly before pressing on to another warehouse. "We'll keep looking until there's nowhere else to look."

Not sparing Raikidan more than a second's glance, I moved in the opposite direction. We hadn't spoken since I had yelled at him. When we had met up with the others and split off into groups of two, he had chosen to work with Rylan. Every time we met up, we'd barely glanced at each other.

"You don't need him."

"Are you and Raikidan fighting again?" Ryoko asked as she caught up with me. I climbed a metal ladder instead of answering, and she sighed. "That's what I thought. What is it over this time?"

"It doesn't matter." I stopped short and exhaled. "Don't do that, Raikidan."

Raikidan kept moving, but as I watched him, I realized he was hyper-focused on something, and not just ignoring me. He hadn't even noticed me this time.

Ryoko leaned over the railing. "What's with him?"

"I have no idea."

Rylan came around the corner of the building and gazed up at us. "He caught a scent and ran off. Keep up with him. We don't need three missing people."

I nodded and followed Raikidan. He was so focused on following whatever scent had crossed his nose, he didn't even notice me once. I placed my hands on his arm and peered around him when he stopped. He jumped, his eyes snapping to me. "How long have you been there?"

A small giggle escaped my lips. "I've been following you this whole time."

"Oh…" He looked away and pointed to the wall of the warehouse. "The scent leads to that wall, but I don't understand why. That woman can't walk through walls, can she?"

I shook my head and took a closer look at the wall. "No, but she is a metal elementalist, making her a great asset for barricades." Pressing on the wall, I searched for a weak point. The metal creaked and eventually a corner popped out. "Bingo."

Grabbing onto the exposed corner, I bent the metal away until a small hole was exposed. Tossing the sheet metal aside, I peered into the hole. The tunnel was dark, but I could make out a small dip where the tunnel curved down.

Raikidan knelt and sniffed. "She definitely went this way, but there's no way we're going to be able to follow. There are no doors or windows to this building, and that tunnel is tiny."

I sat down. "You're such a pessimist."

Placing my gun down on the grated floor, I grabbed onto the top part of the hole and slid myself down the tunnel.

"Eira, no!" Raikidan hissed.

But it was too late. I didn't care where this led me, nor did I care for what lay ahead. I'd deal with it when it came. I stumbled when my feet hit the floor, but didn't let that stop me. Looking around cautiously, I ventured deeper into the dark warehouse, although it wasn't completely dark, thanks to a few holes in the roof that let in the light from the moon.

I jumped and spun around when a masculine hand touched my shoulder. Raikidan held up his hands defensively. "Easy, it's me."

I let out a terse breath and lowered my guard. "Don't do that!"

"I wouldn't have to if you didn't jump into strange holes without thinking."

I crossed my arms. "I was thinking of finding Arnia. She's definitely in here, and we need to get her somewhere safe before it's too late. There may not be soldiers in this area right now, but there will be. She obviously locked this building up to keep them out, so that means they'll come back looking for her." I motioned for him to follow. "C'mon, we need to look around for her instead of argue."

"Her scent is heavy here," he said. "Follow me and we'll find her."

"Your sense of smell is really good."

"Can't you smell her here?"

I shook my head. "I haven't been around her too recently to be able to catch it. If I concentrated long enough, I might be able to pick it up, but it would be faint to me."

"Your sense of smell sucks," he teased.

I pushed him. "Shut up and get a move on."

He muttered something in his tongue and pushed me back before beginning his search. I followed close behind. The two of us stopped next to a large metal crate when we heard boots clomping on the floor, and quiet male voices echoed through the building. Keeping still in the shadows, we waited until two soldiers came into a patch of moonlight.

"This is pointless," one complained. "We've searched this whole place and she's not here. We should bust open a wall and get out of here."

"No," the other objected. "She's here. Otherwise those rebels outside wouldn't be here still."

Raikidan and I exchanged a look but continued to stay where we were.

The first soldier sighed. "I can't wait to get my hands on this woman's throat."

"Don't say that," the other soldier said. "You know our orders. Neither she nor the other is to be killed. Zarda wants to do that himself."

The first soldier kicked a crate. "He gets all the fun. Knowing him, he's just going to screw it up again like that time that commander got away."

The second soldier chuckled. "You mean that freak show that would kill hundreds in cold blood?"

The first soldier nodded. "Yeah, that one."

My arms reached up and held myself out of reflex. I knew who they were talking about.

The second soldier grunted. "Emotionless, bloodthirsty monster she was. Hopefully, whoever is dealing with her now is having fun. Creations like her shouldn't exist. They're uncontrollable."

The first soldier nodded in agreement. "Now there are copies of her that are even worse. That's exactly what we need. More monsters roaming about."

"Make them regret their words."

The two chuckled and my heart ached. Even in my absence, I was remembered as a monster. *Will I ever escape this curse?*

"Kill them."

Raikidan took one of the daggers on my arms and I attempted to stop him, but without words, I wasn't able to do much. I didn't want to risk moving from my spot, and if I made a sound, they'd see us both. All I could do was watch as Raikidan stalked up to them soundlessly. The second soldier ended up walking a little ways ahead of his companion due to his larger stride, giving Raikidan the opportunity to take them out individually.

Raikidan reached up and covered the man's mouth. He thrust the dagger into the soldier's back and then snapped his neck. Laying him on the ground quietly, Raikidan advanced toward the last soldier.

The soldier turned to speak to his companion and stopped moving at the sight of Raikidan and his dead counterpart. The soldier drew his pistol. "Who the hell—"

Raikidan seized him by the throat and lifted him off the ground before he could finish. The soldier dropped his pistol as Raikidan tightened his grip.

"You'd best take back what you said about her," Raikidan threatened.

The man snickered. "So you… know the freak, do you? Why don't you make me take back my words?"

Raikidan pulled the soldier's face close to his own. "You're in no position to be challenging me, you worthless peon."

I noticed the soldier's eyes dart over to me. My grip on myself tightened as he chuckled. "And here I thought she had left. Who would have thought she had been right under our noses all this time?"

Raikidan turned his gaze back to me and then refocused on the soldier. "Look her in the eyes and tell me what you see."

I gulped. I didn't like where this was going. My brain told me to leave. It told me to get away from these words that were going to be spoken, but my body was frozen in place.

The man grunted. "She carries the same look she always did. Cold and emotionless, the look of a monster."

I held myself as my chest constricted. I hated words. I didn't understand why Raikidan was doing this. I didn't see how this was going to help anyone.

"You're a fool," Raikidan snarled. "You know what I see? I see a woman who has felt pain. I see a woman who has been abused and betrayed. I see a woman who has seen the deepest pits of loneliness with no hope of escape."

The man chuckled. "You obviously know nothing about her."

Raikidan thrust my dagger into the man's abdomen. "I know enough to know that not many know the real her. Not many know how normal she wishes she could be. I know enough to know she isn't the cold, emotionless monster you claim her to be."

"The dragon, I might like him," the voice in my head said, surprising me.

I watched in stunned silence as Raikidan dragged the dagger up toward the soldier's chest. Blood splattered all over the floor. The soldier cringed in pain but was unable to scream due to Raikidan's tight grip. Raikidan pulled out the dagger and let the man go. As he did, he slashed the soldier in the chest. The soldier fell to the ground in his own pool of blood and struggled to breathe. He shook as he attempted to keep his entrails from spilling out. I looked away. I couldn't watch this anymore. It wasn't right.

"She… isn't watching…" the soldier whispered.

Raikidan grunted. "Now maybe you'll know how wrong you are. Too bad it's too late for you."

I walked away. I couldn't handle this. Not only was there too much blood in the air, but Raikidan's refusal to see the truth was too much to handle. I wasn't sure how I should feel about it. Finding a small crate, I sat down and waited. Raikidan would follow shortly, but before he arrived, I needed to make sure I was stable.

I glanced up when Raikidan's familiar footsteps approached. He was expressionless, and his left hand was covered in blood. I looked down at my lap. "He didn't deserve that."

"Yes he did, you fool," the voice hissed.

"He insulted you," Raikidan said.

"He spoke the truth. I am what I am. Nothing can change that."

He stepped closer. "His words wouldn't hurt so much if you were a monster."

I held up my hand. "Don't come closer. You need to find a way to clean off your hand."

Raikidan didn't listen. "You'll be fine."

My head pulsed.

"You need to leave."

"It's going to be okay, Eira."

"I'm serious! Don't press your luck with me, Raikidan. I don't… I don't want to hurt you like the others…"

He crouched down in front of me and touched my face with his bloody hand, sending a whirlwind of mixed emotions through me. "I see soft, warm eyes. Not cold, emotionless ones. I see a real person with wants and desires. Not a controlled machine."

"No, you need to leave!"

"It's going to be okay, trust me."

My heart raced and pounded in my ears. He had no idea what he was getting himself into. I tried to pull away, but he refused to allow it.

"Please… Tannek…"

Raikidan's thumb slipped and touched the corner of my lips. I froze as the blood seeped in and touched my tongue.

"Blood!" the voice in my head screamed hungrily.

I tried to fight the monster's urge to kill, but it was too strong. It hadn't been satisfied in so long. It wanted me to go for his throat. It wanted me to tear him apart, but I resisted. I didn't want to hurt him. *I don't want to hurt him.*

"Eira?" Raikidan tried to look me in the eye—big mistake.

My body lunged at him in a crazed frenzy. I pulled back just as my body reached for his throat, and instead I clamped onto his hand with my sharp teeth. I was attacking him in a primitive way I thought I'd never do again. Raikidan cringed in pain but didn't fight back, as if he were completely okay with the situation.

I fought to stay in control of my body, the frenzy slowly taking over. I was too weak to stop it. *I don't want to kill him.* I was starting to lose touch with my reality.

Raikidan pulled me into his lap and held on to me tightly. "Fight it, Eira. You're stronger than it is. I know you are."

"Blood."

I wanted to believe him. I wanted to have the strength, but I couldn't find it.

"Death."

He spoke quietly into my ear. "You're not the monster you think you are. Monsters are ugly and weak. They destroy others out of fear. You are beautiful and strong. You told me you feared nothing."

I froze. Not even the frenzy could get me to move.

"You have the strength to stop it," he whispered.

I wanted the strength to stop. I wanted to stop hurting him.

"I believe in you."

"He's lying. Destroy him before he can turn around and hurt you." The voice was back to hating him.

Shutting my eyes, I fought for the will to stop. My mouth unlatched suddenly and I shoved his arm away. My eyes flew open, and my breath came out slow and ragged.

Raikidan pulled me closer. "I told you, you aren't a monster."

I wasn't sure I could believe him as I stared at his bloody hand—the mark I left clearly visible, and the taste of his blood fresh on my tongue. How could I not be a monster? Sure, I had been able to stop myself this time, but what about the next time? I thought I had this under control. I thought the shamans could help me. But all we did was suppress it and make it worse in the end.

I wiped the blood around my mouth away and buried my face into his shoulder. "You're wrong. I wouldn't have hurt you at all if I wasn't."

"You would have killed me if you were," he replied. "I wasn't going to stop you, Eira." I gazed up at him. "I wasn't going to defend myself. I had tried to hurt you when we first met. I regretted it after. I shouldn't have tried to hurt you in anger."

I stared into his eyes and he smiled at me. He really believed I was a good person. I wanted to be. I really did.

I went to reply, but the sound of scraping metal drew my attention elsewhere. I climbed to my feet, with Raikidan's help, and crept closer to the direction of the noise. I froze when a tiny figure moved from the shadows and into the light. "Arnia…"

She looked terrible. Her beautiful hair was gone, and her face was bruised and bloody. She had obviously been tortured before she was able to escape.

"Arnia…" I stepped closer to her.

My advance triggered something in her mind and she stumbled over to me. I caught her in my arms as she threw herself at me and began to sob. I wasn't sure what to do for her, so I did what I would do if Ryder was upset. Stroking her back gently, I hushed her.

"I–I thought I'd be taken b–back," she sobbed. "I–I thought… I thought y–you guys weren't going t–to find me in time."

"Arnia, it's okay. We're here now," I encouraged. "You're safe."

Raikidan placed a hand on my shoulder. "We need to get out of here."

I nodded and focused on Arnia. "Arnia, do you have the strength to open a small way out?"

She shook her head. "N–no… I used up what I had left to seal myself in here and then hide from those two soldiers I accidentally sealed in with me."

I nodded. "All right. We'll figure something else out, then."

"I could burn a hole in the wall," Raikidan suggested.

I nodded. "It's the only—what the—"

The wall adjacent to us began to creak and warp. Suddenly a section broke off and flew away. Ryoko was left standing in front of the gap with a smile. "Good. I found you. Seda said she lost you two because Arnia was too close. Now let's get out of here. The scanners were picking up strange movement east of here a few moments ago. The military may be coming back to check the area."

I nodded in agreement. "Good idea. C'mon, Arnia. We're going to get you out of here."

Arnia stumbled over her feet several times before we even made it outside. She was so weak, which meant Jaybird couldn't be doing any better.

"I'll carry her," Raikidan offered. "She's not going to make it much farther on her own."

"All right." I attempted to hand Arnia off to him, but she held on tight to my vest. "Arnia, it's all right. You'll be safe with him. I promise."

Arnia eyed Raikidan cautiously. I had never seen her so timid before. It was obvious the people who had tortured her were male. She would have no other reason to be afraid of Raikidan if it weren't so.

Raikidan extended his hand to Arnia, and she hesitantly took it. Being careful not to scare her any more, he lifted her up in his arms and cradled her. Arnia relaxed when she realized he wasn't going to hurt her.

Seda appeared over the top of the warehouse. "All of you, get out of here! They're coming."

"Seda, get the other group to distract them as best as they can while we escape," I ordered. "Ryoko, go find Rylan and meet up with us. If the other team isn't able to hold them off, I'll need you two to help act as another distraction."

Ryoko and Seda nodded. "Right."

They both left and I set a quick pace through the maze of warehouses. Ryoko and Rylan finally caught up with us, and it took us a while to figure out how to get out. We nearly ran into three squads on the way, and each time, Arnia would begin to whimper, almost giving away our position.

Once we were in the back alleys, we were able to move faster. Unfortunately, it did nothing to keep our distance from the pursuing soldiers.

"They have a Hunter," Seda informed me. *"You're going to have to be clever to get rid of it."*

"Great," I muttered. "Seda just told me they're following us with a Hunter. We need to think of something to lose them quickly."

"It'd be wise to run around aimlessly and make sure we backtrack several times," Rylan advised.

"But we don't have that kind of time," Ryoko objected.

"What if you two took something of ours and ran with it?" Raikidan offered.

Rylan nodded. "That would work. It would give you and Laz a chance to get out of here."

The four of us stopped running and I removed my jacket. I handed it to Ryoko and she slung it over her shoulder. Raikidan set Arnia on her feet and removed his vest. He handed it over to Rylan and then took Arnia's hand. "They need this glove."

She nodded and let him take it off her. I hated seeing how submissive she had become. She was never like this before. I didn't understand. What had they done to her?

Raikidan tossed Arnia's glove to Rylan and then picked Arnia back up carefully. Each group wished the other luck and parted ways. Raikidan stuck close to me, and I touched Arnia's shaved head from time to time to encourage her to stay calm. It pained me to see her exposed numbers. I didn't like knowing she had been humiliated so badly.

Arnia cringed. "Jay is in trouble…"

I channeled my communicator's signal to Aurora's. "I need a status report."

"The other groups finally found Jaybird and are now trying to get him out," Aurora informed me. "But they're not doing so hot. The military decided to bring out their own psychics, hindering our advantage."

"Perfect," I muttered. "Just keep tabs on them and give them a hand when they need it."

"Will do. I have Ezhno giving me a hand with this, so they should be able to get him out, no problem, if they listen to us."

"Good. See to it." I cut the connection.

Arnia screamed when a wall burst near us.

"I found you!" a soldier's voice bellowed.

"Go, go, go, go!" I told Raikidan as I pushed him forward.

We took every corner we came across in an attempt to lose the soldier. Every time we thought we had lost him, the soldier would crash through the buildings to close the distance. We took another turn and stopped in our tracks. We were faced with a dead end and no time to turn around. Arnia was visibly shaking now. I couldn't bear to see her like this.

"What now?" Raikidan asked.

"I don't know," I said. "I could climb these walls with ease and you could fly over them, but we wouldn't be able to bring Arnia. We might have to fight."

"We might not have to."

My brow rose. "Say that again?"

Raikidan placed Arnia down on her feet. "I was once told of some dragons being able to transfer some of his shapeshifting ability into someone else for a short period of time."

"A dragon?" Arnia breathed.

"Yes, Raikidan is a dragon," I told her. "But you must promise not to tell anyone."

Arnia nodded vigorously. "I promise."

"Good. Now, Raikidan, what do you mean by you were told? Have you not done it yourself?"

He snorted. "I barely found a reason to shapeshift, let alone find someone to practice forced shapeshifting on."

I chuckled. "Good point. Do you think you'd be able to try once to see if it's possible?"

"It's the only reason I suggested it. I won't guarantee it'll work, but it's a shot." I nodded and waited. Raikidan took Arnia in his arms and held her close. "This might feel a little strange."

Arnia began to shake again, but a few quiet encouraging murmurs from Raikidan stopped them. Raikidan rested his chin on Arnia's head and closed his eyes. I watched his face muscles tense with effort as he tried to do the impossible. I nearly gasped as both he and Arnia began to shift. The process was slow but unbroken. I stared when it was finally done. In front of me were two small rainbow boas. Snapping out of my awed daze, I scooped them up and wrapped them around my neck.

The boa I figured was Raikidan moved until he was securely attached to me, but Arnia was a little slower to react. I didn't doubt the new body she was being forced to take was hard for her to use, especially with her lack of energy. Once she was finally in a good spot, I grabbed her discarded uniform on the ground and rushed for the wall. At the same time, the pursuing soldier crashed into the alley.

Picking up my pace, I scaled the wall with ease and jumped the rooftops. The soldier roared in anger as he couldn't follow, and I laughed. We were in the clear as long as I could get us back to the house, and getting there undetected wasn't going to be easy. I could hear the soldiers rushing around and could see the searchlights they used to attempt to flush us all out.

I ducked behind a chimney when soldiers climbed up on a nearby roof and shone a searchlight in all directions. The light shone over to where I hid, and stayed there for some time before moving away. I didn't move even when the light went out. It didn't matter if I needed to get Arnia back to the house or if Raikidan could hold this shifting technique for much longer. I couldn't chance us getting caught.

When I didn't hear any soldiers after waiting for a little while longer, I crept out of my hiding spot. Unfortunately, I wasn't as alone as I had first thought. The soldiers were no longer on the other roof, instead, they were on the same one as me.

"Stay where you are!" a soldier ordered as he held a gun at the ready.

I stared at the three soldiers for a brief moment and then took off for the building next to this one. The soldiers warned me they would shoot me if I didn't stop, but I wasn't about to stop for them. I cleared the gap between the two buildings just as they began to open fire on me.

"Shit!" I ducked behind a pillar and only stayed out of the line of fire long enough to make a quick judgment call on the direction I should head. The bullets ceased to rain on me when I managed to get a few buildings away, but I wasn't out of the thick of this yet.

Other soldiers heard the gunfire. More searchlights appeared and soldiers began climbing up on more roofs. I was forced to slow down, as I had to sneak around undetected. I ended up having to resort to using the alleys to get around certain buildings because of the heavy soldier traffic. I actually couldn't believe the number of soldiers out here searching. I had never known Zarda to expend so many resources to search for a defect. But maybe it was because he knew Arnia and Jaybird had connections to the rebellion. Maybe he figured we'd be helping and he could get more of us if he did put out the resources for the search.

I scaled a wall and scurried on top of a roof. As I did, Arnia began to squirm. I touched her to reassure her, but she continued. I realized what was going on. The forced shapeshift was wearing off.

"We're almost there," I whispered. "Just hold on."

"Eira." My head snapped in multiple directions, surprised by the sound of Raikidan's voice. *"Eira, Seda is connecting our minds for me. I don't want to sound pushy, but you need to move faster. I can't keep this up for much longer."*

"I know, and I'm sorry it's taking so long," I replied. *"I'm going as fast as I can. I expended a lot of energy back there. Please, just hang on a little longer. We only have a few more blocks to go."*

"I'll do what I can."

I cleared the jump for the next roof and stumbled on my landing. I really was losing energy, far too much for this. I didn't understand. Righting myself, I continued on. There wasn't time to think about it. I had to keep going until my feet couldn't keep me up anymore.

I cleared rooftop after rooftop, and each time my landings worsened. A flicker of hope sprung inside me when the house came into view. I used the last of my energy to push faster. Once we were on that rooftop, we'd be safe. My hopes were dashed when I didn't jump far enough on my last jump.

"Eira!" Raikidan yelled.

Barely managing to grab onto the ledge of the roof, I held on for dear life. Our house was tall, and although a drop wouldn't kill me, it would hurt to hit the ground. One of my hands slipped, and I desperately tried to grab the ledge back. My strength was almost gone. Even though I managed to grab the ledge again, I didn't keep hold of it for very long. *"Raikidan, you have to shift into something that can carry her. I can't pull us up. Something is wrong. I have no strength left in me."*

"But what about you? You'll fall."

"I know... I'll be fine, though. The drop won't kill me."

"I'm not going to let you fall!"

"You don't have a choice," I argued. *"Arnia is your priority. She needs to be safe before anyone else. I'll manage on my own. I told you, I can take care of myself."* My grip on the ledge slipped a little. *"Raikidan, please hurry! I'm going to fall, and neither of you could survive a drop like this in those forms. Even in her nu-human form, Arnia wouldn't make it. She's too weak to survive a fall like that."*

"Eira..."

"Please... do—" I gasped as my grip failed.

"Eira!"

CHAPTER 19

I grunted in pain when a strong hand grabbed onto my wrist, stopping my fall. I gazed up and smiled at the olive-skinned man holding onto me. "I don't think I've ever been happier to see you in my life, Azriel."

Azriel chuckled. "I'll take that as a compliment. Out of curiosity, what's with the snakes around your neck? Did you decide to stop at the local exotic pet store on your way home? And… is one of them bleeding?"

I laughed. "Pull me up and you'll get your answers."

With some effort, Azriel hauled me up and I sighed with relief as my body hit the roof. Raikidan slid off me and shifted. Arnia, on the other hand, didn't have the energy to do more than let go and shift as she fell from my neck to the roof.

Azriel titled his head, his eyes wider than before. "That's not what I was expecting."

"I would hope I didn't get these two at a pet shop," I joked.

"As do I." He looked around. "Now, where are her clothes?"

"I must have dropped them when I messed up my jump," I admitted.

Azriel shook his head with a small chuckle and unbuttoned his shirt. "We'll give her this for now. It'll be long enough to cover her until we can get her inside where it's safe."

I nodded as I accepted the shirt from him and I wrapped it around Arnia. She was out cold now, and I feared we were going to lose her. I attempted to pick her up, but I was too weak to do it.

"I got her," Azriel offered. "You need to take it easy. We'll figure out what's up with you after we tend to her."

Raikidan knelt next to me. "I'll help you."

"I can walk on my own," I lied.

He snorted. "And I was born yesterday. C'mon, it's just until we get inside. It's the least I can do for you almost killing yourself to get us this far."

"Fine," I muttered.

I expected him to allow me to at least keep my feet on the ground, but with typical Raikidan style, he lifted me up off the ground and held me in his arms instead. I was too weak to fight him over it. I just wanted to get inside where it was safe and pray the others were all right and Jaybird was on his way here.

Raikidan laid me down on the couch near Arnia and stepped away. Genesis ran over to Arnia and placed a hand on her forehead. Genesis' brow creased. "She's burning up."

"We need to get her into some actual clothes to regulate her body temperature," I said. "Gen, go get some armor cloth for her. Zane, I need you to go into the back alley and find Arnia's uniform and dispose of it."

"Sure thing," Zane replied.

The two rushed down the hallway. Genesis came back with a strip of cloth and handed it to me. Pulling myself up with my arms, I removed Azriel's shirt from her body and placed the armor on top of her. Without needing to will it, the cloth reacted to Arnia's presence and clothed her.

"Avert your gaze," Azriel said.

I glanced up to see him focused on Raikidan, who blinked. "What?"

"I don't know how things are done where you're from, but here, when in the presence of a naked woman you're not intimate with, you don't stare."

Raikidan, clueless as ever, blinked again. I wasn't sure he'd ever understand this aspect of human behavior at this point. "I'm just checking to make sure my forced shift didn't harm her."

The two stared at each other until Azriel's brow creased. His gaze shifted to me, the unspoken understanding he believed Raikidan's innocent intent clear in his eyes. "Where the hell did you find someone like him?"

I grunted. "The middle of dumb-fuck nowhere."

Azriel laughed and then went to work on checking Arnia's vitals. "Even with the fever, she's stable. I only hope she stays this way. I have no idea what's doing this to her."

"Do you think it could be Jay?"

He nodded. "It's a possibility. He is in the middle of all the fighting."

I opened my mouth to ask for a space communicator to check in with Aurora, when a telepathic message from Seda flooded into my mind. *"Jaybird should be coming up the basement steps soon."*

I let out a relieved breath. *"Good."*

A few moments later, the basement door flew open, and Argus and Blaze dragged a battered man inside. The man had short, styled blonde hair with blue tips and the same shade of green eyes as Arnia.

"Jay, you look terrible," I said.

He chuckled. "Nice to see you too. Where's my sister? Is she okay?"

I looked over at her. "Feverish, but stable and sleeping on the couch over there."

Jaybird stumbled away from the boys and leaned on the couch near Arnia. "She'd better recover. I won't forgive myself if she doesn't."

I hauled myself onto my weak legs. "I'll make sure she gets the help she needs."

Raikidan tried to stop me. "You're not going anywhere."

"Like hell I'm not. Arnia is sick and they both need to get out of here. I know of someone who will help, and you're going to help me get there."

"You're not going anywhere," Raikidan repeated.

I grabbed him by the back of his hair and pulled his face closer to mine. "I don't care about the condition I've been mysteriously placed in. Tell me I can't do something one more time, and I will make you regret it."

Raikidan chuckled, amusement dancing in his eyes. *Did he try to egg a rise out of me?* "Where am I escorting you to?"

I released him. "Do you remember the house where Fe'teline and Tla'lli brought us?" He nodded. "That's where we're going."

In an instant his clothes changed to his Guard uniform. "All right, if you know what you're doing, let's go."

I grunted and used the couch as a crutch to move around it. My clothes changed as I made my way over to the basement door.

Raikidan caught me when I stumbled. "Maybe they can help fix you as well."

"I don't need to be fixed."

"Yeah, you keep saying that," he muttered as he helped me down the stairs.

I sighed. "I hate this."

"Get used to it," he told me. "Because until we figure out what's wrong with you, you're stuck with me helping you."

"You told me you'd only help me to the living room," I reminded him as he opened the hidden door.

"Yes, well, you never said you were going to venture out anywhere else."

I snorted and kept walking.

"It doesn't make you weak," he said. "Relying on others."

I snorted again. "Yeah, and I'll believe that… never."

Raikidan sighed. "There's nothing wrong with getting help."

"I've learned to rely on only myself. I should be able to do this on my own," I replied softly.

"You should also learn to suck up your pride and let someone give you a hand when they offer it," he murmured close to my ear.

"It doesn't happen enough for me to want to."

"You're back on a team now. You might want to start wanting to."

He's right. But I was too stubborn to admit it to him. I didn't want to rely on anyone else. I could barely do it in the past, so why start pretending that would change?

Raikidan opened another hidden door at my instruction, and we headed up the stairs to the main room it attached to. Together we slipped out of the house and slowly progressed to our destination. I sighed mentally when the house came into view. Unfortunately, my bad shape caught the eye of patrolling soldiers.

"Are you two all right?" one asked as he made his way over to us.

"We'll be fine once we get to our destination," Raikidan replied.

The soldiers passed a strange glance to one another.

"Laz'shika!" a feminine voice called out.

I looked up to see a hooded figure running over to us, and smiled. "Fe'teline."

Fe'teline touched my shoulders and looked me over. "You look terrible! If you had told us in your message you were in this condition, we would have sent the healer to you."

I chuckled. "You know me. Why would I do something so smart?"

She laughed. "True. I just can't believe you would put your body though so much torture for training."

I shrugged. "I'm persistent."

"Excuse me," a soldier said, "I don't mean to interrupt, but if you're this injured, why are you walking? Shouldn't you be carried?"

Raikidan grunted. "You don't know Laz'shika. She's stubborn, and even in this condition, she fought like hell to walk here. I wasn't going to have myself torn apart over it."

"Very well," the soldier replied. "We will leave you to your business."

Fe'teline bowed respectfully and ushered Raikidan and me toward the house. She looked back several times to check the distance between the soldiers and us until she figured it was safe to speak quietly. "A psychic contacted us not too long ago to tell us about your surprise arrival."

"Well, I'm glad they did," I said. "Otherwise we could have had a messy situation on our hands back there."

She laughed. "Yes, that is true. Now let's get you inside and checked out. You're in much worse shape than I thought."

I grunted. There was that comment again. *Do I really look that pathetic?* The two of them helped me up the stairs and sat me down on the couch in the living room. There were at least a dozen shamans scattered about. I didn't think so many lived in one house.

Raikidan sat down next to me as Fe'teline went to speak with some of the other shamans. I rested my head on Raikidan's shoulder and let out a relaxed breath.

"Are you all right?" he asked.

I shook my head. I was feeling a whole lot worse than I had before. My eyes fought with me to close and my body grew heavier. Now I knew something was wrong.

Fe'teline came back with a tall nu-human man. He had tan skin, short black hair, and lavender eyes.

"My name is Ven'lar," he introduced in a thick accent that was common for those from the North. "I'll be tending to you."

I barely responded.

"She's even worse now," Fe'teline said. "I hope you can help."

Ven'lar took my face into his hands and examined me. He was gentle, which made me a little more comfortable about the situation. It reminded me of the times Xye would use me as his guinea pig to brush up on his healing. Of course, Xye was much gentler than this guy, but that was because of his wrong feelings toward me. This man was gentle because he was a healer and for that reason only.

"Her life force is weak," he observed. "It feels like it's being drained from her."

A woman walked over to us and crouched down next to him. "Let me see her."

Ven'lar moved aside to allow the woman to examine me.

"What were you doing earlier today?" she asked.

I wanted to respond, but nothing would come out of my mouth. I could barely make a conscious thought.

"Rescuing someone," Raikidan answered for me.

The woman looked at him. "Where?"

"In some warehouses in Quadrant Two. Why?"

"Tell me more about this rescue."

"Nothing to say, really," he replied. "We had to save a teammate and located her in the warehouse she was hiding in."

"Who was she running from?"

"The monster in her closet," Raikidan replied sarcastically. "Who do you think she was running from?"

The woman sighed and switched her gaze to me. "I need to check your leg. Is that all right?"

I blinked in response. The woman moved my cloak and lifted my leg up onto the couch. The movement off-centered me, and I fell over into Raikidan's lap. I let out an annoyed breath, triggering Raikidan to chuckle. To add insult, he curled his fingers around my shoulder, as if he "attempted" to catch me.

The woman touched my leg all over, and I cringed when she touched the inner side of my calf. "This might hurt a little."

I ground my teeth when she yanked on something. I would have screamed from the pain had I not been so weak. Raikidan's grip on me tightened, an aggressive growl rumbling in my chest as blood pooled out of my leg.

"Heal her up," the woman instructed.

Ven'lar positioned himself in front of me again and healed my bleeding leg, and Raikidan calmed down when the bleeding stopped.

"Nela, what did you find?" Fe'teline asked.

Nela held up a small robot that was shaped like a bug and was no bigger than my thumb. "She was being fed upon. This little critter is designed to suck on life energy. The longer it stays on you, the faster it drains you."

"But why her?" Fe'teline asked.

Nela shook her head. "I don't think she was the intended target. This one here stated they were looking for someone. That person was more likely the intended victim, but if Laz'shika's life force was stronger, it would have gone after her instead. From the looks of the settings, this was intended to kill, not weaken."

"So she saved the other person's life," Ven'lar remarked.

Nela nodded. "If the target was weaker than her, yes."

Raikidan eyed her. "You know a lot about it."

Nela sighed. "I wish I didn't."

"What are you not saying, Nela?" Fe'teline pressed.

"The East Shaman Tribe designed this," Nela admitted.

Fe'teline gasped. "But why would you do that?"

"We had to. Our tribe, unlike the other tribes, uses technology on a regular basis. We design things to make life easier, or out of boredom. When we were forced to sign the treaty with this city to be less neutral in Zarda's favor, we were to prove we wouldn't go back on it by designing something. This device is what we designed."

"But... there was... a price..." I managed—my strength coming back already.

She nodded. "My brother designed this stupid thing... and when we handed a working bug over with the plans, they killed him..."

Fe'teline gasped. "But why?"

"To make sure... they didn't make another one," I explained. "They're not smart enough to think... more than one person worked on it, and they're not smart enough... to think they didn't have a secret stash of plans of ways to counter the device."

"I'm sorry about your brother, Nela," Fe'teline said.

"Me too…" she whispered.

I held out my hand. "May I… see the device?"

"Um, sure. Why do you want it?" she asked.

"To destroy it and take back some of the energy it stole from me."

Nela laughed. "You can't take it back. It doesn't work like that."

"You want to bet?"

She pursed her lips. "Even if it were possible, it'd be dangerous. You don't know if this has taken energy from someone else. If it has, you could be harmed by their energy."

I snorted. "Do they teach you nothing… in your tribe?"

"Excuse me?"

"Life energy… it exists in all living things. There is no difference… between the life energy that exists in you and that small flower in your hair. There is no difference between… the energy in me and a small insect. It's all the same. This is why we are able… to have others who can heal. This is why we are able to transfer life energy to… each other when it's needed. No life energy is dangerous. It would only be dangerous if we didn't have it… to begin with." Everyone stared at me and I resisted the urge to get defensive. "What?"

"I don't think I've ever heard it explained so well," Ven'lar said.

Fe'teline nodded. "I agree."

I looked away from them. I wasn't sure how to handle their praise, if that's what it was. I peered at Nela when she handed over the bug. "You seem to know what you're doing, so there is no point in stopping you."

I took the bug and inspected it. Blue lights flashed up a line of bulbs on both sides of the bug. They didn't reach the top bulb, leading me to believe it was an energy meter. Holding the bug in the center of my palm, I took a deep breath and crushed the machine. I could feel the energy escaping its mechanical prison, and I concentrated on harnessing it.

I exhaled as the last of the energy disappeared. I had managed to harness only half of it, but it was better than nothing. The rest that escaped would be absorbed in smaller amounts by everything around us.

"You're a soldier, aren't you?"

I glanced up at a young boy with sandy blonde hair and light-green eyes. "I was."

"How long have you been a shaman?" he asked.

"Many years."

"Is your friend a soldier?"

I shook my head. "No."

"Why is he wearing Guard clothes?"

"Because he's my Guard."

The boy's lips pursed. "But he's not trained as one."

The kid was bright; I gave him that. Even at his age, he could tell a real Guard from a fake one. "No, he isn't trained as one."

"Then how can he be your Guard?" the boy asked.

I glanced up at Raikidan before speaking. "He may not have the right training, but he does as well as any Guard, if not better. I wouldn't trade him for even the best-trained Guard."

"Okay." The boy ran off.

"Don't mind him," Nela told me. "He likes to ask questions all the time.

I smiled. "Children will be children."

"Laz'shika, the psychic who spoke to me earlier told me you were coming here for another reason but couldn't say what it was except that it was urgent," Fe'teline said. "What was she talking about?"

I bolted upright. In my dying state, I had completely forgotten about Arnia and Jaybird. "We need your help."

"Well, I've already gathered that," Fe'teline remarked.

I sighed in aggravation. This wasn't the time for jokes. "What I mean is, we need help from the shamans as a whole. We need your help to get two people out of the city and someplace safe from Zarda."

Fe'teline beamed with enthusiasm. "Does this mean you've reconsidered the offer, and will allow us to help in this rebellion?"

I frowned. "To be honest… I haven't really thought about it."

Fe'teline's eyes darkened, her previous excitement all but vanished. "Then why come to us and ask us for our help? If you won't accept us as allies, then don't expect us to help you when it's convenient for you!"

"Fe'teline!" Nela shrieked.

"You should learn to control your anger, Fe'teline." I cranked my neck to look over my shoulder. *I know that voice.* A man with a muscular build and tawny-beige skin, walked toward the couch. The man still had his hood over his face, but I'd recognize him even if he wore a paper bag.

I smiled as I sat up. "Hey, Ken'ichi."

Ken'ichi pulled his hood down and smiled back, his blue eyes sparkling. "It's good to see you, Eira." He looked at my state. "Though I wish it were under better circumstances."

I chuckled and then accepted a hug when he held out his arms. "What are you doing here? I know how you prefer to protect the town rather than go out on jobs."

He pulled away and frowned. "I couldn't stand being near Maka'shi anymore. Not after what she did."

My eyes softened. "It's really not that big of a—"

"She's losing support," he said. I could tell he didn't want me to be so negative about myself. "Valene refuses to have anything to do with her, going as far as not allowing Maka'shi anywhere near her home. Neither Shva'sika nor Del'karo will speak with her. Alena won't heal her wounds or ailments. Not even Daren wants to deal with her."

My brow knitted. That was quite the loss of support.

"But enough about that. We have more important matters to deal with. Your reasons for not thinking over our offer are your own, and are of little concern right now." He shot a look at Fe'teline when saying that. "What does matter is there are real lives at stake, and it's our job to protect them. So, Eira, are you going to tell me where to find this people, or am I going to have to go on a wild search myself?"

I chuckled. "Eager as always. You're not going to be able to do it on your own. They're both very weak. Arnia won't even be able to walk on her own. When we left, she was resting after recovering from passing out and she's feverish. Jaybird is in better shape, but still worse for wear."

An elven man who had hung back by the kitchen approached us. "There is a merchant caravan scheduled to leave tomorrow. We could get them on that if they're fit enough to travel."

"Where will the caravan go?" I inquired.

"To the North Tribe. It's colder up there, so the military doesn't bother us as often. With summer approaching, it will be warmer. Your friends won't risk catching any sickness in their weakened states."

I nodded. "Thank you. Now we just need to get them there."

Ken'ichi reached into a small pouch he had tied to his pants and pulled out a portal orb. "I don't think that will be a problem."

"I'll be coming with you," Ven'lar announced. "I want to take a look at both of them before we move them anywhere."

I smiled my thanks. Fe'teline roared with anger and stormed out.

"Don't mind her," Nela said. "Fe'teline is stubborn. She had it stuck in her head the next time the two of you met, you'd give her the answer she wanted."

"She has a lot to learn," I said. Nela tilted her head as if to urge me to explain. "Shamans are to make selfless decisions when others need their help. A shaman's needs come second. Fe'teline is putting her needs first. I told her and Tla'lli I was going to think about it when I had the time. I just don't have time right now, and with others needing my help, that decision is a long ways away."

"The spirits were wise to choose you."

I swung my legs over the couch and hopped off. "I hope you're right."

Ken'ichi handed me the portal and I pictured the house before tossing it on the ground. The portal opened and Ken'ichi took the lead. I followed with Raikidan close behind me, and Ven'lar and the elf who had offered to use the caravan as an escape picked up the rear. None of the shamans bothered to lift their hoods over their eyes as we approached our exit, leaving Raikidan the odd one out. I shielded my eyes as we walked through the bright threshold of the exit of the portal. The five of us were greeted by several bewildered faces.

"Welcome back," Seda said. "It looks like your plea was heard."

I nodded and sidled over to Arnia. "How is she doing?"

"About the same as she was when you left," Azriel said. "I was hoping she'd get better with some sleep."

"It's better than worse," I said as I looked over at Jaybird. He slept soundly, sprawled out on the other side of the couch. "He looks comfortable."

Azriel chuckled. "I hope so. It was a fight to get him to move that far from Arnia to just sit down. It didn't take him long to pass out after that, though."

"Well, we're going to have to disturb his beauty sleep if we're to get them both out of here."

"Before we move them, I'd like to take a look at her condition if you don't mind," Ven'lar said, looking at Arnia.

I nodded, and Azriel moved aside to allow Ven'lar to do his job.

Ven'lar lightly touched Arnia all along her body. I noticed he kept going back to her head.

"I'm feeling something is wrong around here." He made a small circle with his hand around Arnia's head. "It's some sort of recent injury."

"A hard blow to the head would cause her body to shut down like this," Azriel said.

"And it could explain why Jaybird was so restless," I said.

Azriel nodded. "You're right. He could sense the issue but not see it directly, so it was making him agitated."

"His body was probably also trying to transfer energy to her in an attempt to help her heal, which would have explained his defensiveness," Rylan commented.

"I'm not sure what's so special about these two, but I do know this injury is bad," Ven'lar stated. "I sense bruising. I'm getting the feeling there was hemorrhaging at one point as well, but it's no longer there, which baffles me."

"Probably a positive result from the healing done by the bond," I said. "Can you heal the bruising?"

Ven'lar nodded. "It's easy. I'll need everyone to be quiet while I do it. I don't want to damage another part of her brain."

"You do and I'll kill you."

I shifted my focused to Jaybird, who was now wide awake. "He's not going to hurt her."

He snorted and continued to glare at Ven'lar. He wasn't going to trust the shaman until Ven'lar proved he knew what he was doing. Ven'lar, ignoring Jaybird's threat, took a slow, deep breath and began the healing process on Arnia. Arnia's eyes fluttered open as Ven'lar pulled his hands away and then began to freak out when she noticed Ven'lar's close proximity.

I placed my hands on her shoulders and hushed her. "It's all right, Arnia. Ven'lar was only helping you." Arnia looked up at me and then back at Ven'lar warily. "He's not going to hurt you."

Slowly, Arnia lay back down and watched Ven'lar.

"How are you feeling?" Ven'lar asked her.

"Fine," she replied elusively.

"Arnia, tell him how you're feeling," Jaybird ordered her.

She looked away and wrung her hands. "Still crappy, but better than before."

Ven'lar smiled. "Good. It looks like the healing has begun, which I'm happy for. Once we get them to the house, I'll do another session and continue to do so during the trip to the village. Even a little progress is good progress."

Arnia's eyes snapped up at me. "Wait, we're going somewhere?"

I nodded. "I've asked the shamans to help get the two of you out of the city. They're going to bring you to the North Tribe, where you'll be safe."

"But I don't want to leave!" she protested. "I want to stay here and help everyone. Why can't we stay with you guys?"

"It's not safe," I insisted.

"I don't care!" Arnia shouted, only to immediately hold her head and moaned in pain.

"Easy," Ven'lar cooed. "You're not completely healed. Too much stress is going to prevent you from healing properly. Come with us. You'll get the treatment you need, and then you can come back here."

Arnia crossed her arms. "Eira won't allow us to come back."

I held out my hand. "You can once you're better."

She blinked slowly as she processed my offer. Normally, I would have agreed with her, but I knew they wouldn't want to come back. Once free, they wouldn't want to feel confined again.

"You mean it?"

I smiled. "Yeah."

Arnia nodded. "All right, I'll go. But only long enough to heal up and be a distant memory to Zarda and his military goons."

I chuckled and flicked my gaze to Jaybird. "You okay with this?"

"Do I have much of a choice?" he asked.

I knew he wasn't happy, but it was the only way. "No, not really."

He sighed and pushed himself off the couch. "Then let's get going before I find the right words to argue."

Jaybird stumbled his way around the couch, refusing any help. Ven'lar, ignoring Jaybird, offered Arnia his hand to help her. She accepted his gesture after hesitating for a moment. She tripped but Ven'lar didn't allow her to fall, and together they made their way over to the portal where the others were waiting for them.

Ken'ichi looked over at me as Ven'lar and the other shaman escorted Arnia and Jaybird through the portal. "They'll be safe with us."

"I know," I replied. "Thank you for doing this."

He smirked. "You know I can't refuse you. When we're about to head out tomorrow, I'll send a messenger hawk. You can keep her once she's here. It'll allow you to speak with us freely without the military getting in the way."

I nodded and watched him enter the portal and disappear as it closed behind him.

"Good luck," Ryoko whispered.

With the weight of emergency now over, I could relax, and I needed to. I felt as though I could sleep for days. Wordlessly I made my way to my bedroom. There was nothing to talk about with the others. Arnia and Jaybird would be safe with the shamans. They wouldn't have to worry about their bond being the death of them in the shamans' care.

I threw myself onto my bed and grunted as my body bounced a few times. My clothes changed without me needing to tell them to. It was as if they knew it was time for me to sleep. It wasn't long before I was pulling a pillow into my body and cuddling up to the rest of them. I liked how soft my bed and pillows were. It was like sleeping on clouds.

"They'll be back, you know," Raikidan said.

I turned to glance at him over my shoulder. "What?"

"Your friends," he clarified. "You don't think they'll be back, but they will. They're loyal to you."

"I hope they don't come back," I muttered into my pillow. "It's safer for them to stay away."

Raikidan sat down on the side of my bed. "That may be, but you're all stubborn and do stupid things."

I chuckled. "That's an understatement."

"Eira, did you really mean what you said about me when you were talking to that boy?"

I rolled over and leaned on my arms to look at him. "I wouldn't have said it if I didn't mean it. I wouldn't trade you for any other Guard."

He pushed his hood down with one hand and grinned at me. "Thanks." I smiled in response. "And thanks for carrying us all the way back here. It was really hard to keep both of us in that shape."

I shrugged. "Don't worry about it."

"Just don't try to make me leave you behind again, all right?"

I laughed. "I won't promise anything."

He gave me a pointed look. "You have to. I won't leave you behind. You don't do it to others, so why should I do it to you?"

I blinked. I had never thought of it that way. Grunting while smiling, I curled into my pillows again. "Go to bed."

He stood and took me by surprise when he placed his hand on my head. "Dream well, Eira."

I snuggled into my pillows some more and sighed with content. "You too, Raikidan."

CHAPTER 20

I grabbed the side of the car trailer and climbed up. We had arrived at the drop-off location, and all the time and work we had put into getting the vehicles up here was now thrown out the window as we removed the securing ties to get them down. It was the one thing I hated about transporting cars to the dealers in the city.

Raikidan climbed up next to me and gave me a hand with the chains. As we worked, a group of three women strolled by. Their giggling and quiet whispers caught Raikidan's attention. He looked down at them and smirked. The three women looked at each other and giggled more. I rolled my eyes and let out an exaggerated sigh. *Looks like he's been playing up his cluelessness.*

Raikidan lifted his brow at me. "What?"

"Nothing."

"Eira, what did I do?" he whispered.

I gave him a side-eyed glance. "Don't give me that. You know what you did."

"No, seriously, what did I do wrong? All I did was smile at them in an attempt to be friendly. I'm trying to be as normal as possible, like you asked. Obviously, I did something wrong by the way you're acting compared with how those females were acting."

I sighed. "Raikidan, that wasn't a smile. That was a smirk."

He blinked. "All right, how was it wrong, then?"

Okay, maybe he really is clueless. "Your smirk said you were interested in them and got them a bit excited. It made them feel a little lucky to even grab your attention for a split second. It's a woman thing."

Raikidan snorted. "Well, that's not what I meant to do."

"Then smile at people. Don't smirk."

Raikidan blinked. "That's the only way I know how to smile." I gave him a look of disbelief. "I'm telling you the truth! My father smiled the exact same way."

"A family trait, then?" I mused.

"Black dragons are the most persuasive of the three dragon colors, so I don't see why it wouldn't be," he said.

I thought this over. That might explain why he had been able to get more information out of me than I would have liked the first few days after we had met. I wasn't on top of my game, which could have made it easier to persuade me. It might also have to do with my strange behavior lately. I made a mental note to be careful of that from now on. "I suppose that could explain it."

"Hey, lovebirds," Blaze called up to us. "Quit your yakking and get working. We have cars to unload."

Raikidan tossed a handful of chains at him. "We're already done, smart one."

Raikidan's choice of vocabulary impressed me. He was really getting the hang of blending in. I wondered if he was reading at night while I was asleep. He had to be. It would be the only explanation for his use of names and other lingo the rest of us rarely used.

"Excuse me? Who is this *we* you're talking about?" Ryoko chimed in. "I'm the one who did all the work. But, Laz, hon, I don't blame you for being jealous. They were hot. Especially the blonde."

"I'm not jealous," I muttered.

Ryoko grinned. "Sure you're not."

I snorted. "If you like her so much, why don't you go after her? I doubt she's made it that far with how slow she was walking."

"Nah, she's not my type. The brunette was, but I'm going pass this time."

Because you already have someone else in mind. I chose to bite my tongue. I knew it was for the best right now.

Zane came around the back of the trailer. "Don't make me tell you two ladies to stop flapping your gums."

Ryoko jumped down. "We're already done with the chains. Not like we're wasting time since only one person can unload the cars at a time. Which has me thinking, who's hungry?"

Zane chuckled. "You know the way to a man's heart, don't you, Ryoko?"

She giggled. "Who doesn't like food?"

Zane laughed and patted her on the shoulder. "I can't disagree there. Go pick us up something and meet us back here. We should be done in about an hour so don't go too far."

Ryoko nodded and then grabbed Raikidan by the wrist. "You're helping, let's go."

"Why—oh okay."

We watched Ryoko drag him off and the boys snickered. Well, except Rylan. He actually looked both confused and irritated.

Blaze nudged him. "Someone's unhappy."

Rylan shoved him away. "I am not. I just don't know why she didn't ask me like she always does."

"You're not her only friend, Rylan," I said as I headed for the truck. "She's allowed to ask someone else to go with her."

"Where you going, Chickadee?" Zane asked.

"Going to sit down. I'm not going to be useful when it comes to unloading the cars."

"Fair enough."

I walked around the truck and sat on the bumper to wait. I watched Raikidan and Ryoko walk down the street while the boys went back to work. The two were laughing about something. Jealousy turned in my stomach. Why couldn't I open up to either of them like that? To anyone like that? Why did I have to be such a recluse freak that couldn't hold a proper conversation without pissing someone off?

I glanced to my right when Rylan appeared—he too watching Ryoko and Raikidan. The bond tugged at the back of my mind. I snickered. "You're pathetic, you know that?"

"You're watching them too," he said. "Makes you no better than me."

"I'm just observing. You're the one getting worked up."

He looked at me. "I see that look in your eye. You want to know what's up too."

I shook my head and chuckled. "I really don't care. The two are friends, so what's there to get all worked up about?"

"You can't fool me, Laz," Rylan said. "The bond has made me very aware of how you've been feeling lately, especially when it's been just the two of you. I'm aware of how you've been feeling while sitting here. You know the bond has always been stronger on my side than yours, for whatever reason."

"I was thinking about something, but it's not what you believe it to be."

"Right." He grabbed me by the wrist and hauled me off my feet. "Let's go."

"What are you doing?" I demanded as he dragged me down the street.

"Getting to the bottom of this."

I stared at him wide-eyed. "Seriously, Rylan? We are not stalking them. Not only is that illegal, it's creepy."

"We're not stalking them. We're investigating without them knowing."

"That's stalking, stupid."

"Shut up and follow with me."

I snickered and complied. I was more interested in observing his behavior than Ryoko or Raikidan's. This was very out of character for him.

"Hey, where are you two going?" Zane yelled out.

I waved him off. "We'll be back."

"But—ah forget it. Be back soon."

I chuckled and followed Rylan as we *stalked* Ryoko and Raikidan. I studied Rylan as he observed Ryoko's interaction with Raikidan. His expression would sour and the bond would tug every time she'd get physically close to Raikidan, especially when her actions appeared flirty. Raikidan didn't reciprocate, but Rylan was sure responding as if he had been.

It amused me at first, but as their interactions continued, I began to feel negative about it as well. I was sure a lot of it had to do with Rylan and the bond, but I knew some of it was me, too. I was aware of the change happening in me about Raikidan. Rylan's observation wasn't too far off as time progressed, and I didn't like it. I knew this couldn't happen and I needed to keep Raikidan at a distance, but as the jealousy rose, the more Ryoko and Raikidan interacted, I knew that was going to be easier said than done.

Rylan abruptly pulled me into an alley and I caught a glimpse of Ryoko looking back before I was pulled out of sight.

"What, didn't want her to see us?" I teased. He hushed me and I snickered. "If you weren't stalking her, you wouldn't have to worry about her finding out you're being creepy."

Rylan ignored me and peered around the corner. I peeked around as well and caught a glimpse of the two turning a corner. Rylan ducked back in case Ryoko looked our way again, but I wasn't going to hide. I suspected I knew what was going on in her head. If I was right, she was trying to get Rylan riled up and Raikidan made for the perfect bait.

"We can keep moving," I said when the two disappeared.

"Did she see you?"

"No, she didn't look back."

"Good. Let's go."

I followed him but he slowed his pace as we came to the turn. I on the other hand, didn't slow down and he hissed at me to not to turn the corner so carelessly and blow our cover. Ignoring him, I turned the corner to find Ryoko looking back. Acting as casual as possible, I continued walking as if nothing was amiss.

"Hey, Laz, whatcha doing out here?" Ryoko called.

I shrugged. "I wasn't useful to the unload process so I figured I'd walk around."

"It's just you?" she asked.

"Only me."

"And you're just walking?"

I nodded and passed them. "Yep."

"You're not going to walk with us?" she asked, clearly confused.

I shook my head. "You didn't invite me and I don't invite myself. You guys keep having your fun and get the food you promised."

"But you can join us," Ryoko said.

"No one willingly chooses to be a third wheel." I hoped she'd take the bait.

"Third wheel? You wouldn't be a third wheel."

Bingo. You're welcome Rylan. I shrugged. "I'm just out for a walk. Don't mind me."

"Laz, if you want to come with us, you can."

"I don't want to."

"Oh, okay…"

I continued my path, but as I went to take a turn to go down a side street, strong hands seized my arm and threw me over masculine shoulders.

"Raikidan," I growled.

"You're coming with us," he said.

"Why?" I asked. "You don't need more than two people to fetch lunch."

"Because you're already here and you're not going to walk around on your own and get into trouble."

I chuckled. "Who said I was going to get into trouble?"

"Me."

"Right."

I looked back to see Rylan standing in the street and watching. I winked at him and he smiled his thanks before heading back to the truck. He had been too fixed on Ryoko's actions to know Raikidan wasn't a new form of competition for him. And even though I didn't want to get in the way of Ryoko's plans to uncover the truth about his feelings for herself, I needed to keep the house peaceful.

"So, Laz, was it really only you following us?" Ryoko asked.

I rolled my eyes. "I wasn't following you."

"But you hid when I looked back because I thought we were being followed."

"Because I left shortly after the two of you and I didn't want you to think I was stalking you or anything. I didn't see which direction you had chosen to turn and hadn't expected to make the same choice."

"And you were alone," she pressed. "Because I was sure I saw Rylan."

"You were sure, or you hoped?" I teased.

Her face flushed. "Laz, don't start!"

"Yeah, she was hoping," Raikidan ratted out.

Her hands curled into fists at her side. "Raikidan!"

I snickered. "I do know he was upset you didn't ask him to join you on your excursion for food."

"I knew Zane would want him to move the cars." She curled a tendril of hair. "He's good at unloading them."

"She's lying," Raikidan said.

Ryoko face reddened and I chuckled. "I know. But, hey, Rai, do you mind letting me walk on my own now?"

"No, because if I do, you'll try going off on your own," he said.

I shook my head. "I'm not going to walk off on you. You obviously want me here that bad, so I'll stick around."

Ryoko halted when her communicator flashed. She placed it on her head and answered. Raikidan put me down on my own feet when she started rolling her eyes. From what I could catch, she was talking to Zane and they were having an issue they needed her help to fix.

"I need to head back," Ryoko said when she hung up. "A part of the trailer is jammed and none of them can get it unstuck."

"Okay, we'll continue to get food then," Raikidan offered. "Makes Eira's arrival a good thing."

Ryoko nodded and started heading back the way we had come. "Thanks. I was just going to a sandwich shop, so it wasn't going to be anything fancy."

I nodded. "Won't be hard to get the order right. I know what the guys like."

She smiled and nodded and continued in her direction while we continue in ours.

"Eira, why were you really following us?" Raikidan asked when Ryoko was out of earshot.

"Because Rylan dragged me with him," I admitted.

"So her plan did work."

I chuckled. "Yeah. He wasn't happy in the least."

"You figured it out and didn't go with it, how come?"

I shrugged. "Because of how irritated he was. He was actually beginning to hate you because he wasn't reading your actions properly, and I don't want discord in this house. Ryoko can figure out a different tactic, or outright tell him."

"How did you feel about it?"

My brow rose. "Why are you asking that?"

"Because it's Ryoko, and she thought it might upset you, too."

"I suspected she may have had an ulterior motive behind her actions, but like I told Rylan, I don't care."

"Really?"

"Yes, really," I snapped. "Why would I care?"

Raikidan reeled back. "I don't know…"

I sighed. "I'm sorry. I shouldn't have snapped at you."

"No, don't be. I should know better than to question your motives."

We were quiet and I didn't like it. I wasn't a good conversationalist and my actions toward Raikidan were honestly uncalled for. It proved I wasn't good around others and made for an overall poor human being.

"Eira, I'm sorry I upset you," Raikidan finally said.

"I'm not upset with you."

"But you're being quiet."

"Well I'm sorry I can't be bubbly and talkative and all buddy-buddy with you like Ryoko can." I sighed, my shoulders slumping. *There I go again.* "Forget that. Let's just get lunch and get back."

"Okay…"

We were both quiet after that. Even when we made it to the sandwich shop we didn't talk to each other. I ordered food for the others and myself, and before I could indicate it was Raikidan's turn, he rattled off what he wanted to the man at the counter. We left the building once we had all our food and, unsurprisingly, silence enveloped our walk back. I knew better than to open my mouth. I was better with silence and I might as well accept that and keep to myself from now on.

"I prefer you as the quiet type," Raikidan said suddenly when we rounded the last corner before making it back to the truck.

"Huh?"

"Ryoko is too talkative," he said. "I would have liked it if she shut her mouth for more than a few seconds." I stifled a laugh. "And there's no way I could handle another person who would talk my ear off like she nearly did. I'd probably bite your head off—literally. I was nearly getting to that point with her."

I didn't believe him. I could see the fun he was having. He liked that Ryoko was open and talkative. He had more fun with her than he could ever have with me. He was just trying to make me feel better, but it didn't change anything. I was boring, quiet, and definitely not open with anyone.

"Eira, please don't go into one of those moods," Raikidan begged. "I'm being—"

"Stop, Raikidan," I said. "Just… don't talk, okay?"

"Okay…"

The rest of the walk was quiet, like I had asked it to be, and when the others greeted us, I did my best to act as normal as possible. Once everyone had their food, I went to hop into the truck.

"Laz, where are you going?" Rylan asked.

I opened the back door. "Into the truck."

"But it's so nice out."

"I'll be in the truck."

"What got her all upset?" he muttered to himself as I shut the door.

I placed my sandwich down next to me. I wasn't hungry. Instead, I closed my eyes, but that made it easier for me to pick up conversations outside. This included the one Raikidan and Ryoko were having on the other side of the truck.

"Your little stunt, didn't go anywhere near as planned," Raikidan whispered to her.

"What do you mean?" she asked. "I was sure she'd get upset."

"Oh, she did, but not in the way you were theorizing."

Ryoko gasped. "No, she didn't start comparing herself to me, did she?" When he didn't reply she groaned. "What have I done? I don't even know how to fix that."

"Do what most people do," Raikidan said.

"Most people would talk it out, but talking will only shut her down," Ryoko replied. "And I can't do a *plan b*—participate in a common interest to build bonds—because Laz and I don't have much in common. It's pretty illogical for us to be friends in the first place. Had we not been part of the same unit in the military, we would have never become friends."

"Well think of something fast, because I tried to fix it, and she told me to shut up."

Ryoko sighed. "Yeah, I'm trying to."

"What's this I overheard you saying you upset Laz?" Rylan asked suddenly. I was quiet surprised, as I wasn't expecting him to be listening in.

"I kinda wanted to see if she'd get jealous if I dragged Raikidan off with me," Ryoko admitted. "But I got a much different reaction."

Rylan sighed. "Seriously, Ryoko? Even I know that was a poor idea."

"Well, I'm sorry that we all can't be perfect like you and just feel out where her emotional state is," Ryoko spat.

I was taken aback by that outburst. I knew Ryoko had an issue with the bond, but that was a rather extreme lash-out.

Ryoko stormed away and Raikidan didn't utter a word. He probably knew it was better if he kept his mouth shut. The front passenger door flew open and Rylan hopped in. He slammed the door shut, and an uncomfortable silence fell over the truck.

"Sorry," I finally said.

He gave me a surprised look. "Why are you sorry? I'm the one who opened my big mouth. I should have just stayed quiet."

"Because the argument happened because of me. Because I make for a horrible bond partner, and that should have gone to someone better. Like her."

"Laz, please don't start comparing yourself to her again," Rylan said. "We've been over this with y—"

"I'm not. I was designed from the very beginning to be an assassin. We're trained to be quiet and kill without question. We're not meant to be good conversationalists or decent human beings. Whoever made the choice to pair you with me was an idiot. She would have been a far better pick for that big of a choice."

"There's nothing wrong with you, Laz, and I wish you'd understand that."

He was wrong, and I was certainly right about the bond. He should have been paired up with her. The two were perfect for each other from the get-go. Me? I was the shadow that got in the way all the time—the third wheel.

CHAPTER 21

*T*he sun was low, casting long shadows across the courtyard. I struggled, but my two captors held me in place. Anger boiled in my chest and there was nothing I could do. I couldn't believe this was happening. After all this time, building everything up to what it was, it was all about to crumble around me. I felt so helpless.

They held her down on her knees some ways off from me. The longer I watched, the more I struggled. I had to get out of this situation. I had to get her away from here. I wished Ryoko and Rylan had been here. I wished they hadn't been sent off on some false assignment that was just a way to keep them away. No one could help us.

The crowd that had formed around us parted, and a tall man with short black hair made his way to the center where she was being held. It was Zarda, and he carried a gun in his hand. My heart stopped. It was too soon. I needed more time to think. My struggling became more vicious as he came closer. I needed to get free. I needed to get her free.

Zarda stopped a few feet away from her and waited. I knew he was waiting for her to look at him, but she didn't.

"This could have been avoided," he told her. "You would have been better off doing as you were told."

She didn't acknowledge him, making him scowl. He lifted the gun. She looked over at me through the aqua hair that hung over her face, and my body froze. My *blood ran cold as I gazed into her aqua eyes. She was so sad—so broken. She wasn't the same woman I once knew. Over the years, something had happened. Something inside her had started to give up. I did what I could to help her, but eventually, even that wasn't enough.*

"You should have listened," he said. "This could have been avoided if you had. There is no room for imperfection. Goodbye, my dear."

She didn't flinch at his words. She didn't look to face the gun as he pulled the trigger. She stared at me instead, as if she was trying desperately to find the words to say something before it was too late. I, too, wanted to say something, but it was already too late.

I watched her body jerk as the bullet entered her skull. I saw the blood. I watched her body go limp. My heart constricted tighter than I'd ever experienced before. I wanted to cry.

"Mother!"

My eyes snapped open and I bolted up in bed. My breath came out in ragged gasps, and sweat dripped down my neck and back. It had only been a nightmare, and yet the breeze—the smell of blood—the gunshot ringing in my ears—it all felt so real. The memory was so vivid and painful. I hated it.

I pulled my legs up to my chest and wrapped my arms over them. I buried my head and tried to control my breathing, to no avail. My chest felt tight and my body ached all over. I dug my sharp nails into my arm, the flesh tearing easily. Blood trickled down my arms. I wanted the pain to go away; I didn't care how as long as I didn't have to feel it.

"Eira?"

My grip on my arms tightened at the sound of Raikidan's voice. Of all the times I could be in pain and not want anyone around, he had to be here. I didn't want anyone to see me like this.

He sat down next to me and placed a hand on my shoulder. "Eira, are you all right?"

I buried my face deeper into my folded body. I couldn't answer him. I knew if I did, I wouldn't be able to lie to him. Raikidan startled me when he pulled me into his arms and held me close to him—the warmth of his bare chest and strong arms enveloping me protectively.

I didn't fight him—didn't want to. I wanted the pain to go away. I wanted to know someone cared, even if it was only for a moment. I curled closer into Raikidan's embrace, and he responded by resting his head on mine and tightening his grip.

"Do you want to talk about it?" he whispered.

I shook my head.

"Okay."

He wasn't going to press, and I was grateful. He respected me enough to give me that privacy. My eyes closed halfway and I sighed with content as Raikidan stroked my hair. It was comforting and relaxing.

"It's painful to remember…" I whispered. "So painful…"

Raikidan hushed me. "It was a nightmare. It's over now. You're safe here."

Safe. I liked the sound of that. I yawned and snuggled closer to him. I didn't care how out of character my actions were. I didn't care about anything I normally cared about right now. For once in my life, I was safe for a night. For one night, I was respected for me and I was okay with it all. I could sleep, knowing that even though it was one night, I had a taste of something I had always wanted. My eyes closed, and I didn't fight the sleep that begged to take me over.

I didn't care I was about to fall asleep in someone's arms. I didn't care if it came to bite me in the morning. I'd deal with the consequences then, but now I would sleep soundly, knowing I was safe from anything as long as he was here.

My breath came slow and steady as I sat on the edge of the roof, thinking while watching the sun sink below the towering buildings of the city. I had been up here alone all day, which helped me. My state and actions last night left me in a haze of confusion when I awoke.

I had woken up alone on my bed. I would have thought what had happened that night was nothing but a dream, had it not been for two small details. I was under my covers, which I was normally never caught under, since I felt too confined and less safe under them. The other detail was much larger and much harder to miss. Raikidan's head lay on my bed while he slept in his natural form. Why he was sleeping like this, I couldn't figure out, but my mind wanted me to believe it had been because of what had happened. Whatever the true reason, I was surprised he hadn't broken that end of my bed.

I had left my room to find something to eat when I'd grown bored of waiting for Raikidan to wake up to question him, and when I returned, he had disappeared, and I hadn't seen him since.

I sighed softly as a small breeze picked up. It carried the faint smell of salt from the far-off coast in the East. I wondered what it was like to live in the harbor cities. Many belonged to Zarda, so it couldn't be much different aside from the ocean water access. I had never been to the ocean. Zarda had always made sure I stayed inland as if he thought I'd disappear otherwise. I snorted at the thought. He didn't care if I disappeared. He wanted to make sure his *property* didn't get into someone else's hands.

Then I thought of Jaybird and Arnia. A messenger hawk with the symbol of the West Shaman Tribe attached to the bird's back arrived earlier in the afternoon. The canister contained a letter with a healing and fire seal—a letter from Ken'ichi to me.

Ken'ichi had written that both Arnia and Jaybird were doing much better than the night before, and were loading into the caravan as he wrote the letter. He had also told me of Ven'lar's growing interest in Arnia, and Jaybird's idiotic jealousy. I laughed when I read that section. Although I didn't know Ven'lar, I had never met a bad shaman. Even Maka'shi wasn't bad, per se. She just had issues. Arnia would be safe with Ven'lar, and if he could get around Jaybird's overprotective nature, he might be able to convince her to stay away from this awful place.

The letter didn't say much more beyond Ken'ichi's plan to leave with them and then come back when Arnia and Jaybird were settled into their new temporary home. I had put the hawk in the greenhouse, where she'd be safe, and made a mental note to feed her in a few hours.

I was taken by surprise when I someone lightly touched my hair. The smell of honeysuckle drifted into my nose, and shortly after, small petals tickled my cheek. I turned my head as Raikidan sat down next to me. I hadn't heard him at all, and even now he was quiet. I could barely hear him breathe. *And here I thought I was good at being stealthy.*

I became confused when he didn't speak. He just watched me, his eyes giving nothing away to any thought that may be running through his mind, but the small upturn of one side of his lips said otherwise. He always had something on his mind, and he was becoming worse at hiding it.

My cheeks flushed and my breath caught when Raikidan suddenly leaned forward. Now I knew what he wanted. The same thing he had wanted from me since the first day he had asked.

I pushed his face away before he got too close. "No."

He pulled my hand away from his face. "Just one."

"No!" I yanked my hand from his grip and swung my legs back to the inside of the roof.

"Why can't you let me have one kiss? I just want to know what it's like."

"You already got one from me when Argus fell into us."

"That wasn't a real kiss. That was an accident."

"Go find someone else who will give it to you," I muttered as I stormed off. "There are plenty of other women out there who would be happy to give you that."

"But not you."

I stopped walking and let out a tight breath. "We've already discussed this, Raikidan. I'm not going to discuss it again."

He didn't reply, but I could feel his intense gaze on my back. I sighed again. I was really getting sick of this. No matter how many times I said no, he didn't stop.

I turned to face him. "If I gave you a kiss, would you stop asking for one?"

He grinned. "It's all I've been asking for. Just one."

I worked my jaw before walking back over to him. I couldn't believe I was about to do this. It was all because I wanted him to stop asking. Anyone else I would have been able to ignore. So why was he so special? Why was I unable to continue to ignore his plea?

Grabbing his chin lightly with my fingers, I leaned down and kissed him on the cheek. I withdrew quickly and attempted to make a hasty retreat.

Raikidan grabbed me by the wrist. "Oh no you don't. That wasn't a kiss."

I chuckled and wiggled my hand free. "You said you wanted a kiss. You didn't specify what type of kiss." He stared at me with disbelief. "I did warn you it wasn't going to be the way you thought it was going to be." I retreated to my greenhouse. "A kiss isn't just a kiss. There are different kisses that mean different things."

Raikidan scowled and followed me. "You know what type of kiss I want. I won't keep my end of the bargain if you don't."

I chuckled. "Yes, you will. You didn't specify what type of kiss in the agreement. Therefore, you allowed me to choose, and now you have to keep your end of the deal since I've lived up to mine."

I ran to my greenhouse, and Raikidan followed. "Eira!"

I slammed the door behind me and locked myself inside. The glass panes shook, but not enough for me to worry about the structure collapsing on itself, although, the greenhouse collapsing because of Raikidan was another story.

Raikidan yanked on the door several times. "Eira, open up. You owe me."

I snickered. "I owe you nothing. You have no one to blame but yourself for not making your rules clearer than mud."

He growled and hit the door with the flat part of his fist. His anger only made me laugh. The loophole was all too perfect. He got a simple kiss and I was able to keep his lips off mine. Sitting down where I was, I went into a meditative trance. I was aware of Raikidan watching me and I could hear his occasional banging, but I didn't move. I only opened one eye when it stopped completely. He wasn't looking at me anymore. Instead, his attention was on the door to the house.

"What are you doing, Raikidan?" It was Ryoko.

"Um…"

I snickered. He knew Ryoko knowing the truth behind this little situation wouldn't be a great idea, and his ruckus had brought her up here. It was going to be interesting to see him worm his way out.

"Why is Laz locked up in the greenhouse?" she asked him.

"Um…" He scratched his head. "I chased her in there. She pulled my hair and… and I… got pissed off…"

I bit my lip. *That's the best excuse he can come up with?*

Ryoko laughed raucously and then turned to walk away. "Don't be mad at her. It means she likes you."

I pursed my lips. *What's that supposed to mean?*

Raikidan, mirroring my thoughts, questioned her. "What do you mean?"

Ryoko giggled. "You'll have to figure that out on your own."

She shut the door behind her, leaving the two of us alone again. Raikidan looked at me and I shrugged. I was as confused as he was.

He rapped on the door. "Can I come in?"

I eyed him, skeptical of his intent. "You're not going to make me kiss you again, are you?"

"You didn't give me a real kiss."

I closed my eyes and went back to meditating.

He let out an aggravated sigh. "Fine. I'm not going to ask for another from you. A deal's a deal."

Grinning with triumph, I stood and unlocked the door. He came in hesitantly, his eyes darting around as if I had some secret trap waiting for him, making me laugh. "You're so paranoid."

He grunted. "When you're involved, it's a good idea to be careful. You're too unpredictable." I continued to laugh. "Why do you come in here all the time anyway?"

I shrugged and retreated to the center of the greenhouse, where a small koi pond was located. "It's peaceful in here. It allows me to stay calm, and escape from the harsh industrial atmosphere of the city."

He gazed around. "Is that why this place is so abnormally huge?"

"Yes and no. I also needed it to be this big because of the various species of plants I've collected. A small greenhouse wouldn't work out. It'd be too cramped."

"You don't like the city much, do you?"

I snorted and sat down in front of the pond. "I hate this place. It smells terrible and it's noisy."

Raikidan sat down next to me. I pulled a flame from one of the small fires that burned on the statue in the center of the pond and played with it. The flame morphed into several different shapes until I settled on a butterfly. Willing life into the fire, it fluttered around the two of us.

Raikidan, enthralled by the insect-shaped flame, reached out and grabbed it. "I was right, it was harmless."

"It's called *Show Fire*," I explained. "It's a false flame that has the same properties as a real flame but without the heat, making it ideal for training. All trained shamans and elementalists know how to use it because it's so ideal."

He held out his hand were the ember barely remained alive. "Basic or not, it's still neat. Can you teach me?"

I lifted a finger and willed the ember into another flaming butterfly. "You can't teach anyone fire control. They have to be a shaman or elementalist themselves."

"I can use fire."

"You breathe fire," I corrected. "It's not necessarily the same."

"Well, then how do you become one?"

"You're born as one."

He snorted. "That doesn't explain how you become one."

"That's because no one knows the qualifications or why. The elemental gods just bestow the power to us."

"What about to be a shaman?"

I pursed my lips. "Some think the spirits choose you since being able to communicate with them is another requirement, and others speculate it's fate."

"Do you believe in fate?"

"Yes."

"So everything that's happened in your life was predetermined? It wasn't some freak thing that just happened?"

"I met you, didn't I?"

He blinked. "I don't understand."

I willed the butterfly in his hand to flutter around for some time while I worded myself correctly. "Why you? Why you, out of so many others, did you find me in the shape I was in? What made you so special? Why were you the only one who wouldn't turn a blind eye to my condition and keep going on in your life without any regret?"

Raikidan gazed down at his hands in his lap and let out a long drawn out sigh.

I scratched my head. "Sorry, that… that came out wrong."

"No, it came out fine," he said. "It's just… I never thought about it that way. I thought fate was bogus. I believed it was some way for others to explain the unexplainable. I thought it was a reason for others to make you not hate. But… but now that you've said that, I suppose I should really think it over. I shouldn't let one or two past events dictate how I see things as a whole without putting serious thought into it."

I studied him. I had a feeling I knew what past event he was referring to. *His mother.* The urge to ask—the need to know what exactly had happened to her—rose up in me, but I kept my mouth shut. It wasn't my business. I knew the kind of pain that came with losing someone like that. I knew not to poke at those types of scars.

"So will you teach me?" Raikidan asked. "I want to try to learn this."

"It's not easy to learn," I warned. "Especially for someone like yourself."

Raikidan shrugged. "The harder it is to learn, the more determined I am."

I laughed and then turned my body to face him. "Fine, but don't say I didn't warn you."

He grinned with enthusiasm and faced me to receive his first lesson.

CHAPTER 22

Raikidan flinched when I dabbed healing ointment on his burn. He wasn't doing well with the training. I knew it would be hard for him, but this was ridiculous. Every time he attempted the most basic technique, he'd burn himself. I was starting to think I'd run out of ointment before he'd finally give up on this crazy idea of his. *Why is controlling fire like this so important to him?*

Raikidan flinched again and I sighed. "Sorry. If I had any skills in healing I'd be using them."

"It'd be a relatively futile effort," Raikidan said.

I peered up at him. "How come?"

"The spirit energy used by priests and shamans doesn't mix well with our draconic power. Some wounds can be healed, but not many."

"So, if you were deeply wounded to the brink of death, no one could save you?"

"Another dragon with healing fire could. That would be easy for them, but a shaman or priest, even with combined efforts with others, would struggle to stabilize a dragon with their healing abilities."

I pursed my lips. "It's a good thing I know something about modern medicine then."

I went back to searching his arm for more wounds. I tilted my head when I found a scar on his bicep. I lightly traced it with my finger. I had never noticed it before. Then again, I had never taken this close of a look at his skin. "I didn't know you had a scar here."

He shrugged it off. "It's nothing."

I chuckled. "I always thought your skin had no imperfections. It's good to know you're a lot more normal than I first thought."

He chuckled. "Nothing is really ever perfect, right?"

I smiled. "How'd you get it?"

"A small scuffle some time ago." It was obvious this scar would look much bigger in his dragon shape. It had to have come from another dragon. I couldn't think of anything else that could pierce a dragon scale.

"You seem pretty okay with having it."

Raikidan shrugged. "I have other ones. They show how formidable I am in battle."

He has more? I knew this one was hard to see because of how faded it was, but he was bound to have more recent ones than this that were more noticeable.

"Why don't I see any other scars?" I asked.

"Maybe your eyesight sucks."

I punched him in the shoulder. "It does not."

Raikidan laughed and rubbed his shoulder. "Then tell me, why do you think you can't see them?"

"Because you're hiding them."

His brow furrowed. "How'd you—"

I snickered. "I didn't. You just told me."

He stared with bewilderment and then laughed. "Cheeky human. Now tell me, how did you really figure it out? You had to have thought about it first to trick me into telling you."

I smiled and checked over his arm once more. "It's simple. If you can shapeshift, why not be able to shift in a way to hide something. Although I'm not sure why you'd want to hide a few scars."

"I knew enough about humans to know many are repulsed by them so I chose to hide them," he said. "And because I chose to do that, I've decided I needed to keep this disguise up. But you appear more interested than anything."

I nodded. "Scars show character, and as you put it, many show battle experience. There are many reasons scars exist, but there should be no shame in obtaining any of them."

"Is that why you are okay with the scars you have?"

I nodded again. "I have seen battle. I have fought formidable opponents, and I have made mistakes. Every scar I have shows that. They map out my life as an experiment."

"But you don't like being reminded you are an experiment."

A puff of air came from my lips and I moved around him to check his other arm. "No matter how much you wish you can, you cannot change who you are. Once you learn that fact of life, you can get by the best you can."

I ran my fingers along his arm to check for tenderness. Even if he didn't have any burns, he might have damaged himself in some other way. I blinked when my fingers touched another scar. As I touched it, another one appeared nearby right before my eyes. He wasn't hiding them anymore.

I traced my fingers over the larger scars, bypassing the smaller ones. They showed signs of deep gouging and long healing times, as if he chose not to heal them himself, couldn't, or didn't know how at the time of receiving them. I could only imagine how large and deep these where if he wasn't in this nu-human shape.

I followed the scars to his chest and traced even larger scars. "These were deep wounds."

"We're not as well protected on our underside," he admitted.

I looked up at him. I almost couldn't believe he had told me that so casually. He had revealed a weakness of his like it was nothing. "You've seen many battles."

He nodded. "I have prime territory. I have to fight to keep it, and there are a lot of other dragons who want it. Corliss and I work together to keep our territories as large as they are."

"Who is Corliss?"

"He's a dragon whose territory borders mine to the West," Raikidan explained. "We work together to keep other dragons from moving in."

"So he's your friend," I said.

Raikidan nodded slowly. "Yeah, I suppose he is."

The corners of my eyes crinkled. "And here I thought you didn't have friends."

He crossed his arms and snorted, causing me to laugh. As I laughed, his frown turned into a small smile. He really did suck at being mad.

I finally managed to get my laughter under control and look up at him. A small scar on his cheek caught my eye, and on impulse, I touched it. It was much different than his other scars. It looked as though he had obtained it in a human form.

"How did you get this one?" I asked.

Raikidan reached up to remove my hand from his face, his gaze falling away. "I'd rather not talk about it…"

"Oh, okay." I knew that tone and it was best that I not press. This scar was a painful reminder of something tragic. I had a sneaking suspicion he didn't mean to let it show up.

He looked at me again, and the two of us stared at each other. I didn't know why I wasn't going back to my burn search. *Eira, go back to your search. It's more important to make sure Raikidan is healed—but I like—*

I tore my gaze from him and looked up at the stairs to the living room when someone thundered down them. Argus ducked his head under the low ceiling when he had made it half way down. "You two need to get up here right now. We have a problem."

Raikidan and I glanced at each other briefly before we bolted over to the stairs and followed Argus up to the living room. Everyone was gathered on the couch when we reached the threshold of the door. Ryoko looked up and motioned for us to join them. When we reached the couch, I noticed they were watching something from a small hologram device.

"They're still looking for Arnia and Jay," Rylan informed us. "And they're not doing raids this time."

I watched in horror as soldiers stormed the streets and killed anyone in their path. They searched buildings before blowing them up and moving on.

Blaze threw his hands onto his lap. "I don't get it. Why would they do this?"

"To flush more than just Arnia and Jaybird out," I replied. Everyone looked at me, but I pointed to the hologram. The hologram showed an average-sized woman with long hair and heavy makeup.

"It can't be…" Ryoko whispered in disbelief.

My anger boiled as I watched her. "Verra."

"There you are, Eira." I gazed down from my perch on my favorite tree to find Amara standing below me. "I would have figured you'd want to say goodbye to Ryoko and Rylan."

"I already did."

She blinked. "Really?"

I nodded. "Just after they were given their assignment."

"Are you okay, dear?"

I sighed and jumped down. "Something doesn't feel right about this. I have this feeling, like something bad is about to happen."

Amara smiled and wrapped her arm around me. "Don't worry. Everything is going to be fine."

"Who is she?" Blaze asked with a little too much interest.

"Someone who will do anything to get what she wants," Rylan growled. "Zarda hates the rebellion, so she will be his faithful bitch and attempt to destroy us without a second thought for civilian lives."

"Kill her. Make her beg for mercy."

"You three seem to know her pretty well," Blaze remarked.

"Unfortunately we—uh, Laz, where are you going?" Ryoko asked as she noticed me make my way to the front door.

The training yard was empty. The uneasy feeling I had kept growing. There were always soldiers brushing up their skills. Amara didn't seem to notice. She kept walking with her arm around me securely.

A woman with snow-white hair and a disgustingly revealing uniform walked into the training yard. She strolled past us with a smug smile. "Enjoy today together. It may be your last."

A growl escaped my lips. Amara tightened her grip to quiet me. I tilted my head, but she wouldn't look at me. She kept leading me, and the feeling of unease grew.

"To battle." I responded. I didn't wait to see if they would follow. I didn't wait to discuss the options. My option was clear. I would fight this demon woman and end her for good. I owed it to Amara. I owed it to her to release Lumaraeon from this vile woman's grasp.

As I stormed down the stairs, I drew my favorite dagger and thought of Amara. I thought of how she would dress and how she would choose her battle weapon. I thought of how she would march into battle with confidence and power. I willed my clothes to shape themselves into the style of her military uniform and willed my dagger to change to her choice of weapon.

The sun was low in the sky. Its low beams created a blinding threshold to the front door as I opened it, but I was not afraid of the unknown. I would fight just as Amara would. Resolve pushed me to fight Verra on her behalf—for the sake of her memory. I owed it to her.

The air was still and smelled of fire, ash, and burning flesh. The military was on a rampage and anything that stood in their way was eliminated. The soldiers didn't care if they were potential rebels or loyals. They killed them anyway.

I wished my feet could carry me faster but I wasn't accustomed to carrying such a heavy weapon. I couldn't see how Amara could use such a weapon in battle, especially during high gunfire situations. Sure, it was strong when used properly, but the weapon was so massive, it was heavy and hard to swing in a small area, but somehow she managed and could make it look easy, even though her strength was no greater than mine.

"Laz, wait up!"

I glanced back to find Ryoko running after me—her dog-ears twitching occasionally when a loud noise echoed through the street. I tried not to cringe as I watched her run. I wasn't sure how she was capable of running without being in pain. She had once told me she learned to ignore the weight on her chest but I couldn't imagine how that was possible.

She carried her large battle wrench, and even with the type of strength she had built up in her body, she was struggling to keep up. Apparently I was still capable of running at adequate speeds even with this burden on my back.

I slowed my speed until she was able to run beside me. "You should be at the house."

She snorted. "Like I'd miss this. The others are coming too. They sent Raikidan and me ahead to let you know."

I blinked. "Raikidan?"

She pointed up and I tilted my head back. Above us flew a black raven. I grunted. Of course he would choose an easy form of transportation. The raven shifted shape and he dropped down to run with us.

"You know, you should learn to pay attention to things above you," he remarked.

I snorted. "Things don't normally drop from the sky at me."

Ryoko laughed. "No, Laz is usually the one doing the dropping."

I laughed and agreed. Aerial stealth attacks were one of my favorites.

"So what's the plan?" Ryoko asked.

I shrugged. "Kill Verra and get out. How's that sound?"

Ryoko laughed. "Not much of a plan."

"I don't care how this goes," I admitted. "As long as none of us get hurt, and Verra ends up dead, nothing else matters. She's destroying everything in her path, so it's not like we can do any more damage to the situation."

"She has a point," Raikidan said.

Ryoko sighed. "I know, but I figured we'd have some sort of plan of attack. I get the feeling Laz is going to be the only one fighting."

"If the other soldiers attempt to attack, they're fair game to you, but you know I have to take on Verra. It's the only way," I said.

"We cared about her too." I cranked my neck over my shoulder to see Rylan catching up in his white wolf form.

"This is a first," I said. "Usually we have to do some heavy convincing to get you shift."

He grunted. "I wasn't going to be able to catch up with the three of you at this point if I hadn't."

"I like it when you shift," Ryoko said. "You're cute like this."

"I am not cute!"

My eyes squinted as I grinned. "Yes you are."

Rylan growled and then shifted to his nu-human form. "You're both wrong and it's stupid to think that I am."

"It is not," Ryoko muttered before picking up her pace.

"Nice going, Rylan," I said.

"What? I didn't do anything wrong," he defended.

I rolled my eyes. "Course not. You're so perfect and never do anything wrong."

"Don't get sarcastic with me."

"I wouldn't have to if you would stop upsetting her. Even if you don't agree with her, the least you could do is be mindful of how sensitive she can get." I gave him a pointed look. "Like, maybe next time not call her stupid."

He swallowed, seeming to realize what I was getting at. I picked up my pace to catch up with Ryoko. She gave me a weak smile when I reached her, but said nothing. I smiled back at her, understanding, and left it at that.

A small building crumbled ahead of us and we stopped dead in our tracks. I could hear the soldiers marching and people screaming. We were close.

"Looks like Argus and Blaze are going to miss the fun at this rate," Rylan said as he and Raikidan caught up with us. He was looking at Ryoko, hoping she'd respond positively, but she folded her arms and stuck up her nose. He sighed. "Ryoko, I'm sorry, okay?"

"Tell somebody who cares." She stalked off.

He exhaled slowly, running his fingers through his hair. His gaze flicked to me. "Chocolates or flowers you think?"

I snickered. Bribery always worked on Ryoko. "For this blunder, I'm going to say chocolates and a spa day."

He let out a breath. "Great."

I dashed off, running past Ryoko, who shouted in objection, and swung around the corner of the street that sounded to have the most activity coming from it. As I rounded the corner, the devastation before us was astounding. Buildings everywhere were in crumpled heaps and bodies of civilians were strewn about. The scent of blood was heavy in the air, and I did what I could to ignore it. I didn't want to lose control but I also refused to turn back. I had to do this.

I narrowed my eyes when the woman I was seeking came into sight. I didn't waste any time. I took the abnormally large great sword and, with as much strength as I could muster, I swung it, letting it fly at her. I knew there was a large possibility it would miss her, but I didn't care. I was going to make a statement nonetheless.

"General, look out!" a soldier warned.

The woman turned and then flattened herself to the ground. My weapon flew over a group of soldiers, who also flattened themselves to the road to avoid my attack, and crashed into the side of a building. The woman I intended to hit stood back up and glared at me, but then her lips turned into a disgusting smile.

She was an average-sized woman, around Ryoko's height with tan skin, long, snow-white hair with bangs that swept over her left eye. A large black rose was tucked in her hair behind her ear on the opposite side her bangs swept. Clasped around her neck was a black choker, and on her body were clothes that I wasn't sure could qualify as armor.

She wore mid-thigh high black-and-white boots and a cropped jacket that clasped at the neck and cut around her bust line. Under the jacket, a black and white micro tube top covered her chest, and around her hips she sported a black and white mini skirt. I couldn't find a scrap of armor on her anywhere.

"Well hey there, Eira," she cooed. Her accent was thicker than I remembered. "What a pleasant surprise findin' you're here. I'm so glad you're alive."

I snorted. "I'm sure you are, Verra."

She snickered. "Why wouldn't I be? It means I have the chance to kill you with my own hands."

"In your dreams," I spat.

She chuckled and her grin grew. I didn't understand why until a group of footsteps approached behind me. Turning to take a look, I spotted Ryoko and the two boys making it down the street. Argus and Blaze were also with them. They all skidded to a halt when they reach my side.

Verra chuckled. "This day keeps gettin' better an' better."

"Stuff it, Verra," Rylan growled.

Verra wagged her finger. "Temper, temper, Rylan. And it's General Verra now."

I snorted. "Finally whored yourself out enough to get promoted to the top?" I sneered. "You're disgusting."

Verra glared at me. "How dare you suggest such a thing?"

Raikidan snorted. "She smells like she's been with a thousand different men."

I snickered. "You were saying, Verra?"

Verra growled. "I'll make you regret sayin' that."

"Suck my dick, Verra!" Blaze challenged.

"I wouldn't ask that of her if I were you," I advised him. "She just might."

"Oh really?" He seemed a little too interested in the idea.

"Again, I wouldn't advise it. She's infested with more diseases than you."

"I told you, I'm clean," Blaze growled.

"Sure, sure, but I can guarantee she's not," I replied.

Blaze grunted. "Pity. She's hot."

Verra drew her sword. "I'm growin' tired of this. If you're here, Eira, then you must know where Arnia and Jaybird are."

"I don't kiss and tell," I remarked. Ryoko giggled and I glared at her but that didn't make her stop right away.

Verra sighed. "You're such a pain. Just like Amara. I don't see why Zarda was so fond of you two."

"Aww, I think someone is jealous," Ryoko teased.

I snorted. "She can have her master's attention and be his little play thing. I'll pass."

Verra glowered. "Such a waste of a design. Zarda created you. He gave you life. And you disregard his existence as if he were a mere pebble on the street. How dare you act this way?"

I stuck my finger in my ear and twisted it briefly before pulling it out and looking at its still clean state to show Verra how much I didn't care. "I prefer not being someone else's lackey."

"I am not a lackey, you impudent wench."

I grinned. "Then let's see if you can back up those words."

Verra growled. "I'll make you regret crossin' my path. I'll send you to where you belong. With Amara and the rest of the failures!"

I glared at her. "You'll regret calling Amara a failure."

Verra grinned. "She got exactly what she deserved. She had no right to have been seen so highly in Zarda's eyes. She had no right to keep his attention and refuse him without a second thought."

"You'll eat those words, Verra."

Verra readied her sword. "Then let's settle this once and for all. Just you and me. No guns."

I grinned. She was out of her league now. "May the better-skilled experiment live."

Verra chuckled. "May the most beautiful prevail. Oh wait, that's me."

Raikidan grunted and muttered to himself. "Delusional bitch."

Verra glared at him. "You'll be next on my list."

I chuckled. "Not like you'll get past the first one on your list, but I will."

Without allowing her to speak, I charged her empty-handed. Verra grinned, seeing my actions as rash and thoughtless, but as she swung her sword, I dodged and grabbed her by the arm. Holding on tightly, I swung her across the street and then took off as she crashed into a crumbling building.

"Bitch…" she muttered as she pulled herself out of the rubble. "You'll pay for that."

I continued to run. I needed to get to my weapon. Soldiers attempted to stop me, but I dodged them with ease.

"Move, fools!" Verra barked as she attempted to catch me.

Reaching my giant great sword, I swiveled on my feet and swung the giant blade. Verra defended herself and the two swords clashed. Verra giggled and I growled when her sword refused to break against the weight of my weapon. *Her sword must be made from a synthetic metal.*

"You'll have to do much better than that, Little Eira," Verra taunted. "Amara couldn't defeat me with that pitiful excuse of a sword, so what makes you think you can?"

I roared with effort and pushed Verra back, taking her by surprise. I advanced and swung the heavy sword with great effort, taking out the side of a building in the process. Verra, unhindered by the weight of a heavy weapon or shield, dodged with ease and came at me.

"Eira!" Raikidan yelled.

I didn't have time to scold him. I was very aware of what was going on and didn't need to be warned. Grinning, and using the size of my weapon to my advantage, I slipped behind my weapon and twisted it sideways to use the flat end as a shield. Verra growled in annoyance and tried to attack again but I countered the same way once more. Amara may have had a much different fighting style than me, but I had seen her fight enough times to know how to fight like her, or as similarly as I could.

Verra backed off, but then charged at me right after. Ducking under her, she was forced to run up my blade. The moment her weight left the blade, I slipped under my great sword and swung it at her. Verra twisted her body, but was unable to get away fast enough. My blade sliced into her side and she screamed as she fell to the ground.

"You'll pay for that, you stupid bitch," she swore as she stood. "You're just like Amara. Pitiful, ugly, and a complete failure. Zarda should have thrown you away when he did her."

I glared at her and tightened my grip on the hilt of my weapon. I was getting sick of her insulting Amara. She had no right. I charged, but as I did I changed my weapon. I wouldn't be able to kill Verra if I kept fighting like this. I had to fight the way I was used to.

Willing the blade into my favorite reverse blade dagger, I separated it into two and held them firmly in my hands. I was going to end this now. Verra's eyes widened in fear at the sight of my magical weapon and attempted to block my attack, but she was too slow. My blade struck her sword as she managed to block, but the defense didn't stop my speed. I swiveled around her and thrust my daggers upward as she spun around to defend herself. Verra choked as the blade entered her soft abdominal flesh and her sword clattered to the ground.

"You forgot one thing, Verra," I growled. Verra grabbed onto my shoulders and squeezed in attempt to get me to pull away. "I am nothing like my mother… I could never be half the person she was. She deserved to live. Not me. Now die."

I pulled my daggers out and spun around. In that moment, I grabbed Verra by the back of her head and sliced my sharp dagger through her neck. Her body fell to the ground and I stood motionless with her head hanging in my hand at my side.

"Laz?" Ryoko asked tentatively.

"Yeah I'm here," I replied. I was actually quite surprised of how in control I was of myself. I couldn't feel the monster inside of me trying to claw its way out at all. It was as if, for this single moment, it respected me enough to allow me to remain this way.

"'Kay, just making sure."

I turned to face the confused army that surrounded us. I tossed Verra's head at them and stared them down. "Anyone else want to end up like your poor general?"

The soldiers wordlessly looked at each other. Although I couldn't see most of their faces because of their helmets, I could smell their fear rolling off of them in waves.

"I thought as much. Now all of you get back to your pathetic cells in that prison you call home. These people are innocent and don't deserve to be punished for something they haven't done."

Someone chuckled, but I couldn't figure out who. Then, a man pushed his way through the crowd and spoke. "Jeez, you've gone soft on us, Commander. I would have at least expected a death threat or two."

I tilted my head in confusion. I thought I recognized the voice but the helmet muffled it enough to make me second-guess myself.

He chuckled again and pulled off his helmet. "Been gone so long you forgot who I was?"

I blinked. I couldn't believe who I was looking at. He was a tall, young and handsome man with ivory skin and hair just as pale.

I chuckled. "Well, if it isn't my pal, Talon. I thought you would have high-tailed it out of the military by now."

Talon chuckled, his deep crimson eyes dancing with amusement. "Nah, I figured I'd stick around and do some recruiting."

My brow rose. "What?"

I watched as more soldiers began to remove their helmets and saluted me.

Talon snickered. "There are more on your side than you realize, Commander."

My head swiveled around. There had to be hundreds of soldiers here and at least half of them had to be showing me respect.

"Traitorous scum!" But before the loyalist had a chance to do anything, someone took care of him.

Talon grunted. "Idiot."

I looked at Rylan and he grabbed my shoulder. "Nice job, Laz."

"But I didn't do anything," I said. "Talon did all of this."

Talon shook his head. "No, you did, Commander. I convinced them because of you, because you led us so well. Without your leadership, I would have been long gone and dead."

"I'm not that great," I muttered.

A young man stepped forward. He smelled of tank water, and I wondered how recently he had been released. "Talon says you are one of the greatest leaders alive. He's told us many stories of the great things you've done."

"How old are you, kid?" I asked.

He hesitated. "Uh… nineteen."

I grunted. "I figured as much. You still carry the heavy scent of tank water. I will tell you something. You're young, so you wouldn't know of who I am or what I've done in the past. But I will tell you, I have done nothing great in my lifetime. I've made mistakes and allowed good men to die. I'd take their place if I could, but I can't, and if I were a good leader, they'd still be around."

The young man blinked. "Why are you telling me this?"

I turned to leave. "Because I won't allow you to blindly follow a fairytale that doesn't exist."

What the young man said next stopped me in my tracks. "Then we won't follow you blindly. We'll follow you willingly, Commander."

I looked around at the body of soldiers who agreed with this young man. Even soldiers who had been on the fence or against our cause removed their helmets and agreed with the kid's words.

I turned a bewildered gazed to Talon, who had a large grin on his face. "What did you do, brain wash them?"

Talon laughed. "I can assure you I didn't do anything nefarious."

The young man spoke again. "Talon told us you were honest. He told us you would give your life for your comrades. You were honest in how you spoke to me. You were willing to admit you've failed in some way. You value your comrade's lives more than you do your own. That's more than anyone can say about the commanding officers we deal with under Zarda's rule. We are no longer loyal to Zarda. We are loyal to you, Commander."

I shook my head. "I guess that settles it then, now doesn't it?"

Talon chuckled. "I guess it does. So what are your orders, Commander?"

I turned and began to walk away. "I want updates on a regular basis. I don't care how you get them to me. And before you go back to Zarda to play faithful soldier, I want you to clean up your mess. This place is a disgusting disaster zone."

Talon chuckled. "Now that's the commander I'm used to. Oh and, Commander Eira."

I turned one last time to look at him. "Yes?"

"The clones of you, the ones Arnia and Jaybird got caught showing you, they're going to be letting them out soon."

I groaned. "You have got to be kidding me."

Talon grunted. "I wish I were. They're terrible when it comes to socialization. They've destroyed all civilian dummies they've come in contact with. They barely have the control right now to keep themselves from killing other soldiers and each other. They're completely wild and savage. Zarda has ordered them to be allowed out by next spring. He doesn't care if they're ready or not."

I walked away. "It looks like we have a deadline now to end this. Now get to work, all of you."

Talon chuckled. "Yes, ma'am."

My team fell in behind me, and no one spoke until we were around the corner.

"What are we going to do?" Ryoko asked. "We can't think of a plan to end all of this by spring, can we?"

"Where there's a will, there's a way," I told her. "We'll figure it out, and come spring we'll be free people."

Blaze grinned. "I like the sound of that."

"Are we going to inform the Council?" Rylan asked.

I nodded. "We'd be stupid not to. I'll have Seda contact them when we get back to the house."

Ryoko placed her hand on my shoulder. "You look nice. You look like Amara."

"She'd be happy you did this in her honor," Argus said.

"I know," I replied. "It was the least I could do for her."

I wish I could do more for you, mother. You know I would if I could. I'll think of something. I promise…

23
CHAPTER

Images flashed by as I messed with the objectives on my planner. Nothing was working together and it was frustrating me. Not that I wasn't frustrated as it was.

The military made their big "apology" announcement to those who were affected by Verra's assault. Someone spoke in Zarda's stead, offering condolences as the filth of a man was claimed to be dealing with the "treason" personally. Supposedly Zarda was disturbed by the betrayal and all the suffering it brought his people, and would do what was needed to make things right.

All words of course, but the majority of the gullible masses would believe anything as long as he compensated the living even a little.

On top of that irritation, there were rebellion matters pressing on my mind. The Council had promised they'd up the ante on our assault against Zarda, and yet nothing had changed. It wasn't surprising in the least though. Their way of working and my way of working were different, and that's what frustrated me. They didn't like to listen to other ideas that were different, even when they promised they would. Even working on these plans would be a waste of time because I more than likely wouldn't be able to use any of them.

I exhaled a tight breath. I needed to talk to Genesis. She was part of the Council, after all, and the leader of this group. I needed to go to her more often with problems I had, rather than try to work them out myself. Tossing my planner on the bed, I scooted to the edge, but as my feet touched the floor, my door opened and Raikidan strolled in.

"Hey, I need to talk to you," he said.

"Can it wait?" I asked. "I need to go talk to Genesis about something having to do with the rebellion."

He shut the door. "Actually that's what I want to talk to you about. Can you hear me out?"

I nodded. "Okay. What's up?"

"I've been thinking about this a lot and didn't know how to bring it up until now. When I offered to help, I thought there'd be more hands-on work. I thought the moment we entered the city we'd be doing something to tear Zarda down quickly, but that's not how it happened. We've done more keeping low and to the shadows than helping the cause. Can you explain to me why this is?"

I sighed. "I can when I'm done talking with Genesis. They're pretty much related."

He blinked and then nodded. "All right."

I walked past him and set a quick pace for Seda and Genesis' room.

"Come right on in," Seda invited as I was about to knock.

I didn't hesitate and opened the door. "Genesis, I need to talk to you."

Genesis sighed and Seda giggled. "Told you she was coming."

My brow furrowed as I closed the door behind me. "Seda, you haven't been eavesdropping on me again, have you?"

She smiled. "Not intentionally. I was discussing with Genesis about what you were thinking about, and told her you were on the same page as me."

I nodded. "Good, at least I don't have to explain myself and I have someone on my side."

Genesis exhaled. "There's nothing I can do differently, Eira. Things have changed; our team just doesn't see them yet."

"Well we need to start seeing them. We need to end this. It's gone on for too long."

"We have limited resources," she reminded me. "We have limited numbers. Zarda doesn't. We need to work with what we have."

"I was gone twenty-two years and we haven't progressed in the least! We're an organized group. We should be better than this."

Genesis' face reddened as her anger started to rise with mine. "I understand your frustration, Eira, but there's only so much that can be done."

Someone knocked on the door, diffusing our anger a bit.

"Come in," Seda called.

The door opened and Ryoko stood in the doorway. Everyone else in the house hung out in the hallway behind her.

"We all should be a part of this discussion," Ryoko said.

Genesis glowered. "There's nothing to discuss."

"Yes there is!" I shouted. "We're not moving this fast enough."

"We're doing the best that we can, Eira. Like I said, we're limited on our resources and numbers. If we exhaust too much, we'll go backward."

"We've barely gone forward."

"And what will you do if things stay the same? Go rogue and attempt this on your own?" she challenged.

"Of course not," I replied. "I'm not suicidal."

"Then you need to be patient. The other teams already have more work and are doing them the best they can. We will have our chance soon enough."

My lip curled. "Don't tell me about patience. It's my job to be patient and wait. And this is getting far too ridiculous to be patient about anymore."

Genesis sighed. "If you want a team transfer, I'll give it to you."

Ryoko looked at me as if she were afraid I'd take that offer.

I shook my head. "That's not what I want."

"None of us want that," Argus said. I glanced to him and he nodded. There was one thing we both had in common and that was how out of place we were on Team Three. "We want this rebellion to end."

"Just talk to the rest of the Council," Ryoko begged. "We're all tired of fighting. If this is dragged out too much longer, morale is going to be what kills our cause, not lack of numbers or resources. We all want real lives."

"And some, like Raikidan here, are offering their time to help even when they're not directly involved," Blaze pointed out. "Still not clear why you're here."

"His reasons are his own," I said.

Blaze held up his hands. "Easy. I was just stating a fact. No one here but you knows why he's helping. We don't exactly get help from the outside."

"Except there are a lot of people who are affected by Zarda's reign," Raikidan countered. "And that's why I'm here."

Nice cover. The others wouldn't be too thrilled to hear his only reason for being here was the satisfaction he got out of revenge, even if it wasn't his own.

Genesis pressed her lips together. "Look, I don't want to argue with all of you about this. I'll go talk to them again, but I'm not promising anything."

"Whatever," I muttered before heading for my room.

I flopped down on my bed and grunted into my blanket. My planner rolled and tapped me on my head, but I ignored it. That talk had amounted to nothing.

"Hey, Eira?"

I turned my head to look up at Raikidan. "Yeah, I promised you an answer."

He sat down on the bed. "I need a lot of answers now."

I laughed. "All right then, ask away."

"Well from what I've gathered, things aren't exactly how I imagined them to be when it came to overthrowing Zarda. Care to explain why I was led to believe this would be a bit easier?"

"'Cause I'm stupid and didn't explain anything to you properly," I said with a half smile.

His gaze darkened. "Don't call yourself stupid." I blinked. He took that a bit too offensively. "Now, explain everything to me now."

I sighed and sat up. "Okay. So, yes, I did make it sound like this was going to be a quick job, but I didn't mean to. It could have been my state of mind back when we met, or I just didn't think about it since I'm used to how the others think. Actually, I'm pretty sure it was my state of mind. Your offer to help put me in a position that made me forget a few things, and then when my mind righted itself, I forgot to tell you the important stuff."

"So are you going to explain it, or what?" he asked impatiently.

I laughed. "Calm down." He sighed playfully and I laughed some more. "So, obviously we're part of the rebellion and we all work together to try to take Zarda down. There's a reason for this. It'd be suicide for a small number of people to go after him. He's too heavily guarded by loyal soldiers and psychics for anyone to pull it off. So we have to resort to being a large organized group."

Raikidan nodded. "Okay. So when you made it sound like it was just the two of us going to take him on, maybe with a little backup, that was a mistake."

"Right," I said. "And since we're an organization, it takes time for us to get things done. And as you can see with my fight with Genesis, it doesn't always go as quickly as most of us would like."

"Yeah, I can see that, and I'm glad to see you have some sense about the time frame it has taken," he said. "Now, tell me more about how the rebellion works. Genesis said something about other teams getting more work, so I'm confused why we aren't."

"I'd be happy to. You know how we're split up into seven teams?" He nodded. "Well, there's a reason. The teams are split up based on types of abilities. These abilities determine what type of assignments they qualify for. Occasionally, you'll get a rebel who doesn't fit into that team's mold, but that's usually because they had an affiliation with someone on that team at the time of joining the rebellion, or they made a transfer.

"Team Three, our team, is comprised mainly of Brutes and foot soldiers. This makes us ideal for head-on conflict, spy missions, and recon, but recon assignments don't come up as often as most would think, and spy missions are spread throughout all teams so our team doesn't get a ton of them. This leaves very few jobs for the team to do, since head-on conflict is typically bad, turning Team Three into an income-based team.

"Large sums of money earned at the shop, the club, and other businesses we run are given to the rebellion to pay for equipment repair, food and medical supplies, ammunition when we can purchase it without raising suspicion, and anything else that would help our cause. This is why we don't do as much as you'd think... or I'd like. If we were on another team, we'd probably be doing a lot more."

"All right. That makes a lot more sense now," Raikidan said. "But that does raise questions about you. By design, you're not a foot soldier even though you had a ranking position over a group of them, so why are you on this team?"

I scratched the back of my head. "I'm one of those variable people. The Council wanted to place me on Team One when I joined. They're the team that deals with… I'm going to say, ninety-five percent of assassin-related assignments. But because of my affiliation with Zane and everyone, I chose to join Team Three."

"They didn't try to force you to join Team One?"

I shook my head. "That would go against what we represent. We fight Zarda so we can be free and have more choices. By forcing people to join certain teams, that would make us hypocritical. It also worked in everyone's favor since Team Three had lost their battle leader a few months prior, due to an incurable illness. Ryoko and Rylan knew I was a good leader, and Zane put in the good word. Although, in the Council's eyes, I'm not the only one who doesn't belong on the team."

"Who else doesn't?" Raikidan asked.

"Argus."

"Really?"

I nodded. "The Council wanted him on Team Six. That team is comprised of the smartest people we can recruit. They create and research new ways to give us the upper hand, and they make attempts at figuring out how to either get us into Zarda's fortress or how to lure him out. But Argus didn't want to leave his friends, so he stuck with our team. He still gets to use his brain in the ways he wants, even if we can't get the resources like Team Six could."

Raikidan nodded. "Just an observation. For a leader, Zarda doesn't show his face often. At all really."

I grunted. "The people of the city will be lucky to see his face even once in their lifetime."

"How does he get them to follow him?"

"Because the people of the city are brainwashed. He's managed to convince the people they don't need to see him in order for him to run the city. Occasionally he'll use images and recordings on billboards or holograms temporarily to bolster his control when he has any inkling it's slipping. The tactic works too unfortunately. People think the suns shines out his ass, and they act like they've met a god when he does appear before them in person."

Raikidan shook his head. "Crazy… but thanks for clearing that all up. Everything makes a whole lot more sense now."

I smiled. "You're welcome. I'm sorry I never explained that. I feel really—"

"Don't"—he warned—"Don't say it. Anyone could have made that mistake."

I sighed. "All right, all right."

Raikidan picked up my planner. "Mind showing me how to use this?"

"Why do you want to know how to use it?"

He shrugged. "Why not? You can use it, and I'd like to understand your technology better. I struggled to understand how the communicators worked on my own; I'm pretty sure the TV was the easiest technology to work, and we both know I wasn't very good at understand that for at least a week."

"I'm pretty sure the microwave is easier."

His face reddened. "I had a harder time with that…"

I laughed. "And yet you were able to figure out driving a car rather quickly. Are you sure you're not a human guy with shapeshifting abilities?"

His face tinted more, and then he muttered, "Just teach me how to use this."

I giggled and nodded. "Sure thing."

24
CHAPTER

Hot water rushed out of the shower head and steam fogged up the mirror. I stripped down out of my dirty clothes and hopped into the stall, a sigh escaping my lips as relief rushed over me. Working hard at the shop, then the club, and two assignments later, I needed this break.

I took my time scrubbing up, not caring if someone else needed the shower. They could wait for me to be done for once, and not the other way around. Not that there were many in the house at the moment to begin with. Seda and Genesis were at some meeting, and Zane and the boys were pulling a late-nighter at the shop to get a custom car finished by tomorrow for a client. That left Ryoko, Rylan, Raikidan, and myself in the house, and Ryoko had been the only one to put up a fuss about the shower situation.

My scrubbing stopped when someone shouting caught my attention.

"Ryoko, give that back!"

I shook my head as two pairs of feet thumped up and down the hall several times. Where she got the energy to torment Raikidan at this time of night was beyond me. I went back to washing, but froze when the bathroom door flew open.

"Ryoko I said—whoa, what are you doing?" Raikidan shouted.

A pathetic girly shrill of scream came out of my mouth when Ryoko whipped the sliding door of the shower open and threw Raikidan in. Raikidan crashed into me, the shower stall barely big enough to fit two people. My body burned with discomfort.

I shoved him and tried in vain to cover myself. "Get out!"

He didn't have to be told twice and attempted to leave, but the door wouldn't budge. I peered around Raikidan and spotted the adjustable security bar holding the door shut. *She did not!*

Ryoko grinned and waved her fingers. "Have fun, you two."

She then pranced out of the bathroom and shut the door behind her. I pressed myself into the corner of shower stall and Raikidan banged on the glass doors. My heart thundered in my chest. Unfortunately, due to our enhancements, we had this stall made with reinforced glass that could handle a beating. Water beat down on him, soaking him head to toe. His muscular form took up more room in the stall than I liked, and blocked off most of the running water.

Raikidan stopped attempting the door and sighed. He began to turn around and I shrieked, "Don't turn around!"

He sighed again. "You're really going to act like this?"

"Don't look at me."

"Why do make such a big deal out of this?"

"I said, don't look!"

He leaned his arms against the glass door and stared at the far bathroom wall. As much as it should have made me feel better, it didn't. In the military, the only shower available had been co-ed. Most got used to it, but Ryoko and I hadn't. We'd shower at odd times so we wouldn't have to deal with others seeing us without clothes.

"You still haven't answered my question," Raikidan said.

"I don't like being looked at in this condition."

"Condition?" He shook his head and chuckled. "You're something else if you think a lack of clothes is a condition."

I held myself tighter and stared at the tile floor. I couldn't talk to him about this. Being a dragon, he wouldn't get it, not that I really knew how to put it in words.

"You're shaking," he said. "Are you cold?"

"I told you not to look at me," I said.

"Forgive me for being concerned when you got real quiet."

"Yes, I'm a little cold," I lied. "You're blocking the warm water and this tile wall cools off quick."

He backed up. "Then take my body heat."

My face flushed and my body warmed up when his back came in contact with my arm that covered my chest. He may have been wearing clothes, but it didn't make this any more comfortable. "Raikidan, this is weird."

"It's not weird if you don't make it weird," he said. "Relax and put up with it until Rylan gets—"

"He's never going to have the balls to stand up to Ryoko," I said. "She's too intimidating for him in multiple ways."

"I don't know," Raikidan said. "Sounds like he's trying to reason with her in the living room."

The two of us grew quiet to listen.

"Ryoko, stop doing this," Rylan said. "It's not good for anyone."

"I'm just having fun," she defended. "No harm done."

"This is Laz we're talking about. You can hear her freaking out in there."

"I don't know; they're pretty quiet now."

"Ryoko, let me pass and let them out."

"Make me." The house grew quiet, though I thought I could hear some shuffling of feet over the running shower water. Then, a *thud* against a wall. "Oh, really, Ry? I never took you for the kind of guy for something like this."

I snickered when she started laughing. I could only guess he thought pinning her would work in his favor, only to backfire with the confidence she exuded. "See it's going to be a while before we're rescued."

"Then maybe you should relax," Raikidan said. "It won't be weird."

I chewed on my bottom lip. Even though I had initially lied about being cold, now that the water continued to be blocked, I actually had cooled off, and the warmth of his skin enticed my body. Eventually, my cold state won out in my internal conflict, and I relaxed a little against him. I attempted to keep body contact to a minimum but as the minutes passed, his offered warmth became too hard to resist. I found myself in a rather embarrassing situation of pressing my body against his for warmth. My cheeks and ears burned and my heart beat hard in my chest every time I let my mind think about it too much. *I need to not make this so weird…*

"Are you warm enough?" Raikidan asked. "I could try to move more so the water can actually touch you."

"N–no, no, this is fine," I stammered. "Moving around in this tight spot will be too much of a chore."

"These wet clothes I'm wearing I guess wouldn't help…" Out of nowhere, Raikidan removed his shirt and dropped it on the tile floor.

"Raikidan, what are you doing?" I shrieked when his pants loosened.

"You'll stay warmer if these wet clothes aren't touching you," he said as both his pants and boxers hit the floor.

I immediately stared up at the ceiling and pulled away from him. "This is *so* not okay."

"Stop making it weirder than it is."

"You're the one who's making it weird!" I hissed. "Be more decent for once."

"Do you want to be warmer or not?"

I continued to keep space between us. That is, until the shivering started. Lip quivering, I let out a tight breath and I had no choice but seek him out for warmth again. With my arms protecting my chest from contact, I leaned against him. The warmth of his body teased and enticed me to get comfortable, but I knew better than to give into something like that.

"Eira, relax," Raikidan whispered. "We're going to be here a while at this rate. You might as well calm down and not make this out to be a big deal."

"I'm fine."

He reached behind him and wrapped his arms awkwardly around me. "You're tense and freezing. That's not the definition of fine. Just relax."

I thought about doing as he said, but the moment the thought came to me, my body burned with embarrassment. No way could I do more than stand here like this so awkwardly.

"Relax," he encouraged. "It's no different than a hug."

"It is *so* not the same."

He chuckled. "I beg to differ."

I chewed on my bottom lip and did my best not to shift my weight when awkwardness flooded over me each time I thought about relaxing against him. *Is it really like a hug? Am I blowing this out of proportion?*

Raikidan didn't move a muscle as I wrestled with my internal conflict. Eventually, the reluctant side of me lost and I started to relax.

My arms moved from being a protective barrier and rested in a more comfortable position on his back as I pressed my chest against him. Raikidan's arms lowered and he pressed on my lower back, squishing my entire body against him. My body temperature rose in an awkward way. Raikidan chuckled and I knew it was because he could feel my heart nearly pounding out of my chest.

As we stood there, I began to calm down. It wasn't all that bad. The situation was weird, unlike he tried to claim, but it wasn't *that* bad. I rested my head against Raikidan's back. *Could be worse, really...*

"See, not much different than an ordinary hug," Raikidan said.

"I don't hug you like this."

"Well, then maybe you should. I wouldn't mind."

I lifted my gaze, wondering. Why would he want a hug from me? Especially one like this?

As luck would have it, the front door opened and several pairs of feet entered the house.

"Ryoko, Rylan, why are you two having a staring contest in the hallway?" Zane asked.

"Ryoko played a dirty trick on Laz and Raikidan," Rylan said. "She shoved Raikidan in the shower while Laz was using it and locked them in the stall."

"Wow, really?" Blaze asked. "Anything happening in there?"

Argus smacked him. "Don't be stupid. She's probably freaking out in there."

At least some of my housemates understand.

"All right, you two, move out of my way," Zane said. "This has gone on long enough."

"Don't rain on my parade," Ryoko whined.

"I will, now move."

She huffed and Zane stormed past her. I pulled away from Raikidan and he quickly pulled his boxers and pants back up. He grabbed his shirt, wrung it a few times, and hung it over his shoulder before leaning his arms against the glass door. *At least he's being decent about this and not making it more awkward.*

Zane flung the bathroom door open and rushed in. He barely looked at the two of us before noticing the security bar and ripped it out of its holding place. Raikidan immediately slid the door open and exited not only the shower stall, but the bathroom, quickly.

Ryoko yelped in pain. "Ow, Rai! Don't thwack my ear. They're sensitive."

"Consider it a warning," Raikidan said. "Don't do that again."

She grumbled. "You guys are no fun."

"You okay, Chickadee?" Zane asked without looking at me.

I nodded and kept myself covered as best as possible. "I'll be fine. I'd like to finish up my shower in peace now if you don't mind."

He nodded and left. A long sigh came from my mouth as I relaxed when the door shut behind him. *Thank the gods they came home finally.* I stood under the water and let the liquid roll down my body. I didn't need to finish cleaning up, but if I left this room, I'd be far too tempted to hurt Ryoko. *And Raikidan too.* No way was I going to be truly okay with that stunt he had pulled, regardless of his supposed reasons.

The bathroom door creaked open and Ryoko's scent wafted in. "Ryoko, you come in here, the gods help you, I'll slaughter you for that stunt."

"Okay, well good night!" she said too cheerfully.

I shook my head. *She's something else.* I stood in the shower for several more minutes before deciding it was time to head to bed and sleep this incident off.

25
CHAPTER

y breath was short and my blood cold. Bodies were strewn around me, and my hands were stained with their life force. The lifeless faces of these people scared me. They were my friends. I watched them die over and over again, and my heart pulsed with pain with each death.

I sensed it then. Death was about tear out my heart once more. Ryoko ran toward me in fear. She glanced behind her as if she was looking for whatever chased her in the blackness of nothing that surrounded us. My heart clenched when she screamed and fell to the ground. Nothing had attacked her. Nothing came out of the darkness, but she bled out and died nonetheless.

Rylan was next. He made it farther than Ryoko, but not by much. I looked down at him as he crashed to the ground in front of my feet. His body lay unnaturally, his face hidden under him like every time before. I shifted my focus in anticipation of Zane, Argus and Blaze. They were always next. The sequence of their deaths never changed.

The boys ran past me, but as they did, they, too, were killed by an unknown assailant. Blood splattered over my chest and the taste of blood seeped over my tongue. New blood dripped off my hands. It was as if I was the one who was killing them. It was as if I was to blame, yet I hadn't moved. I hadn't ever thought of killing them.

Then they started to run past me. Hundreds of people ran in terror. I recognized some people and others I did not. But they all met the same fate in the end. It didn't matter if they made it past me or not, they all died, and each time they did, the blood weighed me down.

Then, something changed. In the crowd of people, a new face appeared. I blinked, figuring when I opened my eyes he'd be gone, but when they opened again, he was still there. He looked around frantically as if he were searching for something, or someone.

"Eira! Eira! Eira, where are you?"

"Raikidan…" I whispered. I wasn't sure if I should call out to him any louder. I didn't want him to end up like the others.

"Eira, where are you?" he called again. "Please, say something!"

I stepped forward, unable to move far due to the bodies scattered everywhere. "Raikidan!"

He looked at me. He was too far away to read his expression but he didn't waste any time running over to me. As he came closer, I noticed the blood on him. It was everywhere. What was going on? I blinked slowly as he crashed into me and held me in his arms. His breath came slow and deep from his running.

"Eira…" he mumbled as he rested his face in my hair. "I thought I'd never find you."

I was too confused to respond. I didn't understand what was going on. Over and over these events played. Over and over the same people died. But Raikidan never showed up at any point until this time. He started to pull away, and I wanted to fight to keep him close. I didn't want to lose him like I had the others.

"Raikidan—" The pain that shot through my abdomen stopped me. I choked as blood rushed up my throat. "Rai…kidan… why?"

He chuckled, but his voice was different now. I pulled away and was faced with the man I hated so much.

"Who is this Raikidan, my dear?" the dark haired man asked.

"Z–Zarda…" I managed.

He smirked at me, his topaz eye glinting with malicious amusement. "Did you really think you could escape me? Did you think you wouldn't screw up again?"

I tried to pull away from him but the pain in my abdomen worsened. I cringed and looked down. I couldn't believe the sight before me. Zarda's hand was speared into me as if it were a sharp blade.

Zarda snickered. "The apple doesn't fall far from the tree. Your heart will betray you."

He pulled his arm free and walked away. I fell to the ground and bled out. His words replayed in my mind over and over.

"Your heart will betray you."

I had been warned with these words before. It couldn't be true. I was alone. A lone heart can't be betrayed.

Strong hands pressed on my back and Raikidan's worried voice echoed through my ears. "Eira? Eira!"

He shook me each time he spoke my name but I was far too gone to respond. "Eira!"

I smelled blood. The scent was heavy and it smelled sickeningly close. I could hear muffled voices all around me but I couldn't make them out. I moaned in pain. Something was wrong, but I couldn't figure out what. A strong pair of arms touched me. *Who do they belong to?* The voices then became clearer.

"Who are you?" a feminine voice that sounded like Ryoko's demand.

"I told you, right now that doesn't matter," another female voice that sounded oddly familiar replied. "Right now, you have to move her away from all this blood and to a spot where I can help her."

Blood? There's blood around me. Is it my blood?

"How do we know we can trust you?" a male voice that sounded like Rylan's asked. "You come out of a mysterious portal, don't address yourself, and tell us what to do with her, and you really expect us to believe you're going to help her?"

The strong arms that had ceased to touch me lifted me up, and I was held close to a muscular bare chest. The movement shot excruciating pain through my body. I screamed.

"Raikidan!" Ryoko screech.

"We need to move her," he said. "I'll put her on the couch."

I managed to open my eyes into slits. Upset wouldn't begin to describe him.

"You're hurting her more!" Ryoko protested. "You need to put her down right now."

"Eira is dying, and if we don't put her somewhere where she can be healed, then we're going to lose to her!"

I'm dying? I cringed and whimpered as more pain flooded through my body as Raikidan carried me out of my room. I felt like I was dying, that was for sure. How did I get hurt? All I could remember was that awful dream. With Raikidan in the room, no one would have been able to sneak in.

Did Raikidan do it? *No, he couldn't have.* If he did I'd be dead already, and he wouldn't be trying to carry me somewhere so I could get healed up, right? I groaned. It hurt to think about this and it hurt to be moved.

Raikidan laid me down on the couch and pulled away from me. I wanted to stop him. I didn't want him to leave but I couldn't find the strength to move. As he moved away I saw all the blood on him. I was bleeding really badly. No wonder they said I was dying.

A hooded figure took Raikidan's place by my side. She had to be the source of the mysterious voice. The only part of her face I could see was her lips. They were deep shade of red, thanks to her lipstick, and they were pressed together with concern.

"I'll have you fixed up in no time," she promised me.

I grunted in pain as a response. I watched her as best I could as she placed her hands over my wound. A green light enveloped her hands, and then part of my body. Something about her gave off a sense of familiarity. Maybe it was the cloak. She was a shaman after all, but there was something about the cloak that made me feel like I knew her. Not to mention her voice sounded familiar as well. I cringed in pain. She wasn't very good at this.

"Sorry…" she whispered. "I'm definitely not as good at my brother."

I grunted. I knew who she was now. I couldn't believe I hadn't figured it out sooner. "You suck… at this compared… to him… Shva'sika. The color of your healing aura even says so."

Shva'sika laughed. "Ouch. You could at least give me some credit."

I grunted again. "I'm dying here for some unknown reason and it feels like you're making it worse."

"Hey, I had no one to teach me."

"Yeah, whatever," I muttered.

She sighed. "You're such a pain."

I snickered. "If I'm such a pain why don't you go back home?"

Shva'sika smirked. "Too late, I'm already here helping you."

"I thought as much. You could never leave me to die."

"You've got me there."

I needed to distract myself. "I didn't know you could heal."

"I didn't either until I tried it one day. When you left, after the village had been attacked five years ago, I felt like I needed to replace Xye's loss, so I gave it a shot. I didn't want to be taught how to do it. Xye never did the first few years of his shaman life, so I was determined to do the same."

"Well you forgot something. Xye was a natural at healing. I remembered hearing how much of a protégé he was from the other healers."

Shva'sika laughed. "That is quite true."

Ryoko lean over the couch. "So you know her?"

I snorted. "Know her? I can't get rid of her!"

Shva'sika laughed. "I don't know why I put up with you sometimes."

I chuckled. "When you figure it out I'd love to know."

Shva'sika laughed more and shook her head. She pulled her hands away when she finished. "There. You're all patched up. How are you feeling right now?"

I exhaled and closed my eyes. "Like shit."

She giggled. "Your strength should come back in a few hours, with a lot of rest."

I grunted. "It'd better."

"Hey, Laz?" Ryoko asked.

I opened my eyes. "Yeah?"

She smiled. "Happy eighty-fifth birthday."

I snorted. "Is it really?"

"Yeah."

I had no idea summer had been so close. With everything going on I had completely forgotten. I grunted. "Some birthday. I've had weird things happen on my birthday but I don't think almost dying has ever made the list until now."

"Birthday?" Raikidan asked.

"Please tell me you know what a birthday is," Ryoko begged.

"Uh, no," Raikidan replied.

"It's a stupid tradition to remind us of how old we are," I explained to him. "It's celebrated once a year on the same day you were born. Mine just so happens to land on the summer solstice."

Raikidan grunted. "Sounds stupid. But how do you all figure when you're born?"

"That's easy," Ryoko commented. "To keep things consistent, and to make sure nothing goes wrong, we're released from our tanks on the year desired that is on the day we were created."

"What's the point of celebrating it?" he asked.

"There isn't one," I said. "It just tells you you're another year older."

"There is nothing wrong with getting older," Shva'sika defended.

"Maybe for you," I shot. "You don't die, you old woman."

Shva'sika laughed. "We do too. It just takes a long time. Don't tell me you're jealous."

I snorted. "Hardly. Everything is supposed to have an end. That's how the cycle works." Sighing, I attempted to pull myself up into a sitting position.

"Oh, no you don't!" Shva'sika placed her hands on my shoulders and tried to get me to lie back down. "You need to rest."

I resisted. "No, I need to sit up."

She sighed and let me do as I pleased. Once I managed to succeed at sitting up, I rested my hand where my wound had been. It had been in the same spot Zarda had attacked me in my dream. As I left my hand there the memories of the dream flooded back to me. I was remembering everything in fine detail and I didn't like it. It was painful.

Shva'sika rested her hands on mine. "Laz, I need you to tell me what happened."

I shook my head. "I don't want to talk about it."

"Laz, please. If this vision was bad enough to nearly kill you, I need to know about it." My forehead creased and she chuckled. "You didn't honestly believe it was a nightmare did you? Dreams don't kill, but visions can."

"That's a little creepy," Ryoko said. "Why would you ever want to have one if it risks killing you?"

"It's not common," Shva'sika explained. "But under the right conditions it can happen. It's not only Laz's element that is enhanced on this day. Her bond with the spiritual plane is also heightened, and if the spirits choose to send her a vision, then it could potentially be fatal, like this one."

"But if they know it could happen, then why not send it when she wouldn't get hurt?" Rylan asked.

"Visions are given when the time is right. There is only one time you can receive it, and you can't get it again once you've seen it," Shva'sika explained.

"That's stupid," Ryoko muttered.

I yawned. "It's fine, and I'm better now. Now everyone can stop worrying and go back to bed."

"Laz, I still need you to tell me what happened," Shva'sika insisted.

I shook my head. "No. Maybe when I'm ready to talk about it, but I'm not right now, so stop pushing me. I don't have to tell anyone if I don't wish to. The vision was for me, and it's my choice to tell or not."

Shva'sika exhaled. "Very well. We're going to have to find you a new place to sleep for the night, though. That blood will have to be cleaned up later today and a couch will not work for your recovery."

I closed my mouth when she told me the couch part. I was okay with sleeping on it but if the healer said no, I was to listen. I yelped when strong arms picked me up.

"C'mon, let's get you back to bed," Raikidan said.

"Raikidan, put me down!" I protested.

"You're in no shape to walk."

"Like hell I'm not."

Ryoko giggled. "Just because you have the energy to yell doesn't mean you have the energy to walk."

I folded my arms and snorted unhappily. I didn't have the energy, but I also didn't want to be carried like I couldn't take care of myself. I watched as Shva'sika moved from her spot and followed Raikidan as he carried me down the hall. I blinked with slight surprise when he brought me into his room.

"You know, there are plenty of guest rooms," I told him as he placed me down gently on his bed. "I can sleep in one of those."

"This room is closest," he said as he sat next to me.

"There's one right next to Ryoko's room!" I protested.

"Shva'sika will sleep there. She'll need a place to rest too, you know."

I wanted to smack myself. Of course she would. What kind of person would I be if I made her go home at this hour after saving me?

"Raikidan?" Shva'sika asked quietly. "Would you mind letting me speak with Laz in private for a moment?"

He nodded and stood. He closed the door behind him when he left, leaving us alone.

Shva'sika sat down next to me, taking Raikidan's previous place. "How are you feeling?"

I laughed. "That's all you wanted to ask? Did you really need to force Raikidan to leave for that question?"

Shva'sika huffed. "Answer my question please?"

Something was up. "I feel fine. My energy is low but it's coming back slowly, and I'm alive. I have you to thank for that, though I'm surprised you're here. It's like you knew this would happen."

Shva'sika nodded. "I did."

Now I knew why Shva'sika wanted to speak to me alone. This was shaman business. "Go on."

"I was given a vision a few days ago," she explained. "You were dying and all your friends were around you. I knew I was the one who was supposed to save you."

"But you didn't come right away," I observed. "That's not like you. You've always jumped head first without thinking about consequences when the spirits are involved."

Shva'sika nodded slowly. "I would have been here sooner, since the spirits didn't tell me when it would happen, but Maka'shi found out about my vision."

I didn't like where this was going. "Shva'sika, what are you beating around the bush about?"

She sucked in a tight breath. "Laz, is it all right... if I stayed here with you? Like, permanently?"

I forced myself to stay calm. "You can't be serious? Maka'shi didn't make you choose, did she?"

"It was either I stayed in the village and not help, or come to your aid and never be allowed to come back."

"Shva'sika!" I shouted. "How could you choose me over everything you had? That's your entire life you left behind. That's everything your family ever owned. That's the only home you've ever known! Why would you do it?"

She looked at me. I could tell, even though her hood shadowed her eyes, by the frown on her lips, this decision hadn't been made lightly. She had struggled with this choice, knowing the very words I spoke were the deciding factors. "I did it because I cared about you more than any one object I owned. You're my family now, Laz, and I'll be damned if I ever forget that for a moment. I'd rather have you than something that belonged to a dead person, any day."

"Shva'sika..." I didn't know what to say. She and I had been close, much closer than I would have let anyone outside of my select group of comrades come close to, but not even I had thought she would choose me over everything she had. "You can stay. I'm not sure what you can do here, since I'd rather not see you fighting alongside us, but you can stay as long as you wish."

She smiled and hugged me. "Thank you. I'm not sure if I'll be of any help, but I would like to assist in some way. I'm no longer a member of the West Tribe, so I can't put them in any danger." I pulled away. She cocked her head. "What?"

"I have this weird feeling you're still not telling me something," I said.

Her lips twisted. "It's nothing really. I just have this feeling that I haven't accomplished what the spirits told me about. It feels like this night wasn't the incident they were referring to. Sure, this vision could have killed you if it weren't for me, but it also might not have if your friends had been able to get you help fast enough." I looked away from her for the first time this night. I didn't want her to see what I was thinking. "Laz, what is it?"

"It's nothing, forget about it."

"You're thinking of something. What is it?"

"I have a feeling you're right," I told her honestly. "I have a feeling this isn't the incident they were talking about, but I also think that you won't be able to help me when that day comes."

Shva'sika touched my shoulder. "What are you talking about? What do you know, Laz?"

I shook my head. "It's time for me to go to bed."

"Laz, please! What do you know?"

I looked at her without expression. "Leave it be, Shva'sika. It's not important."

"But—"

"Shva'sika, we both need sleep now. The room next to Ryoko's will be yours if you want it."

She sighed. "Very well. I'll leave you to rest up."

Shva'sika slid off my bed and left. Raikidan entered almost immediately after and closed the door behind him. He stared at me. "What did you not tell her?"

I pursed my lips. "It's rude to eavesdrop."

"Answer my question."

I slid up higher on the bed until I reached the pillows. "It doesn't matter."

"What do you know that everyone else doesn't, Eira?" he asked. "What happens to you at the end of this?"

I laid my head down on the pillows and curled up. They weren't as comfortable as mine, and neither was the bed, but they would do for the night. "I'm removed from the picture. I already told you that. Now, good night."

"Eira—"

"I said good night!"

He sighed and shifted forms without another word. I curled up tighter and closed my eyes. The end was coming up soon, much sooner than I had thought. I wasn't sure if I was ready for it, but then again, I wasn't sure if I ever would be.

26
CHAPTER

I wiped my eyes groggily as I opened the bedroom door with a foggy mind that had me contemplating climbing back into bed. I was surprised to be met with a wall and not an open living room, but after a few moments of standing in place and waking up more, the memories of this morning's earlier events flooded back to me.

"Good morning," Shva'sika greeted happily as I entered the living room. She sat on the couch near Ryoko, with the hood of her cloak still over her head, sipping on a cup of tea.

I chuckled. "You know you can take your hood off. No one here bites… much."

Shva'sika laughed and pulled down her hood. Her long, navy blue hair spilled out around her shoulders.

"Whoa. She's an elf," Blaze commented.

"No, really?" I replied sarcastically, my night's grogginess almost completely gone now. "I thought she was a gargoyle."

"Oh, fuck you," he retorted.

I sat down on the couch next to Raikidan, who I hadn't noticed was sitting here, and not in the bedroom, until now due to my tired state, and yawned. "I'll pass, thanks."

Blaze snorted, triggering Ryoko to giggle.

I turned to Shva'sika when she handed me a cup of tea. "Why haven't you changed?"

She smiled. "I left in such a rush, I didn't leave with anything more than the clothes on my back."

I sighed. "Figures."

Ryoko's eyes sparked. "That means we get to go shopping!"

I groaned. "Shva'sika, why couldn't you have been a more normal height? Now she's going to torture me, which I don't want to deal with especially, after my ordeal this morning."

Shva'sika laughed. "Oh come now. Shopping isn't that bad."

Rylan looked up from his magazine. "You've never been shopping with Ryoko then."

Ryoko gasped in defense. "You guys are horrible! It's not that bad shopping with me."

Rylan and I both gave pointed looks. "Yes, it is."

She folded her arms and huffed. "Well, whatever. Laz, you still have to go with me. You're the only one who knows what will fit, err, Shva'sika, right?"

Shva'sika smiled. "That's right."

I worked my jaw. She was right, and until we could get Shva'sika some proper clothes she'd be stuck in the house wearing her shaman clothes all the time. I handed Raikidan my cup of tea and stood.

Raikidan looked up at me. "What am I supposed to do with this?"

I shrugged. "Drink it. Put it in the kitchen. I don't care."

"No, you take this back and deal with it," he said. "It's not mine."

"Is now," I replied as I walked down the hall. My clothes changed as I walked. "I'll go get some money, Ryoko, so we can leave."

She cheered. "I like that plan!"

Reaching the wall at the end of the hall, I moved the large hand-painted painting that hung on the wall and placed it on the floor. A small vault door was left where the painting had once hung. It was a real cheesy way to hide the vault, but it worked, so there was no reason to complain or change it.

Typing in the passcode, the vault door unlatched and I pulled on the small handle to open it. Inside were several leather bags and pouches that contained money, but one in particular caught my eye. I picked the bag up to inspect it.

It didn't match the other bags in quality or size. This one was by far larger and of higher quality. It was also tied off with a red rope instead of a basic, brown, leather one, and was embroidered with red thread on the top. Curious, I untied the red rope and peered inside. I couldn't believe what I was seeing. The bag was filled with gold coins. I sifted through the bag, hoping to find some silver and copper pieces, but I was unsuccessful, which meant this wasn't just a bunch of money thrown into a decorative bag.

Clenching the bag tightly in my hand, I slammed the door of the vault shut and stormed down the hall. I knew exactly who put this in there, and I wasn't at all pleased with him. I grabbed Raikidan roughly by the back of the head as he left the kitchen and dragged him into my bedroom, slamming the door behind me.

"What the hell is your problem, Eira?" he shouted.

I threw him away. "What's my problem? What's yours?"

Raikidan rubbed his head. "What are you talking about?" I held up the bag of coins and his eyes grew wide. I had been right. He knew exactly what this was. "E–Eira, I can explain."

"You can explain why you deliberately disregarded my words and left the city without telling me?" I bared my teeth. "If you can, I'd love to hear it!"

I watched him swallow and try to find something to say. When he had made me wait long enough, I lost it. He didn't care about what I had told him. He didn't care that he could have put all our lives in jeopardy. I lifted my arm and, with all my strength, I slapped him across the face—the bone cracking on impact. Raikidan cried out and held his face with his hand. My senses came back to me just then. *Shit.* That was extreme and uncalled for, even if I was angry. *Too late now.*

I spun on my heels and stormed out, grabbing Ryoko by the arm on my way to the basement. "Let's go."

Ryoko blinked. "Wait, is everythign okay?"

"Don't worry about it."

I stomped down the stairs, hearing Shva'sika gasp. "Oh my, what did she do to you? Here, let me check you."

Ryoko yanked on my arm, her eyes wide. "What did you do? I heard soemthing hit skin, but you didn't…"

"Let it go, Ryoko. Doesn't matter."

She frowned. "All right."

I lounged on the couch as Shva'sika dressed in her room. Ryoko and I had spent over four hours looking for clothes, and it wasn't because I didn't think she would wear them. Shva'sika was so tall it was hard to find clothes that would actually fit her. Even Seda had an easier time shopping for clothes since she was still within a normal nu-human height range.

Ryoko bounced next to me in excitement. I couldn't help but roll my eyes at her. She was acting like a child in a candy store and for no reason. I didn't get what was so amazing about Shva'sika trying on new clothes.

"Ryoko," Zane said from his spot in the kitchen. "This woman isn't going to dress any faster if you keep bouncing."

"I know, but I want to see what she decided to wear!" Ryoko complained.

I lay down on the couch and propped my feet on her lap. "Well you're not going to have to worry. Shva'sika has a pretty good grasp on fashion."

Ryoko grunted. "Well I figured that, what with those painted dots on her head, the way she does her hair, and the neat necklace she wears."

"It's called a torc." I sat up when Shva'sika spoke.

Ryoko squealed with delight. "You look so good!"

I chuckled. Ryoko really was something else, but she was right, Shva'sika did look nice. She wore a loose green, long sleeved, off-the-shoulder blouse, and a green and black underbust corset. On her lower body, she sported blue denim pants and black knee-high boots. Around her neck she wore her metal torc, and her lips were coated in a thin layer of red lipstick. Her eyes were dusted with a light coating of eye makeup, and her hair was still wrapped with beads and cloth, but it didn't hinder her look.

I frowned when I noticed she still hadn't removed her painted dots and pointed to my forehead to emphasize what I was about to say. "Um, Shva'sika, you're going to want to remove those."

She frowned and touched her forehead. "Oh… I guess I was hoping to keep my mark."

"It would be best not to," I said. "The soldiers here are stupid, but they're not that stupid. They'll know something is different about you, besides you being an elf, and it could draw unwanted attention."

She sighed. "I suppose you're right. I knew I shouldn't have left without my circlet."

"What's so special about the dots?" Ryoko asked.

"They're a symbol of my full shaman status," Shva'sika explained. "Full-fledged shamans have some sort of mark, and most rarely go around without them."

"What do you mean by most?" Ryoko asked.

Shva'sika tapped her lips, working out her words. "Tradition calls us to let go of our past and embrace our new life. To do this, we're given new names when we agree to take on the path of the shaman. When we achieve full status, we're given our marks. However, there are many, especially in more recent decades, that don't partake in the tradition, either with the name, mark, or both."

Ryoko nodded. "Are the marks always on the face?"

"No. It depends from shaman to shaman."

"So the marks are unique?"

Shva'sika laughed. "Well they're supposed to be, but it's not always the case. The mark represents who we are, and if two shamans are similar they may get similar marks, if not the same."

Ryoko scratched her head. "I think I was better off not asking. My head is starting to hurt."

Shva'sika and I laughed at her before Shva'sika disappeared into the bathroom.

"Hey, Zane, you all right?" Argus asked.

When he didn't receive a reply, I looked over at Zane. He was staring at the wall where Shva'sika had been standing, with a blank expression on his face.

"Zane?" Argus asked again as he waved his hand in front of Zane's face.

Zane still didn't respond. He didn't even blink.

"Uncle!" I shouted.

Zane jumped, hitting his bowl of soup in the process, and blinked.

"You all right?" Argus asked.

Zane blinked some more and then shook his head. "Yeah, I'm fine. I must have spaced out."

I snorted. "Now I know you're getting old. You never space out."

"I'm not old." He narrowed his eyes at me. "And I'm not bald either."

I closed my mouth. I wasn't going to win either battle. He was stubborn—a family trait. But I had something bigger to figure out. Zane never spaced out. Something wasn't right here.

Ryoko nudged me and then handed me a notebook of paper. On it were quickly scribbled symbols and a smiley face at the end. Taking the paper, I read them.

He likes her.

I rolled my eyes and tossed the notebook back at her.

"I'm serious!" she whispered.

"You're delusional," I mumbled.

She snorted and scribbled some more symbols on the notebook and handed the book to me.

Then you explain to me why he was spacing out at the same exact spot where Shva'sika was standing.

I huffed and tossed the notebook down on the couch. I hoped she was wrong. Zane had taken little interest in most women who crossed his path. My mother claimed only a handful had ever caught his eye in his entire life, but it never worked out. Zane always came up with these lame excuses, but everyone knew he was picky. Normally I'd be all right with his new found choice, if it weren't for the fact it was highly unlikely those feelings would ever be returned.

Shva'sika finally came out of the bathroom, rubbing her forehead.

"You okay?" Ryoko asked her.

She nodded, a frown on her lips. "Yeah, I'll be fine. I'm just not used to not having them there."

"I'll make you something to replace it," I offered.

"Like what?" Shva'sika asked.

I grinned. "It's a surprise. But I'll give you a hint. It'll be crafted out of metal."

Ryoko looked at me. "I forgot you could craft metal."

I snorted. "Who do you think taught Ryder how to make stuff? Not Argus."

Ryoko laughed but stopped when someone sighed.

"Why can't you have friends who aren't freakishly tall, Eira?" Blaze asked as he walked into the room.

Shva'sika blinked. "I'm not freakishly tall."

"Neither am I," Seda said from her mediation corner.

Blaze snorted. "Woman shouldn't be any taller than Eira and definitely shouldn't be close to Zane's height."

"Not our fault you're intimidated by women who are taller than you," Ryoko muttered. I bit my lip so I wouldn't laugh, and he glared at her.

Shva'sika shrugged and headed for the couch. "Then you've never met my people. I'm considered short."

"How is seven feet short?" Blaze asked.

Shva'sika laughed. "I'm only six-four."

Blaze rolled his eyes. "Close enough."

Seda chuckled. "Now I don't feel as tall."

"So tell me, how tall are you elven kind?" Blaze asked.

Shva'sika thought for a moment. "On average, men stand at seven and a half feet tall and women stand at about six-eight."

Blaze's face paled. For a moment I thought he might faint. "It's a people of giants!"

I shook my head. "Blaze, just shut up."

Blaze glowered at me but did as I said. Shva'sika giggled and sat down on the couch where everyone was avoiding. It was the spot where I had been bleeding to death earlier this morning.

I scrunched my nose. "How can you sit there after you cleaned it with that awful-smelling solution?"

Shva'sika smiled. "My nose isn't as sensitive, remember?"

I snorted. "Then you must not have a sense of smell at all if you aren't bothered by it in the least."

She laughed. "I had to put up with Xye designing it. I suppose… I've become desensitized to it."

I blinked. I had forgotten Xye had invented the solution. It was the only solution I knew of that could remove any trace of blood. Not even a faint smell was left for even the most skilled Hunters to track. The military would kill to have something like that. "So it's safe to assume I won't be sleeping in my own room tonight, right?"

Shva'sika nodded. "Your room was the worst to clean. With your nose, you might not be able to go in there for a few nights."

That comment made my stomach turn a little. I didn't want to know how much blood I'd lost for her to say it like that.

"Hey, Shva'sika. Not to sound rude, but is there another name we can call you by?" Ryoko asked. "This one is a little complicated."

Shva'sika blinked. "I think it's all right. Don't you, Laz?"

I shrugged. "I'm on Ryoko's side, but for a different reason. Shamans come and go in this city enough for soldiers to get a feel for our naming conventions. Using your elven name would be a better choice."

Shva'sika laughed. "But my elven name is even harder for others to say."

I snorted. "No kidding."

"It can't be that bad, can it?" Zane asked.

Shva'sika smiled. "Elarinya."

Ryoko blinked. "What?"

I laughed and Shva'sika giggled. "It means Morning star."

Ryoko scratched her head. "I'm still trying to get the pronunciation down in my head."

I laughed some more and then spoke flawlessly. "Elarinya."

Ryoko blinked. "Now you're just being mean."

"Our human equivalent would be Danika," I said.

Ryoko looked at Shva'sika with pleading eyes. "Can I call you that?"

Shva'sika nodded. "Sure. Elven isn't easy for most to learn. It was hard enough getting Laz to get the concept."

"Since when can my niece speak anything but common?" Zane asked. "I remember it was hard enough getting her to speak that."

I leaned my head back, gazing at him. "Since two elves made me learn."

Shva'sika laughed. "You make it sound like we bullied you."

"Because you did!" I defended. "You and Xye would constantly speak to me in your tongue as if I knew it, refusing to use common in the least. Not to mention, you would force me to learn how to read your tongue by giving me books to read with a deadline, and if I didn't meet them you'd come up with some sort of extra chore or training time."

She raised the back of her fingers to her lips as if she was pretending to think about the memories. "Oh yeah, that's right."

I rolled my eyes and then blinked when Ryoko bolted to her feet and dashed over to Shva'sika. She grabbed Shva'sika's mouth and pried it open. "You do have a tongue piercing! I thought I saw it."

I smacked myself on the forehead. "Ryoko…"

Shva'sika laughed and pushed her away. "She reminds me of Valene and you."

I chuckled and flashed my sharp teeth at her. Her eyes widened in wonder. Then, before I knew it, she was on her knees, and her hands were prying open my mouth to inspect my teeth.

I laughed. "No kidding. She had that weird obsession with my teeth when she was a child."

"Your teeth are so sharp! Like a tiger! Or maybe a raccoon."

Shva'sika laughed. "She really was a strange child."

"Who's Valene?" Ryoko asked.

"Laz's daughter," Shva'sika explained.

Zane's eyes widened, as if alarmed. "Daughter? What?"

I shook my head. "Calm down. I didn't hook up with someone while I was gone. Valene is not biologically related to me. Even calling her my daughter is a stretch."

Shva'sika shook her head. "I disagree."

"Hard seeing Eira as the parent type," Blaze remarked. "Let alone the adopting type."

"She has a son," Ryoko reminded him. "And she does a good job with him."

"I suck at parenting," I said.

"You do fine," Ryoko argued.

I snorted. "I'm never around for my son, and I kill for a living. Yeah, I get the parent-of-the-year award."

"You did well with Valene when Velessa died," Shva'sika pointed out.

Ryoko looked at Shva'sika. "Was that her real mom?"

Shva'sika nodded. "She was sick, and when she died, Laz took Valene in since she had become so attached to her over the years."

"Daren took care of her," I said. "He adopted her long before I came around."

Ryoko sighed, clearly bored of this back and forth, and then focused on Shva'sika again. "You don't come off as the type who would go out and get her tongue pierced."

Shva'sika smiled. "I had gotten it when I was younger as a test. It didn't work out so well."

I snickered. "Younger? What do you mean by younger? Fifty years or two hundred years?"

She laughed. "I was only one hundred and seventy-five."

Blaze choked on his drink. "Only? You say that like that age is so insignificant. How old are you?"

"Only six hundred," she replied with an innocent shrug.

"And here I thought Zane was old," he muttered.

"I told you two and a half centuries wasn't old," Zane said.

Shva'sika laughed. "You're only a child to us."

Zane laughed. "I'm not sure what's worse. Being old to a nu-human or a child to an elf."

"I suppose it's a compliment on our end," Shva'sika observed. "I'm more or less a young adult."

"Don't look like it," I teased.

Shva'sika glared at me. "Don't make me shock you."

I laughed at her threat. She may have appeared around Zane's age but she was beautiful and seemingly ageless, and I doubted it'd change anytime soon.

"Six hundred…" Blaze mused. "Sound like a lot of time to have fun."

Ryoko grunted as she sat back down on the couch. "There he goes again. His mind goes right down into the gutter without fail."

I grunted in agreement.

"The answer is no, Blaze," Shva'sika said.

He stared at her. "Seriously? I didn't even get the chance to ask."

"Laz told me all about you," she explained. "And my answer is no."

"Oh c'mon. It'll be great," Blaze urged. "I promise."

"Drop it, Blaze," I told him. "You're not going to win."

"Give me one good reason you won't," Blaze said.

"I'm chaste," she replied as she relaxed on the couch.

Blaze blinked and then looked at me. "What the hell is with you and your friends being virgins, Eira?"

"Who said we all were?" Ryoko crossed her arms. "Pretty big assumption if you ask me. Just because we don't sleep around with people we don't know doesn't mean we haven't been with someone in the past."

Blaze's face screwed up. "Well I know Eira hasn't been with anyone. She scares them all away."

Pain twinged in my chest and Ryoko glared at Blaze. "Why do you have to be such a dick?"

"Why are you taking such offense to this?" Blaze asked. "I'm just stating a fact. She scares away any guy that shows remote interest in her. And then there's you."

"Me? I have had a boyfriend before," Ryoko said.

"Oh yeah? Why have we never met or heard of him?"

She bared her teeth. "Because he's dead, jackass! You think you know everything, but you don't know what happened in our lives while we were in the military. You were too busy living your comfortable civilian life and sleeping around with any woman you could get your hands on to know what happened to any of us. You don't know who we've been with, who we've lost, what we're not willing to go through again, or why we're so selective with those we give our time to. You don't know jack shit!"

I sighed internally. He would push her to this point. It didn't help, that any time Zeek came up, she got upset. This was only going to get worse now. Or so I thought. Blaze was actually quiet now. There was this weird look in his eye as if he understood he'd crossed a line that should have never been touched.

He then stood and walked out without a word. That was not what I was expecting from him. It wasn't like him at all. Which part of Ryoko's outburst had put him in this state?

As I watched him leave, I realized Raikidan wasn't in the room. Thinking about it, I hadn't seen him since I slapped him. It made me wonder where he was.

"So you said you got your tongue pierced as a type of test," Ryoko said, reinitiating the original conversation in a clear attempt to get her mind in a better state. "What was the test?"

"Being a lightning shaman, I wanted to find new ways to utilize my abilities, and since metal is a conductive I figured I'd give it a shot to see if it would help me to shoot lighting from my mouth." Shva'sika laughed. "It didn't work out. I wasn't able to transfer the charge from my hands to my mouth. I never found a reason to get rid of it after."

"What compelled you to have that sort of idea?" Ryoko asked.

"I saw a dragon do it once."

"Dragons don't exist anymore," Argus argued. "You couldn't have seen one."

"I've seen a few in my life and met three face to face within the past century," Shva'sika objected. "One was within the past decade."

"That's impossible," he replied. "They died out decades ago."

"Just because you can't see them, doesn't mean they don't still exist."

"We were told they were all dead."

Seda chuckled. "Do you always believe so blindly?"

Argus blinked but couldn't manage a good comeback, so he remained quiet. I wanted to laugh but I knew it wasn't his fault. The stories said they were gone now, and they didn't know about Raikidan's true identity.

I yawned real loud suddenly. I needed sleep. My energy was still low from the loss of blood, and shopping all day with Ryoko didn't help me one bit. I stood and headed for my temporary room. I flopped down on the hard bed and grunted. I wanted my own soft bed back, but thanks to my vision, I wasn't going to be able to get that yet so Raikidan's bed would have to do.

"You didn't have to hit me so hard."

I sat up. Raikidan stood in the far corner, in the shadows, with his arms folded. His eyes were expressionless, giving me no hints if he was angry with me or not. *So this is where he's been hiding.*

I fell back on the bed. "Well if you had just listened to me in the first place I wouldn't have hit you." *I also could have not resorted to violence.*

"You fractured my jaw, and cracked three teeth! You didn't have to go that far."

I bolted upright. "And you left the city when I specifically told you not to unless you spoke with me! You deliberately put everyone's lives in danger so you could grab a stupid bag of gold."

"Well if you had waited to let me explain why I did it, you would understand."

"You were taking forever to say something. Obviously you didn't have a reason."

Raikidan threw his hands into the air. "I did! I was trying to figure out how to word it so you wouldn't be mad."

I snorted. "I was already mad."

"No, really? I wouldn't have figured that out from my painful healing session. You're lucky Shva'sika could heal that injury with her shaman healing. I thought I'd have a bad jaw for the rest of my life because you can't control your anger."

I resisted the urge to wince and folded my arms. "Then tell me, why did you leave?"

He relaxed against the wall again. "I overheard Zane talking to Argus. He said that thing you call a tax was being raised and you'd be short on a lot of money soon. So I thought I'd grab some gold from my hoard to help."

"That's it? That's your reason?"

Confusion clouded his face. "Yeah, that's my reason. Why is it that you don't sound happy about it?"

My anger from earlier boiled up again. I wanted to choke him. "Why? Because you put everyone's life at risk to get money! We were going to be fine, Raikidan. We've dealt with shortages before and it wasn't like we weren't going to have any money."

"You act like you knew about this tax."

I sighed. "Of course I knew. Zane told me about it. It's why I've been working so hard at the club. It's the sole reason I've forced myself to attempt to flirt with every guy that walked into the club to get extra tips. It's not like I actually like having to act so desperate."

"But why are you so mad at me? All I'm trying to do is help!"

"Because you risked everyone's lives for something that wasn't going to be an issue! The least you could have done was talk to me about it first. If it was going to be a problem, I would have shown you a way out that would have been safe. That way, there would have been no risk of anyone being hurt." I fell back on the bed and rubbed my palms over my face. "Forget it."

I was tired of fighting with him. It was all I seemed to do with him anymore. This human-dragon barrier was really starting to get tiresome. Was it worth it anymore? Was he going to learn that the others' safety was primary over anything else? Should I cut my losses and tell him to leave now? He was a great asset, but if he was going to risk everyone's lives then was it really worth it?

Raikidan let out an annoyed breath. "You obviously don't get what it means for me to take gold from my hoard and give it to all of you."

I curled up and closed my eyes. "I'm not a dragon, so why would I?"

Silence fell over the room, though my mind was anything but. I was to blame for this as much as he was. I didn't need to lash out like this. Why was it my gut reaction to act so poorly? Bad people skills? Defense mechanism to keep others away?

I sighed and opened my eyes. Raikidan still hadn't uttered a word. I had honestly thought he'd make some sort of snarky comment, even a hurtful one. He still leaned against the wall watching me. I didn't get it. Why did he watch me so much? Was I honestly that interesting to him?

"I'm sorry," I mumbled out. "I shouldn't have harmed you in my anger. I'll work on my behavior."

Without saying a word Raikidan pushed off the wall and shifted. I was surprised by his size. Was my room really that much bigger than this one or was he choosing not to take a smaller dragon shape?

I sat up when he curled around the bed and rested his head on the soft surface. My head cocked. His eyes were closed and his breath came slow and deep as if he were already asleep. With my legs close to my chest, I watched him in hopes that some sort of answer would jump at me, explaining what was going on. I knew he wasn't asleep so I assumed at some point he would open his eyes. I was wrong. I waited and waited, and yet he didn't open his eyes.

Growing bored of waiting for nothing, I sighed and curled up on the bed, or what was left of it, thanks to Raikidan's giant head, and closed my eyes.

My eyes snapped open only moments later when something heavy pushed on my back. I turned to find Raikidan's tail pressing hard against me. I pulled myself a little closer to his head thinking that would help but his tail moved in the same direction and still pushed against me.

I looked at Raikidan, whose eyes were now open and watching me. I raised an eyebrow at him and he responded by pushing me with his tail again. Playing along, I scooted closer to him until I was only a few inches away from his face. He stopped pushing me then and let his tail drape over the side of the bed. Confused, I eyed him skeptically and lay back down.

I wiggled a little bit to get comfortable and closed my eyes. Raikidan exhaled and inched his face closer to me until his nose and hot breath touched my leg. I grunted with a slight smile and let my mind go blank. I had no idea what he was doing but I also didn't mind. It felt like he was making a protective circle around me, but as I thought it, it didn't make any sense for him to do so.

I snuggled deeper into my arms. It didn't matter. He wasn't in his nu-human shape and trying to sleep next to me, so it wasn't a big deal. Whatever he was doing was his own business and if I really needed to know he'd tell me in the morning. Right?

CHAPTER 27

The stench of blood and burning flesh filled my nose. No more than a few hours after I had fallen asleep, Raikidan and I had been woken up. Team Two had been caught during an assignment and now needed backup. As I scanned the situation from my temporary hiding spot behind a dilapidated building, I attempted to figure out the reason for the failure.

This was the third failed assignment and Team Two was a good team. They were always cautious and made sure they were doing everything right. It didn't make sense for them to be caught. Had they just been unlucky and messed up this time or was there something on the military's side giving them the edge?

I exhaled slowly when a dud rocket landed several feet away from me. Aiming my gun, I shot at several approaching soldiers, but it did nothing to stop them. Raikidan then came out from his hiding place on the other side of the street and exhaled a blast of fire. This stopped the soldiers and they screamed in pain.

This had been a major issue throughout the battle. These soldiers were oblivious to bullets unless it was going through their head, and even that sometimes took more than one to take them down. Fire and other elemental attacks were the only real effective way to take these soldiers down and only some of them would feel the effects. I wasn't sure why either. These weren't the new experiments everyone had warned us about. I knew that for sure but their pain tolerance was abnormally high. It was like they were dead or had no nerves.

I sighed and put my gun away. Spitting fire into my hands I formed the fire all around them and pushed away from the wall. I threw the fire as large balls and watched the soldiers scatter. Those who were hit continued on moving.

"This is getting stupid," I muttered.

"I'm starting to think these guys are using some sort of pain suppressant," Rylan called in. "I had a guy survive three shots to the head."

"If they were foaming at the mouth, I'd say they were rabid," Ryoko complained. "Some of these guys are trying to bite in self-defense."

"Do you think a psychic has something to do with this?" someone from the other team called in.

"It's a possibility," I replied as I threw more fireballs. "In the end, we'll never know, and it doesn't matter. We either have to keep fighting or fall back."

"I'm not failing this mission!" the commander of the other team shouted.

"Sometimes you have to take a loss to win," I replied.

"Running is for cowards," he shot back.

"Living to fight another—"

"Eira, look out!" Raikidan shouted.

His cry came too late when the building I was hiding behind exploded. I fell to the ground and pain raked up my body.

"Eira!" Raikidan ran over to me as I struggled to get up. "Eira, are you all right?"

"Peachy," I muttered through clenched teeth.

"I'm sorry," he apologized. "I didn't see the tanks until it was too late."

"It's fine. It's not your fault. I should be paying attention to the battle and not arguing with some nitwit who is too stubborn to see the benefits of retreating when needed."

He chuckled and helped me drag myself over to where he had been taking cover. Soldiers shot at us but Raikidan retaliated with blasts of fire. He set me down and checked me over.

I bled all over. Large chunks of skin were missing where bricks and other debris had slammed into me. I watched in quiet amazement as

Raikidan used his fire to heal me up. *How can he use fire to destroy as well as to fix?*

When he was done, there were no signs of injury anywhere. It made me wonder why I had a scar from the first time he healed me. Raikidan placed his hands on my shoulder. "When the time is right, get everyone to run."

My brow creased. "What are you talking about?"

He handed me his headset and stood. "Just do it, okay?"

I grabbed him by the arm. "Raikidan, what are you doing?"

He stared at me for a moment without speaking. "I'm done being a burden to you."

My eyes widened and he pulled away from me. What was he talking about? He wasn't going to get himself killed, right? "Raikidan, stop!"

I tried to get up and stop him but I was too late. He was already out in the street and running headfirst into the line of fire. I prayed to Satria I was wrong. Then I heard it—the unmistakable roar. The burden he was talking about wasn't his existence. It was the secret I'd forced myself to keep.

"Dragon!" a soldier shouted.

The sounds and smells of crackling flames filled the air, along with the screams of soldiers as they died.

Regaining my composure, I put Raikidan's headset on my head. "Everyone fall back and don't get caught in Raikidan's flame."

While I waited for the others, I watched Raikidan from the safety of my hiding place. He torched everything in sight. His flame was so hot it burned white at times and was melting metal within seconds. I had never seen such a hot flame burn from another creature before. It was mesmerizing to watch.

"Laz!" My attention as pulled away from his destruction at the sound of Ryoko's voice. I watched her dash down the side street I had been taking cover in before. She eyed Raikidan once she reached the open street, but her reaction wasn't what I was expecting. She appeared more in awe than in fright or confusion.

"What's going on?" she asked, carefully picking her way over to me.

"I'll explain everything later. Right now we need everyone together so we can get out. Raikidan is going to buy us some time."

She nodded. "Okay. The others should be here soon."

Just then, both Argus and Blaze dashed around the corner. They looked like they wanted to ask about the situation, but kept their mouths shut. It wasn't long after Rylan joined us with a few other people from both our team and the other.

"Commander Innon is already pulling the rest of our team back," someone informed. "One glance at the dragon and he was more than willing to hightail it."

Everyone laughed but me. I was more focused on the situation. "Let's move out then. The others will catch up."

No one questioned me, or my choice to move out without Raikidan. They just moved. Our ragtag group headed away from the battle with haste but I started to lag behind. It wasn't until I stopped following that anyone noticed.

"Laz?" Ryoko asked.

I didn't answer her, only watched Raikidan fight. He thrashed his giant body and his tail against the buildings, causing them to crumble. He set everything ablaze and fought off anyone who tried to stubbornly fight back.

"*…get everyone to run.*"

Everyone but him. I never let someone stay behind. If someone was to stay behind, it was always me.

"*I'm tired of being a burden to you.*"

With great conviction I took off in his direction. I didn't leave anyone behind, and that included Raikidan.

"Laz, what are you doing?" Rylan yelled after me.

"Keep going!" I shouted back. "We'll catch up."

I forced the fire from my mouth into my hands and engulfed them with it. Timing myself correctly, I jumped onto the base of Raikidan's tail and ran up his back as best as I could. His thrashing stopped once my feet touched him.

I slipped on his smoother scales but I wasn't willing to put my flames out or risk burning him so I willed my shoes to disappear, allowing me to use the hidden spines under my skin to grip him better. Using the spikes on his neck as leverage, I bolted up his long neck, and once I reached his head, I let loose fireball after fireball.

Soldiers attempted to jump out of the way, but those who escaped my flame were incinerated by Raikidan's. I stopped my attack when a tall, muscular man, standing still caught my eye. His actions confused me until I realized I recognized this man. He and I had much in common but our ideals set us apart. He was an old general who refused to believe Zarda would kill those worthy of living, whereas I believed in the truth.

The two of us stared at each other for several moments before he held up his hand and shouted his command. "Fall back!"

"But, sir!" a soldier protested.

"I said, fall back," he growled. "We cannot win against a dragon and a demon."

The soldier looked up at me warily and I narrowed my gaze at him, fire still burning in my hands. This frightened him and he ran off. Slowly, the general turned and stalked off with his retreating company. I stood there on Raikidan's head and watched him leave. I knew I should stop him. I knew he shouldn't leave alive. I knew if he left, he would tell Zarda and it would complicate things, but for some reason I couldn't find the will to move.

I turned my attention behind me when I heard hesitant footsteps, to find Ryoko and the others making their way toward us. From the looks of it, Innon's team had run off with him, but it didn't bother me much. They weren't my problem now that the battle was over.

I gasped when Raikidan jerked his head and I went flying into the air. I was so surprised, I was having a hard time recovering to right myself in time to land properly. I was going to kill that dragon.

I grunted when I was caught by a pair of strong arms. I glared at Raikidan and he grinned back at me. "Don't do that!"

He snickered. "Scare you?"

I snorted. "Hardly. Now put me down."

Raikidan thought for a moment. "No, I think you're fine."

"Put me down you jerk." I struggled against his grip when he ignored my order. "I said put me down, Raikidan. Now!"

He chuckled but did as I demanded. I stumbled away from him and punched him in the shoulder.

"Ow!" he complained as he rubbed it.

"That's for tossing me carelessly," I muttered.

"I knew what I was doing."

I smacked him in the back of the head. "And that's for not putting me down when I told you to."

"Can you stop hitting me?"

I smacked him hard across the face. "And that's… for everything else."

He grunted but didn't say a word—getting the hint. I stalked away from him and past the others.

"Laz?" Ryoko asked quietly.

"We need to get back home," I instructed. "I'll answer all of your questions then. It's too dangerous to stay here much longer."

"All right," she replied.

I sat on the windowsill, leaning on my legs with my arms, and waited for someone to say something. Raikidan leaned against the wall near me.

"So you knew this whole time Raikidan was a dragon?" Rylan asked.

I nodded. "Yes."

"Shva'sika, did you know?" he asked.

Shva'sika nodded. "Yes."

"Genesis and I knew as well," Seda informed.

"Why didn't you tell us, Laz?" Rylan asked, looking at me again.

I shrugged. "It wasn't my place to say. Seda knew because she's a psychic and therefore Genesis knew, and Shva'sika knew because he shifted at the village for basically the same reason as tonight."

Rylan nodded. "I see."

Argus scratched his head. "So when we were told dragons were gone, we were lied to?"

"There are plenty of us out there," Raikidan said. "Hundreds, maybe even thousands. We're just secretive. When Eira told me you all thought we were dead I was baffled. I didn't think we were that secretive."

"Is that why you never told us?" Argus asked.

Raikidan shrugged. "Sorta. At first, yes, but then I figured there was no need to tell you unless you really had to know."

"Makes sense."

Blaze grunted. "Why does this all matter? He's still the same guy… dragon… whatever. We just know a little more about him. Why is everyone getting so weirded out by it?"

"No one ever said we found it weird," Argus argued. "We're just trying to piece things together."

Blaze grunted again but stayed quiet. I sighed and rested my hand on my chest. My eyes widened when I could only feel soft skin and no hint of leather or bone. I looked down and noticed my necklace was gone. Jumping up suddenly, confusing everyone, my head swiveled frantically. I even resorted to unbuttoning my long shirt in attempt to find it stuck in there somehow.

"Laz?" Ryoko asked. "What's up?"

I stopped my frantic search and rest my hand on my chest again. "My necklace is gone…"

Rylan looked at me. "Are you sure?"

I nodded. "Yeah…"

Blaze snorted. "What's the big deal about this necklace? It's just a necklace."

"Shut up, Blaze," Rylan growled. Blaze blinked but didn't say a word. Rylan gazed at me again. "I can make you another one."

I shook my head. I didn't want another one. I wanted that one. It was special.

"It must have been cut when that building crumbled on you." Raikidan stated. "You had a cut on your neck when I healed you."

Ryoko blinked. "You can heal?"

He nodded. "I use fire to heal. It's not guaranteed to work and can leave scars behind, like the first time I healed Eira, but now with her it works like it's supposed to."

"Because she's a fire shaman," Shva'sika informed. "Her body can accept that kind of treatment because it knows how to handle fire. You might have used too much the first time or, since she had never been healed in that way before, it could have shocked her body and it rejected the healing, like the average body would, creating the scar."

I tuned everyone out and headed for my room. I couldn't believe I was so careless tonight. I lost my necklace on the battlefield and I allowed a general to see me. Slamming the door behind me, I slid to the floor and pulled my legs up to my chest. I didn't care how bad it smelled in here, I just wanted to be left alone.

I ignored the knock on my door and didn't answer when the voice on the other side tried to speak to me. They knocked again but still I ignored them. What I wasn't able to ignore was the heavy feet on the fire escape outside. I looked up as Raikidan landed on the windowsill. He didn't enter right away, as if he wasn't sure if I'd freak out at him, but when I didn't speak he came in the rest of the way.

"You going to be all right?" he asked as he came closer. I rested my chin on my arms, dropping my gaze. "Eira, if you really want your necklace back, I can go find it for you."

I shook my head. "The place will be scoured by a military cleanup crew. It's too dangerous and my necklace isn't worth it."

He crouched down. "It's the least I can do for being a burden to you."

My head tilted to the side. "Raikidan, you're not a burden."

"I made you lie to your friends so they wouldn't know what I really was because I was so unsure of how they'd react."

I shook my head. "You didn't make me, Raikidan. You didn't utter a word about keeping your identity secret. I chose to say nothing and I chose to beat around the bush when answering certain questions because it wasn't my place to say."

He placed his hand on my head. "All right, if you say so. But I can go looking for it if it'll make you feel better."

I shook my head. "I said it's not worth it."

"Then there's another reason you're upset," he said.

I sighed and pulled my legs closer to my chest. "I screwed up. I screwed up real bad. I'm… I'm going to have to leave again."

He blinked. "What are you talking about?"

"That general leading that military assault, I knew him and he saw me." I swallowed hard. "I can't stay anymore. If they come looking for me it'll put everyone in danger. I didn't tell the others because I didn't want to upset them."

"Eira…" He rested both his hands on my shoulders. "You don't have to leave. We'll figure something out. We'll figure out how to make it so you can stay, no one will get in trouble, and you can get your revenge."

Revenge. That's why he was here. He wasn't really here to help us. He enjoyed exacting revenge, and once we got it he was gone. *Just like me.* I was gone after this—maybe even sooner. I couldn't stay here and let the others suffer for it.

Raikidan stood and headed for the window. "We'll figure something out. Now, when Ryoko knocks on the door again, you should let her in. She really wants to talk to you."

I watched him head up to the roof, and then looked at my door when someone knocked on it softly.

"Laz…" Ryoko said with a quiet voice.

I rose to my feet and opened the door. She hesitated as if unsure if I was willing to talk, but when I opened the door more she smiled and came in.

"You going to be okay?" she asked once the door shut.

"Yeah, I'll be fine."

"Rylan said he could make you another one," she said.

I shook my head. "It wouldn't be the same."

"I could give you mine," she offered. "It's not on a leather thread or anything, just in a box where I keep it safe, but I could give it to you to make into another necklace."

I shook my head again. "That's yours, Ryo. You keep it."

"But—"

"I said no, Ryoko. It's not a big deal. I just wish I had been more careful. I promised him I'd never go anywhere without it and I've already broken that promise once. It sucks to have done it again."

Ryoko blinked. "When did you do it the first time?"

"About eight years ago," I explained. "It broke while I was training and I couldn't fix it until my training was done which was three years away."

"That's a long time to wait."

I chuckled. "In the end I waited eight years because when I was finally able to fix it, the village came under attack and I had to leave. I ended up leaving without it. I felt really bad. I don't like breaking my promises."

Ryoko smiled and placed her hands on my shoulders. "Don't worry about it. I think he'd understand. And he understands now. It's not like you meant for it to break."

I sighed. She was right and Rylan hadn't been upset when we found out it was missing.

Ryoko smiled. "You look a little better now."

"I feel a little better," I admitted. I wasn't going to tell her about my other mess up. I couldn't worry her like that.

Ryoko nodded. "Good. Now I have to find Raikidan and apologize to him."

My brow rose. "For what?"

"For insulting him by saying I hated serpents that day you had him change into a replica of Argus' pet snake," she explained. "When he told me he was a dragon, I forgot to let him know I only hate snakes and not his kind."

I stared at her. "You knew?"

"Yeah," she said. "Based on how you reacted when I was hanging around with him, I figured he hadn't told you. So if he hadn't said anything, I wasn't sure if it'd be okay if I did, so I kept quiet."

"Wait, back up. If you knew, all those weird things I caught you doing with him—"

She laughed. "What, did you really think I was into him or something?"

"No—maybe—I don't know! I couldn't understand what you were doing for the life of me. Especially when the two of you were in the garage."

Ryoko giggled. "I was trying to make him shift into his dragon form."

I stared at her. "Seriously?"

"You got to see it whenever, so I wanted to." She pouted. "But he was being a butt-head about it. So I tried to make him."

I smacked myself in the forehead. "By the gods…"

She grinned wickedly. "Admit it. You thought I was trying to do dirty things with him and you didn't like that."

I rolled my eyes. "Don't even start. As a matter of fact, since you know he's a dragon, you shouldn't even have that idea in your head anymore and you should apologize for trying to push us together."

"And why would I do that?" She placed her hands on her hips. "I'm human and wogron. If that can work, why can't a human and dragon?"

"Because wogrons were once human," I reminded her. "They were human until… whatever happened to them happened. Dragons have never been human. They're not compatible with humans. I'm not even compatible with humans. I'm not compatible with anything. This crazy idea of yours that I'm going to find someone isn't going to work."

Ryoko grunted. "It will. I'll make sure of it. Even if it kills me."

I groaned. "You're going to be the death of me!"

She laughed and headed for the door. "I'll make it work and you'll thank me in the end." She winked. "And then you can share the juicy details with me." My face flushed several shades in response to the unwanted image she placed in my head and she laughed. "See. You want him. But we can discuss this later. I need to find that dragon."

"He's on the roof," I muttered.

She blinked. "So that was him I heard?" I nodded and she tilted her head. "Why was he in here?"

"He was making sure I was okay."

She smiled. "That was sweet of him."

I nodded and then smiled at her. "If you're still insistent on seeing his dragon form close up, ask him to shift as a favor to me."

She eyed me. "He'd do that?"

"I'm pretty sure he would. But probably only once."

She grinned. "See, he likes you."

I pointed to the door. "Just get out."

She laughed and opened the door. "Be that way, but I'm not giving up on you two."

I fell onto my bed once she closed the door. I sighed with content as I enjoyed the softness of my bed and pillows. The smell of the solution was present but faint enough to be tolerable. Maybe I'd get a good night sleep tonight. It'd be a first but I could dream.

CHAPTER 28

The sun was beginning to set and I had done nothing all day except worry. Raikidan told me not to and he told me I wouldn't have to leave, but as time passed I knew he was wrong. I screwed up and I wasn't going to get the others in trouble because of it.

I clenched my fists tighter. Tonight I'd leave. The longer I stayed, the easier it'd be for them to find me, and the higher the chance of the others getting dragged into the mess. I'd make a scene like last time and then escape. Raikidan would be free to live his life normally and the others would be safe.

"You don't have to leave," Seda voiced.

"Don't argue with me, Seda. This is how it has to be. I have to deal with my mistake and I'm not putting everyone in danger because of it."

"We'll figure something out. Be patient."

"I'm leaving tonight, so unless you can think of something by then I'll be gone by the morning."

I figured she had something to say but the sound of heavy boots clomping up the entryway stairs pulled our attention to that area. I almost panicked thinking they were soldiers, but I pushed the idea away. The boots weren't rushed enough to belong to them. I was getting paranoid now and that wasn't good.

Ryoko burst through the doorway and rushed to her room. Rylan was next to appear, with Argus and Blaze close behind. Raikidan, curious about the commotion, came out of my room. I watched Ryoko run out of her room and into the bathroom and then back again. Rylan then entered the bathroom, rummaged around in the closet, and was out again with a matter of seconds. What was going on?

Shva'sika glanced up from her book and watched the commotion for a moment before looking to me. I shrugged. I had never seen them act like this before. Zane finally made his way up the stairs and looked around. He was much calmer than everyone else, as if the others were overreacting about something.

I went to ask him about the situation, but Ryoko bolted out of her room and ran over to Raikidan. She grabbed him by the wrist and yanked him toward his room. "Let's go. We need to get you ready, and I'm not sure if I've bought anything for you that will work."

"What are you talking about?" Raikidan asked. "What the hell is going on?

"Yeah, Zane, why is everyone acting like headless chickens?" I asked.

Zane scratched his head. "We had an unexpected visit from the military today." I swallowed. I didn't like the sound of this. "The military is throwing a party, and as supposedly active military supporters, we are obligated to go."

I blinked. That was it? That's why everyone was freaking out?

"Okay, that doesn't sound bad," I said. "So why is everyone in a freaking frenzy?"

"The party is tonight."

"Not very kind of them to tell you so late," Shva'sika commented.

He shrugged. "We're used to it. It happens every time there's a party."

"So this party thing isn't new?" I asked.

Zane chuckled. "Not in the least. They started doing it about two years after you left us. Now it's common for the military to have two or three a year. Sometimes more."

"All right, so why is Ryoko dragging Raikidan to his room?" I asked.

He smiled. "Because the two of you are going with us."

"What?" I couldn't believe he said that. "No!"

"You two work for me from time to time," he reminded me. "That means you're obligated to go."

I folded my arms. "I don't do parties."

Ryoko stuck her head around the corner of the hall. "You're going. Now get your ass in your room and start looking at dresses to wear."

"I'm not going!"

"But it sounds like a lot of fun," Shva'sika objected. "I'd like to go if that's okay."

Zane smiled kindly. "I wouldn't say no."

Ryoko laughed. "Well since Danika is going, that means you have to go, Laz."

I snorted. "No."

"Raikidan is going to need a date."

"Shva'sika can be his date. I'm not going."

Shva'sika laughed. "I think I look a little too old to be his date."

"There, so you're going," Ryoko stated firmly.

"No!"

"Yes!" I flinched when everyone yelled. Even Seda had joined in on it. I was completely outnumbered.

"Can I have a say in this as well?" Raikidan asked, poking around the corner.

"No," Ryoko said. "Both of you are going and that's final. We don't have time to argue this."

I sighed in defeat. Seemed I was going whether I liked it or not.

Shva'sika shifted focus to Ryoko. "I don't think I have anything to wear to this party."

Ryoko nodded. "We didn't buy you anything fancy, but that's okay. I went through Raikidan's closet and I never bought him anything either so the three of us are going to have to go out and get something real quick."

"Make that four," Rylan said as he entered the room. "I ripped the sleeves off of my suit in my rush."

"I'll go get some money," Ryoko offered as she headed down the hall. "You and Raikidan can go to the tux store while Danika and I go to a dress shop for her."

Rylan nodded. "All right."

Shva'sika looked at me. "You might want to get working on picking out a dress or we'll do it for you when we get back."

I grumbled to myself and stood. I wasn't going to weasel my way out of this, so I might as well have a choice in my clothes. If I didn't, I knew I'd be even more miserable.

I sat in the car trying not to bite my lower lip and go into a panic, while Shva'sika and Ryoko chatted happily about everything and nothing as Zane drove us to our destination. The boys left earlier than us, since both Shva'sika and Ryoko felt the need to fuss over every little detail on me.

I hated the dress they made me wear. It was a shimmery ruby red, floor length, one-sleeved dress with a small slit on the right side starting at the hip, exposing too much skin in my opinion. The one I picked out wasn't good enough for them, which didn't surprise me in the least.

I hated the black stilettos they expected me to walk in. I hated all the makeup they put on me, the fake freckles they added to my face since the cover-up did too good of a job in their eyes, and I hated how tightly wrapped my hair was. I didn't like the earrings they forced me to wear, and all in all, I was uncomfortable.

Ryoko and Shva'sika, on the other hand, looked amazing. They both exuded the confidence I didn't have. Ryoko wore a nice yellow, floor length wide V-neck dress that cut down to her navel and had large cutouts on the sides from her shoulder to her hips. Shva'sika had insisted on Ryoko getting it while they were shopping for a dress.

To accompany Ryoko's dress, she wore black stilettos and changed out the two small hoop earrings in her ear for hanging crystal ones that matched the pair they had forced me to wear.

Shva'sika's dress was a shimmery dark blue, floor length one-shoulder dress with a draped shoulder scarf. The top part of the dress appeared form-fitting due to the ruching, as the girl called it. The dress then flowed freely from the hips down, splitting in the center and draping longer in the back, showing off her legs and giving her a light, airy feel when she walked.

On her feet she wore black stilettos that matched mine and Ryoko's, and she wore some gemmed rings on a few fingers. Around her neck was her favorite torc, and on her ears hung a pair of crystal earrings, also matching Ryoko's and mine. Her hair still had her typical cloth wraps and beads, but she somehow was able to pull it off.

The limousine slowed when we neared our destination. Once we were parked, Zane cut the engine and stepped out of the car. Around the same time the door nearest me opened and a tall man extended his hand to help me out. Based on Shva'sika and Ryoko's quiet giggling, I knew they had put me here on purpose.

Letting out a mental sigh, I accepted the man's offer and stepped out of the car. I took in my surroundings while I waited for Ryoko and Shva'sika to climb out of the car. The mansion this party was being hosted at was enormous and elegantly designed, with large white pillars, giant front steps, large windows, and a mahogany and gold front door. Vines grew on the walls and pillars, giving the mansion an older look.

The large yard was well landscaped and maintained. Along the outside of the circular driveway was a line of trimmed shrubbery, and in the middle of the driveway was a large fountain depicting the six peacekeepers, surrounded by more tended shrubbery and flowers.

The building hid the back yard, but I figured it looked as nice as the front. A tall black, fence with a single entry gate surrounded the entire property. It was obvious we were in Quadrant Four.

My fingers entwined with each other in front of me as I waited and fought the urge to jump back into the car and leave. My anxiety lessened once Ryoko and Shva'sika were both next to me, but it was short lived when Zane strolled over to us after handing the keys off to someone and extended his hand to Shva'sika. "Danika."

Shva'sika smiled back and accepted his gesture. "Not Elarinya?"

He chuckled and spoke low as he tucked her arm into his. "I didn't want to offend you by butchering your name."

She giggled. "It's light on the tongue like the wind. That's where most mess it up. Now try saying it."

He swallowed. "Are you sure? It's not going to sound pretty in the least."

She laughed. "I can assure you I've probably heard worse."

Zane sighed and tried. "El–r–i–ya–na."

I cringed. It wasn't the worst attempt I'd heard at least. Not even mine was much better.

Shva'sika smiled at him. "That's one of the best first tries I've heard. With a little practice you'll be great at saying it."

Zane chuckled. "I'm not sure I want to risk butchering it again."

Shva'sika tilted her head. "I think you should practice. I'd prefer hearing you calling me by my real name."

I blinked. *Is she… flirting with him?* It did appear that way, which was out of character for her. I had only seen her flirt with one other man, and that was to swindle money out of him since we ran out on a three-month journey. I was sure, at the time, it wasn't the proper shaman thing to do, but since we hadn't been traveling as shamans I hadn't minded, and it was a better, more legal, choice of action than my idea.

Zane smiled at her. "All right, if you insist."

Ryoko giggled when they were out of earshot. "They're cute together. You think something will happen between those two?"

I snorted. "Doubt it. Zane is picky. That's why he hasn't even attempted to date a woman as long as we've known him. And Shva'sika… well… let's just say in six hundred years she hasn't made a single attempt to settle down."

"So basically you're saying she's just as picky."

I nodded. "It's the only thing I can think of. She never cared to talk about it, not that I felt the need to ask."

Ryoko went to say something when Rylan showed up and offered his hand with a smile. "Ryoko."

She smiled back and accepted his gesture. "I suppose you're my date tonight."

Rylan's smile turned into a grin as he folded her arms into his. "I suppose you'd be right. You look nice by the way. Your dress really suits you."

She blushed and murmured her thanks as they walked away. My new lone status, in a place I'd rather not be at, with several pair of eyes on me everywhere now and then, sent me into a near self-conscious panic. Raikidan was supposed to be my date for this stupid thing, but it didn't look like he was going to escort me in like the others were kind enough to do for their dates. I sighed. *I guess I should go in myself before a bold soldier tries—*

Raikidan stretched out his hand to me. "Eira."

I assessed him before taking his hand. He looked good in his suit. A little uncomfortable, but good. He had gelled up his hair, offsetting the high-class look he was supposed to be achieving, but I didn't mind. I preferred it this way.

"About time you came over here," I grumbled.

He raised his eyebrow as he folded my arms into his. "You act like I was late. I wasn't going to leave you standing here alone."

"I was about to escort myself in."

His expression lowered. "Sorry. I didn't want to interrupt the conversation you and Ryoko were having."

"Rylan did."

"He left to take Ryoko before the two of you started speaking," he defended.

"And you didn't go with him why?"

"I…" He sighed. "I didn't exactly know what to do. I didn't want to make myself look like an idiot in front of you and then embarrass you."

"Raikidan, you overthink things sometimes. I wouldn't have been embarrassed. I would have preferred it over standing alone. And for the record, you could have asked the guys. They know you're pretty much clueless when it comes to stuff like this."

Raikidan grunted. "You make me sound stupid."

I laughed. "Well only someone stupid would leave a woman waiting."

"I won't do it next time," he promised.

"I hope to the gods there won't be a next time," I muttered.

"Why do you hate these things so much?" he asked.

I sighed. "I'm forced to dress in clothes I don't particularly feel comfortable in, and I have to be around tons of people. And I don't have any say in any part of the matter. I didn't even get a say in anything I'm wearing, down to the jewelry. The least the girls could do is to give me that."

"I'm sorry I didn't fight more to say no," he said quietly. "I should have realized that was the reason to your initial opposition."

I shook my head. "Don't be sorry. Nothing was going to change anyone's mind. We're stuck doing it whether we like it or not."

Raikidan was quiet for a moment while we climbed the long steps. "How come Argus kept refusing a date for this party every time Blaze offered to find him one? He even refused when Blaze's date offered to call one her friends, not that I blame him. His date looks like he picked her out at a bar."

"It's because Argus has this weird code he goes by," I explained. "He won't take a woman to a social event unless he's interested in her, and since the person he's interested in is babysitting a seven-hundred-plus-year-old child, he's here alone."

Raikidan blinked. "Seda? You can't be serious."

I laughed. "Quite serious actually."

"Even when she acted all detached and inhuman?" he asked.

I nodded. "Yep. I can only guess he had inklings from the start that it was a façade."

"Then why doesn't he do something about it?" Raikidan asked.

"Because of what his last girlfriend did," I said. "He was with her for at least a decade and then she tore him apart. He's not ready to take the new risk yet."

"Do you think Seda knows?" he asked. "With her being what she is and all."

I smiled. He knew not to say what she was with all these soldiers around. At least I knew I could trust him not to blow our cover any time soon. "I don't doubt she knows. Or she at least has some speculations."

"You know something," he observed as he led me through the large front doors.

I laughed. "I know many things."

"Spill it. What are you hiding?"

"Some things are meant to be a secret."

He let out an exasperated sigh. "Eira."

I laughed. "All right, all right. Let's just say his feelings aren't one-sided."

Raikidan blinked. "Seriously?"

"I have no reason to lie."

"About time you two came inside!" Ryoko yelled at us as we approached, shutting down our conversation.

I snorted. "Raikidan was being slow, like always."

"Me?" Raikidan half laughed. "You're the one wearing shoes you can barely stand in."

I wanted to laugh. He was right. We had taken forever to get up the stairs because I was so unstable in my shoes, but he was the reason it took forever to get to the stairs in the first place. "Hey, I didn't pick out the shoes. I was forced to wear them."

"Whatever you say, Butterfly."

I focused on Argus, noticing something odd about his behavior. "Argus, you okay? You look tense already and this party has barely started."

"I've been listening to what these soldiers have been conversing about," he said. "It's all been the same topic. It's been about a violet-haired woman whose innocent civilian identity is now in question."

I gulped. It would be my luck that the others would find out about what happened. Everyone looked at me. They weren't stupid.

"Why didn't you tell us?" Ryoko asked.

I sighed and dropped my gaze. "I didn't want to worry you."

"Please don't leave us again," she begged. I did my best not to react. She knew me all too well.

"She won't have to," Raikidan said. "We're going to fix it."

My gaze flicked to him from the corner of my eye. He knew something. I couldn't say how I knew, but I had this weird feeling that he was hiding something.

"Well it's good to see that you actually chose to show up, Zane." I wanted to shoot myself at the sound of Zo's voice.

Zane chuckled and shook Zo's hand. "We've never missed one of these parties yet, we're not about to know. Though, a little more notice next time would be great."

"Yeah," Ryoko muttered. "Four hours to get ready was not enough time."

I snorted. "Not like you needed those four hours. You spent two on me alone, which was completely uncalled for."

Ryoko wagged her finger at me. "Perfection takes time."

"Then what about you? You took all of five minutes to get ready."

"Years of practice," Ryoko justified. "You on the other hand, don't have that and need help. A lot of help."

Raikidan snorted. "Someone needs to get a reality check."

I laughed, although Ryoko, on the other hand, didn't find his statement as funny.

Zo chuckled. "Well at least I know you're all enjoying yourselves already. Now, Zane, if I may ask, who is your beautiful date?"

Zane hesitantly glanced to Shva'sika, unsure if he should attempt her elven name again. With a smile, Shva'sika extended her hand in greeting. "Elarinya Lightshine. It's a pleasure to meet you."

Zo took her hand and planted a small kiss on it as if he were some sort of gentleman. "General Zo, and the pleasure is all mine. It's an honor to meet an elf of such status."

Shva'sika smiled kindly at him. "A rare find you are, General. Not many know my family name anymore."

"I've done a lot of traveling in my time," he admitted. "Though I must say, none have come close to comparing to your beauty."

I wanted to wretch, and one look at Ryoko told me I wasn't the only one. I couldn't see how Shva'sika could stand it. She showed no signs of disgust at all as she spoke with Zo.

I looked around when the music softened suddenly and the lights dimmed. Several groups of couple moved onto the floor and began dancing.

"Shall we?" Zane asked Shva'sika.

She smiled. "I'd love to."

I watched the two walk off. I had to resist the urge to laugh. Zane's shiny bald head reflected the dim lights, making him a tiny beacon. Ryoko, on the other hand, was more inclined to giggle.

Blaze was next to take his date away and then Rylan stole Ryoko away leaving Raikidan, Argus, Zo, and me. I observed the three couples float across the floor. It was interesting to watch. I had never really learned to dance even though it had been a requirement in the military. I thought it was stupid and no one wanted to dance with a monster like me so I didn't see the point in learning.

I blinked when Zo offered me his hand. "I would be honored if you'd dance with me, Eira."

"I… I um… uh…" I couldn't think of anything that would be good enough to say no. "I don't think that's a good idea, Zo. I have two left feet."

Zo chuckled and kept his hand outstretched. "It's easy, I promise."

I let out a quiet breath and reluctantly took his hand. Apparently the lack of dance ability wasn't a good enough no. I tossed a glance back at the two men as Zo led me away. Raikidan looked at a loss and I didn't blame him. Like me, he had no idea how to dance so how was he supposed to help? My only hope was Argus. I gave him my best pleading eyes but he only returned my plea with an apologetic look. He wasn't going to help me. He was going to stick to his stupid code and I was going to suffer.

Zo pulled me closer to him and placed my hands in the correct spots. I prayed to the goddess, as he placed his hands on me, he would keep them in the appropriate places. I knew I'd end up slapping him if he didn't behave.

He pulled me along as we began to dance. I stumbled several times and became more and more uncomfortable by the minute. Not only was I being forced to dance with a man I hated, I had to endure overhearing what the soldiers were saying about me. I listened as they compared me to rebel me.

"Relax, Sweetcheeks," Zo said. "Follow my lead and you'll be fine."

"I'm trying," I said. "I'm just… not good at this. Sorry."

He chuckled. "Why are you sorry? There's no shame in not knowing how to dance."

I gazed at him through my lashes. "I'm making you look like a fool."

Zo laughed. "Trust me, hon, you're not making me look like a fool. My company can and does, but you, you make me look good."

I wanted to gag. He was gloating about something that didn't exist. Instead I half smiled.

Zo frowned. "Something is bothering you."

"Bothering me?" I blinked. "Nothing is bothering me."

"You don't seem happy like you usually are."

I'm never happy, you oaf. "It's nothing really."

"Eira, why don't you tell me?" he asked. "I hate to see you so upset."

Why did he sound so concerned? It was creepy. I sighed. "I'm not good with crowds in small places."

Zo eyed me skeptically. "That's not what's bothering you."

I wanted to smack him. He couldn't get the hint I didn't want to talk about it. "It's just the things the others here are saying. They're talking about me. They're comparing me to someone and it doesn't sound good."

Zo smiled at me. "Don't listen to them. They're wrong."

Was Zo really that dumb? "Who are they comparing me to?"

"A rebel who was spotted last night."

"Why are they comparing me to her?" I asked. "What did I do?"

Zo sighed. "They think you look like her."

I furrowed my brow. "That's it? That's their reason? They're comparing me to a trouble maker because we look similar?"

His lips twisted. "You also share her name."

Shit. I knew I should have come up with a fake name. I looked down at the floor. "My parents named me because of the time I was born. We had seen peace in the village for so many years they wanted my name to reflect that. I never thought anyone else shared my name…"

"Don't listen to them," he said. "You're nothing like this rebel. She's cold and heartless, which I know you're not. And the name thing can be a coincidence. It's a beautiful name and it suits you. Not to mention you admitted you dye your hair and Azriel vouched for it. You have nothing to worry about."

I nodded. He really was dumb, but I wasn't about to complain. The more people I could convince I was a civilian trying to get by in life, the better.

"Besides, she doesn't wear leather and ride motorcycles."

Oh man… I was hoping he hadn't seen me that day. "I don't know what you're talking about, Zo."

"Oh don't be like that, Eira," he teased. "I saw you on the back of that bike with your friend. You seemed to be enjoying yourself."

I forced heat into my cheeks. "D—don't tell anyone okay? I don't like a lot of people knowing."

"Guilty pleasure?" he guessed.

I nodded. "It's not the bike part. I drive that all the time."

He chuckled. "I get it. It's the leather. But if I'm allowed to say, you looked good."

I forced myself to blush more, instead of gagging, and averted my gaze. I didn't need any images of him fanaticizing about me running through my head.

"So, tell me about your elven friend," Zo said, changing the topic.

"What about her?"

"How did Zane end up with her as his date?" he clarified. "How do you know her?"

"Oh, that's easy." I smiled. "Elarinya is a longtime friend of mine."

Zo blinked. "I'm a little confused."

I laughed. "It's all right. I confused everyone else too when she showed up. Elarinya, Rai, and I lived in the same village. She's an old friend of my family's; though acts more like my older sister."

"So you remembered her after you lost your memory?" he questioned.

I shook my head. "It took me three weeks to remember her."

"I see," he mused. "What is she doing here now?"

"She's living with us now," I explained. "I bought a messenger hawk from a traveling caravan a few weeks ago and sent her a message about my progress. She was so excited and missed me so much she gained citizenship and now lives with us at the house."

"Your family is very lucky to be so close with a member of the Lightshine family," Zo commented.

I shrugged. "We've never seen it as anything special. I've always seen it as a normal thing."

"Practice in humility." Zo smiled. "An excellent trait to have. A trait the rebel you are being compared to doesn't share."

I wanted to sigh and leave. Zo was so stupid and I hated him insulting the real me. What he was saying about me may be true, but it still hurt. I hated who I was and his words only made it worse.

I gulp when Zo pulled me closer and lowered his hand closer to my ass. I pulled his hand back up to my lower back. "Please don't do that, Zo."

He chuckled and tried to move his hand again. "I'm not going to hurt you."

I let out a tight breath and forced his hand back to my lower back. "I'm being serious, Zo, stop. It makes me uncomfortable."

"All right, all right, s—"

"May I cut in?" Raikidan's voice asked out of nowhere. The two of us turned to find him holding out his hand and waiting patiently.

Zo nodded. "I guess I don't have much of a choice. She is your date after all."

Zo moved away from me, much to my relief, and allowed Raikidan to take me by the hand. Zo retreated a little ways off but didn't disappear into the crowd of party attendees. He stayed near the dance floor and watched.

Raikidan put his arms around me and pulled me along the dance floor. I exhaled slowly. "Thank you for saving me from him, but can we not dance?"

Raikidan chuckled. "I'd like to have my turn with you now. Besides, it's the least I could do for being late and letting him take you. I shouldn't have done that."

I shrugged. "You didn't know how to dance."

He hesitated. "It wasn't just that. I didn't want to make you look like a fool for choosing me as a date for this thing, and I can't even dance."

I laughed. "What are you doing now?"

He smirked. "I had time to watch Rylan and Ryoko."

"Is that why you finally came to save me?" I asked.

Raikidan thought for a moment. "Partially. I also didn't like how grabby Zo was getting. It was… disrespectful."

I fought a real blush that tried to surface. He was sounding so protective of me, which normally I hated, but the way he said it, it was nice.

Raikidan spun me around, surprising me, and pulled me along on the dance floor. I had no idea where he learned all of this. Rylan couldn't have done these moves with Ryoko, could he? He did like to show off for her sometimes, even if they were subtle most of the time. Where had he learned to cut in properly for that matter?

Raikidan spun me out to arms' length and then spun me back to him. "You have something on your mind."

"Trying to figure out how you knew how to cut in on my and Zo's tortuous dance correctly, and not all caveman style," I admitted.

Raikidan chuckled. "A brave male tried to cut in on Rylan and Ryoko but Ryoko refused and insisted on dancing with Rylan only."

I smirked. "Rylan must have loved that."

"He didn't complain, that's for sure," Raikidan said with a grin. "And may I say, Zo is a horrible dancer and leader."

My brow rose. "What?"

"You tripped at least half a dozen times with him, but here you are with me, not tripping."

I blinked. He was right. I hadn't tripped once since Raikidan took me as his partner. "I suppose you're a better leader than I thought. Thank you, for not making me look like a fool."

Raikidan pulled me close and dipped me with a grin. "You're welcome."

Startled, I wrapped my arms around him. "Don't do that!"

He chuckled. "I'm not going to drop you."

"I don't care."

He sighed and pulled back up. I went to hang my hands over his shoulders when Ryoko's shouting caught my attention. Raikidan and I looked at each other and then Ryoko. She had a communicator held up to her ear and she was speaking frantically with someone. Raikidan and I rushed over to her to find out what was going on. Zane, Shva'sika, Argus, Blaze and his date also rushed over.

"Ryoko, what's going on?" I demanded.

"Hold on," she told the person on the other end of the communicator. "Seda says the military is raiding the house!"

My heart sank.

"What the fuck?" Zane shouted. "Why the hell would they do that?"

My eyes bulged. It wasn't often Zane swore so freely.

Zo strolled over to us. "What seems to be the problem?"

"The problem? I think you know the problem, Zo!" Zane shouted. "What right does the military have to raid our house? What have we done?"

Zo blinked. "I have no idea what you're talking about."

"My babysitter is on the line," Ryoko barked. "My daughter is freaking out and there are soldiers all over our house destroying our belongings! Don't you dare tell me you have no idea what is going on."

I was taken aback by the amount of anger rolling off Ryoko. This was not good.

"I honestly don't know what's going on," Zo insisted.

"That's because not everyone was let in on it," a soldier stated as he approached. From the way he held himself, he was a high-ranking officer, but since he wasn't wearing a uniform, I wasn't sure how high of a rank.

Zane narrowed his eyes. "I demanded to know what's going on."

The officer pointed a firm finger at me. "She's the reason."

I flinched and shrunk back. This was bad. Raikidan stepped in front of me, creating a shield.

"What proof do you have to justify it?" Argus snapped. "All I've been hearing all night long is how Eira resembles some low-life rebel. There's no proof she is, just speculation, and it's solely based on how she looks. That doesn't justify a raid!"

The officer snorted. "I received a status report showing they couldn't find any identification cards. Not on any of you. That's suspicious in its own right."

Zane growled. "I lock those away so they don't go missing."

"It doesn't change the fact that you are possibly harboring a criminal," the officer said.

"But we also don't have enough proof showing that she is one," a soldier said.

The officer glared at the soldier in attempt to silence him, but he didn't back down, and other soldiers backed him up on his claim. Then the shouting began. People were pointing fingers, shouting and fighting. I hated this—hated knowing I was the cause. *This is my fault... I should have just left...*

The room was completely divided. There were those who were opposed to what the military was doing, those who thought the military was in the right, and then the rest who were trying to stay out of it. When the fighting escalated, I left. I couldn't deal with it. I pushed past anyone who was in my way and headed for the balcony.

"Eira?" Raikidan called. "Eira!"

I didn't stop. Not when I stumbled and not even to find out who Raikidan had punched. I didn't stop until I was outside. I leaned against the railing of the balcony and held my arms close. What had I done? This was all happening because of me. If I hadn't been so stupid I wouldn't have put everyone in this situation. *I've risked everything...*

"Eira?" Raikidan asked as he walked out onto the balcony. I didn't answer him. He approached and leaned against the railing. "Eira, talk to me."

I looked away from him. "Just go away."

"No. I'm not going anywhere." I continued to look the other way. "Eira, please."

Raikidan tried to place his hand on my shoulder but I shrugged it off. "Don't touch me."

He let out a tight exhale and pulled me into his arms. I sighed and didn't fight him. There was no point. "It's going to be okay."

"No, it's not. Look at what I've done. I'm a horrible person. The others don't deserve this."

"Eira, stop," he growled. "You're not a horrible person. This is going to get fixed."

I shook my head. "It's not, and I'm going to have to leave again."

Raikidan's grip tightened. "You're not going anywhere. You hear me?"

He's wrong. I pulled away from him, but as I was about an arm's length away Raikidan pulled me back. I yelped when I fell a little farther than I expected and then blinked with surprise when something beneath me cracked. I glanced up at Raikidan, who looked as confused as me. When I realized my feet felt different from each other, I peered down at them and half-laughed at what I saw. When Raikidan noticed what I was looking at, he let me stand on my feet.

I took off my left shoe and held it up. The tiny heel had snapped and hung loosely from the bottom of the shoes. Raikidan began to laugh.

"You broke my shoe!"

"Not like you mind," he said through his laughter.

I joined him. He was right and I was glad I didn't have to wear them now. Once I had my laughter under control, I took off the other shoe and tossed them both somewhere. I leaned back on the railing and gazed out at the city.

Raikidan sidled closer to me and copied how I stood. "Feel better?"

I shook my head. "No."

He sighed and touched my chin with his finger, forcing me to look at him. "It's going to be okay. Believe me when I promise you this."

I pulled away. "Even if it does miraculously work out, what these soldiers have said… really hurt."

"Eira, they don't know what they're talking about. They don't know you." He forced me to look at him again. "They don't know you like I do."

I blinked as my cheeks warm a little. I didn't know what to say. Then I did something I didn't expect. I smiled. "You're right, they don't."

Raikidan grinned and let go of my chin. He looked out at the city. "So your name means peace, huh? Didn't know humans put meanings behind their names."

I nodded. "Most have some sort of meaning, but I don't deserve mine."

"Why do you say that?" he asked, setting his eyes on me again.

I gave him a pointed look. "When have I brought peace to anyone?"

He smiled. "You've brought it to your friends, for one. And, I can't believe I'm going to tell you this, but you've brought it to me, too, and I'm glad for it."

I looked at him funny. What did I do to bring peace to his life? Certainly not enter it. I never made anyone happy or peaceful. *He's just trying to make me feel better.* With a shake of my head I gazed back out at the city.

"Eira, I'm being serious."

"Raikidan, I don't bring peace to—what is that?"

Raikidan peered at the billowing black smoke I pointed at. It appeared far off, like it was coming from Sector One. Or somewhere close to it.

Raikidan furrowed his brow. "What in Lumaraeon?"

"Either that's a really bad fire or something is going on."

"Stay here." Raikidan dashed off before I could say anything.

I watched him speak urgently with some soldiers who took one look at the smoke and ran off into the mansion. The sounds of soldiers shouting below me caught my attention. Soldiers, now in full uniform, rushed down the driveway and into the city. Only time would tell what was going on.

Raikidan returned and stood by my side. He looked at me for a few minutes and then shifted his focus out at the city.

"What?" I asked him.

He shrugged. "Nothing."

I grunted and let my gaze wander. The sky was uneventful. The light and air pollution blocked out most of the stars. "You haven't tried to compliment me on how I look tonight."

Raikidan's eyebrow cocked. "Uh, is that a problem?"

I shrugged. "No, just an observation that's all. I know I don't look all that great."

"Eira, don't say that," he said. "You look great."

I eyed him. "Then why haven't you insisted on complimenting me? I've become accustomed to you trying it at least once and since you're stubborn, I never imagined you'd give up trying so soon."

He gazed down at his hands, his jaw working back and forth. "Honestly, I was going to but I couldn't find the right words. The ones I thought of either sounded like something Blaze would say or couldn't justify how you really looked."

"So, you're being picky," I teased.

He scratched his head. "I guess so. I'm trying to figure out the most appropriate human way of explaining it."

I leaned one arm on the balcony, facing him to give my full attention. "Then why not describe it in a way that would work best for you and not me or another human?"

Raikidan chewed his lower lip, my eyes briefly drawn to the action. "You… look like a gem."

I fought furiously to stop the flush threatening to burst onto my face and tried to keep the burning of my ears down. I knew what that type of compliment meant for him. Dragons thought of treasure for their hoards. They thought of gems and other priceless object to own and being compared to a gem had to be one of the better compliments he could have thought to give me, not that I deserved it.

Afraid I wouldn't be able to hide my embarrassment, I went to look away but Raikidan grabbed my chin with his fingers and made me look at him again. "The only thing that has to be done with you is to polish that makeup off. You'd feel more comfortable and be able to express the real you. Then you'd be a perfect gem."

I couldn't hold back my embarrassment anymore. His gaze and the conviction in his voice made it too difficult. Raikidan's thumb caressed my cheek, setting my body's temperature ablaze and my heart racing, but I didn't stop him. I had no willpower to do so, as if I was being hypnotized or compelled by some unknown force.

I snapped out of my daze when a masculine voice cleared his throat. I looked to see Zo and the officer who had accused me of being a rebel standing near us.

"What do you want?" Raikidan growled.

"To apologize," Zo said. "That smoke you two saw was from a rebel group who chose to destroy a small military compound. The woman Eira was accused of being was with them."

I blinked. How was that possible? This couldn't be right.

Zo nudged the other officer. "Don't you have something to say?"

The officer swallowed as if he were swallowing his pride. "Miss, I owe you an apology. I was quick to accuse you of something without proof. I'm sorry I've caused you so much grief this evening."

I stuck up my nose and turned away. I was not going to accept it.

Raikidan chuckled. "Eira holds grudges and they don't end within a few days."

"You sound like you've been on the receiving end," Zo commented.

Raikidan grunted. "She didn't talk to me for five months."

"You deserved it," I mumbled.

He snorted. "Hardly."

The officer cleared his throat. "Well if you two would excuse us, we have work to do, thanks to those rebels."

Zo and the officer excused themselves. My shoulders slumped, my built up stress leaving me all at once. I was off the hook. I didn't have to leave, and I could finish what we started.

Raikidan chuckled low. "You're welcome."

My brow knitted. "Raikidan, what did you do? What's going on?"

He edged closer to me. "Seda and I created a fake you to throw the military off. It just took longer to implement since they raided the house."

I blinked in disbelief. They had done that for me? They went through all that trouble to get me to stay?

"You're welcome, Laz," Seda quickly messaged.

Without any thought, I wrapped my arms around Raikidan's neck and gave him a tight hug. Raikidan tensed, taken aback by the sudden gesture, but soon relaxed and squeezed me back.

"You're welcome, Eira," he whispered.

"Hey, guys, don't mean to interrupt your hug-fest, but we gotta go!" Ryoko yelled to us as she ran out onto the balcony. "Zane got back with the car and he says we really have to see the damage."

I let out a heavy breath and pulled away from Raikidan. I was not looking forward to this.

Raikidan folded my arms into his. "It's going to be all right. We'll get everything fixed."

I pressed my lips together. "I hope so."

Raikidan guided me back into the mansion and then down the front steps to the car where everyone was waiting for us. Blaze was now dateless, and I could only assume the woman ran off with someone else during all the commotion.

"I can't believe you broke those designer shoes," Ryoko grumble.

I snorted. "Designer my ass. They were uncomfortable and not made to be walked in."

Ryoko sighed in aggravation and got into the car. I followed close behind her and Shva'sika was in next after me. The boys climbed in after us and before they were seated Zane was driving off. Raikidan and Rylan were the unfortunate two who were still standing up, and Ryoko and I were the two unfortunate victims to be fallen onto.

Raikidan gazed up at me as he partially lay across the floor and partially across my lap. "Sorry."

"It's fine," I replied tersely.

"Crazy driver," Rylan muttered. "Sorry about this, Ryoko."

She laughed. "Not your fault."

The two tried to get up and sit down in an actual seat, but the limousine hit a bump and the two fell back on our laps. They attempted again, but Zane took a sharp turn and they fell once more, only this time Raikidan took me with him when he fell on the floor. Blaze, Argus, and Shva'sika found great amusement in this, and weren't afraid to laugh the whole time it was happening.

I'd barely managed to climb back up on the seat before having to hold onto the back of it when Zane took another sharp turn. "Zane, slow it down! Stupid old man." When Zane didn't listen, I pounded on the window blocking us from him. When he didn't listen to that, I smashed it with the flat side of my fist. "Zane, slow the fuck down before I wring your neck!"

"I'm trying to get home," he defended.

"I don't care!" I bellowed. "You're driving like a crazy old lady. Now slow it down or you're going six feet under."

He sighed and took his foot off the accelerator.

Argus snickered. "Whoever said violence wasn't the answer never met Eira."

Everyone laughed. Even Zane and I were laughing. It was a good thing. It was lifting up our spirits and we were going to need it to deal with the problem to come.

CHAPTER 29

I woke to the early morning sun peering through the skylight, much to my displeasure. After we had gotten home a few nights ago and assessed the insane amount of damage the military had caused to the house, Genesis had sent me out on an assignment, which turned into three more, and five more after that. I was lucky to get a quick nap between requests.

I had initially taken the first one since she had told me to. Then I took the next few assignments in hopes it would make me feel better, but then it got out of hand after that.

Raikidan and Seda's effort to keep me here was well-planned and thought out, and it worked like a charm, putting me in a better mood and all, but with the ridiculous number of assignments Genesis had insisted on piling on me, accompanied by my missing necklace with broken promise, and previously torn-apart house, their gesture had become insignificant.

I snuggled deeper into my new soft pillows. Thanks to Shva'sika, most of the damage done to the house had become a non-issue. I didn't know she was so well connected until she explained it to us. Apparently, she came from a wealthy working-class family who made the best hand-carved products in all of Lumaraeon, and many of them were also highly sought-out contractors.

She'd never told me her family had come from the North, or that she had actually been born there when her father and mother had been visiting family. It didn't bother me, though, because I was so grateful she was willing to speak to her family about the matter. I had gotten a new bed out of it, as well as an exceptionally well-crafted dresser and nightstand, and an enormous walk-in closet. I wasn't the only one who had received this treatment, but because I had been gone so often on assignments, I never found out what everyone else had received.

My stomach growled and I sighed. Apparently I wasn't getting my way this morning. Sitting up, I threw my hair up into my hairclip and headed for the door.

"Well good morning, sleepyhead," Shva'sika greeted as I entered the living room. "Tea?"

"Let me just grab some breakfast," I said as I entered the newly renovated kitchen.

After preparing a bowl of cereal for myself, I sat down on the couch next to her and accepted the cup of tea. The sweetness of the honey and pomegranate tantalized my taste buds eliciting a pleased hum from my lips. "Where are the others?"

She shrugged. "I believe Ryoko is still sleeping, and Rylan and Raikidan might be downstairs. The rest, I'm not sure."

"Figures Ryoko would be asleep. I am surprised however, that Rylan and Raikidan are working together."

"Ever since you left for those endless string of missions, Raikidan sat around doing nothing, unsure of what to do with his free time," Shva'sika explained. "So Rylan figured he'd teach Raikidan a few tricks to using the guns and from then on they've been doing all sorts of things down there."

I almost choked on the tea. "You make it sound like they've progressed their relationship beyond friends."

Shva'sika laughed. "Well from some of their sparring matches it would make you wonder."

We were both laughing now.

"What's so funny?" Ryoko was now in the room, rubbing her groggy eyes.

"Well good morning to you too, bright-eyes." Shva'sika smiled and held up her cup. "Tea?"

Ryoko shook her head and shuffled her way to the kitchen. "Coffee…"

I snickered. Ryoko could not function well in the morning without her cup of coffee. My attention was brought to the basement door by the sound of footsteps. Rylan and Raikidan came through the door, shirtless and sweaty.

"Looks like you two had fun," I remarked as I took a sip of tea, although I wish I hadn't. Shva'sika giggled, causing me to choke. I glared at her. She looked at me apologetically but couldn't control her giggles, which then sent me into a giggling fit, too.

Confused, Rylan and Raikidan exchanged glances, which made us go from giggling to full out laughing. We were horrible people.

Someone behind us cleared their throat, causing us to calm down rather fast. Turning, I almost dropped my cup of tea when I saw the young man behind us.

"Laz, who's this?" Shva'sika asked. "A friend of yours?"

"Ryder…" I whispered.

"What are you talking about, Laz?" Ryoko questioned. "Ryder is like ten-years-old, or at least, looks that young. This guy is definitely not that young."

"Hey, Mom," Ryder greeted, proving Ryoko wrong.

I rose to my feet slowly, taking in his appearance. I guessed him to be around seventeen, with white hair, an athletic build, and unique blue-green heterochromic eyes with rings around the pupil. *It's definitely him.*

"What are you doing here?" I asked.

He crossed his arms. "Jeez, don't sound so unhappy to see me." I gave him a long, stern look and he laughed. "Chill, I'm teasing. I came to see you. I figured you needed to see what the scientists figured out. And I also have a favor to ask of you."

"Do you realize how bad of an idea this is?" It sounded a little harsh, but I didn't want him hurt, or worse.

"Calm down, Mom. No one is going to find out about this. Now can I be welcomed in?"

I rolled my eyes and waved him in. "Forgive me for being concerned for your wellbeing. Not get your ass over here."

He smiled and joined me on the couch. He embraced me in a tight hug. "I missed you."

"I missed you too," I murmured. I was the first to pull away, but one of my arms remained around him, encouraging him to sit. "Now you said you had something to share?"

Ryder rolled up his pant leg and removed a long, plastic canister strapped to his leg. He handed it to me. "They figured out the problem." I opened the canister and slid out the rolled paper. Unrolling it, I inspected the symbols scribbled everywhere. "This is only a copy, and it wasn't easy for the scientists to smuggle it out."

"You know I can't read," I said.

"It's the code to enable the aging process in experiments like me. I'm the first they tested it on, and in a week my body aged seven years. Auron says they'll put me under another test to bring me up to a more appropriate-looking age, but they want to wait a little so my body isn't put under too much stress.

"I remembered you saying someone else was like me in that sense so I figured this may be of some use. I know you guys don't have the high tech equipment the scientists used with me, but you're all smart enough to figure out how to use it without them."

"Thank you, Ryder. This will be a lot of help."

He smiled. "Good. Now I was wondering if I could borrow the dagger I made you. I promise I won't have it long."

"Um, sure." I went to reach for it but realized they weren't there. None of my daggers were. I shot a questioning glance at Raikidan.

"On your dresser," he stated, tossing his head in the direction of my room.

I entered my room and grabbed the dagger from the dresser. Remembering I still needed materials to make the gift I promised Shva'sika, I rummaged through a drawer for a pencil and paper and scribbled down a checklist. When I came out, Ryder was waiting near the doorway and he took the items gratefully when I handed them over. "If you could, I need these supplies for something. If it's too much to ask for don't worry about it."

He smiled at me. "I'll get them for you. Nothing is too much for you. And I promise you won't regret giving me your dagger. But I should get going before someone gets suspicious."

"Be careful," I said, wrapping my arms around his neck for a hug. He was tall like Rylan and I hoped he wouldn't get any taller. "Go to the shop before you head back. That way it looks like you were look-ing for Zane."

He pulled away. "I will."

I wished he could stay here but I knew it was best that he didn't. Ryder nodded respectfully at Rylan and Raikidan, who returned the gesture, and then he left. Jumping over the back of the couch, I sat down.

"When are you both going to tell him?" Ryoko asked when the front door shut.

"When he asks," I said.

I picked up the paper Ryder had given us and slipped it back in the canister. *Genesis will want this.* I watched Rylan silently walk to his room. Even though he didn't show it, I knew how he felt about my answer. I had to believe my decision was best, even if Rylan hadn't agreed to it.

Ryoko leaned over the bar and watched as well, but obviously for a different reason. I looked at Shva'sika the two of us started giggling.

"Shut up," Ryoko muttered, going back to her coffee.

I tossed her the canister. "Give this to Genesis. If anyone can figure out that gibberish, she can."

"And then meet us in my room," Shva'sika put in, pulling me off the couch.

"Why?" Ryoko and I asked in unison.

Shva'sika laughed. "I want to talk to you two about something."

"Um, okay." Ryoko watched Shva'sika pull me into her room before she headed to see Genesis.

Shva'sika left me standing in the middle of her room as she went about her business of looking for something. I peered around to pass the time. Her room was decorated in a way that made it look like it had been plucked right from her house at the village. I wondered if she bought all this stuff or if she had snuck back to the village using a portal to grab it. I was about to ask her when Ryoko opened the door and joined me.

Once Shva'sika noticed Ryoko had joined us, she grabbed three towels from a shelf and pushed us toward a wooden door that never existed before Shva'sika moved in. Entering the room on the other side, she closed us in. Ryoko and I gazed around. We were in a bathing room. Much like the baths at the inn at the shaman village, this one had vine-covered stone walls, floors made of natural soil with beautiful plants growing from it, and a cobblestone path leading to a stone bathing pool and a stone sink with mirrors wrapped in what appeared to be roots. There was even an artificial light source that mimicked the sun during the day and moon at night. The only difference between the inn room and this one, this one was far larger.

The air was warm and steam rose from the hot bath water.

"Wow, this is cool," Ryoko whispered.

Shva'sika gestured for us to follow as she made her way to the largest pool. Stripping down, she entered the water. I did the same without hesitation, but Ryoko was a little more reluctant.

I rolled my eyes. "C'mon, Ryoko. There's no need to be self-conscious around us."

Hesitantly she undressed. She relaxed once she sank into the water.

"So why are we here exactly?" I asked.

"Well, since you all, mainly you, Laz, have been busy almost killing yourselves with few breaks between, I thought maybe the five of us could head out of the city for a little while to get away from all the stress. It would also help keep you all under the radar."

"Five?" Ryoko asked.

"The three of us and Raikidan and Rylan," Shva'sika clarified.

I thought this over. "I'm not so sure. While I'd love to take a break, we really need to focus on the rebellion. We're not at a point where we need to keep low yet, and if we take a break we won't be able to push our position as fast. We may even lose it. Each member of our resistance is important for our success."

Shva'sika sighed. "You need to relax. You could have killed yourself on those assignments and you need a break. You're the one I was thinking of most when coming up with this idea."

Ryoko nodded. "Yeah. We don't need to lose you, Laz. Take a small break. It won't hurt."

I exhaled through pursed lips. "All right, all right, we'll go on a small vacation. How do you propose we leave? Soldiers don't exactly let people out all willy-nilly."

"They let shamans out," Shva'sika reminded me.

I grinned. *Clever.*

"So you want us to pose as shamans who wish to leave?" Ryoko asked, mirroring my thoughts.

Shva'sika nodded. "Exactly. They can't look at our faces or stop us, so as long as only Laz, Raikidan or I speak it should be fairly easy to leave."

"I like the idea." I sank deeper into the water. I could use the break. "When do you plan for this to happen?"

"I was thinking tomorrow."

"That doesn't give us much time," I said. "But I think it's doable, that is, if you figure out how to design Ryoko and Rylan some clothes and, after this is all done, make Ryoko and me a baths similar to this one for our rooms."

"Deal," Shva'sika agreed.

"Leave the boys out of the loop?" Ryoko asked with a grin.

Shva'sika and I grinned and nodded. It would make this a little bit more fun.

"I will let Zane in on this though. He'll need the boys until late afternoon anyway so we can prepare tonight and tomorrow without them knowing," Ryoko explained. "Rylan will not be so enthusiastic about this surprise so it might be a battle to get him to switch clothes."

I laughed. "If I know Shva'sika as well as I think I do, that won't be much of a problem. She can push anyone into doing what she wants."

"Except you," Shva'sika commented.

Ryoko laughed. "You can if you corner her."

The two laughed some more and eventually I joined in. I didn't care if they were picking on me. It was all in good fun and quite true. I was stubborn and fought if there was even a glimmer of hope of winning.

I stuffed another empty jar into my bag. Since we'd be out of the city I wanted to stock up on herbs and other supplies that were hard to obtain here.

Ryoko came into my room after knocking on the doorframe. "You all set?"

I glanced up when I placed the last jar in the bag. "Yep, you?"

She nodded. "I have everything I need. Danika finished my outfit a few hours ago and is now finishing up Rylan's. If I may say, if your outfit looks anything like mine, then I'm surprised you wear them."

I laughed. "I don't enjoy wearing them, if that's what you're trying to ask."

She grunted. "I figured as much. I'm not too thrilled with mine either."

"What kind of bottoms did she make for you?"

Ryoko thought for a moment. "I think it was a short skirt that tied off on one side showing off my thigh."

I grunted and headed for my closet. "Consider yourself lucky."

"Care to elaborate?"

I pulled out the thong I was supposed to wear and showed her. "I'd rather have the skirt." Ryoko placed her hand over her mouth to stop herself from laughing. It didn't work. "Yep, keep laughing."

She shook her head and tried to stop. "I'm… sorry. It's just… I could never see you wearing that."

"Join the club," I muttered. "I didn't have much of a choice. It was this or go with nothing at all."

Ryoko's brow rose. "Seriously?"

I laughed. "No. Shva'sika isn't that cruel. She just bullied me into it."

Ryoko shook her head and giggled. "I can't see anyone bullying you into doing anything." I gave her a long, stern look and she laughed. "All right, all right, with the right number of people, sure, but only one person? That's a long shot."

I chuckled. "You've never seen Shva'sika's demanding side."

"Fair enough, but are you seriously going to wear that thing? It looks like something you'd wear to bed or use to seduce a guy, which, as much as I wish it were different, I doubt you have any plans to do in the future."

I laughed. "Well I have nothing else to wear with the top. I might have to wear it."

"Why not use the armor clothes? For the pants at least. That should work out for you a little better."

I blinked and then grinned. "Ryoko, you're a genius. Shva'sika is going to kill me when she finds out but it'll be worth it."

Ryoko's ear twitched. "Sounds like the boys are coming."

I checked the clock. "They're early. I wonder what's up."

"Not sure," Ryoko mumbled. "But I'd better check with Danika to see if Rylan's outfit is ready."

I nodded. "Good idea. It's going to be a fight to get him to agree to do this, let alone get him into the clothes."

"I don't think the clothes for guys are that bad. They look real nice actually."

"Neither do I. But Rylan is worse than a fashion diva in a thrift store."

Ryoko laughed. "Good point."

She shut my door and left me to change, though it didn't take me long, since upon picking it up, I found the top for my outfit bent in several places. I was worried about damaging it further, so I chose to go full armor cloth. Seda had disguised the outfit during the raid, but that didn't mean it was safe from harm.

Fastening my cloak around my neck, I opened the door. As I did the boys were coming up the stairs.

"You guys are home early," I said as I headed for the kitchen. "Raikidan, go change. We're going out."

He nodded and went into my room.

"The power went out," Rylan muttered. "And Zane is having issues with the military."

I bit into an apple and leaned over the counter. "How so?"

"They're refusing to pay for the damages they caused to the house," Blaze said as he sat down on the couch. "And they're adamant about not paying for the damaged cars since they are so expensive to replace."

I snorted. "That's what they get for raiding our house for no reason."

Blaze smirked. "Well not for no reason, but we're not going to tell them that."

I shook my head and finished my apple as Raikidan came out of my room and headed my way.

Rylan eyed him. "How can you wear that?"

Raikidan shrugged. "I see nothing wrong with it. It's better than those things you call a suit."

Argus chuckled and took a seat at the bar. "He's got a point."

Rylan folded his arms. "I still think it looks stupid. The pants are outdated, the shoes are weird and what's up with a vest with a hood?"

"Shamans need to hide their faces somehow," Ryoko said as she came out of her room with a cloak fastened around her neck and a bag in hand.

Rylan raised an eyebrow at her appearance and then looked at me. "What's going on?"

I grinned. "We're going on a little vacation."

Raikidan stared at me. I wasn't sure if he knew was vacation meant but he seemed to know something good was about it happen.

"I could use a vacation," Blaze said.

I laughed. "Sorry, Blaze, but you and Argus aren't going. Shamans traveling on foot only travel in small groups."

"That bites."

Argus relaxed on the bar. "Fine by me."

"City boy," I teased.

"Country bumpkin."

"Nerd."

"Xylophile."

The two of us stared at each other with neutral expressions, before bursting with laughter.

"What do you mean by vacation and traveling shamans?" Rylan asked.

"She means we're getting out of this stupid city for a little while," Shva'sika elaborated as she made it down the hall. "And that means you have to dress like us whether you like it or not."

Rylan stepped back. "Like hell I am."

Shva'sika clicked her tongue against her teeth. "Look, I'm in no mood for games. So either you go into your room and dress yourself or I'll dress you myself."

He crossed his arms. "I'm not doing it."

Shva'sika narrowed her eyes and then grabbed Rylan by the shirt. Everyone watched in stunned silence while she dragged him down the hall. My attention was pulled away from them by the sound of angry footsteps heading up the front steps. Zane appeared in the doorway but his foul mood switched to puzzlement when he noticed Shva'sika shove Rylan into his room and then follow him, slamming the door behind her.

"What is going on?" he asked.

I bit into another apple. "You'll see."

As we waited we could hear a lot of muffled yelling and complaining. It got so bad Genesis ended up poking her head out of her room to figure out what was going on. Finally the shouting stopped and Rylan's door flew open. We all watched as Rylan was shoved out of his room and Shva'sika calmly walked out after him.

You couldn't see what he was wearing thanks to the cloak, but I could tell by how the cloak covered him there wasn't much on his body.

Blaze snickered. "How does it feel, Rylan, to be forcibly dressed by a woman?"

"Violating…"

We all laughed at him.

Shva'sika shook her head, mumbling to herself, "Bunch of mollycoddles."

Rylan walked into the living room, muttering to himself. I exaggerated an eye roll. "Suck it up, buttercup."

He growled. "I don't see why I have to wear these stupid clothes."

Annoyance flared up in my chest. "You know what, for being such a baby about all this, Ryoko is going to be your Guard."

Ryoko perked up. "Really?"

"What?" Rylan's eyes went wide. "You can't be serious."

"Dead," I replied.

Ryoko squealed with excitement. "Yay!"

Rylan groaned. "Why do you guys hate me?"

"We don't hate you," Shva'sika said. "You're just acting like a child and, even though normally I'd object to this idea because the soldiers will have a hard time believing it, at least I know Ryoko will act accordingly and pull off the Guard demeanor, unlike you."

Rylan sighed but didn't voice an argument. He knew when he had lost.

Shva'sika clapped her hands together. "All right, get your bags and we'll head out."

I slid off my barstool and headed for my room to grab my bag. Raikidan followed. He had a question for me. I knew it.

He closed the door behind him. "You said we weren't allowed to leave the city. And I figured our cause was too important to leave anyway even if we could."

I picked my bow and quiver up off the bed and slung them over my shoulder before snatching up my bag. "I said if you needed to leave the city, we'd need to be careful. And Shva'sika had too many good points in favor of a vacation so I agreed to it."

His lit up. "So this isn't a bad joke?"

I giggled. I knew he'd like this idea. "No, I'm being serious about this vacation. It'll be good for us."

Raikidan took my bag from me and slung it over his shoulder. "Good, because if you were messing with me I'd have to hurt you."

I snorted and headed for the door. "You couldn't hurt me."

Raikidan invaded my personal space. "Oh yeah?"

I pushed him away and opened the door. "Yeah, you'd feel bad if you did."

Raikidan only grunted in response, proving me right. The others were already waiting for us, and we all wordlessly headed down into the basement.

"Have fun you guys!" Argus called after us.

Ryoko opened the door to the hidden passage and we set a quick pace to the safe house. Once there, we left through the front door of the building and headed for the front gate. Rylan started to lag behind in his sour mood, so Ryoko resorted to grabbing him by the hand and guiding him the rest of the way.

I watched how he'd react to her move and smiled. Ryoko's back was turned, so she was unable to see the redness in his face. Rylan could talk to her like nothing was going on, dance with her as if she was just another friend, or pretend he was indifferent about how he felt, but a small bold move on her part, no matter how simple, gave away the truth.

As we approached the gate several soldiers positioned themselves in the way.

"State your business," one soldier ordered.

"We are shamans from the West Tribe," Shva'sika said. "We request free leave on business."

The soldiers looked at each other, Shva'sika's formal speech throwing them off a bit. Rylan fidgeted catching their attention.

"What's your problem?" one of the soldiers demanded.

Rylan stepped back and Ryoko took a protective stance in front of him, confusing the soldiers further.

"He's mute," I stated. "He won't be able to answer you."

"Is she his Guard?" one soldier asked.

"Yes," Ryoko stated.

"Something isn't right," one soldier whispered to the one who was speaking with us. "Only men are Guards."

Raikidan snorted. "And who told you that, a shaman? Or did you all come up with that moronic idea on your own?"

"Watch what you say, shaman," one soldier threatened. "We can choose to not let you out."

I snorted. "No, you can't, now move." I pushed passed them before I gave them a chance to speak.

Shva'sika sighed. "Laz'shika, what are we going to do with you?"

Raikidan snickered and followed. The rest soon followed his lead and the soldiers didn't argue.

Shva'sika led our little group south for several hours, utilizing a portal when we were an acceptable distance away from Dalatrend. Ryoko and Rylan found fascination with the unusual form of transportation, though voiced their distaste of the disorientation after prolonged exposure to the spiraling magic. When it dumped us out in the Forest of Marior, their discomfort was forgotten about, and the two insisted on bombarding Shva'sika with all manner of questions. Raikidan listened in, his curiosity for knowledge getting the better of him.

While that went on, I paid attention to our surroundings. I had been here once, when I had first gone on the run, but hadn't had the chance to really get a good look at the forest. The Forest of Marior spanned for several miles and was one of the few remaining forests to have held up through the War of End. Because of this, the trees grew to enormous sizes and the animals and other plant life flourished.

"So, do we have a designated location in mind?" Ryoko asked. "Or are we going to wander around in this forest forever?"

Shva'sika giggled. "This is the forest I had in mind, so we just need to find a good clearing to set up camp."

Ryoko's cloak snagged on a bush. "Well I hope we find some place soon."

I halted in my tracks and scanned the forest. The others also stopped and Rylan opened his mouth to ask, but I held up my hand to keep him quiet. The forest had grown quiet. Not a bird or insect made a sound. Only the rushing of a river couldn't be controlled into silence. Ryoko and Raikidan tensed when they realized this as well and scanned the forest. *What's lurking in the shadows?*

I turned when the canopy leaves above rustled, and barely managed to dive out of the way of the figure crashing down on me. I scrambled to my feet and Raikidan reacted quickly, taking a protective stance in front of me.

Our attacker kept his distance from us and I did my best not to recoil from his hideous features. *Definitely a Hunter.*

"Who are you?" Shva'sika demanded. "What do you aim to get from attacking shamans?"

The hunter chuckled. "You are the only real shaman here. I have no quarrel with you." His gaze flicked to me and he licked his lips. "I'm just here for my quarry. No disguise will ever hide her delicious perfume."

He then dashed into the shadows of the forest and disappeared from sight. Raikidan flexed his muscles in preparation to pursue but I stopped him. "No, he's trying to lure you out."

"I can take him," Raikidan said.

"Just wait. He'll be back."

"Is it just me, or did the hunter look uglier than normal?" Ryoko asked.

"I'm more concerned with his comment about Laz's scent," Rylan said.

I hushed them and listened. This Hunter's looks and comment didn't matter. His presence here in the first place did. Zarda would know I'm in the city again. He'd have no reason to keep Hunters beyond the city walls looking for me anymore. So why was this one here?

Scanning for this Hunter proved difficult with my hood up, so I pulled it down. Given there was no tricking this Hunter, I found no reason to worry about my identity. When that didn't improve my odds of locating him I backed up in attempt to lure the Hunter out. He was after me, after all.

Raikidan tried to protest, but I placed a finger to my lips and gave him a stern "trust me" look. He nodded, though he clearly wasn't happy about it. I continued to back up and look around in hopes to catch even a glimpse of this Hunter, to no avail.

"Got you," a whisper came from behind me.

I gasped and my eyes widened when an arm reached around my body and pinned my arms to my side. An ugly, talon-like hand reached up and grabbed my neck and jaw. The others froze, his sudden appearance catching them off guard.

"How?" I asked through gritted teeth.

He chuckled. "I'm a bit different than the other Hunters. A new breed, if you will. We're able to conceal ourselves much better, but we have one fatal flaw. We hold on tighter to the scents we're told to follow—too tight in my case. Your scent is so delicious, even after I was ordered to give up on it, I couldn't." He inhaled deeply near my neck and grinned. "I couldn't help but track you down in the city and follow you."

I tried to struggle out of his grip but his hold was too good.

He chuckled. "You'll only tire yourself out. My joints lock, allowing me to hold on much better than others. I need this scent of yours. Zarda wants you back, but I'm selfish."

I struggled more. *What a creep!*

Raikidan growled and took a step forward. "Let her go."

"She's not yours anymore, Dragon," the Hunter sneered.

The Hunter tried to force me to back up, but I resisted. No way was this thing taking me anywhere. My resisting worked in my favor as Raikidan took advantage of the small struggle and ripped the Hunter off me. The act scraped the Hunter's talon-like hands over my cloak, ripping it, and wounding my arm, but I couldn't have cared less. At least this freak wasn't touching me anymore.

Raikidan stood between the Hunter and me, his muscles tense with anger. "You'll pay for touching her like that."

"It'll be you who pays, Beast," the Hunter snarled. "No one gets between me and my quarry."

The Hunter then ran into the forest, but Raikidan wasn't going to stay put this time. He shrugged his vest off his shoulders and bolted after the Hunter, his body taking on another shape as he did. The rest of us watched his dragon form thunder into the forest after the elusive Hunter.

"Stupid dragon," I muttered. "He won't catch the Hunter like that." I looked at Ryoko, brow furrowed, when she sputtered out a laugh. This really wasn't the time to find something funny. "What are you laughing at?"

"Raikidan," she admitted. "Did you not see his face when that hunter grabbed you? He was absolutely livid."

Shva'sika placed her fingers over her mouth as she attempted not to laugh either. "He also didn't need to take his shirt off. It would have handled his shifting just fine with that enchantment applied."

Ryoko continued to giggle. "He was so showing off."

My cheeks started to burn. "He was not!"

"Oh yes he was. And you know it. That's why you're getting embarrassed."

My eyes narrowed into slits. "You really need to get this delusion out of your head."

Ryoko shook her head. "It's not a delusion. I know what I saw on Raikidan's face when that creep tried to claim you. There's something there."

I looked to Rylan. "Help me out here."

He held up his hands. "Look, I'm not getting in the middle of this."

Before I could shoot off a reply, a high-pitched, painful scream echoed through the forest. The sound sent a small chill up my spine. I couldn't be sure who screamed, but whatever happened to them, had to have been extremely painful. The four of us waited as the forest remained silent.

I let out a breath of relief when the familiar sound of dragon footsteps echoed through the air. I didn't care what he had done to the Hunter to make him scream like that. I was just glad he wasn't the one who had been hurt.

Ryoko cheered the moment Raikidan came into sight. I smiled at him as he lowered his massive head toward me.

I rested my hand on his snout. "Thank you."

Raikidan shifted. "He won't bother you again."

I barely heard him as the blood staining his lips and teeth distracted me. "Let's get you cleaned up. You look ridiculous with so much blood in your mouth."

"I want to see your arm first," he said. "I know you were harmed during that."

I turned myself so he wouldn't be able to see through the holes in my cloak and see me clutching my upper arm where I had been gashed. "I'm good, don't worry."

He reached for me. "C'mon show me."

"Raikidan, seriously, it's nothing. Just a scratch."

"I can smell all the blood, it's not," he insisted. "Now stop being so stubborn and let me see your arm."

Ryoko giggled and heading off in a random direction. "We'll let you two lovebirds figure this out."

"We're not lovebirds!" Raikidan and I shouted in unison.

Ryoko snickered as an awkward tension fells between us and led the others away.

"Eira, can I please see your arm?" Raikidan asked after we had been alone for a moment.

"Raikidan, it's seriously not a big deal."

"I don't care if it's only a scratch. I was careless when removing that filthy thing off you and you were harmed in the process. Please let me look at it."

I sighed and complied. How could I not with that reasoning? He scowled when he found out exactly how bad of scratch it was and then proceeded to heal me up. When he was done, he allowed me to dig through my bag to find water and a rag to clean his mouth, and for me to clean my own skin of my blood. Then we headed in the direction of the others before they could get any other funny ideas about us.

❦

I examined the clearing we stood in. It was big enough to make a camp but had enough cover to ensure it stayed secluded and private. After the run-in with the Hunter, we'd need a place like this.

Rylan sat down and let out a heavy breath. He had finally calmed down when we reached the Forest of Marior, but after the ambush, his anxiety levels rose back to their original level. I couldn't blame him for being on edge. He'd only ever been out of the city while in the military, and during that time we had been forced to wear tracking devices so we wouldn't be tempted to run off. The Hunter's attack didn't help him with separating his past and present. *Hopefully he'll calm down now that we were able to make camp and relax.*

I took my bag from Raikidan and rummaged through it. The sooner we arrange camp the better. Pulling out the materials needed to assemble the tent I probably wouldn't use, I laid them out so it'd be easier to grab what I needed as I worked. Unclasping my cloak, I took it off and, in a matter of seconds, had it folded in my arms and then I worked with the body cloth that matched my mouth veil.

The veil was next and I was forced to fix my hair when it came loose from my hair clip during the process. Ryoko removed her cloak and handed it to me in hopes I'd fold it for her. I laughed, shook my head, and complied.

After I folded it, I took a good look at her outfit. It was cute on her and rather fitting since it was made of wolf hide. The top was a strip of hide that wrapped from her back over her breasts and threaded around a small metal ring that was attached to a multi-layered bone necklace. Clasped to the cloth, holding the two sides together to keep her breasts in place, was a circular pin that was painted to look like the full moon. Her skirt only went down mid-thigh and tied off on one end, exposing a lot of skin on that side from the hip down. On her feet were leather, toeless boots with teeth and claws from various carnivorous animals threaded through them.

I glanced back at Rylan to see his reaction and I wasn't disappointed. His hood was down, and he happily, and not so subtly, checked her out.

"So how long am I going to have to wait for you to pitch the tent so I can change out of this stupid thing?" Ryoko complained.

I rolled my eyes. "You can go change behind a bush if you're in that much of a rush."

Ryoko laughed dryly. "Funny, real funny."

"It's not that bad. It's not like it's going to kill you."

Ryoko snorted. "Please. I'm not changing out in the open. I mean not even"—she looked around—"where did Danika go?"

"She mumbled something about changing into clothes that would be better for hiking," Raikidan replied as he sat under a large oak tree.

Ryoko clasped her hands together. "That sounds like fun!"

"Then go change," I told her.

She folded her arms. "Not until the tent is up."

I gestured to the tent pieces. "By all means, set it up."

She grumbled to herself and went to work. I knelt and rummaged through my bag again. Raikidan was going to need to change his clothes and I had no idea where I had put the cloth armor I had stuffed into the bag before I put the jars in.

Shva'sika's sudden shriek pulled my attention from my bag. She stood by the tree line staring at me. She looked absolutely horrified.

My brow creased. "What?"

She pointed at me. "What did you do to the outfit I made you?"

I blinked. "What are you talking about?"

"You changed the bottoms!"

I laughed and peered down at the skirt I wore. It was a thick strip of cloth that wrapped low behind me. The two ends crossed in the front and attached to black bikini bottoms. I would have preferred pants but I knew better to wear this. This skirt allowed more movement where pants didn't, plus it still had that revealing look to it, making it match up to Shva'sika's criteria.

"That's your issue? Of course I changed them. The ones you gave me were repulsive."

"I wouldn't say repulsive, but they certainly weren't walking-in-public material," Ryoko piped in, waving her hand.

"That bad?" Rylan asked.

Ryoko nodded. "It'd be perfect to seduce someone though."

Rylan's eyebrows rose and then he let it be.

Finally finding the armor cloth, I pulled it out of my bag and held it up. "Here, Raikidan, I knew you'd like this more than regular clothes."

Raikidan got up from where he sat and came over to take it. He was out of the clearing before I could blink. If I didn't know any better, I would have sworn he didn't like being in his shaman outfit.

"Hey, um, did either of you pack me something?" Rylan asked.

Ryoko glanced up from her work and smiled. "Oh yeah, I forgot I did that for you, sorry."

He smiled and waited as she rummaged through her bag. Once she had all his clothes in a pile for him, he got up and took them off her hands.

"Wait!" she called to him before he disappeared into the tree line.

"What?" he asked.

"Could you take off your cloak so we can see the style of your clothes?" she asked quietly. "Danika wouldn't tell us."

He scratched the back of his head. "I don't know…"

Ryoko tucked her hair behind her ear and looked away, glancing back at him only briefly. "Okay that's fine. I don't want to force you to do something you don't want to."

I noticed his gulp as he thought over his options. Ryoko's coy gestures put him in a situation he wasn't planning for.

He sighed and took off his cloak. "All right, you can look."

The two of us turned our gazes on him and blinked. His shirt wasn't much of a shirt. It was more like a long, thick, strip of cloth that wrapped around his torso several times and then over his shoulder.

His pants and shoes were exactly like Raikidan's and his hands were wrapped in cloth until mid forearm. The chains around his wrists were wrapped up tight inside the cloth, preventing anyone who didn't know him from knowing they were there. Around his right thigh he had a small belt with a few pouches. *Was Shva'sika going for an unusual healer look?* I honestly didn't understand the first thing to the shaman style. If there was any concrete style.

Ryoko smiled and went back to working on the tent, tucking her hair behind her ear once more as it broke free from the movement. "You look nice. I don't see why you were complaining."

Rylan stared at her like a deer in headlights. Shva'sika snapped her fingers and he jumped. I bit my lip trying hard not to laugh.

He turned and made a hasty retreat into the woods but just before he disappeared he spoke. "You shouldn't complain either, Ryoko. You look very nice."

Ryoko immediately stopped what she was doing and her face flushed. I couldn't help but laugh now, and Shva'sika was sure to join in.

"If this was one of those cartoons all of you watch in the morning, I swear his tongue would have been hanging out," Shva'sika teased.

"Danika!" Ryoko screeched.

"Trust me that was nothing," I said. "You should have seen him when she first took off her cloak. I swear he was about to drool everywhere."

Ryoko's face reddened more. Our laughter increased. Raikidan stumbled out of the brush, his foot having snagged on a stubborn branch, and he looked at us funny. I waved him off and he understood it would be best not to ask.

He dropped his shaman clothes at my feet and knelt next to Ryoko to observe her tent setup. I sucked in a tight breath and folded his clothes. I needed to teach him how to do it himself. I felt like his maid.

Rylan returned, his clothes folded in his hands, and handed them to me carefully so they wouldn't spill everywhere.

"Rylan, you have to be the only guy I know who can actually fold clothes," I said as I stuffed them into Ryoko's bag, making his folding efforts pointless. "Unlike a certain dragon."

Raikidan grunted. "I don't know how to fold clothes. I don't even know how my clothes go from that thing you call a hamper to my dresser and smell better in the process."

Ryoko laughed. "That's because I do your laundry."

"You do what now?"

She shook her head while laughed some more. "I clean your clothes."

"Oh… well… thanks, I think."

I rolled my eyes and shook my head. *He's something else.*

Shva'sika clapped her hands together. "There, done."

I turned my gaze onto her tent she stood in front of and laughed at the dilapidated sight. "You still suck at that."

She scratched her face. "Yeah, I do. You mind giving me a hand?"

I nodded and helped her fix her tent. By the time we finished, Ryoko had hers taken care of, thanks to the help the boys ended up giving. Ryoko grabbed her bag and dashed inside the tent. She was back in a matter of seconds. Shva'sika and I exchanged glances in stunned silence. Apparently Ryoko's years of shopping and trying on clothes did some permanent damage.

"So who's ready for some hiking?" Ryoko asked.

"Not, Laz," Shva'sika teased.

My clothes changed within a matter of seconds. "What are you talking about?"

Shva'sika blinked and Ryoko laughed. "I thought you were going to wear a regular top?"

"I was," I admitted. "But when I went to put it on, it ended up being damaged from that damned raid and there wasn't enough time to have Shva'sika fix it."

Ryoko shrugged. "Fair enough. Let's go that way."

I didn't hesitate to head off in the direction she pointed in. A hike sounded nice.

"Laz, don't you want some shoes?" Shva'sika asked.

I stopped walking and looked at her. "Why would I do that?"

"Because you'll callous your feet if you don't."

I lifted my foot to show the calluses that had already built up over the years. "Too late."

She snorted. "Were going to have to fix that. Soft, pampered feet are what you need.

"Soft feet make for weak feet," I replied as I turned on my heels.

Ryoko discarded her boots before she caught up with me. Shva'sika sighed and muttered to herself. "Looks like I'm the only one here who cares about their feet."

I resisted the urge to laugh. She had no idea how good it was for you to walk barefoot.

Ryoko's ears twitched. "I hear running water!"

Before I could say anything she was grabbing hold of my arm and dragging me in the direction of the water.

The soft grass cushioned my feet as we traveled alongside the river Ryoko had found. The wind, a mere light breeze, moved the warm air. The sun sat low in the sky, casting long shadows over the forest. Ryoko spotted a protruding grass covered ledge and ran over to it.

"Ryoko, be careful," I said. "It might be unstable."

She waved me off. "It's fine. I mean there's grass growing on it."

"That doesn't mean it's safe," I muttered.

Ryoko happily looked around at the scenery. This vacation idea was a good one. She and Rylan deserved to be able to get out of that hellish place for once. Even Raikidan was enjoying himself in his own way. I hadn't seen him this relaxed since we entered the city. Not even the park did this to him.

My ears pricked at the sound of crunching rock. "Ryoko, move."

She switched her gaze to me, her head cocked. "What?"

I sprinted toward her. "I said move!"

Suddenly the earth beneath her crumbled away. Ryoko, taken by surprise, froze up. I grabbed her by the arm and tossed her back where Rylan caught her.

"Eira!" Raikidan cried.

The wind rushed around me as I fell. There hadn't been enough time for me to get back to the others before the ground fell away completely. Raikidan reached out to try to grab me but I was too far away. Pain shot through me when I crashed into the water.

Everything looked green and bubbles floated up all around me. The voice that spoke to me was now gone. In its place was a loud buzzing noise.

The strong current pulled me downstream until I smashed into a large boulder. My hands latched onto the smooth surface in reflex, allowing me to fight the strong current.

My eyes darted back and forth frantically as I struggled, and my long hair moved in slow motion around me.

I tried to struggle to the surface, but before I could move much a large boulder from the falling ledge crashed into me. The pressure released all the air I had in my lungs and I thrashed violently. I was pinned with no hope of escape.

I couldn't breathe. Whatever gave me the ability to breath in this liquid substance I floated in, fell off and now I couldn't breathe or get out. I didn't know what was going on.

I pushed against the boulder with what little strength I had, using up the last ounce of oxygen reserve, but the current was too strong. It pushed the boulder harder than I was able to push back.

I flailed my arms and they hit something solid. I pressed my hands against the solid surface and realized it was some sort of barrier. I pressed on the barrier in several areas. I was trapped. I struggled more and banged on the barrier. The green liquid substance I floated in flashed a pale red color repetitively and the buzzing sound got louder.

I coughed and water rushed into my lungs, choking me up. I struggled more even though I knew it wouldn't do any good. There was no one around to open a glass tank. There was no one to wake me from this nightmare. It was happening all over again but this time, there was no one to save me.

My struggling became more violent. Why couldn't I get out of this barrier?

My vision blurred and darkened. I fought to stay alert but my body was shutting down. I never thought I'd end like this. I never thought my fate would change. My eyes hooded and numbness fell over me. The sound of a loud splash hit my muted ears and I could see a dark figure swimming around in the water.

As a last ditch effort I forced the last of my energy into my arms. I reached out to whatever was brave enough to enter this water. The creature glided through the rushing water toward me, but before it was close enough to see well, my eyes shut almost into slits. The creature swam even closer and changed shape. Raikidan's blurred face briefly graced my sight before my vision failed and the numbness overtook me.

I wanted to be free. I wanted to breathe. I wanted to stop feeling like I was drowning—like I was dying.

30
CHAPTER

y mind was foggy; spinning even. I didn't know if I was up or down, alive or dead. A man leaned over me and smiled. He was tall with olive-tan skin, brown eyes, trimmed facial hair, and appeared transparent as if he weren't really there. He looked a lot like Azriel, dual set of ears and all, but I knew he wasn't.

"Wake up, Chickadee. Wake up."

"Tannek?"

His smile deepened. "It's okay. You're not dead. I'm just here to make sure you don't move any further toward the spiritual plane."

"I'm not... dead?" I squinted, the heaviness in my mind making it difficult to understand.

"He saved you, you're safe now. He'll protect you." Tannek began to fade. "I'm sorry, Chickadee. I can't stay any longer. I know my presence upsets you. I'll try to stay away from now on, as hard as it is. For your sake."

"Tannek... wait." I reached for him. "Don't leave... Don't leave me... again..."

Darkness enveloped me. Tannek was nowhere to be found, and yet, I could still hear him. "He'll keep you safe, like I once did. Now, wake up."

The numbness was ebbing. A fire crackled and popped close by, its warmth teasing my skin. An owl hooted in the distance, crickets chirping their night song. Two people whispered a little ways off and

I was sure I could hear someone breathing close to me. *Am I dead?*

My body ached, especially my lungs, making breathing painful. My head spun and pulsed, and I feared the numbness would return. That was, until the back of a masculine hand caressed my cheek. His fingers ran across my skin and brushed away a stray hair. This sparked a small ounce of energy to flow through my body and I opened my eyes into small slits.

A campfire flickered in front of me as I lay on my side. On the other side of the fire Ryoko and Rylan chatted while they ate something off small plates. The flames cast harsh shadows over their faces, clashing with the blanket of the night. *No, I'm alive.*

Shva'sika came out of her tent and knelt next to them to speak with them briefly before heading around the fire and out of my sight. Those three were accounted for, so Raikidan had to be the one sitting next to me. He was the only one missing and the only one to be stupid enough to touch my face like that.

"How's Laz doing?" Shva'sika asked, kneeling next to me.

"I think she's awake," Raikidan said. "Her breathing has improved tremendously, and I noticed a shift a few moments ago. Though I don't know if she's strong enough to acknowledge us."

"Well it's better than her condition before," Shva'sika said. "I was afraid she wasn't going to respond to my healing treatments."

"We all thought that for a while." I thought I caught pain laced in his words.

"I brought you over some food," Shva'sika said. "It's fish and wild nuts. I wasn't sure if you were hungry yet."

"No, I'm fine."

She placed a ceramic plate and metal utensils on the ground. "All right. I'll leave it here for you. Let me know when Laz fully wakes up."

"Sure."

Shva'sika walked off, leaving the two of us alone. Raikidan placed his hand on my shoulder and began murmuring rhythmically in his tongue, washing a sense of peace over me. *Is he praying?* As he did, he slid his thumb over my skin that felt a lot like a light caress. The stroking didn't last long though, as his grip tightened and his murmuring became more urgent. His grip hurt actually.

I tried to muster up the ability to speak but the only sound that came from my throat was a pathetic gurgled moan.

Raikidan's grip lessened. "Eira?"

Another gurgled moan came from my mouth. I needed more energy to communicate. The fired danced in front of me and I smiled. I reached for the flames but Raikidan grabbed my hand.

"Eira, what are you doing? Don't touch that."

"Raikidan, let her go," Shva'sika called over.

"Are you crazy?" he asked. "It'll burn her."

"No it won't," Ryoko said. "Trust us."

He hesitated but eventually released my hand. I reached for the fire again and begged for it to come to me. A small flame licked my fingers and I grabbed hold in fear I'd lose it in my weakened state. Pulling my arm back to my body I brought my hand up to my mouth and forced the fire down my throat.

"Eira!" Raikidan yelled in horror.

"Raikidan, it's all right," Rylan said.

"She shoved a flame into her mouth! How is that okay? She isn't a dragon. That'll torch her insides."

"Just watch."

I finished swallowing the hot flame and embraced the warmth that rushed through my body as the fire healed me. I coughed violently when the flame entered my lungs, startling Raikidan. As my coughing continued, water trickled out of my mouth with each expulsion of air.

When my fit subsided I let out a relaxed sigh, feeling much better than before. My senses weren't as dull and my strength was returning.

Raikidan touched my face. "Eira?"

I rolled onto my back and smiled at him, croaking out, "Morning."

He chuckled and shook his head. "What did you do?"

"I can use… fire for energy," I said. "I just… have to eat it to do so."

His mouth opened but he didn't speak right away. He blinked and shook his head again. "You're just full of surprises."

I closed my eyes as energy pulsed through my body.

"Eira, you okay?" Raikidan asked.

"Yeah, just recovering," I said. "It's a… slow process."

Raikidan brushed a stray hair out of my face. "All right. You hungry?"

I shook my head. "Not yet. You?"

"No."

"Were you praying for me?" I asked.

He nodded. "Yes."

I smiled. "Thank you. And thank you for saving me from drowning."

He shrugged awkwardly and avoided eye contact. "It was nothing, really."

A giggle escaped my lips. He picked such strange times to get weird about attention placed on his actions. "Go find something to eat."

"But—"

"Dummy, don't even start with me. You need to replenish your energy." I glance over at the plate of food. "And just one fish and some nuts isn't going to cut it for you." My gaze fell on him again. "Please. I'll be all right now, thanks to you."

He hesitated but then nodded and stood. In the blink of an eye, he shifted into his dragon shape and disappeared into the starlit sky. I sighed and closed my eyes but opened them again when someone approached.

Shva'sika smiled as she crouched down next to me. "Now that you've gotten him to go eat, are you up for something?"

I shook my head. "Maybe in a bit. I still need some more time to recover."

She nodded. "All right, I'll leave you to rest. You'll need it if Raikidan comes back and starts bothering you again."

I chuckled before closing my eyes to rest some more.

I sighed and continued to draw in the dirt out of boredom with a small stick I had found. I had already sharpened my daggers—twice— and was out of ideas on what to do with myself. I had recovered the last bit of my strength completely last night, thanks to Raikidan, who had brought me some red meat to eat, but Shva'sika didn't want me doing anything today, just in case.

"Cheer up, Laz," Shva'sika insisted as she mixed some sort of herbal medicine in a small bowl. "It's only today. Tomorrow you can go and do what you want."

"I know." It didn't make me any less bored though. Rylan and Raikidan went off to do something together, and Ryoko wandered away on her own not long after. That left Shva'sika to babysit me, so I wouldn't be tempted to do anything strenuous. I didn't even know why she was being so cautious. But I knew better in this situation than to argue with her.

Maybe I can find some good wood to whittle on. Better yet, if I could find something of good size, I could practice carving. It'd been a while since I'd done that.

I got to my feet and ventured toward the campsite edge, only to stop when Shva'sika called out, "Where are you going?"

I gestured to the underbrush. "Just going to search for some sticks."

She shook her head. "Oh, no. You need to relax."

My brow furrowed. "Collecting sticks isn't strenuous."

"I said you're not doing it. You need to recover and moving around isn't recovering."

I threw my hands up in the air. "What is your deal? Do you expect me to sleep the day away? Because that's not going to happen!"

Shva'sika's lips pressed into a thin line, the corner of her eyes tightening. Before she could respond, the brush near us rustled. Ryoko popped out a moment later. She blinked when she noticed the tension, as if she hadn't heard the arguing, and then smiled at me. "Let's go!"

I cocked my head. "Go? Go where?"

Ryoko grabbed my wrist and pulled me out of the campsite. Shva'sika started to protest, but Ryoko dragged me away too quickly.

When the camp was out of sight she released me and stopped walking. "Stay here. I'm going to go smooth things over with Danika before we go any further."

I shoved my hands in my pockets and nodded. *So she had heard the argument.*

She dashed off. I kept my mind busy by looking around and identifying plant and animal life by name. Xye was the source of this knowledge. I thought I had known a lot back then, but he had proven me wrong.

A cluster of yellow and orange-pedaled daisy-like flowers caught my eye as well as some white daisy-like flowers.

"These are calendula and chamomile."

"They're flowers."

"Not just any flowers. Calendula is great to use as an antifungal and antiseptic. Their petals also can be used to sooth the skin. And Chamomile is great for treating colic in infants as well as a great relaxer for those who are nervous or tense."

I didn't care to know about remedies at the time, but my lack of interest didn't deter him and he told me anyway. Xye would even get Shva'sika or Del'karo to make me go searching for herbs and other wild plants with him so he could try to teach me.

I spotted a patch of wild peppermint and smiled.

"Xye, where are you dragging me off to now?"

"I told you. I need help picking some herbs. It's prime season for this herb and I need to get as much as possible."

"Then why not ask your sister instead of wasting my time?"

"Because she told me to bring you."

"Fine. What are we picking?"

"Peppermint."

"You're dragging me out here to pick peppermint? Why the hell would you waste my time with that? You can grow that yourself!"

"But wild peppermint is better."

"Right… What's it even used for? Besides freshening your breath."

"It helps with indigestion and vomiting."

"That's weird."

But in the end his tactics wore off on me and I started asking about what he was doing or if a plant was good for medicine.

I touched the flaking bark of a birch tree.

"What are you doing, Xye?"

"Taking bark from this fallen birch tree."

"Why?"

"Because of the healing properties. Birch bark is great for dealing with indigestion, fevers, urinary system problems, and so much more."

"Okay. Why from a dead tree?"

"Because taking bark from a living tree will kill it."

I even asked about animals and how good they were to eat. I was actually quite interested in that—maybe a little too much.

"Are squirrels good to eat?"

"They're pretty good, but you need a lot of them to get a good amount of meat and catching them is a bit of a pain so it's not really worth the effort."

"We would shoot them."

"Yeah, well, guns are in short supply here, remember?"

I sighed and stopped looking around. There were reasons I pushed memories away. The past was too painful. It reminded me of what was and teased me about what could have been but never would.

"Laz, you okay?" Ryoko asked as she approached.

"Yeah, I'm fine."

Skepticism flashed over her eyes but she didn't voice an argument. Instead she grabbed onto my arm and dragged me away.

I chuckled. "Ryoko, where are you taking me?"

She smiled. "I found a smaller river up this way that has a low current. It'd be a great place to bathe and just hang out."

"Didn't Raikidan say something last night about finding a better river?" I asked. "And didn't they say something earlier about going to bathe?"

Ryoko shrugged. "I dunno. I wasn't really pay attention." I eyed her warily and she laughed. "Don't worry, Laz. Even if it is the same river, I found this spot myself and the guys weren't there. I'm positive we won't run into them."

"If you say so." Though, I was anything but convinced.

She laughed. "Speaking of boys…"

"No!" I threw out my arms. "We're not discussing that."

Her shoulders slumped and she threw her head back. "Please, Laz?"

"No."

"I want to be able to talk to you about normal things like normal women do. And talking about women is off the table with you. Please?"

"Ryoko, if you really haven't noticed, I'm anything but normal. Talking about normal things isn't something I can do. And not all women talk about men, especially not as much as you'd like to."

She tugged on my arm. "Please!"

I let out an exasperated sigh. "All right, all right, I'll talk to you about something *normal* people talk about." Ryoko squealed with delight but it was cut short when I continued. "But I'm not talking about men."

She pouted. "Why not?"

"You know why not…"

"Laz, you need to let go. You need to let *him* go."

A sorrow filled sigh left my lips. My eyes darted away. "Easier said than done…"

"You need to let go of the past. You can't have a future if you linger where you no longer are."

"Ryoko…"

"And don't let Zarda control you anymore either."

The muscles in my neck tensed. "You weren't there, Ryoko. You didn't see what he tried to do."

She held my hand. "Rylan told me." I glanced at her. "He told me what happened, Laz. I know what he tried to do but you can't keep living in fear. You can't let him keep his hold on you."

"I don't fear."

She snorted. "And pigs fly. Everyone is afraid of something, Laz, and that means you are too. Jasmine told me she purposely didn't make your DNA right, and you know that as well. You know you're not exactly what Zarda wanted, because Jasmine cared enough not to make you that way. Now, talk about this with me. Just once."

I sighed. "Only once." She squealed with delight. "But you also have to participate in this." She laughed and latched onto my arm. Confusion fell over me when she didn't speak. "Well?"

"Give me a minute. I'm trying to figure out how to word it so you'll be willing to answer." I blinked. I didn't like the sound of that. Ryoko grinned wickedly. "'Kay, we're going to figure out the perfect guy for you."

"We're not doing you're stupid male ordering menu activity, are we?" I hesitantly asked.

Her grin widened. "Yep!"

"Shoot me," I muttered, my head tipping toward the sky as if I were asking the gods themselves to pull the trigger.

She laughed. "It's not that bad. Now, body type."

"You first." If I was going to have to stomach doing something so shallow, and frankly idiotic, I wasn't going to answer first.

"Hey, none of that!"

"I said you had to participate in this too so you answer first or I'm not answering at all."

"Fine," she muttered. "Muscular or athletic. Now you."

"You answered for me, next question."

Ryoko stomped her foot. "You can't do that!"

I laughed. "There's no rule saying I can't, now deal with it and ask another question."

She grumbled to herself and I laughed some more. "Long or short hair?"

"Short," I said. Though if I was honest, long wasn't bad on some men I'd met. Course, Ryoko didn't need to know that. The quicker I answered, the faster this "game" would end.

Ryoko cocked her head. "But long enough to style it with gel from time to time?"

My brow twisted. "Sure?"

"Yes or no."

"I see it as still being short hair."

"All right, that's fair I guess, and to make you happy my answer is the same. Now, hair color?"

I shrugged. "Dark."

Ryoko raised her eyebrow. "Really?"

I nodded. "Yeah."

"I would have thought you'd dislike anything close to Zarda's hair color."

My shoulders lifted again. "He has dark hair. A lot of people have dark hair. Not something that reminds me of him anyway."

"So your like of dark hair, is it why you didn't have feelings for Rylan?"

I shrugged. "I just didn't find myself attracted to him."

"And what about Zo?"

I rolled my eyes. "Let's not talk about him."

"I'm surprised you deal with him so well. I half expected you to scare him off by now."

I sighed. "I put up with him for the team. Otherwise I'd avoid him at all costs. Now, your turn. Hair color preference?"

She smiled. "Light hair."

I grinned. "Not white?"

Her face reddened. "Don't start."

I chuckled. "All right, eye color, missy."

She blinked with surprise, not that I blamed her. I hadn't planned on asking any questions, but I was getting into this a little. Of course, I'd never admit that to her. She wouldn't understand that didn't mean I would do it again if she asked. The whole activity was wildly inaccurate, given so many could answer one way and end up with a partner that didn't fit the game's results.

She tapped her lips with a finger. "That's a tough one."

A wicked grin spread across my lips, creasing my eyes in the corners. "Just say two toned and I'll understand."

Her face flushed more. "Laz, stop it!" I laughed. It was fun getting her all flustered. "You know what, for that I'm not answering that question."

"Oh, no you don't! You're going to answer."

She folded her arms. "No, you answer it."

I stayed quiet. I shouldn't have asked this question. I really didn't want to answer it.

"Laz, you have to answer," Ryoko said.

I held my head high. "You didn't."

"Because you were being mean! Now answer the question."

I sighed. "Blue."

"Blue?" I nodded and she grinned. "That choice wouldn't be influenced by a certain someone, now would it?"

I glared at her. "Don't even go there."

She laughed. "All right, all right. Facial hair?"

I scratched my head. "That's a weird one, but okay. Let's see…"

Ryoko giggled. "I didn't think it'd be that hard."

"Choosing isn't hard," I defended. "Wording it right is."

"Say what you don't like then."

"No beards and no mustaches."

Ryoko laughed. "Too old looking for you?"

I nodded. "Full beards at least. Mustaches just… they're creepy on most."

She chuckled. "Point taken."

"Your turn to answer."

Ryoko shrugged. "I think it depends on the guy. I'm not usually in favor of the clean-shaven look. But I'll take it over a beard grown out of laziness and isn't well maintained. Though, mustaches creep me the hell out."

I laughed when she shuddered at the word mustache. "Any more questions, or are we finally done with this?"

Ryoko placed her hand on her cheek. "Well I figure it's safe to throw back hair out."

I gagged. "That's disgusting. Why would that even cross your mind?"

Ryoko shrugged. "I don't know. Hmm…"

I blinked when her lips upturned into a grin. I had a bad feeling about this.

"How about shaven or lo—"

"Above the belt!" I shrieked. "Above the belt."

"Oh, c'mon, Laz. Where's your sense of fun?" Her eye brow raised up and down. "Or in this case, adventure?"

"I said above the belt! Please?"

She snickered. "Your face is getting red."

I hid my face in my hand. "Ryoko, stop."

"Just answer it. It's not that bad. Stop being such a prude."

My face grew warmer by the second. "I don't want to talk about this…"

Ryoko chuckled. "Just answer the question. It's not that hard. Shaven or not?"

I shook my head.

"C'mon, say it," she urged.

The warmth in my face migrated to my ears. "Trimmed."

Ryoko laughed raucously and I wanted to hide. My face and ears both burned with embarrassment and her laughter wasn't making me feel any better.

"Ryoko, please stop laughing at me…"

"I'm sorry, but I can't help it. I can't believe I got you to say it. You're the most prude person I know and here I got you to say it. Your face is so red right now!"

I hid my face in my hand. I never thought I'd ever feel this embarrassed. "Ryoko, please…"

She quieted her laughter. "Okay, okay, I'm sorry. I'm just glad you're being a good sport about this."

"Define, good sport," I grumbled. "Now it's your turn. Answer your own question."

Ryoko grinned and winked. "I don't mind a man with some hair. Though I won't say no to a little 'scaping."

A hot flush emerged on my face again, reaching my ears. Her answer was so… brazen. I didn't know how to react to it really. "Um… well…"

Ryoko laughed, clearly enjoying messing with me some more. I swallowed, trying to focus. "Is, uh, that all the questions we're going through?"

She gazed up at the sky, clasping her hands behind her back. "Yep. Now I have to piece Mister Perfect together to get a good idea of what you're looking for."

I sighed. "I'm not looking for someone."

"You sure?" She winked. "Because a certain someone fits your criteria quite well."

I pinched my nose. I knew this was where she was going with all this. "Don't even go there. I already told you, he's not an option."

"Oh, c'mon, why not?"

"Because he's a dragon? It wouldn't work."

"And how do you know? I mean, how do you *really* know?"

"How?" I threw a hand out. "Because inter species relationships don't work! You should know that better than anyone, Ryoko."

"But it can. Minus some spats here and there, you two get along super well. How can it not work?"

I sighed. "I get along with you but that doesn't mean anything. It doesn't work and it's not going to happen. Now drop it, Ryoko. I don't want you to bring this up again."

She frowned. "Okay, okay, sorry. I just want you to be happy…"

"Pushing something on me isn't going to make me happy."

She raised her eyebrows a few times, a grin on her lips. "You mean someone?" I shoved her and she laughed. "C'mon, I can hear the river. It sounds like it's just beyond these tr—"

She stopped dead when she pushed through the line of shrubs and trees. I looked at her as I stepped into the open. Her eyes were wide and her face turned several shades of red. Confused, I shifted my gaze. *Bad idea.*

Standing in the shallows of the river were Raikidan and Rylan, the water barely coving her lower halves. The two boys glanced at each other and then back at us with a grin.

"Ladies," Rylan greeted.

"Sorry to inform you but this part of the river is taken," Raikidan teased. "Unless you feel the need to join us."

My face burned. This couldn't be happening. I grabbed Ryoko by the arm and pulled her back into the safety of the woods. The boys howled with laughter, making the situation more embarrassing.

"I can't believe that happened," Ryoko muttered. "That was—" She gasped.

"What?"

"What if they heard what we were talking about?" she asked worriedly.

I gulped. "Don't even think that."

She whimpered. "But what if they did? We being so loud because I didn't think they'd be over here. I thought we were going in the same direction I had gone the first time. I only wanted that talk to be between the two of us."

I let out a tight breath and kept walking. "Pray to the gods they didn't."

We entered the clearing of the campsite and were greeted by Shva'sika cooking like crazy.

My brow rose. "Shva'sika, don't you think it's a little early to start dinner? It's maybe a few hours past mid-day."

She smiled. "It's never too early. Besides, I thought I'd make a big meal tonight."

"Do you need any help?" Ryoko asked.

Shva'sika smiled. "I could always use help. I have a lot of herbs and vegetables that need to be prepped if you two want to do that."

The two of us agreed to help hoping it would distract us from the mishap earlier. Ryoko dashed off to collect some supplies to work with while I sat down in a soft patch of grass and reached for my favorite dagger, only to remember I gave it to Ryder. I shrugged. We weren't preparing a meal in a five star restaurant. It didn't need to be perfect.

Ryoko rejoined me and handed over a few pouches that smelled like herbs, a small wooden cutting board, and a bowl to put the herbs in once prepped. I handed her my remaining arm dagger and reach down to grab another one from my leg for myself. Ryoko accepted it and retreated to her own spot she had set up near the oak tree by the edge of the campsite. Looking down at what I had to work with, I went at it.

My working slowed when someone knelt behind me. My face flushed when Raikidan chuckled. "Go away, Raikidan."

"Why would I do that when I enjoy watching you do weird things?" he asked.

"Because I don't want you near me. Now git."

He snickered low in my ear. "Your face is red." I shoved him and he fell backward. "Now that wasn't very nice."

I went back to cutting my herbs instead of responding, and glanced over at Ryoko, who was having worse luck than me. Her face was positively scarlet, and I didn't see any reason for it not to be. Rylan had completely pressed himself up against her, pretending to be *helpful*.

He whispered something low in her ear and she turned around and slapped him. He yelped but it didn't deter him from bouncing back and trying to *help* her again. Shva'sika shot me a questioning glance and I shook my head once. She got the hint and went back to working on her meal prep.

Raikidan moved back to his spot behind me and I tried not to sigh. He reached around to grab a hold of my dagger but I swatted him away.

"I was just going to help," he defended with fake innocence.

I grunted. "Yeah, I'm sure you were. Now go away."

"Maybe I'll stay so you can look at my blue eyes since you like them so much."

My face burned. They had heard us. When Raikidan chuckled in my ear I lost it. I punched him in the face and jumped to my feet. My freshly cut herbs spilled everywhere but I didn't care. I stormed into my tent. I could hear Raikidan moaning in pain and Rylan laughing at him. Even Shva'sika couldn't control the giggles that escaped her lips.

"If I wasn't so nice, Raikidan, I'd let you suffer with that injured jaw," she told him. "Especially since you were asking for it."

Locating my bow and quiver filled with arrows I was searching for, I left my tent. Ryoko pushed Rylan away from her and dashed over to me. "I'm coming with you."

I didn't argue. The more space we put between the boys and us the better. "You can carry back whatever I kill, okay?"

She nodded. "Just make it something worth carrying."

I laughed and nodded.

"Bring back something that will work with the rest of the meat I have if you can," Shva'sika called after us. "And don't worry. I'll put the boys through their paces for you for being jerks."

I waved my thanks and the two of us disappeared into the underbrush.

31
CHAPTER

It was hot. Too hot for me to be cooled by lounging in the shade of the large maple tree I sat under, but I didn't want to swim with the others. Instead, I chose to wear a cropped tank top and shorts and sucked it up. Raikidan lay under the trees near me in his dragon form and watched the others.

As I observed him from the corner of my eye I wondered if he was warm or cold blooded. A strange thing to wonder, since he was a serpent and all, but because he could shift into a warm blood creature it made me curious.

He also didn't seem to be affected by temperature change like either a warm or cold-blooded creature would be, and at present he didn't appear hot in the least, nor did he when he was in his nu-human shape. Normally this would indicate he was cold blooded, but because I'd never seen him need to use the sun or some other heat source to warm himself, I wondered if he was able to create his own body heat like a warm-blooded creature and had a high heat tolerance. *Or maybe he's a hybrid of both…* I resisted the urge to rub my temples. I was giving myself a headache for no reason.

"C'mon you two, come join us!" Ryoko called out. "The water is refreshing."

I waved her off and closed my eyes. The breeze teased my hair and the flame in my chest taunted me. The awful voice in my head attempted to provoke me, but I blocked it out. I was here to relax, and I wasn't going to let that other side of me ruin it. My eyes fluttered open when water splattered and dripped on my legs.

I raised an eyebrow at Ryoko as she towered over me. "What?"

"Get your ass off the ground and come join us," she said.

I glared at her. "I don't want to."

"You don't have to come in all the way. You could also sit on the bank and dip your feet in."

"Then I'd have to go into the sun, defeating the purpose," I pointed out. "I'll stick to the shade."

"Stop being a scaredy cat. Now come join us and have fun."

I got to my feet and in her face. "I said no! Now leave me alone."

I stormed off before she had the chance to react.

The cool water of the small pool refreshed me from the summer heat as I sat at the edge, submerging my legs. In my anger, I had stumbled upon this secluded alcove and, as I sat here, my anger had slowly dissipated. The trees and other plant life that grew in this location were thick and beautiful. Birds warbled in the distant foliage and bees buzzed nearby. A fat, fuzzy bumble bee *bonked* my leg, misjudging the clearance needed to fly to a patch of flowers.

My fingers dug into the carpet of moss beneath me, releasing its subtle, earthy and fresh scent into the air. The sun barely peeked through the dense canopy above, reducing its oppressive heat and casting specks of light dancing over the water's surface.

The pool itself was lovely, made up of a small, multilayered rock face with pools in each layer that fed into a bigger one below it by small waterfalls. The last pool I was in trickled out and I could only guess it fed into the river.

I giggled and flexed my toes as small fish nibbled on them. When they weren't deterred from my movement, I allowed them to continue. My eyes focused on the deepest part of the pool again. A suffocated stillness crushed my lungs and chest, and the hairs on the back of my neck rose the longer I looked, but I couldn't tear my gaze away.

The bushes rustled behind me, breaking me out of my trance. I glanced back to see Raikidan standing a few feet from me. I looked away and back at the deepest portion of the pool. I didn't want him here. I didn't want to answer any questions. I didn't want to talk. *I want to be alone.*

From the corner of my eye I noticed him sit down on the edge of the pool and enter the water, scaring away the fish. He pushed away from the edge and moved in front of me—the water only coming up to his hips. When he extended his hand to me I eyed at him skeptically. "Trust me, Eira."

"Don't trust him," the malevolent voice hissed.

I continued to stare at him with apprehension. He wanted me to go into the water, which I definitely didn't want to do.

"Eira, take my hand. Nothing bad is going to happen."

I put my hands on the ground to get up to leave, but Raikidan moved faster and secured a grip on my hip and lower back. I clung to his neck and shut my eyes tight when he pulled me into his arms.

"Eira, it's all right." My grip didn't loosen. "Eira, you don't have to be afraid. I'm not going to let you drown."

My eyes snapped open. "I don't—"

"Everyone is afraid of something. Everyone. It's okay to be afraid, Eira."

I stared into the deep area of the pool again and my chest tightened. Shyden, my mentor, taught me how to be the perfect soldier—the perfect assassin.

"Fear is a weakness. To fear is to be weak."

My grip tightened.

"Bury all signs of fear and push through all ordeals. Never give into any signs of such weaknesses. Never be weak."

The memories wouldn't stop.

The man stared up at me, petrified and unable to move as I brought up my blade to end his meaningless—pathetic—weak life.

"Eira, it's time to let go," Raikidan whispered.

A suffocating stillness crushed my lungs and heart as I stared at the rushing river before me. Sweat dripped down the back of my neck and my palms clammed up. I swallowed, to rid myself of the dryness that plagued my throat, to no avail.

"I can't swim…" I whispered.

"Tell me why."

"Don't tell him," the annoying voice in my head whispered. *"Don't admit to anything."*

I shook my head. I wasn't afraid. I wasn't weak.

"You're afraid of drowning," he voiced for me. "You're afraid someone won't be able to save you the next time it happens. Eira, I won't let you drown, I promise. Let go and trust me."

"Don't trust him."

I didn't want to admit my weakness. I didn't want to let go because I knew if I did, I'd be weaker than I was before.

"Trust me," he whispered in my ear.

"Only a weak fool would trust him."

Slowly, my grip loosened and I allowed some space between us. I gulped when that pitiful feeling crept up. Raikidan forced my hands to slide down to his arms as he moved away. The sensation worsened.

My grip on his arms tightened. "Raikidan, my feet can't touch the bottom here."

"It's okay. Just kick the water so you stay afloat."

"You said y—"

He smiled. "I won't let you drown. I did promise that and I mean it. But you have to face your fear on your own in some way."

"I'm not afraid," I muttered.

He chuckled. "You're cute when you pout."

I looked away from him, my cheeks burning a little. I wasn't cute. I was anything but that.

"You're doing well. Are you okay with—"

My gaze snapped back to him, panic flooding through me. "Don't move away!" I tightened my grip on his arm. "Please…"

"I was only going to have you move your hands to mine to give you more control."

I eyed him warily but in the end allowed my grip to loosen. I slid my hands to his. I started to sink and the panic returned.

"Eira, it's okay. Stay calm and force yourself to stay afloat."

I gulped and tried. It was hard and I sank a few times, but Raikidan kept his promise and helped when I needed it the most. Minutes filled with pitiful treading attempts passed before I had a breakthrough and comprehended the concept. Then, Raikidan did something I was afraid he'd try. He withdrew his hands and moved just out of reach. I was on my own and I didn't like it.

"Told you not to trust him."

I shrieked and tried not to sink. "Raikidan, you promised!"

"I promised I wouldn't let you drown, and I won't. Now try to reach me."

"You're going to die."

I reached for him but I dipped so I went back to treading water, which I was terrible at. I'd have to swim to reach him and I wasn't sure if I could. Raikidan flexed his fingers, teasing me, and I was not okay with that. I needed to figure out how to swim so I could smack him.

My breath caught when water rushed past me. *I moved.* I repeated what I had done and moved more. Raikidan grinned and kept his hands outstretched. I tried to swim closer, but the more attempts I made, the more it appeared I wasn't going anywhere. I wasn't getting any closer to him, but I was sure I was moving.

Then the realization dawned on me. He was swimming backward every time I swam forward. Determined, I kept at it. I wasn't going to play his game. Putting more strength into my strokes, I started to notice the gap between lessening. This realization strengthened my determination and I kept at it.

My heart leapt when my fingers grazed his. I reached out my hand again and grabbed a firm hold on his. The water around me rushed past, and Raikidan placed his hand firmly on my lower back as he pulled me closer to him. In reaction to the sudden movements, I instinctively wrapped my arms around his neck and held on tight.

Raikidan chuckled. "You did well."

"You tricked me," I muttered. "I should hit you for that."

He chuckled again. "Look around and tell me what you see."

Slowly, I let go and looked at him. He gestured with his eyes to look around, so I did out of curiosity. My mouth fell open. We were in the center of the pool. He had gotten me to swim all the way out here. *He got me to swim.*

I set my gaze on him again. Raikidan had gotten me to face something I wasn't willing to admit—something I thought was better to pretend didn't exist in my fear of weakness. He made me face something weak to make me strong.

I pulled my arms tightly around his neck again. "Thank you."

He placed both his hands on my back and then water rushed over my head. He had stopped treading, submerging us. My chest tightened; the instinct to survive flooding my brain. One of Raikidan's hands left my back while the other tightened its hold as he struggled to bring us back to the surface. I tried to help but I was too new at this to be of much help.

I gasped for air when we finally surfaced. Raikidan laughed hysterically and I realized he had done it on purpose. I smacked him in the chest. "That wasn't funny!"

He quieted his laughter to a chuckle. "What, scared you?"

"Don't say it!"

"Yes!"

I froze and Raikidan grinned at me. "Really?"

I looked down to avert my gaze. "Yes…"

Raikidan lifted my chin with his fingers and then wiped a stray wet tress of hair away from my face. I stared into his eyes. *Blue eyes.* My favorite-colored eyes. Dark blue eyes being preferred. *His eyes…*

"Get away from him."

I blinked. No, that wasn't right. I looked around. None of this was right. I pushed away from him.

"Eira?"

"Get away."

This was all wrong. I paddled backward a little bit.

"Eira, what is it?"

Turning, I swam to the edge of the pool. Launching out of the water I bolted for the tree line.

"Eira!"

"Run."

I kept running. I didn't stop until I knew I was far away from him. I leaned against a tree and breathed heavily. I placed my hand on my forehead and tried to stay calm. This was all wrong. It wasn't supposed to be like this. Why wasn't it going like it was supposed to?

He was only supposed to help. He was supposed to want to keep his distance. He was supposed to—I was supposed to remain alone. I wasn't supposed to make a connection. I was supposed to make sure I didn't have something else to lose. I was supposed to protect myself. *It's best if I'm alone…*

"Eira!" Raikidan called. "Eira, where are you?"

I pressed myself against the tree and hid. He pushed through the underbrush some ways off and I quieted my breathing. When he burst through the trees and stopped to look around near me, I prayed he wouldn't find me. I shouldn't have taken such a direct route.

"Eira, please."

I shut my eyes and held my breath. He sounded desperate, and I hated how much I wanted to answer.

"What did I do to upset her?"

I place my hand over my mouth to prevent me from speaking. I wanted to tell him it wasn't him. I wanted to explain it was all me but I knew I couldn't. It would only complicate things.

Raikidan yelled in frustration and hit a tree. The tree cracked but it didn't fall.

"Forget it," he muttered. "I can't do anything right with her."

I sunk to the ground when he left. *I'm an awful person...* I pulled my legs up to my chest and rested my arms on top of my knees, hiding my face in them. The faint flutter of wings from a small bird landing in the tree above me graced my ears, but I ignored it.

I held my head tightly with my hands. "Why am I such a horrible person?"

I slammed my head against the tree, causing small immature acorns to fall—several bouncing off my face, but I didn't care. I stared up at the top of the tree, where I should have been able to see the sky, had the canopy not been so thick. The small bird that had landed on the tree jumped around and chirped angrily.

I frowned. "Sorry little bird. I didn't mean to upset you. Unfortunately, it's the only thing I'm good at."

Slowly, I rose to my feet and walked off somewhere. I didn't know where I'd end up but I didn't care. I wasn't ready to go back and face the others yet. I knew I couldn't look Raikidan in the face and not worry about telling him the truth. It would only complicate things.

CHAPTER 32

I moaned and curled up tighter. My assailant shook me again. Sighing, I opened my eyes. It was still dark out, the only light coming from the moon and the embers left in fire pit.

"Eira, c'mon, wake up," Raikidan urged.

"What do you want?" I grumble.

"Get your stuff," he said in a hushed voice. "We're going somewhere."

I sat up and rubbed my eyes. "What are you talking about?

"You'll see. Now grab your stuff so we can go. And don't wake the others."

I was so confused, probably because I was tired, but I got up anyway. I doubted I'd had much sleep; maybe two or three hours at most. The embers in the fire pit told me that. I hadn't come back to the campsite until after dark, and even then I had stayed out of sight until everyone had gone to bed.

I snuck into the tent and stepped over Ryoko and Rylan, who was shifted in his wolf shape and being used as a comfortable pillow by Ryoko. Snatching my bag, I quickly ducked out of the tent.

"Get dressed," he said.

My brow furrowed. I was dressed—in shorts and a tank top, but dressed nonetheless. Then I noticed he was in his Guard uniform. We were going somewhere far. Forcing my clothes to shift, I pulled my cloak, veil and body cloth out of my bag and put them on.

Raikidan grasped my wrist and pulled me to the edge of the campsite. "C'mon, let's go."

I sighed. "Raikidan, what's the rush?"

He hushed me. "Keep your voice down. I don't want the others knowing we're leaving."

My face scrunched as I tried to figure out why he was acting so strange. "Why are you being so secretive?"

"It's a surprise."

"I hate surprises."

He chuckled. "I think you'll like this one. Come, let's go."

I let out an exasperated sigh and followed him. Once we were out of the campsite, he took my bag and set a quick pace. I struggled to keep up. My night vision was better than most nu-humans, but it still wasn't the best, not that Raikidan noticed. He was too set on his mission.

I gazed around at the enormous trees around us. They looked thousands of years old, making them older than the trees in the Forest of Marior. At first, I didn't think that to be possible, but then I thought about how Raikidan and I had been traveling south for days, and I wondered if we had made it to the second oldest forest in Lumaraeon. *Could we have traveled to the Velsara Wilds?* Asking Raikidan would be pointless. No matter how often I had asked, he refused to tell me anything.

Raikidan came to a halt and took in our surroundings. I sensed his anxiety, making me nervous, and it only grew worse when he started growling. Suddenly, a large figure moved from behind some trees in front of us. I stepped back when I realized I was in the presence of a red dragon.

He was a massive creature, maybe even towering over Raikidan in his largest form. Large, plated scales that looked more like crimson bone lined his green eyes like a mask and merged with the heavy plating over his curved, ivory horns. These heavy plated scales also curved over his cheeks and protruded in two locations like faux horns. He had long spines on his throat and small spines clustered on various places of his face. Large plated scales cascaded down his back and tail, almost covering the barb on the end.

I couldn't say how he had hidden so successfully behind the trees, or how other dragons were appearing all around us in the same manner as he had. Raikidan took a protective step in front of me and growled. The dragon in front growled back; Raikidan growled more.

I glanced around and noticed only the dragon in front of us was being aggressive. The rest of the dragons appeared more curious than anything. When Raikidan shifted his body weight, my attention was brought back to him and the hostile dragon. The two continued to growl at each other, making me want to sigh. That is, until I heard something. It was quick and hard to decipher through the growling but it was definitely a word. These two weren't just acting aggressively; they were speaking. Raikidan had muttered his tongue under his breath many times around me, but had only spoken it twice for me to deliberately hear, and even the few words he had spoken had been hard to distinguish from typical grunts, growls, and hissing.

I rested my hand on Raikidan's shoulder and leaned closer. "Do you mind telling me what the hell is going on here? You dragged me out all this way for something, and I know it wasn't so you could argue with this dragon."

"Stay quiet and let me deal with this," he murmured.

I glared at him, even though he couldn't see it well behind my hood and veil. "How many times do I have to tell you not to order me around?"

Before Raikidan could respond, the red dragon he quarreled with shifted into a nu-human form. He had tan skin, red hair and light facial hair, green eyes, and appeared to be the same age as Raikidan, but I had this strange feeling he was much older. His hair was two tones of red and styled as an unsupported long mohawk, but the sides of his head were trimmed down short instead of shaved or plucked out.

I expected him to be naked when he shifted, but to my surprise, he was fully clothed. *Druid allies, maybe?* If we were in the Velsara Wilds, the thought would be more than plausible. Both the South Tribe and several druid villages resided in these woods.

"State your business here, Human," the dragon ordered, his word drenched in a thick accent more commonly found in the southern wetlands on the west side of the Larkian Mountain rage.

"I thought red dragons were supposed to be friendly," I commented to Raikidan. "Did he not get the memo, or did someone spit on his deer carcass this morning?"

Raikidan chuckled and several of the dragons around us also found my words amusing.

The upper lip red dragon in front of us lifted. "I said state your business, Human."

I jerked my head at Raikidan. "Ask him. He's the one dragging me to the gods knows where."

"I'm askin' you, not the half-color."

Pulling an ember from my lips, I pushed Raikidan aside and threw a ball of fire at the dragon. He jumped out of the way and glared at me.

"Insult him like that again, and next time I'll actually try to hit you," I threatened.

Raikidan chuckled. "For your sake, Zaith, I wouldn't piss her off. Now, let us pass and pay our respects."

"Rogue shaman," Zaith muttered. "My answer is still no. Now leave my colony's territory."

Pay our respects? Now I needed to know what was going on. But of course, since Raikidan was being so secretive, I was going to have to figure it out on my own. He had dragged me south, and he obviously came into this colony's territory on purpose. Raikidan never did things on accident, or at least, I didn't think he did.

But the biggest factor was this paying respects topic Raikidan brought up. Paying respects was for the dead. *That's it!* Turning to face Raikidan, I snatched my bag from him and headed in the direction we had been walking.

"Eira?" Raikidan asked.

Zaith stepped into my path in an attempt to stop me, but I wasn't having it. I twisted his arm and tripped him. He howled in pain, making Raikidan laugh and I continued on.

Raikidan began to follow, but he stopped a few steps later to speak to Zaith. "I warned you. Never get in her way or piss her off. You're lucky she's in a nice mood today."

Zaith growled at Raikidan and Raikidan was happy to oblige with a similar comeback before following me. The trees thinned more as we walked, and I was very aware of the dragons following us. They kept their distance, but that didn't stop Raikidan from being uneasy and walking too close to me. No matter how many times I pushed him away and reminded him about my personal space, he'd come right back.

I came to a stop when we reached a large clearing. In the center of the clearing rested a large pile of bones, but they weren't just any bones. These were the bones of a fully-intact dragon skeleton. *Peacekeeper Pyralis…*

I made my way over to the skeleton. Kneeling down in front of the skull, I placed my bag by my side and steepled my hands in front of my face to pay my respects. Raikidan knelt next to me, but instead of paying his respects he watched me. Ignoring him, I continued my attempt, but I couldn't think of what to say. I didn't know the best way to go about this. I knew the stories and I knew what he had done for everyone, but no words seemed good enough.

I sighed. Words would never be good enough for me. I needed something that would show how grateful I was for what he had done. Allowing my hands to fall, I turned and reached for my bag. I rummaged around and tried to find the large bag buried under all the other supplies. *I know I left it in here. Where did it go?* Finally finding both bags of the same size, I looked at the individual hemmed embroidery to figure out which one I wanted.

Pulling the small bag out, I handed the pack to Raikidan. "You're going to want to back up."

"What are you—Eira, where did you get that?" he demanded to know as I pulled out the red dragon's eye from its leather bag.

"It's mine," I said. "Now back up so I have room."

Raikidan complied but kept a careful eye on me. Collecting myself and then taking a deep breath, I tossed the gem high into the air. The afternoon sun sparkled against the surface of the gem. Unclasping my cloak, I tossed it aside and released the veil from my hair clip, making sure my body cloth and hair didn't come loose in the process.

Taking a deep breath to keep me calm, I pulled a few embers from my lips and willed them to grow in my hands. Swirling the fire around me, I moved my body in a slow dance-like motion. The gem finally reached its zenith and began to fall, and when it came back within reach I snatched it. The fire in my hand engulfed the gem, illuminating and reflecting light all around me.

Using all my will and power, I took the gem and slammed it into the forehead of the skeleton. The skeleton cracked and several dragons reacted with anger. Ignoring them and their potential to attack me, I focused on tapping into the crystal's power. Forcing more fire and some spirit energy into the crystal, it began to glow. It glowed so brightly I had to close my eyes, but I didn't pull away. This was my tribute and I wouldn't back down.

I stepped back when the skeleton moved. I watched as it came to life and repositioned. As it moved, the gem I had planted into the skull distorted and formed over the bones. Taking a deep breath, I forced my body to move and willed the skeleton into a shape I wanted. I needed to make sure this gem wasn't wasted and this tribute wasn't ruined.

The skeleton reared up on its back legs and its mouth opened as if it were breathing fire. The gem continued to engulf the skeleton and as it finished at the feet, it reached across the ground. The gem-like matter shot skyward creating the image of a man with a sword in his hands, thrusting its blade down into the ground.

Weakness flooded over me and I fell to one knee, my breath coming out in heavy bursts. I took in the statue I had created and was a bit disappointed with myself. In creating the human version of Pyralis, I had accidently made him a nu-human. I was so sure I was thinking of him correctly. *Guess I really can't do anything right…*

Then I noticed something peculiar behind the statue. Just a few feet away, stood two gravestones. Raikidan had said they didn't bury the dead; Pyralis' bones were proof of that, so what were two gravestones doing in a place like this? It was possible they buried baby dragons if they didn't make it, but their kind didn't come across as the type to create gravestones. I could only guess some humans had died here once before the dragons claimed the area as their territory. It made the most sense, as the stones appeared rather old.

"Eira?" Raikidan asked hesitantly, pulling me from my questioning.

I glanced back and smirked. "You look pale, Raikidan. Something the matter?"

"I, uh, can you now tell me where you got that gem?"

"It was a gift."

He glared at me. "That's your answer for everything."

I chuckled. "That's because that's how I get all of my stuff."

"No one just gives something that valuable to someone."

I shrugged. "It's how I got the green dragon's eye."

Raikidan stared at me in disbelief. "You have two of the three?"

"Had," I corrected as I looked up at the new statue. "I had two."

Raikidan took a stand by my side. "I can't believe you knew how to use it."

"I didn't. I just went with a gut instinct."

He glanced down at me with a narrowed, scrutinizing gaze. "That's not like you. You always think things out before you act."

I laughed. "You really don't know me at all then."

Raikidan raised an eyebrow in my direction and then focused on the statue. "Could you really not be okay with just saying something? Did you have to use such a rare gem?"

"You know me and words. We don't get along."

Raikidan chuckled in response. I glanced at the red dragons that watched us from the safety of the tree line.

"They don't know what to make of you," Raikidan said. "They're impressed with what you've done. They never thought such a tribute was possible. Being dragons, they would have hoarded the gem for themselves, but you chose to do something nice with it. They expected a human to want to try to tap into the gem's power for their own gain, but you've done the complete opposite."

"I have no use for it," I replied with a shrug. "Zaith, or whatever his name is, doesn't look impressed with what I've done."

Raikidan chuckled. "He's still dealing with his damaged pride."

"Well the buttercup can suck it up. It's his damned fault for getting in the way."

A masculine voice chuckled close by and I looked at Raikidan only to find him as confused as me.

"Eira, you were always rough with the males," the voice said. "No wonder they were always afraid of you."

Raikidan took a step back. "Pyralis."

I blinked when Raikidan said the dead dragon's name and chose to look in the direction he was staring. I was startled to see an incredibly tall man with short, unnatural-red hair, and emerald green eyes standing before us. He looked identical to the crystal man that stood beneath the crystal dragon statue, right down to the nu-human ears. He was translucent, making me aware of his nonliving state.

I dipped my head respectfully. "Sir."

Pyralis grunted. "This is why I've always hated soldiers. You're all too formal. Well, ex-soldier in your case."

"Great, everyone is uneasy now that they know you're an ex-soldier," Raikidan muttered.

I snorted. Not like I didn't expect it.

Pyralis walked around his new memorial. "Impressive work. You really knew what you wanted to do. Thank you for this, but words would have sufficed."

"You obviously don't know me if you thought words would have gotten the job done." I felt like a broken recording.

Pyralis chuckled and faced me. "Yes, words don't come easy for do they, Eira? It's because of that you don't fit in with your own."

I took a step back. I didn't like how he said that. It didn't feel good.

Raikidan, seeing my unease, took a step forward. "Watch it."

Pyralis held up his hands. "I apologize. I didn't mean for it to come off in that way." He walked closer to me. "You look tired, Eira. You should rest."

"I'm fine," I replied, still wary of him.

Pyralis smiled and then faded from view. I spun around when I sensed a spiritual presence behind me, to find Pyralis had appeared there.

"It takes a lot of elemental and spiritual power to use the dragon's eye gems," he said. "You're very good at hiding your weakened state. You need your rest after the wonderful job you've done."

"I said I'm—"

I didn't get a chance to finish. Pyralis reached out and touched my forehead with two fingers. My vision faded and I lost all feeling in my body. The last thing I heard was Raikidan yelling my name as I collapsed.

33 CHAPTER

The breeze was light and the afternoon sun's rays filtered through the think canopy, casting dancing light spots across the forest floor. Songbirds trilled happily as if there were no evil in the world.

I stood in the shadows of a large tree, unsure where I was. Nothing looked familiar, but that didn't worry me at the moment. I was too preoccupied with watching a tiny black dragon playing all by himself. I didn't understand why he was alone. Shouldn't he be playing with other dragons his age? Brothers or sisters; cousins or clan friends even?

He seemed oblivious to the fact he was alone. I watched him circle a flower and then pounce on the unfortunate plant. He held his head high, proud of his triumphant kill, though it was short-lived when a violet butterfly flittered into view. *An amaranthine?* I expected the little dragon to reach out and attack the poor insect, but he followed it with curiosity instead. Intrigued by the dragon's actions, I followed him.

The little dragon hopped around happily as it followed the fluttering creature. I remembered Raikidan telling me black dragons didn't care much for any life beyond their own, but watching this dragon it was hard to believe that was true. If they weren't born with that attitude, what made them think that way later on?

The little dragon put his front legs on a tree when the amaranthine landed on the trunk. He gazed up at it and whimpered. The more he cried the more I pitied him. He really like this butterfly and it was just out of reach for him.

The little dragon placed his front legs back on the ground and walked in a tight circle a few times before looking back up at the butterfly and whimpering again. The butterfly fluttered off and the dragon happily tried to follow it but stopped. He turned around and jumped a few times before scurrying off in the new direction.

I watched as a large red dragon moved into sight and bent its head down. The little dragon made a delighted squealing sound and touched his nose with the larger dragon. I covered my mouth so I wouldn't giggle. The sound was cute, but I couldn't figure out what a red dragon was doing with a baby black dragon. From what I could tell dragons weren't the adopting types, at least not cross color. Their bad relations with each other would deter that. But this red dragon didn't care and I wasn't sure if it was male or female.

The wind picked up, shaking the canopy leaves and scattering more light over the floor. That's when I noticed something on the baby dragon. I couldn't believe what I was seeing, and I blinked to make sure I wasn't crazy. The little dragon had a small red stripe down the center of his back that started near his eyes.

Raikidan? I shook my head of the thought. It couldn't be him. Could it? Was the stripe he had unique, or did all black-red dragons have them? Whatever the case was, if this was in fact Raikidan, that would make this red dragon his mother.

The red dragon turned and headed farther into the woods. The little dragon started to follow, but stopped and looked back to where the butterfly had disappeared. The red dragon turned her head and called to the little dragon and he reluctantly followed after a few moments of hesitation.

Curiosity tugged me to follow, but as I did the world around me blurred and when it stopped I was at the edge of a clearing next to a large cliff. The red dragon and small black-red dragon came out of the forest nearby and climbed a small path that led up the cliff. The two stopped when the sounds of loud growls and roars erupted from the top.

Above them, two black dragons thundered out of a cave onto the crag ledge. They acted aggressively, but as I watched them neither inflicted any wounds on the other. It occurred to me these two were arguing and one of them wasn't a full black dragon at all. As he moved, I noticed red scales in a stripe-like pattern all along his body. That indicated half-colors did have unique patterns; that also meant this little dragon I'd been watching was, in fact, Raikidan. But I didn't understand why I was seeing all of this. What was the purpose?

The black-red dragon roared at the black dragon and then took to the skies. As he did, Raikidan scampered up to the top of the cliff and ran to the ledge where the other black dragon stood. Raikidan called out to the fleeing dragon, but his small cry went unheard.

Raikidan hung his head and retreat into the cave the two older dragons had come out of. My feet moved on their own and climbed the path to the cave entrance. Peering inside, I watched little Raikidan glare at a cave cricket as he lay facing a cave wall. I half expected him to snap at it when it hopped too close but he continued to brood.

I examined the cave. There were no other dragons in here. It didn't make sense. Why was Raikidan the only baby here? Raikidan sighed and flopped over on his side. He no longer looked mad. I knew the look on his face. He was sad and alone. He wasn't oblivious to the lack of other baby dragons around him. He just made the best of it because he had to.

Kneeling down next to him, I couldn't help but reach out and touch his head. I blinked when a strange sensation rushed through me.

"Why did he have to break the promise he made to his brother?"

I looked up when the feminine voice penetrated my mind. It was rough, as if it were partially growling. I watched the red and black dragon and they sat next to each other. The black dragon had his neck draped over the red dragon's neck and his head rested on her shoulder. I recognized that posture. Raikidan had done the human equivalent at the club.

"He has never been good with keeping promises," the black dragon stated.

I blinked. I could understand them. That must have been what that weird rush had been.

The red dragon sighed. *"But now Raikidan is alone."*

"*He has Corliss,*" the black dragon said.

"But they do not come over often, thanks to you fighting with your brother," she accused.

I gazed down at baby Raikidan. He had told me about Corliss once, but he had said he was a friend. I wondered why he didn't say Corliss was his cousin.

The black dragon exhaled. *"We are going to have to manage. You had insisted on keeping his egg warm for a century and a half longer, knowing full well this would happen."*

I blinked. A century and a half longer? How long did these guys stay in their shells?

"Hush!" she hissed. *"You make it sound like we should not have done it, and he can hear you."*

"I am not saying that," the black dragon growled. *"I am merely saying we knew what would happen if we kept hoping. His siblings grew up without him. That is the simple truth."*

A low, sorrowful moan came from her throat. *"Yes, but why could they not have all stayed?"*

"Because they have the instincts of black dragons. They do not want to live in small clans or large colonies."

"But it would have been safer!" the red dragon cried. *"Most of them would still be alive if they had stayed..."*

My heart sunk. Raikidan told me it was a hard life for half-colors but from the sounds of it, they were killed in cold blood, which he had never mentioned.

The black dragon looked as though he was planning to respond but a roar echoed from the sky. Curious, I ventured out of the cave to take a look. Ascending from the sky was a massive black dragon and a beautiful emerald green dragon. The two dragons on the ledge moved, allowing the dragons in flight to land.

When they landed I noticed a squirming green and black bundle of scales in the green dragon's mouth. The green dragon lowered her hand and she barely managed to open her jaws before her precious bundle scampered off into the cave.

I turned to watch the little green dragon bowl over Raikidan. Raikidan, forgetting why he was sad, wrestled with his new companion. I smiled as I watched them. They were so innocent. I noticed the interesting pattern on the little green dragon's body as they played. Although his scales were predominately green he had black ones scattered across his body like stars in the sky.

I wondered if this was Corliss. Raikidan never mentioned to me he was a green-black dragon but as I took in the two black dragons who were sizing themselves up against each other in front of their mates I could see the resemblance between the two. *They're practically identical.* It could also explain the choice in different colored mates but I didn't know enough about Dragon mating habits to be sure.

The two little dragons chased each other out of the cave and down the path leading to the woods. Not wanting to lose sight of them, I followed. As I did, the world around me altered little by little, and the two wrestling dragons grew older each time. By the time the two split apart they were enormous. They couldn't be less than three times my size, but I could tell by Raikidan's size neither were full grown yet. Or at least, not to the size of his current age. Raikidan was easily three times this size now, if not more.

The two dragons sized each other up but as they went to lunge, a roar pierced the sky. Corliss sighed and flicked his tail before jumping to the skies and flying off with his parents. Raikidan exhaled through his nose and headed up the path to the cave. Once he reached the top, his mother greeted him.

"It is time for your shifting lesson," she said.

Raikidan let out an exasperated sigh. *"Do I have to?"*

I blinked at the difference in his voice compared to what I was used to hearing. It was higher, as if he was significantly younger than my Raikidan.

His mother chuckled. *"Yes. Now shift into a human."*

He groaned. *"Can we do a different shape? I hate that one."*

"You have been listening to your father again."

"There is nothing good about humans."

His mother snorted. *"And how would you know? You have never met one."*

"Father has."

"As have I. And your father is wrong. There are nice qualities about them. Your father just refuses to see them. Now shift."

He grumbled and moved to the ledge. Closing his eyes he forced himself to concentrate and his body reacted. The process was slow, much slower than what I had seen when I first watched him shift, but eventually he made it into his human shape.

He was much younger than I expected—looking no older than seventeen. *No wonder he has such an attitude.*

"*You should allow me to cut your hair to a more acceptable length,*" his mother teased.

Raikidan snorted. "*I will pass.*"

"*Your shifting needs work,*" his father chided as he emerged from the cave.

Raikidan huffed and then looked bored. Obviously that wasn't what he wanted to hear from his father.

"*He is still learning,*" his mother said.

His father snorted. "*He has been learning for the past few years, and still he has not mastered shifting to the most basic creatures.*"

"*You need to go easy on him.*"

"*I did not go easy on the others and he will not get any special treatment,*" his father growled.

"*And they resented you for it!*" She turned to head back into the cave. "*As do I.*"

Ouch. On the surface, Raikidan's father looked completely unfazed by her words, but then I noticed his body posture, which said otherwise. Even Raikidan appeared upset by her words.

My head swiveled when everything suddenly started going dark. My blood ran cold when a gunshot rang out and Raikidan's mother cried out in excruciating pain. I gulped when the cave faded away and the three dragons were left standing where they were. Except Raikidan's mother wasn't standing anymore. She lay motionless on the ground with blood pouring out of her from the underside.

Raikidan took a step forward. "*M—mother?*"

Raikidan's father bent his head down and nudged his mate's motionless body. Raikidan ran to his mother's side and placed his hand on her head. He appeared older, about the age I knew him to look, and I could see a large cut on his cheek as he tried in vain to get her to respond. *That cut...* Its location was the same as the scar I had found when inspecting him for wounds after his fire training.

Raikidan's father roared with anger and turned away from the two. He laid down some ways off and as he did his mate faded away and Raikidan shifted to his natural shape. I was still floating in darkness, but they were now inside a cave. It was dark out and a storm hammered beyond the cave mouth.

Raikidan moved to the mouth of the cave and stared out into the night.

"You are finally deciding to leave?" his father muttered.

"There is no reason for me to stay anymore," Raikidan said. *"You blame me for what happened when you are just as guilty."*

Raikidan's father stood and growled at him. *"You did not protect her."*

Raikidan rounded on his father. *"And you were not there to even try! You refused to go with us, upsetting her by telling her it was pointless to go, and you try to blame me? At least I tried to protect her. At least I tried to make her happy."*

"Do not dare accuse me of not trying to make her happy," his father spat.

"Nothing is ever good enough for you. Nothing I did ever pleased you. Nothing she ever did ever pleased you. You did not care about me, or about her. You only cared about yourself! You did not deserve her. She would have been better with another dragon as her mate."

"Then you would not exist if that were the case."

Raikidan turned away. *"At least then she would have been happy."*

Raikidan took to the skies and didn't look back. His father didn't try to stop him and he didn't watch his son leave. Instead, he retreated back into his cave, which faded away soon after. I observed the events that unfolded after Raikidan's departure. I watched him battle storms in flight and fight for his life against other dragons. I witnessed as he tried to find his place in the world.

Now he lay on the ground, battered, bruised, and bloody while rain hammered down on him. He had fought for everything leading up to this point and now he looked like he couldn't defend himself. Raikidan exhaled slowly. His eyes showed his defeat, both physically and mentally. He wanted to give up—saw no reason to continue trying. My chest tightened. I knew that mindset all too well. I felt the need to be near him and encourage him to keep fighting but I couldn't move.

Raikidan tilted his head up, and as he did, a familiar-looking large green-black dragon landed in front of him. Raikidan growled and the other dragon laughed.

"You look pathetic, cousin," the green dragon teased.

"C–Corliss?" Raikidan managed.

Corliss laughed again. *"Of course it is me. I must say you are damned lucky to have landed in this condition in my territory and not a territory belonging to another dragon."*

Raikidan grunted. *"Had I known where you had run off to, I would have done it on purpose."*

Corliss chuckled. *"Let us get you somewhere dry so you can heal properly without getting an infection."*

Raikidan snorted. *"I was joking when I said I would have come looking for you."*

What looked like a possible smile appeared on Corliss' face. *"But I am not joking about helping you. We are kin, Raikidan, and real kin stick together no matter what. Besides, I need someone I trust to share my large territory with. It is getting to be too much for me to handle and I cannot think of a better dragon I would rather split it with. So what do you say?"*

Raikidan chuckled. *"I am not going to pass up free territory."*

Corliss laughed. *"That is the Raikidan I know. Now let us get you to my lair until we can find you one of your own."*

I watched as Corliss helped Raikidan stand and lead him away. Time progressed and flew by again as the two split the territory and worked together to keep it. Each day they would meet up and speak about what happened, and every once in a while they'd size each other up and enjoy the closeness of their kinship.

Then one day, Corliss didn't show up like he always did. Raikidan waited and waited, but he still didn't show. Slowly, Raikidan ventured into Corliss' territory to look for him. Raikidan stopped when he found him, but Corliss wasn't alone. He was following a green dragon around, but from the looks of it, he wasn't being aggressive. It seemed he was actually quite interested in this new dragon, and it didn't appear one-sided.

Raikidan hung his head and headed back the way he came. A somber aura emanated from him. I didn't understand it. From what I could tell Corliss had chosen a mate. I would have figured Raikidan would be happy for his cousin, but he didn't look happy in the least.

I watched as Raikidan lay down with a sigh by the river that ran over his lair. The hours passed and he remained like this. He was finally roused when Corliss walked out of the woods near him, with his new mate timidly following behind.

"Raikidan, I wan—"

"I have seen your new mate already," Raikidan interrupted.

"But how? This is the first—"

"I came looking for you."

Corliss lowered his head. *"Sorry. I meant to meet up with you but everything started happening all at once."*

Raikidan grunted. *"I can see that. Now get off my territory."*

Corliss blinked. *"W—what? What is with you today?"*

Raikidan rose to his feet and crossed the shallow river. *"You do not need me anymore. You have her now. I hope she makes you happy."*

Now I knew why he'd been so upset. *Raikidan, don't think that way.*

Corliss and his mate watched Raikidan climbed down the cliff face and disappear behind the waterfall that hid his lair.

"Corliss, what did I do wrong?" his mate asked, her voice low.

"Nothing," he assured her. *"You did not do anything wrong. He just thinks I have abandoned him."*

"But you did not."

"He does not see it that way." Corliss sighed. *"And with everything he has gone though in his life… I do not blame him."*

The two faded, and the world changed so I was able to see Raikidan again. Time passed, and he didn't do much other than lie in his cave and do nothing on a bad day and lay on top of his lair when it was nice, or force himself to monitor his territory. He was willing to speak with Corliss again, but it took quite a bit of time to pass before that happened.

The two would talk and wrestle from time to time, while Corliss' mate watched from a distance, but I could see why Raikidan never mentioned any relation between the two of them. Their relationship was never the same after Corliss took his mate. They didn't act like family anymore. They acted like friends, but not close ones.

I blinked at the scene in front of me when it changed again. It was now of Raikidan lying by the river, like he normally did, with a bored expression. As he laid there, an amaranthine butterfly fluttered past him. This caught his eye and he watched it intently. It resembled the one he had followed when he was only a baby. *Actually, now that I think of it…* It also looked like the few that had appeared from time to time in these time-lapsed visions. Each time Raikidan had taken an extreme interest in them as if each one was his favorite thing in the world. *Is there something significant about the insect? Or did Raikidan really see the rare creature that often?*

But this time he did something different. He got up and followed it. He followed it down the cliff and into the woods. He pursued it until it landed on a woman who sat under a tree. Raikidan looked at her with interest and she peered back at him. I blinked. I knew the woman. She was me.

Raikidan shifted, fully clothed this time unlike the others, and extended his hand. The woman who was me accepted the gesture and he pulled her up. Without hesitation, she walked past him and he turned to follow.

I observed as he tried to talk to her. At first, she was reluctant to communicate back but, as time passed, she was more willing. He then got her to laugh and he laughed with her. She tried to put some distance between them by picking up her pack, but Raikidan grabbed onto her wrist and pulled her back. He twirled her around as if they were dancing, and the woman smiled the entire time.

I couldn't see why this woman was being portrayed as me. I didn't smile and I didn't laugh. And even if I did from time to time, it was definitely not like that. What was the significance to all of this? *What message am I missing?*

Raikidan pulled the woman close, as if the dance was done, and the two stared at each other. The woman's expression changed then. A frown took the place of her smile and her eyes reflected fear and confusion. The woman pulled away from him and backed up. Raikidan tried to bring her closer again, but she kept her distance.

Raikidan looked so confused. He reached for the woman, but she turned away, and as she walked, she turned to ice. I couldn't do anything but watch. I didn't understand what was going on.

"Stop pushing him away, dear," a voice whispered.

My neck cranked in several directions. "Mom?"

"Don't push him away anymore," she told me.

I continued to look around for her. "Mom, where are you?"

"He doesn't want to be alone anymore."

I regarded Raikidan, who looked sad and confused as he stared at the frozen version of me.

A pair of feminine arms wrapped around me. "He doesn't want to be alone, just like you."

"Mom…" I touched her hands as they rested on my collarbone.

"There's nothing wrong with letting someone in," she whispered. "It's not a sin to rely on someone. He wants to be your friend, Eira. You don't judge him. You accept him as he is. That's all he's ever wanted. He wants something like that to hold onto. Like you do."

My gaze lowered. "It's best if I—"

"It's best that you find peace. It's best you find happiness."

"Happiness isn't for me."

"It can be, if you let it."

I shook my head. "I can't feel happiness."

"Yes you can. You did once, and you can again if you let it."

My lip quivered. "It just leads to more pain."

"It won't if you truly believe in it." She pulled away. "Stop pushing him away so neither of you is alone anymore."

I spun around. "Mom, don't go! Please, not yet!"

But it was too late. She was gone, and so was Raikidan and the frozen version of me. I was alone and, in all honesty, I didn't like it.

CHAPTER 34

A fog clouded my mind as I roused from my slumber. The sun's warm rays bathed over my skin, enticing me to wake up. And although I didn't want to, I wasn't sure if I could face another dream like that again. Shaking my head of its fogginess, I stretched and a small squeak escaped my lips. My eyes fluttered open and were greeted by a pair of curious green eyes.

I stared at the little dragon who perched his front legs on my bent knees. He tilted his head and watched me and I looked back at him. He had red scales and a heavily plated crest that also covered his tiny horns, which were still growing in. Frills lined his hips and trailed down to the tip of his tail.

I reached out and touched his head. The little dragon squealed and jumped around everywhere. His red scales sparkled in the late afternoon sun. A smile crept onto my face as I watched him.

I grunted as air left my lungs suddenly when the little dragon jumped on me. *Good thing I wasn't planning on having kids.* He was a big baby; that was for sure. I turned my head when Raikidan growled. He sat a little way away from me, under the statue I had created. That's when I realized someone had moved me under the memorial, into a soft patch of grass and flowers.

The little dragon lowered his head submissively as Raikidan growled.

I narrowed my eyes. "What's your problem?"

"He's not being careful," Raikidan said.

I snorted. "He's only a baby. What'd you expect?"

The little guy didn't look like he could speak or even fly. His wings looked too immature to be of any use to him.

"He still needs to be taught to be careful," Raikidan muttered.

I shook my head and rubbed the baby dragon's head to reassure him. He chirped happily and tried to nip at my fingers.

Raikidan growled again and I rolled my eyes. "Will you shut up? He's just—"

I cringed when the baby dragon chomped on my hand, angering Raikidan. I smacked the little dragon hard on the nose. He let go and whimpered as I scolded him quickly before looking at my bleeding hand. Blood oozed out of three of my fingers. The little guy had sharp teeth; that was for sure.

The little dragon slowly lifted his head and began lapping up the blood. I could see little sparks shoot from his mouth as if he were trying to create fire, but none formed into a flame. It was easy to understand what he was trying to do. *It looks like Raikidan isn't the only who can heal with fire. It must be a red dragon ability.* But this little guy was too young to make fire, let alone heal with it.

Pulling my hand away, I gave my fingers a quick, clean lick, and then pulled the little dragon into my lap. Bracing him with my arm, I used my other hand to rub his stomach. The dragon chirped and squirmed with delight. I was astounded by how soft and unprotected his underside was. It was still scaled, but the scales were leathery instead of a polished shell.

I stopped rubbing his stomach when I noticed the dark scales that went up the center of his body. The little dragon whimpered when I traced the line. I stopped touching the black scales and rubbed his head to reassure him. I didn't judge Raikidan for being a half-color and I wasn't about to with this dragon.

The little dragon perked up at my touch and flipped over. His next behavior surprised me. He rested his front legs on my shoulder and rubbed his face against mine like a cat did with its owner. Occasionally he'd lick my face and a small purr-like grunt would escape his throat. I wasn't sure how to react to this behavior. He was happy, but that's all I knew. A few quick glances at Raikidan told me he had no intention of explaining it to me either, at least, not with all these dragons watching us.

He was unusually quiet and cold. He tended to be distant when the others were around, but this was a new level with me. He almost seemed angry. I sighed mentally from the headache that was building. I didn't understand him.

I grunted when the little dragon on my lap nearly knocked me out when he headbutted me. "Easy there, killer."

A masculine voice chuckled above me. I gazed up to find Pyralis perched above me on the knee of the dragon gem statue—a grin spread across his face and amusement shining in his eyes.

He jumped down from his spot and crouched next to me. "He likes you."

"I kinda figured that," I said. "I see you're enjoying your memorial."

He smiled. "You put a great deal of spiritual energy into this. It's rather impressive. Not many shamans with only partial training have such power."

I grunted. "I was told I was a protégé."

"You don't believe them."

"I think you know the answer to that."

Pyralis chuckled. "Humility, an excellent trait to have, but with you it doesn't seem to be humility, now, is it?"

I stroked the baby dragon's chin instead of replying. The little dragon pulled away from my touch and looked at me with his head tilted. The dragon may have been young, but he wasn't stupid. He could tell I was avoiding the topic Pyralis presented.

"I'm glad my son has found someone to like," a feminine voice said warmly.

I peered up to see a sultry, red haired nu-human woman standing in front of me. She had spectacular light green eyes and freckles scattered across her light skin like paint on a canvas. She was beyond compare in every way and I didn't feel comfortable being near her. It didn't feel right for me to be near something so… perfect.

The woman smiled at me. "My name is Xaneth."

"Eira."

She continued to smile. "Beautiful name. It suits you."

I looked down at the baby dragon. She was wrong but it didn't feel right telling her that. The little dragon nudged my hand with his nose and I scratched his cheek in response.

"Thank you for being so kind to him." Xaneth knelt. "He doesn't deserve to be hated for my choice. None of my children do. Looking more red dragon than black, Rimu even has a hard time getting along with his siblings."

I peered past Xaneth and searched for these siblings she spoke about. On the far side of the clearing, seven small black dragons played together around a large oak tree and a massive black dragon I could only assume was their father watched nearby. Rimu was definitely different from them. I would have figured all half-colors would have similar coloring among siblings, at least within the same clutch.

Rimu looked over at his siblings and snorted. Obviously he didn't like them much. They probably bullied him for being so different. I scratched Rimu on the cheek and he chirped at me. I was surprised by how vocal he was, but this was also the first time I'd been face to face with a baby dragon.

My brow furrowed in confusion when a red scale under Rimu's eye fell off when I scratched it. I curiously touched the shiny black one that was revealed.

My eyes flicked to Xaneth, who looked as bewildered as me. "Is that normal?"

"Scale shedding allows growth, but you probably figured that out since reptiles do that same," she said. "As for a scale to shed to another color, I've never seen it myself, but it seems it's quite possible to happen during growth periods."

I shifted my focus to Raikidan.

"What are you looking at me for?" he muttered.

"Hmm, I wonder."

"Leave me out of this."

"Two faced ass," I muttered.

"I am n—"

I glared at him and he looked away.

Xaneth giggled. "At least someone has figured out how to put you in your place, Raikidan."

Raikidan set a wary gaze on her. "How do you know my name?"

She smiled. "How could I not? My mate is a cousin of yours."

I blinked. That wasn't something I had been expecting to hear.

Xaneth stood gracefully. "C'mon, Rimu. It's time for you to take a nap and let Eira have some peace and quiet for a little while."

Rimu grumbled and stayed put. His mother chuckled and shifted into a magnificent red dragon. Frills lined her jaw and two sets of horns grew from her skull, one set curling back toward her face, while the other pair grew in a wave behind her.

A mix of large and small plated spikes lined her back starting at her shoulders and boxed in a large frill that rolled down her back down to her arrow point spaded tail.

Xaneth grunted at her son before heading for the far end of the field where her family resided. Rimu grumbled to himself and followed her with his head low. I had to resist the urge to laugh. I couldn't lie to myself; he was cute.

He stopped abruptly and ran back to me. Before I could scold him for not listening he picked up the small scale that had shed from his face with his mouth and dropped it into my hand. With a smile I rubbed his head. He chirped at me and then ran off to catch up with his mother.

"Eira." I almost jumped at Pyralis' voice. I had forgotten he was still kneeling next to me. "I apologize. I didn't mean to startle you."

"You don't breathe," I said. "It makes it easy to forget you're there."

He chuckled. "I suppose that's true. But I do have a request I'd like to ask of you."

"Depending on what it is, I might agree to it."

"I'd like to speak to you in private."

I nodded. I knew what that meant. I'd just be speaking with him on his plane. It couldn't hurt, right? Besides, I was curious to see what he wanted with someone like me. Pyralis faded away before I had the chance to change my mind.

Clutching the dragon scale in my hand, I closed my eyes and centered myself. Slowing my breathing, I pushed my spirit through the threshold of the spiritual plane. I opened my eyes slowly when the pressure around my body disappeared. I was greeted by Pyralis, who sat rather close in front of me.

I pulled back. "Uh, do you mind? Personal bubble here."

He chuckled. "That's right, I forgot. I apologize."

"So, why did you want to talk to me?" I asked, cutting to the chase.

He studied me. "I'm trying to understand why you did it."

"Did what?"

"Use one of the dragon's eyes to make a memorial for me," he clarified. "They're powerful gems; only the gods can remember where they came from or how they were made. Very few are able to use them, and even fewer are willing to use them since once they're used, they are gone forever. The power of these gems is remarkable. They can give the user almost anything they want, power, riches, happiness. But you didn't use it for those reasons. You didn't use it for yourself. Why?"

"Because the only thing I want, can't be given by these gems," I said. "And... and it was the right thing to do. For what you did for everyone... it... it just... seemed right."

"No one knows I'm out here," he said.

"I didn't do it to show off. I did it because I wanted to. I did it..." I looked away from him. "...because you deserve it."

"You're a very selfless human," he complimented. "Even Raynn wasn't this selfless, and knowing him on a personal level, that's... well I think you get it."

"Yeah... I get it," I mumbled.

Pyralis laughed. "And horrible at taking compliments. I can assume it annoys Raikidan."

I shrugged. "I guess."

He snickered. "I can see through his uncaring façade. I wasn't born yesterday."

"Or died yesterday, for that matter."

Pyralis' head tipped back as a hearty laugh tore through him. "You have such a crude sense of humor. I see why the boy is willing to put up with you."

I worked my jaw. "Why are you asking me all this? What's the point? Or are you just bored and trying to pass the time?"

"I'm trying to understand you."

I snorted. "Good luck with that. Raikidan has been following me around since early spring. Go ask him if he's learned anything."

"Even if the boy did know anything, he wouldn't tell me. He's at that age where he likes his privacy—his solitude. Well, unless you're involved."

"He likes all that even when I am around. And I like it too."

Pyralis smiled. "He cares about you. Even now, as you sit on this plane with me he has moved to sit by you. He's noticed your slowing breath and his concern grows each time. He's completely ob—"

"Stop. Just…" I sighed, my shoulder dropping. "Just stop. Please."

"Why, child? There is nothing wrong with wanting kinship. There is nothing wrong with any type of closeness with another. Tell me, what are you afraid of?"

A muscle in my neck twitched. "I fear nothing."

"He doesn't know what you are, even though it's obvious." I eyed him suspiciously and he chuckled. "Yes, I know exactly what you are, and Raikidan is too thick-headed to figure it out on his own."

"And that's how it'll stay."

"There is nothing wrong with what you are." Pyralis stood. "You must let go of all your fear in order for destiny to move in."

I bared my teeth. "I know my fate!"

"You do, do you?" He chuckled. "Are you sure? Or do you only know one side of the fate you were told?"

I narrowed my eyes. "What are you talking about?"

"Destiny—Fate—Neither is truly set in stone. They are woven in with time and as time branches infinitely by choice, so does destiny." Pyralis began walking away. "It's time to end our little chat. I don't want you dead. You have my thanks, Eira. I am in your debt for what you have given me."

"You owe me nothing."

He cranked his head over his shoulder. "You've given me the chance to walk with my family once again. You've shown Zaith there is still good in this world." He smiled. "You have proven to my colony that what I and the other five achieved so long ago hasn't vanished completely. I may have helped save lives with the other five, but you… you have done so much more in one gesture. And for that, I am in debt to you."

I studied for a moment. "If I ask a question, would that fulfill that debt?"

Pyralis smirked. "Not likely, but you should ask anyway."

"Your clan takes the shape of nu-humans. I would expect that of them, in order to blend in easier, but I didn't expect that you, too, would take the shape of a nu-human. Why is that?"

Pyralis chuckled. "Fair question for someone as observant as you. Nu-humans came about in the last years of my life, and I came into contact with many of them enough that I became attached and found myself liking their form until it stuck. This then trickled through the clan and before I knew it, most took the nu-human shape, even after I had passed on."

I thought about this. "How long have you been dead?"

"Not long," he admitted. "Roughly five hundred years."

I stared at him. Only five hundred? The War of End had been two millennia ago. "How old were you?"

He laughed, and I could only assume it had to do with some weird facial expression I'd made. "I was only two centuries old when I assisted the others bring peace to Lumaraeon. Reckless and uncaring of danger, it made me the ideal candidate for the job. That would place me just a few centuries shy of two millennia. A decent age for a dragon."

I laughed. "Decent? That's ancient!"

He snickered. "So little you know, young Eira."

My head cocked, but before I could say anything, I was pulled back to the living plane. Not experienced enough yet, I couldn't stay on the spiritual plane as long as I'd have wanted to. I breathed deeply as air filled my lungs.

"Eira?" Raikidan asked tentatively.

I looked at him from the corner of my eye in acknowledgement. Pyralis hadn't been lying. Raikidan had repositioned himself next to me. He grabbed my faced and turned it every which way, as if he were looking for some sort of wound.

I pushed him away from me. "Don't touch me."

He fell back and stared at me with confusion bewildered expression. "What did I do?"

"Where is my bag?" I asked, ignoring his question.

He lifted it up. "Right here."

I went to reach for it but he pulled it out of reach.

"Tell me why you're angry with me and I'll give it to you," he bartered.

"If you're really this stupid, you don't deserve to know why," I hissed. "Now give me my bag."

Before he could react, I snatched my bag from him and rummaged through it. I could hear low growling from the trees and figured it was the dragons talking, so I ignored it. Finding the bag that once carried the red dragon's eye gem, I dropped the red scale Rimu had given me in the bag and tied it up. Rummaging around some more, I found the other bag that contained the green gem. Opening it up a little I attempted to stow the bag containing the scale into it without Raikidan seeing the gem, but I failed.

Raikidan snatched the gem from the bag and examined it. "You weren't lying. You do have another one."

All of the dragons turned their attention to me and I didn't like it. "Yeah, I was telling the truth, now give it back!"

"How the hell did you get two? And don't tell me they were both given to you. No one just hands these off to someone."

"It's none of your business. Now give me back my gem!"

"Not until you tell me—"

"Give it back now!" I half shouted, half growled.

Now I knew everyone was watching me. That growl hadn't been human. I snatched my gem, and Raikidan flinched as my nails sliced his fleshy hand. I stuffed the gem into its bag and buried it deep inside my pack. I stopped when I noticed my hand.

My nails were elongated and my hand was getting close to transforming like that day in the Underground. Taking a deep breath, I slowly exhaled and my hand went back to normal. I didn't understand why this was happening. I put a great deal of energy into hiding that side of me, and had succeeded in keeping it secret for this long. But now I was losing control so easily, as if I wasn't trying at all to hide it anymore on some subconscious level.

"Eira, what—"

"We're leaving." I rose to my feet. "At least I am. You're more than welcome to stay."

I bent down and grabbed my cloak and veil. I was already walking away before I even had my cloaked clasped.

"Eira, you're going the wrong way," Raikidan said.

"I'll go where ever I dam well p—" I stopped dead, my eyes darting around.

"What is it?" Raikidan asked.

I shushed him and stood still—sniffing the air. *Fear.* I turned when my ears caught the sound of someone running. Raikidan ventured closer to me and gazed in the same direction I was. Suddenly, a young woman with mocha skin and a trihawk burst into the clearing and looked around with fear stricken eyes—visibly exhausted from her run.

"Tla'lli?" This confirmed it, we were in the Velsara wilds.

"Laz'shika!" Relief washed over her face. "Thanks the gods I found you."

She took a few steps forward but lost her footing in her exhausted state. I dashed over to her, managing to catch her before her body hit the ground. "Hey, take it easy."

She shook her head. "There's no time."

"Tla'lli, what has you so shaken up?" I asked.

She gazed at me with wide eyes. "Soldiers are marching to the village and they're not making a friendly visit."

"How do you know? Did you see them?"

She nodded. "I almost ran into them on my way here, but we knew about them sooner. About a week ago they sent us a message claiming we had broken the pact but never stated what we did wrong. No one believed the message since we figured it was a way to scare us, but then a few druids from the neighboring village spotted them marching and they came to warn us."

I swallowed. "They're not from Dalatrend, are they?"

Originally it had only been Zarda who forced a pact onto the shamans. But with the growing issues, and Zarda's continued conquest, other territories and kingdoms had enacted their own forms of cooperation from the tribes.

Tla'lli took a breath of air. "I'm afraid so. I got a good look at the insignia on the uniforms to verify."

I chewed my lip. This was bad. These shamans didn't stand a chance against these soldiers. All cities had soldiers and war experiments, but only Dalatrend modified humans to such extremes.

"Laz'shika, please help us," Tla'lli begged.

I nodded. "Of course I'll help. But, how did you know to find me here?"

She pointed at the statue where Pyralis stood. "He told me."

I eyed Pyralis suspiciously. Why would he tell Tla'lli where to find me? What did he or his colony gain from helping the shamans?

"You should hurry," Pyralis said. "You're running out of time."

I narrowed my eyes. He was right, but I couldn't shake the feeling that he was up to something.

"Take care of her," I ordered Raikidan as I ran off.

"Eira, hold on!" he yelled after me.

He sighed when I didn't stop and Tla'lli laughed. "Does she always leave you behind?"

"When she's mad at me, yes," he muttered.

Tla'lli laughed again. "You must be really stupid to make her mad."

He let out an exasperated breath and muttered to himself before speaking to her. "Let's get you on your feet so we don't fall too far behind."

"All right."

I continued on at a fast pace. The forest was a blur as I followed Tla'lli's scent. My bag snagged on a low tree branch and I allowed the tree to steal it. It wasn't a concern to me. I'd come back for it later.

I choked when another low hanging branched snagged on my cloak. Unfastening it, I let it stay captive in the tree and continued on. It wasn't long before my loose, delicate body wrap was also snagged and I muttered to myself. The forest was out to get me today.

Knowing full well my shaman clothes wouldn't protect me from bullets or any other weapon, I chose to think of something else to wear. I wanted them to know exactly who I was and I wanted to instill fear into them for what they were doing. I knew the exact outfit.

The cloth around my chest morphed into hard but flexible black and dark gray carbon fiber and leather and made its way up to my neck and face as well as extending out to my shoulders. A patch of skin above my chest and around my collarbone area were the only spots on my chest left exposed as the clothing crawled its way around my body to cover me. Carbon fiber and leather covered my neck above the patch area, creating great protection for such a vulnerable spot and connected to the material forming on my shoulders.

My shoulders were covered by small carbon fiber and leather pauldrons and around my wrists, metal and leather vambraces formed. Armored gloves were created under those, and ran up the length of my arm until they connected with the armor protecting my neck, ultimately covering my hands and arms completely. The carbon fiber that crawled up to my face wrapped around my mouth and nose, creating a half-mask, while on my lower half, my skirt changed into black pants, and my sandals morphed into knee-high plated black boots.

Several belts wrapped around my hips where bags of supplies would have hung, had this been a real uniform, and the leather dagger sheaths on my arms and legs prevented my uniforms completion by getting in the way of the belted sheaths I would have worn to carry not only my main assassination daggers but smaller throwing ones as well.

In the past, generals were the only ones who wore black uniforms. Foot soldiers wore white and assassins wore red, and medics were a mix of the two colors. It was never understood why, and had been challenged many times, since it made each unit or individuals—in the case of the generals and medics—distinguishable targets. But it had taken a long time for Zarda to allow change in the uniforms and in the end, only assassins were given dark uniforms. Our case was strong enough since we needed to be capable of staying hidden to perform our tasks effectively.

A determination stirred deep in my chest when the military company came into sight, and it grew stronger when I spotted the wooden walls of the South Village. Soldiers marched fast, but I ran faster, and I was going to make sure they didn't reach that wall.

When I drew closer, a soldier lagging behind a little turned and looked at me. Surprise rushed through my body. It was Talon. For a moment, I seconded-guessed his vowed loyalty to me. But when he smirked and gestured me to draw closer, I knew I had been foolish to question him. They were here because they were still soldiers—because they were ordered to. They had no other choice, and I was a fool to jump to rash conclusions.

I picked up my pace, creating more noise in the process, but I didn't care. At this range, the enemy soldiers wouldn't have enough time to react, still giving me the upper hand. Talon stopped walking when I was close, grabbing the attention of nearby soldiers. The soldiers yelled out to their commanding officer, but it was too late. Talon dropped his gun and, by clamping his hands together, he vaulted me into the air.

The company of soldiers readied their guns, but none of them shot at me. I could see the fear in the eyes of many of them. It was that terror that caused them to hesitate, and it was that fear that gave me the advantage. The general leading the platoon was the first to fire at me. The bullets bounced off of my armor and I grinned.

Pulling embers from my mouth through the small slits in my mask, I formed fire around my hands and threw them down at the invading army. Men and women scattered to avoid being hit, breaking up the tight marching line. Landing on my feet in a crouched position in the center of the gateway of the wall protecting the village, I stood and faced the army.

The general stood wide-eyed with his gun at the ready. "It's you."

I chuckled. "It's me."

He narrowed his eyes. "I knew it. I knew these good-for-nothing savages were lying and were harboring a criminal like you."

"What are you talking about, Rick? This is the first time I've been near this place filled with *savages*. The sound of the military marching boils my blood and bolsters my thirst to kill."

"Make his death slow and painful."

"So you're saying you just so happened to be in the area and decided to drop in on us?" Rick snorted. "Like I'd believe that. Men, fire at my command."

I grinned when only half of the soldiers did as they were instructed.

Rick's eyes narrowed at the soldiers who refused his command. "What's wrong with you? I said aim."

I snickered. "They won't listen to you."

Rick's eyes swept over the soldiers who refused to listen and then glowered at me. "So you have been recruiting for your filthy cause. Fine, they'll die with you."

Gazes turned skyward when dragons flew over-head. Many started to panic and whisper amongst themselves.

Rick narrowed his eyes as he watched several of them shift into humans and land inside the village. "So, they still live and have made themselves at home here. Zarda will love to hear this. Once I'm done dealing with you and all the traitors, I'll be sure to let him know when we return."

"Slice his neck."

I laughed and drew the dagger on my arm. "You won't make it out of here alive, Rick."

"It's General Rick to you," he snarled. "And it will be you who won't make it out alive. You or these traitors."

I taunted Rick by casually spinning my dagger in my fingers and he took the bait. He aimed his gun at me, but before he could shoot I was already moving. Loyal soldiers open fired and rebel soldiers retaliated. Villagers stayed hidden in their houses while Guards left their sanctuaries to do their job. Most of the dragons stayed out of the way and watched the scene unfolding, but a few shifted back into their natural forms and used their plated bodies as shields against rogue bullets.

Pulling embers from my tongue, I threw balls of fire at the army. Those unlucky enough to not being paying attention, or too slow to react, caught on fire and burned a painful death. Once I was satisfied with the destruction I had caused, I focused on Rick. He was reloading his gun and I snickered. Rick had no abilities. He was an old experiment that knew how to weasel his way around to keep himself alive. He also happened to be an excellent tactician, which added to his favor with Zarda.

Rick shot at me, but the bullets bounced off my armor as if they were mere pebbles. I easily shook off the small amount of pain they caused. I didn't see how he was so smart or how he was great with tactics. If he were intelligent he would have aimed for my head or the exposed area on my chest. Rick glared at me and pulled the trigger again but the result was the same.

"Off with his head!"

Growing bored, I spun my dagger in my fingers and chuckled. Before Rick could think to reload his gun I moved with great speed to close the gap between us. I used the trees to my advantage, jumping onto them and utilizing their branches to stay up high. Rick attempted to keep up with me, but he wasn't able to handle my advanced engineering.

Landing on top of the wooden wall, I watched with silent amusement as Rick frantically searched for me.

"General, above you!" a soldier cried out.

Jerk, ruining my fun. Rick turned to face me, but I was already pushing myself out of the tree. He managed to dodge my attack, but I was quick and maneuvered behind him again. I grabbed a hold of his head with my hands. "Good night, Rick."

With one swift movement I snapped his neck and let his body fall to the ground. The enemy soldiers ceased to resist soon after. My men took their weapons and forced them to cluster up.

Talon made his way over to me. "Nice work."

I nodded. "Thanks for the lift."

He grinned. "Just doing my job."

I turned around, allowing my men to figure out who would join us, and who would be loyal to Zarda and die. It would be an unfortunate task, but we couldn't exactly let them go back and reveal our secret. While they did that, I walked back over to the entrance of the village and took it all in, since it was the first time I had ever stepped foot here.

The village was mainly made up of large hardwood trees far larger than any of the other trees in the forest. The houses of the villagers were built high in the enormous branches of the trees, while the shops rested in carved-out holes at the bases. Wooden stairs spiraled up the tree trunks and connected to a platform that wrapped all the way around the tree trunks and lay under the houses. These platforms connected the trees to each other with wooden bridges, allowing the villagers to mingle about in the village as they pleased.

The trees were spread out in a way that you could identify where the center of the village was, if it wasn't obvious by the floating spiritual crystal that looked identical to the one in the West Tribe. Behind all of that was the largest tree of them all with a ridiculously large house. I could only assume that was the home of the leading family. I remembered Del'karo telling me they called their leader a *chief*, which didn't surprise me due to their customs and traditional tribal ways.

The large wooden wall set up to protect the village was merely for show. It was long, but it did end at some point, and there weren't any other walls I could see on the other sides of the village. That of course didn't mean there weren't some out of sight, but I didn't think it was likely, since I was standing in what was to be believed as the main entrance.

I was forced to focus on the villagers now. They were all watching us with apprehension. This was where the fun started. I could see it now. They'd come out of their shock and start screaming, thinking we were going to hurt them next. Talon shifted uneasily next to me as if he were thinking the same thing.

But we were wrong. Smiles started to appear on their faces and one man approached me. He was a tall and muscular elven man with dreadlocked black hair and black tribal tattoos littered across his dark-skinned body. White and blue paint streak diagonally over his face. His golden eyes made me think of someone but I couldn't place who.

"Thank you, Laz'shika," he greeted in an accent so thick I almost didn't understand him. "Without the help of you and your men, we wouldn't have been able to defend ourselves against those soldiers. As much strength as the Guards have and as much skill as we druids and shamans have, we are no match for your guns and advanced engineering, as you've proven with your superior speed and agility."

I tilted my head respectfully in response. I still didn't know who he was, and his open kindness was throwing me off.

The man cocked his head. "What's wrong?"

"She doesn't know who you are, Father," a woman behind me said.

I turned to see Tla'lli making her way through my men and over to us. I locked eyes with her and realized why this man's eyes looked so familiar. They were identical to each other.

"I never got the chance to tell her what you looked like."

"Or a name," I added.

Tla'lli laughed. "Well you weren't all that cooperative that day."

"You expected me to go with an outrageous proposal right off the bat."

She stood by her father. "True."

I noticed she wasn't carrying anything with her. "I suppose it's safe to assume you don't have the belongings I tossed along the way?"

She shook her head. "Raikidan grabbed those while I kept going. He should be—"

"We got a runner!" a soldier cried out.

Talon and I turned to see a young man hightailing it into the trees, but just as a soldier aimed his gun to stop him, a large black tail swung out of the trees and tossed the man into the air.

"Not anymore," I said.

"Dinner time."

As the man plummeted back toward the ground, the large black and red head of the dragon who owned the black tail shot out of the tree tops. His teeth clamped down on the man, his victim unable to even scream, and blood splattered everywhere. Raikidan spat the limp body onto the group and moved toward the village. My men staring up at him more than happy to move out of his way.

"He should have eaten him."

In an instant he shifted to his nu-human form and kept walking without skipping a beat.

Raikidan tossed me the bag he had been previously carrying in his claws. "You're welcome."

"Took you long enough."

He grunted and stood next to me. "You try to untangle that mess. I don't know how you managed to get all of that stuck the way you did."

"I'm skilled like that."

Raikidan folded his arms while rolling his eyes.

Tla'lli's father chuckled and then motioned for us to follow. "You and your men are welcome here, Laz'shika. Please make yourselves at home."

"I'd like it if you called me Eira."

He nodded. "Very well. Mine is Ir'esh."

"A pleasure."

"What is your business here?"

I gestured to Tla'lli. "Your daughter requested my help."

He nodded. "Yes, I figured as much, but what is your reason for being in the area? She wasn't gone long before she conveniently ran into you."

"My business is my own." Shaman leader or not, it wasn't my place to discuss what happened at Pyralis' grave. Even if they knew of its existence.

The man's lips pressed into a line as if he were put off by my elusive behavior. "Very well. Then why do you still stay?"

I grinned. "I have a proposition for you."

Ir'esh grinned back. He knew what I was about to propose.

CHAPTER 35

Both Talon and Raikidan eyed me curiously. Tla'lli looked like she was about to burst with joy and Ir'esh grinned from ear to ear.

"What are you talking about?" Talon whispered. "What proposition?"

I unclipped half of my mask so it hung loose in front of me and moved closer to Ir'esh. "I've chosen to think over your offer again and I've changed my mind."

"You changed your mind?" Ir'esh laughed. "What made you do that?"

"When Tla'lli and I first met, I thought it was best not to involve you. I thought as long as you were sticking to your end of the pact, you and your people would be safe. Then, a little while ago, someone said those outside the walls were affected by Zarda's rein more than many wanted to believe. This had me think over my initial opinion. Then this attack… Talon, what was Rick's reason for coming here?"

"He claimed they were breaking the pact," Talon explained. "Rick couldn't show any physical proof but he was convinced they were, so he ordered a bunch of us to follow him out here and, if ordered, kill."

"Why didn't I hear about this?" I asked. "I wanted status reports."

"You were gone," he defended. "I sent a report and was given one back telling me you had left the city, and no one knew when you'd return. I had no other means to relay the massage so you could cut us off."

"Very well." I faced Ir'esh. "Do you accept my offer?"

"You have proven to be reliable. You have proven to be trustworthy. You are strong and use great wisdom to cast your judgment." Ir'esh grinned. "Our tribe will ally with you."

I glanced to my left when movement caught my eye and I watched Zaith move from his resting spot on top of a building over to us.

"What do you want?" I asked.

"We are allied to this village," he stated. "You ally with them, you ally with us."

I assessed him for several long minutes. Was it right to involve them as well? What type of help could they offer our resistance? Could I trust them to help, for that matter?

Furthermore, why was Zaith so quick to make this offer? He didn't want me in his territory and tried to stop me by force, and now he wanted to work alongside us. What did he truly want?

Xaneth stepped forward. "It may not seem it, but we are as much involved as you are. We are bound to hiding instead of choosing to blend in. No one is uninvolved. No one is safe."

I thought over what she said and then looked at Zaith. "Very well. With the way the resistance is laid out, the Council will more than likely have you reporting to me. I expect you to listen, only questioning where it's really warranted."

"No," Zaith said, shaking his head. "I ain't takin' orders from a female."

"You want to be allies but won't take orders from a female?" I laughed dryly. "Then we don't have an alliance, Red."

He stepped forward and growled. "Don't insult my color."

With a few quick steps I closed the distance between us and wrapped my hand around his neck. Dragging him over to the nearest tree, I slammed him against it. Zaith grabbed onto my wrist as I squeezed his throat and got right up in his face.

"I will insult your color all I please since you have no reservations regarding insulting my comrade," I said. "Don't insult him and I won't insult you. Do I make myself clear?"

Zaith struggled against my grip and struggled to breathe. This might be a little extreme to those around me, but from what I'd learned from Raikidan these last few months, this was a necessary action to get a dragon as prideful as Zaith to listen.

Taking his struggling as a small sign that he understood I wasn't to be pushed around, I threw him away and watched him stumble.

I turned on my heels and stalked away. "Weak. How no one has taken your leadership from you is beyond me."

"I'm not weak, you—"

"Save it, Zaith," Raikidan said. "You've gotten your ass handed to you by her twice today and she barely lifted a finger doing so."

"Shut it, half—"

Xaneth let out a malicious snarl, making Zaith flinch. I couldn't stop myself from grinning. She looked absolutely livid and who could blame her? I could also spy her mate from his perch on a house roof and he appeared no happier than she did.

"Really, Zaith?" A masculine voice sighed. "I'm beginning to wonder how you've kept my clan together this long."

Zaith looked over to where the voice originated from and gulped. "P–Pyralis."

Pyralis stepped out of the shadows and locked his gaze on me.

I dipped my head in respect. "I didn't think I put that much spiritual energy into your tomb."

Pyralis pointed to the floating Spiritual Crystal in the center of the village. "You didn't. I'm using that as an anchor."

I nodded. "I see, so you must have something to say then."

"I request you ally with my clan. They can be a useful asset to you, even if Zaith is less than willing to listen to you."

"Females don't fight," Zaith muttered.

"But we do," a female voice chimed in behind me.

I turned to see a small group of my men stroll into the village. The woman leading them in stopped when she was several feet away from us and pulled off her helmet. Her long wavy black hair rolled over her shoulders upon its release from the confinement of her helmet. More soldiers followed her lead showing that most of this small group that entered were all women.

Zaith climbed to his feet and examined them. "But why?"

"Because we have no reason to see a difference," Talon said. "Both men and women have strengths and weaknesses. We have no reason to treat one sex differently than the other because of it."

"Just deal with it, Zaith," Raikidan muttered. "It's how they do things."

"Don't—"

"Enough!" Ir'esh faced Zaith. "It's how it is, kid, and whether you like it or not you're going to have to get used to it. I may be elven but I won't live forever. My wife died of illness many years ago but I have forced myself to hang onto life for my tribe and my daughter. However, there will be a time where my body won't allow me to fight any longer and my daughter will take my place as our traditions state. Would you break our alliance because she would take over?"

Zaith let out a tight breath. "No."

"Then what seems to be the problem?" Pyralis challenged.

I was grateful for the elder dragon's support, but I did understand Zaith's reluctance. I'd dealt with Raikidan long enough to understand the struggle, even if I didn't completely agree with it.

Zaith bowed his head to me. "I apologize. I wasn't thinkin' clearly. My will is yours to command."

I folded my arms. "You were thinking clearly. For a dragon that is." Zaith eyed me. "But now that type of thinking ends. With this alliance we are no longer separate. We are no longer humans and dragons. We are no longer black or red. We are no longer shaman and soldiers. We are one alliance. One way of thinking. One goal."

"Well said, Eira," Ir'esh complimented. "Now shall we unite this alliance?"

I nodded. "What did you have in mind?"

"An ancient tradition that hasn't been used in a century. A physical reminder of what we are doing. It requires an offering. Something unique from each of us."

Something unique? I thought this over. If this was a physical manifestation of what we were creating and we needed something unique to ourselves to act as a type of offering…

"*Life Fire.*" I nodded as I processed my choice. "I give Life Fire."

Ir'esh grinned. "I was hoping you'd offer that. I give *Life Earth.*"

Ir'esh and I looked at Zaith expectantly.

His eyes flicked between us both. "What you two talkin' about?"

"*Life Elements,*" Ir'esh told him. "The source of our life and the spirit of our element."

"One cannot exist without the other," I added. "They are connected and if one were to cease existing and disappear we'd cease to exist as well."

"They are manifestations of our inner selves," Tla'lli concluded.

Ir'esh held out his hand and, showing no signs of movement, lifted a small group of rocks on the ground by his feet. "Earth."

Tla'lli tilted her head skyward and whistled. The wind picked up and battered everyone before dying down to a gentle breeze. "Wind."

Lifting my hands up gracefully, I threw them down to my side with force and ignited the small flames on my fingertips. The fires burned large and hot. Many took a step back and eyed me with shock. Even Zaith didn't hide his surprise. "Fire."

"All right, Commander, I think you can stop showing off now," Talon teased.

I chuckled and let my fires die.

"My element…" Zaith mused as he recovered himself. "Fire, like you, only stronger."

I pursed my lips, looking him up and down. "We'll see."

He snorted. "So, how we do this?"

"Everyone who isn't a part of this will stand back," I ordered. "Once a Life Element is released it begins a chain and anyone in close proximity will be affected. Therefore, Zaith, the only thing you have to do is stand where you are."

"Why must we stand back?" Xaneth questioned. "What would be so bad if this inner element came out of us?"

"It's painful," I said. "An elementalist has one point in their body in which they can release their elemental abilities. With training they can learn more ways of releasing their element, but it can only be one point of the body at one time. But life elements are different. They're forced out of the body unnaturally, causing excruciating pain."

Xaneth looked worriedly at Zaith and he appeared to be doubting his choice now. It was painful but necessary. I had released my inner element only once before to see what shape it took, and it took commitment to feel that type of pain. If he really wanted this alliance to happen he would have to put himself through this to prove it.

Zaith took a deep breath. "Let's get this over with."

I nodded and went to motion to my men to move back when Ir'esh held up his hand. "Before we start, we need one more thing."

"Nothin' else painful, I hope," Zaith muttered.

Ir'esh chuckled. "I can assure you that this won't hurt. We need a host object."

"A host object?" I knew of Life Elements but this ritual Ir'esh was having us do, I was unfamiliar with.

Ir'esh nodded. "This ritual takes our offerings and combines it with a host object to manifest the physical bond of our alliance."

The image of Pyralis' new tomb flashed through my head and I had a feeling I knew what this ritual was about to do. "Does the host object have to be something specific?"

Ir'esh shook his head. "No. It just has to be something solid and preferably good to look at."

I thought this over. What could we use? I wasn't going to use my last dragon's eye, that was for sure. This wasn't the right time for it. I popped of my thought when a young boy, carrying a large rock in his arms, came over to us.

"You could use this," the boy offered. "It speaks differently than the other rocks around here."

Zaith's eyebrow rose. "It speaks different?"

"Elements manifest differently in everyone," Tla'lli said. "It doesn't have to come out in an aggressive form. The boy can hear the earth as I can hear the wind. I would have figured you'd know this by now since we've had our alliance for so long."

Zaith averted his gaze and muttered to himself.

I knelt and extended my hands to the boy. "May I?"

He nodded and handed the large rock over to me. I held the rock gently in my hands and examined it. Visually it didn't come off as anything more than an ordinary rock. But there was something off about its weight. Holding it in one hand I knocked on it and was surprised to feel the hollow vibrations. The boy and I looked at each other, his eyes wide and curious.

Switching my gaze to Talon I spoke, "I need a laser."

He nodded and searched through the pouches on his belt. He pulled out a small, silver, cylindrical object and tossed it to me.

I caught the object and went to press the small button on it to activate the laser but stopped and looked at the boy. "I'm going to cut this open. Is that okay?"

He nodded enthusiastically, curious himself about the mysterious stone. Pressing the button, a short, thin red laser shot out of the silver object and I slowly sliced the rock open. Once I made a complete rotation around the rock, the side I wasn't holding fell to the ground, revealing the hollow amethyst crystal center.

"A geode," Ir'esh mused. "Those are quite rare in these parts. Where'd you find it, kiddo?"

He picked up the portion that fell on the ground. "By the river."

The boy tried to hand the half he had back to me, but I refused and closed his hands over the crystallized rock. "You keep it."

He smiled at me. "Thanks."

I rubbed his head before he ran off. I watched as a dragon from Zaith's colony stopped him and tried to barter with him, but I wasn't going to have that. "You take that from him and I'll put you six feet under."

The dragon narrowed his eyes at me but moved away from the boy. The boy smiled and waved at me before disappearing into the trunk of a tree.

I noticed Zaith glaring at me, pulling my attention. "What's your problem?"

"You had no right to threaten him," he said.

I chuckled. "I had no right? Your kind has no right to be greedy and try to steal from children."

"My kind?" His lip curled "How dare you say that!"

I grunted and flicked my eyes to Pyralis, who was still watching the events unfolding with quiet interest. "Are you sure he's the right one to lead your colony?"

"I'm beginning to seriously think that over," Pyralis muttered.

Zaith looked between the two of us in confusion.

"Idiot," Raikidan said. "She purposely tried to piss you off."

Xaneth giggled as Zaith groaned and almost pulled out his hair in frustration.

"Maybe I should give leadership to you, Eira," Pyralis offered. "You're quite the capable leader."

I laughed dryly. "And I think that's a bad idea."

"And why's that?"

I pointed to myself. "Not a dragon."

He let out a hearty chuckle. "Very well."

"She acts enough like one." Someone muttered as I walked over to Ir'esh.

"Will this do for a host object?" I asked.

Ir'esh took it and nodded. "It will work perfectly. Due to its size the end result will be quite large as well."

"Very well, we'll follow your lead, then."

"Not always a leader?" Ir'esh teased.

I grinned and backed away. "Only when there is someone more qualified."

Ir'esh chuckled and placed the geode on the ground between of the three of us. He backed away and prepared to start the ritual but he stopped and peered at something behind me. I turned to see Rimu scampering over to us, his gaze focused on the geode.

Knowing full well he had plans to snatch it, I grabbed a hold of him when he came close enough. "Oh, no you don't. We need that." I struggled to keep my grip, but was finally able to subdue him by picking him up and cradling him on his back. I let out a hard breath. "I'm really glad you're not any bigger or this might be difficult."

Soft chuckles echoed through the village at my joke. Rimu looked over at the geode and then back to me with pleading eyes.

I snickered. "That doesn't work on me."

Rimu snorted and tried to squirm away but I wasn't having it. "Rimu, c'mon knock it off."

I laughed when he broke free of one of my arms but ended up upside down. Rimu made small grumbling noises and tried to stretch his neck far enough to reach the geode that was definitely too far away from him. Finally giving up, he looked at me and snapped his jaw.

Not liking his attitude, I touched his belly with my free hand and began tickling him. He grunted, snapped his jaw and squirmed, but it did him no good. When I determined he had been punished enough, I stopped. Rimu grunted one last time and then gazed up at me. His eyes sparkled, showing his enjoyment of his torture, and I thought I could see a small smile on the corner of his mouth.

He surprised me when his tail moved and wrapped around my neck. His expression remained the same and he gave no hints of the meaning of the gesture, or what he wanted from me.

I shook my head and chuckled. "All right, I'm going to put you down now and you'd better behave."

Rimu exhaled slowly and I loosened my grip to allow him to slide down to the ground. He laid partially on the ground and partially up my leg, staring up at me with pure cuteness for a little while before he flipped over and eyed the geode again.

"Rimu," I warned.

He tilted his head to glance at me before taking a few steps toward the rock and then looking back at me. I folded my arms, my eyes stern. He sunk low to the ground and crept closer to the geode.

"Rimu." He swiveled his head back at me and then continued to creep forward. "Rimu, get back here!"

Rimu hung his head and peered up at me. I knelt and held out my hand, keeping stern eye contact with him. Slowly, he crept back over to me and rested his head in my hand. He gazed up at me with sad eyes and I reassured him by stroking his cheek with my thumb.

He had instinctual urges he couldn't control. I understood that. He was young, and listening wasn't a part of what a child liked to do. I also understood that. Rimu glanced back at the geode and I smiled. It didn't matter how stern I was with him. His instinct to hoard was stronger.

"I'm going to make you a deal," I said as I pulled my hand away. Rimu tilted his head as I reached up and took out a pair of stud earrings from my ears. "These are the only pair of ruby earrings I own. They're not exceptionally special, but if you leave that geode alone, so we can use it to finish the pact for our alliance, you can have them."

Rimu looked at the tiny earrings, at the geode, and then back at the earrings, trying to figure out what he liked more. Finally he chirped at me, took the earrings and scampered away to a far-off tree to lie down. His siblings came over to investigate his new treasure but Rimu curled around the tiny earrings and shooed them away.

I found this amusing and could have watched for a little while longer, but there were more pressing matters at hand. Standing up, I had my clothes change into my favored casual city clothes. If this ritual went anything like I thought it was going to, I wanted to make sure I wasn't remembered in my military uniform.

I looked at Ir'esh. "Let's finish this."

Ir'esh watched me as I took my place in our triangle. He was curious about the clothes, that much was obvious. It wasn't every day you saw transforming clothes. "I'll answer your questions after."

He nodded. "All right, let's begin then, shall we?"

I motioned for those around us to move back as Ir'esh began to chant. Everyone was still and waited in anticipation. Ir'esh's chant became lower and lower until it was no longer words, but vibrations that rumbled through my chest.

My body reacted to the chant and convulsed. I clenched my teeth as fire rushed up my throat. My action forced the fire back down my throat, causing me to choke. My body heated up, and I wrapped my arms around myself as it began to ache and pulse. I managed to glance up at Ir'esh to see him on his knees.

He was in obvious pain, but his experience allowed him to continue the chant even while his own body summoned his Life Element. Zaith was in the worst condition out of us all. He lay on the ground in a crumpled heap, holding his head and body with his arms—barely keeping himself from crying out in pain.

The ground shook. I choked again on fire and pain as my body reacted to the ground's sudden movement. The ground in front of me cracked and split apart, and loud snarling came from its dark depths. It wasn't long before a large wolf made of rock and other earthy material climbed out from the depths of the earth. I didn't have long to look at it, however.

Fire was now forcing its way unnaturally out of my back. As the fire pushed its way out, I couldn't stop myself from crying out from the searing pain that took over my flesh. My cry was drowned out by the piercing screech of a large bird, and then the roar of a dragon.

"A phoenix…" someone whispered.

I gasped for breath as the fiery spirit left my presence and shot skyward. My gaze flicked up weakly, watching a white, blue, and red fire phoenix soaring into the evening sky with a flaming dragon.

My eyes fell on the earth wolf prowling around the host object. It was a massive creature that left small bits of debris behind as it moved.

"Eira." Ir'esh took a deep, weak breath. "I'm unable to touch fire, and Zaith doesn't have the training or the strength to command his Life Fire. You must do it. Are you up to the challenge?"

"I've harnessed dragon fire before," I said. "By the looks of it, this fire is weaker. It's even weaker than mine. Shouldn't be too hard."

Zaith snarled, then muttered something under his breath in Draconic.

Raikidan chuckled from afar and that only soured Zaith's mood further. Ignoring the two testosterone-driven males, I took in a strong breath and reach my hands skyward. The power from both Life Fires teased me and I forced them to bend to my will. Linking them to my hands, I used the last of my strength and pulled them toward the geode host.

As the two spirits plummeted to the ground, Zaith's dragon linked its back claws with my phoenix and the two spiraled down until they collided with Ir'esh's wolf, which was now curled around the tiny geode. The collision brightened our part of the village and I was forced to shield my eyes. Strong arms grabbed me and threw me to the ground as a rush of power shot through the village. When the power was gone, I opened my eyes to see Raikidan using his body as a shield.

He pulled away. "You all right?"

"Yeah, thanks," I said.

He nodded as he rose to his feet and extended his hand to me. I took his offer and allowed him to help me up. Once I was on my weak feet and dusted off, I shifted my focus to where I had been standing for the ritual. My eyes were greeted by a large amethyst statue. Slowly, I left Raikidan's side and wandered closer to the sparkling monument. Even in the low light of the early evening, it gleamed with great intensity.

The statue was comprised of three figures. Ir'esh was in the front, standing calmly and welcoming with his inner wolf prowling around him. To his right was Zaith, who stood proud with a large dragon behind him. And lastly, to Ir'esh's left, was me. I stood with my hand extended toward the sky with a flame that turned into a phoenix with wings spread for flight and a long tail that flowed around me.

To my surprise, I wasn't wearing the clothes I had my armor change into. Instead, a cloak with its hood down hung over my shoulders, one side pulled behind me due to my outstretched arm, revealing my clothes underneath. My torso was adorned with a top shaped like a bikini, with a wide band instead of tie strings, and a thick halter-like collar that framed my face. It was made of what appeared to be leather and scales that ran up my breasts and around my collar, and in the center of the top, between the breasts, was a circular pendant with a fire engraved into it.

My hands and forearms were covered by cloth sleeves styled similarly to the ones I liked to wear a lot, and those too were covered on top by layered scales.

On my lower half I wore shorts made of a thin form-fitting material, and over that I wore a long skirt made of cloth with intricate embroidery that draped to one side of my body. The skirt was clasped together on the open side by a pendant identical to the one on my top. Knee-high boots with layered large-scaled plating in the front covered my feet. Strapped over the top of the foot and ankle for each boot were a leather guard with a large pendant with another fire engraved into it.

My daggers were in the typical place I always carried them, but they had new sheaths and bands that also carried a few small throwing daggers each. Feathers decorated my hair and new jewelry adorned my body, including a necklace I'd never seen it before, a mysterious ring on my left finger that had a meaning unknown to me.

All the figures were clustered closely together, sharing the same base. In certain areas, the crystal showed no signs of carving.

Small children screeched and giggled with excitement as they left the safety of their parent's side and ran over to the statue. They pawed every inch of the sculpture they could reach with their little hands as they inspected the new village decoration. I tore my gaze away when someone approached me from behind.

Talon dipped his head in greeting. "I don't mean to interrupt your admiring but we still have some work to do. Do you have enough strength after that ritual to continue?"

I nodded. "I'm fine. We have pressing matters to be dealt with first before we worry about me."

"Very well." He looked back to where most of the men stood outside the village. "The others won't enter unless you say so. They don't want to upset the villagers."

"Give them word to come in then," I ordered. "There is no need for them to sit out as strangers. What of the hostages?"

"The hostages have all agreed to join us," he explained. "Most were more than willing right off but after that little display the three of you showed, the rest soon followed."

I nodded. "Very good. Have everyone come in and then come and see me. We have battle plans we must discuss."

"Of course, Commander." Talon excused himself and headed off to complete his assignment.

Ir'esh and Tla'lli were next to approach me. I greeted them with a small nod.

"Excellent display," Ir'esh complimented. "Del'karo taught you well."

I pursed my lips. "How do you know Del'karo taught me?"

Ir'esh chuckled. "How could I not? He and Ne'kall talk about you all the time."

I smacked my forehead. "Right. I forgot about that."

A new voice called out. "Oh, I see how it is."

I turned to see a young man approaching us and I couldn't believe my eyes. Olive skin, mohawk, piercings and tattoos, he could pass off as a younger-looking Del'karo.

"How could you forget about us?"

I folded my arms. "You mean how could I forget about you, Ne'kall? Easy, you're a second-rate elementalist that ran off ten years ago after an argument with your father and eloped with the woman your father said you were moving too fast with, with no plans to ever return."

"Ah, how I missed the attitude." He grinned. "It's good to see you, Laz'shika."

I bumped the side of my fist with his and nodded. "Same to you. I made a passing visit to the West Tribe a few months back, and your mother said you two finally patched things up when you started a family."

Ne'kall chuckled. "She's not wrong. I thought she would die from excitement when I broke the news. Oh, and speaking of parents, you just missed my father. He was here a few days ago."

"That would figure. It would have been nice to see him again. He wasn't around when I was at the village. What was he doing here anyway, may I ask? Don't tell me you're getting another sibling."

Ne'kall shrugged. "Okay, then I won't tell."

"Oh for the love of—" I smacked my forehead. "When are they going to stop? That's what, twelve now?"

He chuckled. "Thirteen, actually."

"Damned rabbits," I muttered.

"It's not that bad."

Tla'lli held up a finger in protest. "Yes it is. Especially for elves. Since we live so long, we choose small families. At least the sane ones do."

Ne'kall grunted. "You don't get an opinion in this. You're an only child and you're single."

Tla'lli snorted. "And I like being both, thanks. I just hope you don't take after your father in that respect."

"Please tell me you won't," I begged him.

"I already have four."

The amount of time he and his wife had been together flashed through my mind and I groaned. "You are going to be just like him!"

"Hey, give me a break. Two of them are twins. That counts for something right?"

"No."

Ne'kall chuckled. "Whatever. You'll understand when you settle down some day."

I snorted and folded my arms. "I have more important things to do than waste my time with someone."

"Ouch. A little harsh, don't you think?"

"No," I replied as I watched my men make their way into the village.

"Ten years go by and you're still a stubborn pain in the ass," he teased.

"Ten years go by and you're as soft as ever," I shot back with a sly smile.

Ne'kall laughed. "And for that I'm going to kick your ass."

I shook my head. "Never have, never will."

"I've gotten better."

I grunted and looked him up and down. "Doubt it."

"You know what, for that, I'm really going to kick your ass."

Before I could say something back he came at me but I was faster. I moved back and tripped him. He stumbled and spun around to glare at me when he caught his footing.

I chuckled. "You're too slow. Give up now."

Ne'kall came at me again and I grabbed him by the arm and threw him onto his back. He grunted and rolled in pain.

"Had enough yet?"

He shook his head and let his hand light on fire. "Physical combat was never my strong suit."

"Then why would you attack her like that?" Tla'lli asked.

"Cause he's stupid," I said causing her to laugh.

"Do you really have to insult me?" Ne'kall asked.

"Always."

"She's never been one to say nice things all the time," Talon said as he walked over to us. "Rare if she does actually."

I chuckled. "Someone decided to use his brain today."

Talon laughed. "Point proven."

"I never said I was nice."

Ne'kall got to his feet. "No, that's quite true. But you're not cruel either."

"She is when she has to be," Talon said. "But if she has to be then you're pretty dumb."

Placing my hands on my hips, I shook my head and chuckled.

"So what do ya say, Laz'shika," Ne'kall asked. "One match for old times' sake?"

I flicked my gaze to Ir'esh for approval. It was his village, after all, and I had no right picking fights here, regardless of how harmless they were.

Ir'esh nodded. "It's fine by me. I'd like to see what you're made of anyway."

I grunted. "Not like you'll see much. It won't last that long."

"Hey, give me some credit it will you?" Ne'kall begged.

I chuckled. "Ne'kall, tell me, our last match, how long did it last?"

He sighed. "Ten minutes."

"Ten minutes…" I mused as I started to put some distance between us in preparation. "And was that the longest match we had?"

"Yeah…"

"And I can tell you're out of practice. So it would be safe to assume it's not going to last very long if our longest match has been ten minutes with you at your peak."

Ne'kall let out an exasperated sigh. "Just fight me already."

I laughed and faced him. "Very well. Ready when you are."

Ir'esh waved his hand and the ground shifted. Cylindrical pieces of ground shot out of the earth near villagers and soldiers alike, allowing them to have a place to sit and watch. My men gratefully took the offer for the chance to sit. Many who still had their helmets on took them off, showing how relaxed they were becoming, and they all waited for my short fight to begin.

Ne'kall lit the fires in his hands and waited but I kept him waiting. I wasn't going to release my fire right off. I liked making him wait. Soon he grew tired of waiting, like I figured he would, and he threw a large blast of fire at me. Holding up my hand, I forced the fire to obey my will and took it as my own.

"I hate it when you do that," he muttered.

I snickered. "That's why I do it, especially when your flame is so weak and easy to control. The domestic life hasn't been nice to you."

He shook his head with a small sigh and prepared himself. "All right, do your worst."

I smirked. "I don't think you want me doing my worst."

He laughed. "You're probably right."

Taking a deep breath, I flicked my hand and shot the flame back at him. Ne'kall sidestepped and let the flame fly past him. Not letting him have too much time to think, I pulled an ember from my lips and ignited the flame in my hand. Ne'kall prepared himself but I wasn't ready to release this flame yet.

Instead I held up my other hand and used my strength to compact the flame into a solid ball. Before Ne'kall could figure out what I was doing, I shot it out at him. Ne'kall's reflexes were slow, but they were just fast enough to stop the ball of fire before it touched him.

His muscles tensed and veins bulged as he used all his strength to keep the hot mass under his control. My flame was strong, and once it was compact, it made it even harder for another to control and use against me in battle, but it took longer to make. It was a balanced exchange.

Ne'kall took a deep breath and heaved the ball of fire back at me. I sidestepped the flame and paid no mind to where it was headed. The two of us stared each other down.

"What is the point to this?" Tla'lli whispered to someone.

"They're sizing each other up," her father explained.

"I don't understand."

"They're testing the strength of each other's flame," he explained. "It happens most often with old friends who are accustomed to dueling each other. They're seeing how much stronger the other has gotten and by the looks of it, Eira isn't too impressed with Ne'kall right now."

"Who would be?" she muttered. "He stopped practicing once his first kid came around. It's a wonder he remembers how to make a flame at all."

Talon laughed. "I can see why you and the commander get along so well."

"We don't actually know each other all that well," Tla'lli admitted.

"Destined friendships are like that," he said. "You can get along as if you've known each other forever, and yet not even know the other person's first name. Or in the case of this guy next to me, get on each other's nerves all the time and still live to see another day."

Raikidan grunted at Talon's mention of him and Tla'lli giggled. "Yeah, I guess you're right."

Taking a deep breath, I focused on the battle at hand. Ne'kall ignited a flame in both his hands again and I was happy to copy him with the small ember I held in my fingertips. Ne'kall wasted no time shooting off fire at me once he saw my flames. Utilizing my speed and agility, I dodged the flames and blasted him with some of my own. Ne'kall moved away and then fought back. As we fought, the distance between us lessened, and soon hand-to-hand combat was added into the fight.

Ne'kall's skilled improved as we fought, and soon he was doing better than I remembered him doing in the past. I had to admit, I was impressed. All he needed was a reason to utilize his skills. There was nothing wrong with him choosing a domestic life, but it did make him soft. It was like that for all shamans who settled down. They took on fewer tasks, trained less, and spent more time doing passive things with their family, but Ne'kall was bouncing back much faster than most. Most of the time, it took a shaman several fights or training sessions to get back to their former skill level.

Ne'kall threw punches, flaming kicks, and blasts of fire at me but I was still too fast for him. This was where he always failed. He was strong and his fire showed it, but he was slow just like Del'karo. It wasn't until now did I realize how similarly the two fought. Del'karo was much more patient than Ne'kall, but that was the only major difference.

Knowing we had important issues to deal with, I figured it was time to end this fun little duel. Using my short stature in comparison to him to my advantage, along with my speed, I got underneath him and tossed him several feet. While he lay there, stunned from the impact, I mustered up a large blast of fire and shot it into the sky. When it was high enough, I pulled it back down directly over Ne'kall.

Ne'kall, still paralyzed, closed his eyes and waited bravely for the impact. But it would never come. When it was close enough to him, I pacified the fire into show fire and dispersed it into thousands of tiny flaming butterflies.

Ne'kall opened his eyes and watched the butterflies flutter around and then sighed. "You win… again."

I chuckled and walked over to him through the mass of butterflies. Children giggled and screeched as they chased the harmless flying fire creatures. Even several of Rimu's siblings found delight in chasing them, and even more interest when they'd burst into several smaller ones once crushed.

I extended my hand to Ne'kall, who gratefully took the help up. "You did better."

He chuckled. "How would you know? You ended it far sooner than the other times."

"I just know. Though, my old mentor would have done better."

Ne'kall grunted. "Don't go comparing us now. You know I hate that."

"Daddy! Daddy!" a little girl called out to him before I could respond. She was young, maybe no older than five, with brown eyes, and a dual-colored mohawk that matched Ne'kall's.

He chuckled and picked the little girl up. "Hey there, sweetheart."

"Look, daddy!" She held out her hand showing him a small flaming butterfly. "Look at what this pretty lady made."

I did my best not to react to her words and Ne'kall chuckled. "I see it. It's very pretty."

"Daddy, how come you were fighting with this lady?" his daughter asked.

Ne'kall shook his head. "Laz'shika and I weren't fighting. We're old friends and we were catching up."

His daughter nodded. "How come you lost?"

Ne'kall chuckled. "Because I always lose to her."

His daughter smiled. "How long have you known her, daddy?"

"A long time. Before your older brother was born."

She scrunched her nose. "Daddy, you're old."

I laughed. She was cute. She reminded me of Ryder.

"Lady, how old is you?" the girl asked innocently.

"Selena, that's rude," Ne'kall scolded.

I chuckled. "I'm eighty-five."

Selena tilted her head. "You don't look that old."

"Well does your father look two hundred years old?"

She looked at Ne'kall and nodded. "Yes, but that's cause he's old. But that's okay. Daddies are supposed to be old."

I laughed and Ne'kall joined in.

"Are you sure you don't want this life?" His lips twitched up into a smirk. "You'd like it."

"I don't do kids."

"You have a son."

"Tank-born, not the same."

"What's a tank-born?" Selena asked.

"Someone who is created; not born," I said.

She cocked her head and blinked. "I don't get it."

A small smile spread over my lips. "You will when you're older."

"M'kay." She looked at Ne'kall. "Daddy, can I go play again?"

He kissed her on the head and set her down. "Of course. Go have fun."

Selena giggled and ran off to play with the remaining fire butterflies. I shoved my hand into my pockets and headed back to where Raikidan and the others waited.

"So how is he doing?" Ne'kall asked as he followed.

"Ryder?" I shrugged. "Fine I guess. I don't see him often. The geneticists figured out the aging problem and now have it partially fixed."

Talon snorted as he overheard us on our way over. "He's a pain in the ass like you."

"Somehow I doubt that."

"He doesn't listen, like someone we know," he said, shooting me an accusatory glance.

My eyes narrowed. "Don't look at me like that."

"Why shouldn't I? You're the one who is covered in self-inflicted scars."

I snorted and folded my arms. "Your point?"

"Wait, those scars are self inflicted?" Tla'lli asked.

I nodded. "Some of them."

"All of them," Talon corrected.

"Most of them," I ended.

"Why would you do that to yourself?" Tla'lli asked.

"As punishment," Talon explained. "It's designed into us to obey orders without question and if we disobey any order we're to feel pain as a type of deterrent from doing it again, and that pain is usually self-inflicted. But, even though it's supposed to be a deterrent, that doesn't mean *some* people like to listen to it."

I snorted. "I don't take orders."

"And neither does your son."

"It's not my fault," I retorted. "I tell him to listen."

Talon blinked. "Wait, really?"

I nodded. "It keeps him safe."

Talon shook his head. "Well, he needs new listening skills. He'd rather run off and build something than do something as simple as patrol the city."

"He's a maker, not a destroyer."

Talon nodded. "That, I can agree with."

"What does he make?" Tla'lli asked.

"He's a metalsmith," Talon explained to her. "And one of the finest ones I've ever seen at that. He specialized in weapon making, but boy can he craft some other interesting things. He made a real fascinating dagger for Commander Eira, but she doesn't appear to have it on her."

"He dropped by before we left the city to take it for some special project he wouldn't tell me about," I said.

Talon smiled. "That would figure. He's always doing something for you."

"He's always trying to please me."

"More like make you happy."

I grunted. "Not possible. Now we really should get to work. We're burning daylight on stupid subjects."

Talon sighed. "Very well. Where will we start?"

"Show me a tactical map. Explain where we stand. What Zarda's power status is. Anything will do at this point. I haven't gotten a single report from you."

Talon held up his hands. "All right, all right, I get it. You're not happy with me. Here…" Talon pulled a metal cube out of a pouch that was attached to his belt. "We'll start off with the tactical map. It'll help with explaining just about everything. We just need a table to rest it on."

"A table you say?" Ir'esh chuckled. "That's simple."

With a flick of his hand the ground between us shifted and a large, oval cylinder piece of earth shot up, creating a type of table. Talon walked up to the table and placed the cube down onto it. I joined him and stood on his right and Raikidan moved from his place to stand to my right. Ir'esh and Tla'lli took their place at the table opposite of us but we were still missing someone.

"Zaith, you're a part of this too," I called over to him. "Get over here."

Zaith muttered to himself and moved from where he had been observing everything to join us.

Once he was at the tactical table Talon reached for the object he'd placed down on the table but Ir'esh stopped him. "Before we start, Eira promised to explain these clothes of hers."

I shrugged. "I won't, but Talon will."

"Oh, well thanks for volunteering me," he replied sarcastically.

I grunted. "I know nothing about them. I was told they were bullet proof and change into whatever I want."

Talon nodded. "That's the basic gist of it. The ones we're using now are a bit different than the one you're currently using. The ones Arnia dropped off for you were new prototypes. They're supposed to be resistant to the most current firepower and sharp weapon damage like your daggers. It was said they could possibly even withstand plasma weapons but no one knows because we can't get a working gun right now. The one the rest of us are using can only protect us from the most common gunfire and has a tendency to fail against sharp weapon damage. Other than that, not really much else to it."

"But how does it do it?" Tla'lli asked. "How does it know how to protect you and how does it know what to look like? Is it magic or is it science?"

Talon chuckled. "It's definitely not magic. The cloth is alive."

I tilted my head. "Come again?"

Talon chuckled again and placed his hand on his chest. The chest-plate reacted to his touch and shifted to its dormant cloth state, leaving his torso exposed. He handed the cloth over to Ir'esh to take a look at. "Looks and feels like an ordinary piece of spandex right?"

Ir'esh nodded and waited for Talon to go on. Talon rummaged through one of his pouches on his belt and pulled out a small cylindrical object.

"You have a lot of stuff in those pockets," Tla'lli observed.

Talon smiled at her. "I'm Eira's highest ranking tactician. If I'm not prepared, then there's going to be a problem."

Tla'lli laughed and waited for an explanation about the cloth her father held. Ir'esh handed the cloth back to Talon when he asked for it, and he pressed a button on the cylindrical object. A small laser appeared out of one end. He pointed the laser at the cloth and the top of the object projected a magnified view of the cloth.

"Like I said, the cloth is alive. It's made up of organic material that is enhanced for durability." Talon ran his thumb across the material and it reacted defensively. "As you can see, it reacts to touch and as a way to protect itself, its individual cells cluster and harden. Inadvertently, this protects the one wearing the cloth."

Zaith cupped his chin. "So you use the protective nature to your advantage."

Talon nodded. "Exactly."

"But how do you get it to change?" Tla'lli asked.

Talon chuckled "I'm getting to that." He placed the cloth back onto his chest and it reacted to his will and changed back into his chestplate. "Because the material is living, it requires a food source. This is where science takes its big hold. The material has been manipulated to feed off of electrical charges, in particular neural electrical charges.

"This is the energy that passes through all the neurons in your body, and is the energy your brain works on. This being said, the cloth taps into this limitless energy, connecting it right to your brain, allowing someone to control it as easily as it is to breathe."

"What's the catch?" Zaith asked.

"Well it has a limit of what it can change into," Talon admitted. "Because the cloth doesn't exactly have a brain, it doesn't have memory, so it can't store any information. This means in order to change into something, it's forced to feed off the memories of the user. So if the user doesn't know everything about an item to be worn, the material can't change into it."

"So you need to know the item by sight, texture, smell, and the works," Tla'lli mused. "But it's impossible to remember all that."

Talon chuckled. "Just because you can't think of it consciously doesn't mean it's not stored subconsciously."

Tla'lli nodded. "Okay, I think I get it."

Ir'esh rubbed his chin. "Our tribe is unique. Not only are we shamans, but we're druids as well. We must enchant our clothes so we don't lose them if we choose to take our animal form. Can these clothes you have handle that?"

Talon scratched his head. "I don't know. We don't currently have any shifters to test that out on."

"They won't," I piped in. "You still need the spell."

"You've tested this then?" Ir'esh asked.

I nodded and gestured to Raikidan with my thumb. "On him."

Ir'esh chuckled. "I'll accept that."

"Are we done talkin' about these stupid clothes yet?" Zaith muttered. "Seems to be the least of our worries, no?"

"Very well." I motioned Talon to begin.

Talon stored his magnifying tool and started up a holographic map from the cube he had placed down on the tactical table.

Talon pointed to the map. "This is the most current information we have. As you can see, this shows the land and who controls it. The blue circles are the shaman tribe and the green are the druids. Orange shades are the various nu-human power cities not yet taken over by Zarda. Violet are the elves, yellow are the small wogron packs we know of, and brown are the dwarves. The large red areas belong to Zarda."

Ir'esh leaned closer. "That's a lot of land he controls."

Talon nodded. "And he still craves more. He won't be happy until he has it all."

Zaith narrowed his eyes. "Where are the dragons and gypsies?"

"Gypsies are nomads, so they have no land to speak of," I said.

"And we have no data on dragons," Talon concluded. "As far as we were aware, you were all dead."

Zaith's brow creased, his head cranking to the side. "Say that again?"

"It exactly as I said it. Nothing else to it." Talon shrugged. "Frankly, we were surprised to see you flying over us when we first arrived."

"That don't makes no sense. He would know because of…" Zaith trailed off and stared at the ground in thought.

Talon looked at me and I waved him off. Zaith knew something, but right now wasn't the time to find out what. Talon nodded and continued explaining where we stood. By the time he was done, the sun was a mere sliver on the mountainous horizon.

"And that's it," Talon finished. "That's the best I can explain everything, so I hope no one has any questions."

"I have one but it's not related to anything you just talked about," Tla'lli said.

"Very well, what is it?"

"What are we going to do about the events that transpired earlier?" she asked. "I doubt Zarda didn't know about this many soldiers leaving the city."

Talon nodded. "You're right, he did know. General Rick requested permission to come out here with this company, on the count you had broken the treaty in some way, even though he had no proof."

"And the way we fix it will be easy," I said.

I walked away toward the entrance of the village. My men parted for me, and as they did, a soldier handed me his elven-crafted sword. I took it gratefully and left the village for Rick's body. With great swiftness, I sliced the blade through his neck, severing his head from the rest of him.

Taking the head and leaving the body, I headed back into the village. I tossed the elven sword back to its owner and headed for Talon and flung Rick's head to him when I was close enough. He caught it and kept it away from his body in disgust.

"You couldn't have put it in a bag first?" he muttered before he pulled a large leather bag out of a pouch and stuffed the head inside.

I rolled my eyes. "Don't be such a baby. Show that to Zarda and tell him Rick defected. It's that simple."

"I didn't kill him," Talon said. "I can't present him with this unless I did it."

"Then lie."

"You know I'm terrible at that."

I sucked in a breath. "Then learn fast. It's the only way you're going to be able to get him to believe Rick was lying and not killed by me."

Talon sighed. "All right. I'll do my best but if I'm killed I'm blaming you."

I snorted. "If you can't lie well enough that's your problem."

"What if I went with him?" Tla'lli offered. "If I explained our side would that help?"

I thought this over a moment and then nodded. "Yes, it would help but it would be best if your father went instead."

Tla'lli shook her head. "Due to his health I have to say no. I must go in his place."

I contemplated this. "Very well, but be careful. Zarda will expect your father, so you'll need to explain yourself for your appearance and not his. Be tactful in what you say, and give no signs of weakness in the tribe due to his illness."

Tla'lli nodded. "Don't worry about that. I'm good with words."

I nodded. "Good."

I glanced down and blinked as a young boy approached me with a small wooded bowl filled with a foul-smelling clear liquid.

"It's to wash your hands." He shuffled his feet. "Sorry that it smells bad."

I smiled at the boy and gratefully washed my bloody hands. When I was done, the boy ran off to dispose of the solution.

"Remarkable solution," Ir'esh remarked. "We received a supply a few months ago from your tribe. It's quite handy. You wouldn't happen to know the person who made it, would you?"

"I did," I stated quietly. "Now if you excuse me, I must speak with my men before I leave and go about my usual business."

I turned on my heels and went to speak with my men. As I spoke with them, I listened to their worries about our plans and heard ideas they shared to aid us. Some of them were absolutely terrible, while others were quite good.

As I was speaking with one soldier who was worried about safety, we were interrupted by someone near us calling out. "Watch out!"

CHAPTER 36

Before I could think to turn and see who the warning was for, something heavy hit me in the back and I fell to the ground.

"Ow…" I complained. My assailant chirped and I sighed. "Rimu…"

My men laughed at me.

"She can take on monsters, armies, and adult dragons, but she's taken down by a single baby dragon with ease," someone teased.

I grunted. "You all will shut your mouths if you know what's best for you."

They continued to laugh but didn't make any more comments. I grunted when Rimu shifted his weight as he sat on my back.

"Rimu, get off me," I muttered.

Rimu grunted in defiance and planted his front claw on my head, pinning me more. Xaneth giggled and then knelt beside me.

"I apologize. He's been eying that hair clip of yours for a while now. I didn't think he'd actually jump you though."

"He was eying my—that's what this is about?"

Xaneth's eyes squinted as she smiled. "I'm afraid so. The urge to hoard is hard for our young to resist especially something like that—Rimu, don't you dare!"

I blinked with confusion with her sudden warning. What was Rimu about to—

"Hey!" I shouted when my hair fell free and Rimu jumped off me. "Give that back, you little punk!"

I scrambled to my feet and chased after him. Soldiers jumped out of the way as Rimu charged through them in an attempt to escape me, but I kept with him. Rimu tried zig-zagging, making sharp turns, and even turning mid-run to run around me, but I wasn't deterred from getting my hair clip back. By no means could he have it. That was one thing I would never part with.

I crashed to the ground with a *thud* as something heavy slammed into me. I grunted and tried to get up, but whatever hit me was still on me. My assailant hung his face in front of mine and chirped. I huffed. It was one of Rimu's siblings. Taking a good breath, I forced myself against his weight and started to get up, but I was thrown back down when more weight jumped on me. I let out a tight breath when a new voice chirped. I was being ganged up on by baby scaly critters, and losing.

Their weight disappeared and the two little dragons grumbled. I turned to see Raikidan holding them by their tails and staring the two down, who showed no fear and stared back defiantly. Not taking my freedom for granted, I scrambled to my feet and ran off, looking for Rimu.

"You're welcome!" Raikidan called after me.

I pushed through my men and searched for Rimu. He had gotten the chance to get pretty far, but I doubted he was old enough yet how to be tactical in his hiding.

I grinned when I found him trying to hide behind a rock seat that was much smaller than him. "Found you, Rimu."

Rimu snatched the hair clip from between his feet and took off again. I followed, but slower. I needed to be aware of his siblings and figure out where he was going next for me to cut him off. Rimu ran and hid behind his mother but she stepped aside, exposing him. "You're not going to hide behind me."

He whimpered and tried to hide behind her again but she moved once again.

"This is your problem. You've upset her by stealing her treasure, so now you deal with it."

It sounded weird hearing her talk to him like that. It sound like something you'd say to an older child, but Rimu could be older than I thought. I wasn't familiar with the dragon age-to-growth ratio. Of course, they could just parent differently than humans as well.

Rimu looked at me and then back at his mother. He then looked at the entrance of the village and then back at me. He hesitated for a moment and then dashed for the gate. Unfortunately for him, that hesitation was all I needed to gain the upper hand. I cut him off and snaked my arms around his abdomen, grabbing a firm hold of him. He wiggled and writhed, but my grip held and I hauled him into the air and into my arms.

I sighed. "You're the size of a medium sized dog, but you sure aren't as light as one." Rimu grunted and continued to try to get away. "I'll let you go when you give me my clip back. There's no negotiating this."

Rimu grunted and shook his head. He had stopped squirming now, much to my relief, but it didn't look like he intended to hand the clip over any time soon.

"Rimu, I'm not playing. Give it back to me," I ordered.

Rimu lowered his head submissively but shook his head again in defiance. I let out a frustrated breath. I wasn't going to hurt him, but asking wasn't working for me. Just then, a small child ran up to us with her hands held out to Rimu. I watched her with interest, keeping careful eye on her motions. Rimu looked up at me and then suddenly tossed the hair clip to the girl. Shocked by his willingness to hand it over, the girl was able to get several feet away before I reacted.

Placing Rimu down, I dashed after the girl. "Get back here, kid."

She squealed and giggled and continued to run. Picking up my pace, I closed the distance between us and grabbed her. She squealed and giggled with delight but didn't fight me. I hoped she'd hand the clip over to me without a fight, but quickly became confused when I noticed she no longer had it.

The girl giggled and then another girl giggled. I turned to see another child with my hair clip in hand before she disappeared into the crowd of soldiers. I placed the child back on the ground and ran after the other. Just as I picked my way through the crowd of men and reached her, she tossed the clip to another child who lay in wait. I went after him, but he too tossed it to another child when I came too close.

I huffed and pulled my hair to one side. I was starting to get annoyed now. These children didn't see any harm in this but I wanted my hair clip back. I didn't want it getting broken.

I chased after a young child, maybe four or five, and watched her bump into one of the Brute soldiers. The little girl fell down and began to cry.

"Hey, hey, don't do that," the soldier cooed as he knelt and pulled her onto his knee. "See, you're okay."

She sniffled and he smiled at her. His smile was genuine and warm and she smiled back at him. Slowly the little girl held up my hair clip and offered it to him. The soldier took the hair clip with a grin and then put her on his shoulders before standing up. I advanced toward him, thinking he'd be wise and hand it over, but I was wrong.

With a large grin, the soldier tossed my hair clip to someone else. I growled and spun on my heels. This just got worse, and my worry about my hair clip being broken was looking to become a reality.

"Give it back," I ordered.

The other soldiers refused to listen and laughed as they tossed the hair clip around.

"I'm not joking. Give it back."

"Aw, lighten up, Commander," someone said. "We're just havin' fun wi' ya."

I bared my teeth "I said give it back!"

Most of the soldiers stopped laughing. With that tone, they knew I wasn't going to play, but there was one soldier in particular who wasn't going to comply with my order. He also happened to be the one with my hair clip.

"Dude, give it to her," one soldier told him in a hushed tone.

The soldier with my hair clip grunted and tossed it carelessly between his hands. "Why? It's just a hair clip. It's not like it's something special."

"You're wrong," another soldier argued. "Amara gave that to her. If anything happens to it, you're a dead man. Just give it to her."

I threw out my hand. "Give it to me now."

"Lighten up, Eira. Nothing bad—"

I watched with horror when he fumbled my hair clip and it flew out of his hands. Even though the hair clip was made of emerald, it was over half a century old. I wasn't sure if a short fall would break it or not. It wasn't like I could easily get it fixed, and it definitely wasn't replaceable.

I prepared for the worst as gravity pulled it down, but it never hit the ground. Several ivory spikes soared through the air, penetrating the ground and cradling the hair clip. I breathed a relieved sigh and watched as Talon strolled over to where my hair clip was being held captive. I eyed the long ivory spikes sticking out of his arms and watched as more grew out as if replenishing the ones he'd used.

Talon knelt and picked up my hair clip and gave it a quick once over before standing back up and holding it out to me. "I think you dropped something."

I grunted and walked over to take it from him. "Thanks."

Talon smiled and nodded and headed back to the tactical table. I took a step to follow him, but was stopped when Tla'lli tossed a bow and quiver filled with arrows to me.

"Hunting, you in?" she asked. "Can't rightfully allow you to leave without filling your belly. And we'll need some more with all these extra mouths to feed."

I tossed the items back to her. "Don't need them."

She grinned and handed the bow and quiver over to her father, who glanced at the tool and then at me.

"I see you don't have the one I gave you"

"I left it back at my campsite," I said. "I hadn't realized I'd be gone for so long."

He nodded. "Fair enough. Have you used it for more than just hunting?"

"Once. It took me a while to figure out its unique trait but it was useful. Though, it's a bit clunky for what I do so I can't use it all that much. Something smaller, like a hand crossbow or even a smaller bow, would work better for me."

He nodded. "I understand. Unfortunately that's the only one in existence, and we don't know how to recreate it."

I was a bit shocked. I couldn't believe he'd give me something so rare.

Tla'lli grabbed onto my arm and pulled me toward the village entrance. "I don't mean to interrupt you and my father, but we need to hurry before he—"

"Don't be too long!" Ir'esh called. "You can't be late."

Tla'lli let out an exasperated sigh. "Yes, father."

I chuckled. "Late for what?"

She frowned. "Today is my coming-of-age celebration. It's been in planning for months. It's probably what made that general think we were planning some sort of rebellion or attack."

I raised an eyebrow. "You have celebrations for coming of age?"

She nodded. "It's a big elven tradition. Once an elf reaches a century old, they're considered mature enough to be of marrying age, and since I'm the only one to reach a century in a while, it's a really big deal."

My eyes squinted as a teasing smile slid up my face. "Careful, your father might start trying to marry you off right after the ceremony with all these men here to choose from."

"He's already started," she muttered. "I don't want to think about what he'll do with all these new men here."

I laughed and threw my arm over her shoulder. "Then let's hurry up. Can't make you late for your own bachelorette party."

She sighed. "Please make me late."

I laughed again. "Not a chance."

"You're horrible," she muttered.

I grinned. "I try."

She shook her head and laughed. "Hey, where are you going?"

I pointed to the new direction I'd chosen to take. "Hunting, remember?"

"Best hunting places are this way."

"There's prey this way. I can smell it."

She shook her head. "We don't hunt over there. There's never anything good."

"I know what my nose is telling me."

She snorted. "And I know these woods like the back of my hand. You don't know what you're talking about."

"You wanna bet?" I challenge.

Tla'lli grinned. "May the best hunter win."

She turned to continue heading down the main path that lead out of the village and as she did, the wind picked up and she changed shape. I watched as she went from woman to cougar within seconds.

"Commander." My attention was pulled away when a young soldier spoke. "What should we do?"

I shrugged. "I don't know. Just make yourselves useful, I guess."

I headed down my intended path without another word. Hearing soft crunching noises behind me, I stopped walking and turned around. Behind me, Rimu tentatively followed.

I chuckled and motioned him to follow. "C'mon, maybe I'll teach you something."

Rimu chirped happily and trotted close behind me as he followed me into the woods.

The bonfire crackled with life, burning bright, lighting up the forest around us and reaching high for the starry sky. My men and I sat amongst the shamans as equals, the shamans going above and beyond to make us all feel welcomed. My men laughed, drank, ate, and were merry. It was nice to see them like this. Such a needed change for them; a moment in time where they didn't have to worry and could feel like normal people.

"You're smiling," Talon observed. "That's not something I've seen in a long time."

I gave him a sidelong glance. "Don't get used to it. It'll be gone by the morning."

He laughed and went back to conversing with Tla'lli. I smiled. It was nice seeing him getting along with her. Talon was usually awkward around women in his attempt to never offend them, but there was no awkwardness between these two. It had to be a Tla'lli thing. The two of us had gotten along well today, and we didn't really know each other. I had never bonded so fast with someone. Maybe Talon had been right. Maybe it was a destined friendship waiting to blossom. Or maybe it was just her. She was quite strange compared to most of the other village women. She dressed like them, but she didn't act like them.

She was more trusting and curious. After we had gotten back from hunting and everything started moving with the party, she had boldly asked Talon about his ability. She was anything but shy and she liked getting her way, which meant she hated losing. I almost laughed, remembering what happened when we had come back from our separate hunting trips.

I had dragged back a decently-sized deer, surprising her. She really hadn't expected me to bring back anything, but she wasn't completely impressed because she figured her two deer, which Rimu attempted to steal right from her hands, rivaled my catch. She tried to tease me, thinking I had made the wrong hunting spot choice, and made a worse choice by bringing Rimu with me, but it backfired in her face when I left and returned with a large black bear.

She almost fainted at the sight of me dragging it back, and even Rimu had a small rabbit in his jaws, although I wasn't going to tell her he had actually caught it when I was retrieving the bear. Rimu had made it difficult to hunt. He was too eager and tended to scare the prey off, but after watching me, he managed to get the concept of waiting without bouncing around, allowing me to finally land a kill.

When Tla'lli had recovered from her shock, she refused to believe I had caught the bear in that location. No matter how much I insisted I'd hunted in the spot I'd intended, she struggled to accept her defeat.

A masculine voice pulled me back to the present. I looked up to find Ne'kall holding his hand out to me. "C'mon, let's go."

My brow rose. "Go where?"

He chuckled. "It's time for the fire dance. Now get up."

I shook my head. "Oh no. I don't prance around."

Ne'kall snorted. "It's not prancing and you know it. Besides, there are few fire shamans in this village, and even fewer who know any of the dances. And that few includes you."

"I don't care. I'm not doing it."

"I vote you do," Tla'lli said.

"I vote you don't have a say," I mumbled.

Tla'lli grunted. "I do too. This is my celebration and you're going to do it."

"This is the celebration you begged me to keep you from. And since you didn't want to be here in the first place, I'm not going to listen to you."

"I'd like to see what this dance is," Talon said. "Especially if you're supposed to be a part of it. You always liked to say you didn't know how to dance."

"C'mon, don't be a chicken," Ne'kall teased.

I sighed and reluctantly took his hand. What was the harm? It wasn't the kind of dance Talon likely thought it to be. Unfamiliar with tribal dances, he'd think this dance would be like those seen in the city.

Following behind Ne'kall, we headed for the bonfire. As we did, I figured it'd be more appropriate to wear my shaman outfit, so I had my clothes change. Once we arrived at the fire, a shaman with a large moose skull on his head handed me a large bear skull with large, colorful plumage attached to the back.

My brow rose and he chuckled. "Just wear it."

I eyed him skeptically, but when a young woman came over and offered a deer skill to Ne'kall and he allowed her to a place it on his head, I put the bear skull on my own head. Another woman joined us with two wooden bowls in her hands. Curious, I peered into the bowls, to find green and red paint. This intrigued me, although all of this aroused my curiosity. I was familiar with the dance, but never had I performed it in an actual celebration setting, or with this tribe.

This tribe's customs were much different than the West Tribe; embracing their primal roots, where the West Tribe didn't. The West Tribe was self-sufficient, but they also had a firm hold in modern living.

I stepped back when the man in front of me dipped his fingers into the bowl with the red paint and then reached for me. He chuckled and then motioned for me to come back. Eying him, I did as asked and waited as he painted my face with various marks. When he was done, he pulled away and cleaned his fingers. I glanced over at Ne'kall to see a woman finishing the process of painting his face.

He glanced at me when she was done. The two of us, and the man who had been painting my face, moved into our positions around the fire with two other shamans. My body reacted instinctively as drums began to beat and people chanted. My feet moved without me having to think much, and my fingers pulled the bonfire flames to dance to my will.

I could feel the rhythm of the drums in my chest and the heat of the flames as they licked my skin. The world faded and it was just me, the flame, and its warmth. I couldn't feel the eyes of anyone watching. I couldn't feel the stillness of the night summer air. I was lost in a world I knew but hadn't visited in a long time. I was lost in a small sense of security and peace.

Then they all came back, flowing into my senses like an unstoppable wave. That feeling was gone, but for good reason. Now I simply couldn't dance alone. I shared my fire with the others, working together to keep the flame alive. We bent the flames to our will and they danced without protest.

Then, when the time came, three of the shamans backed out, leaving Ne'kall and me to finish the dance. We had been elected to perform the duel that ended this particular dance, and that was a lot of pressure for me.

Ne'kall's dancing mirrored mine on the opposite side of the empty bonfire pit. His motions were stiff, unlike my more fluid ones, making this part of the dance harder to do, even though it wasn't his fault. The way I used fire was different than most. Most used power and force to control their fire, creating jerky or stiff movements, but my movements were fluid, like an elementalist using water.

I knew the reason. It was because of my mother. She had taught me how to control my ability. She had taught me how to ease the burning, but she could only teach me in the only way she knew how. She knew water and water was fluid. She didn't know fire but she knew it couldn't be much different than water so she taught me her way without hesitation. She had been right and, in the end, it had been more beneficial for me to learn that way. It helped me ease the hunger and ease the loneliness caused by my difference from others.

Ne'kall's movements became more aggressive but my pace remained the same. The fires stopped merging, and we ceased sharing. My fire spun around me, and his around him, and it moved faster as the beat of the drums increased. The fires continued to swirl around until the drums abruptly stopped and the fire we controlled suddenly burst outward.

My breath came slow and steady, and I held my crossed arms over each other elegantly. Small butterflies that were once my flame, created by the flame's death, fluttered around illuminating small bits of the night sky and surrounding forest. Ne'kall's embers rolled on the ground, and as they touched they formed into larger flames until they shaped into small bear cubs that tumbled around his feet.

The will of the flame butterflies pulled on my fingertips, and I secretly watched them flutter over the villagers and my men. I observed their awed faces and I watched as many of them tried to reach up to the tiny flames. Some flames landed, lighting up smiles everywhere.

Then a drum beat and my fingers twitched. The butterflies reacted, and then reacted again, when the drum beat again and my will to respond was forced into them. The drums beat more, its slow-building rhythm vibrating deep in my chest. The beat picked up, moving quicker, and I pulled my flames with great force back to me.

Ne'kall's flames reacted to the beat as well and merged together creating, larger and larger bears. Ne'kall and I danced once again but this time our fires began to merge and form into a completely different shape. Ne'kall relinquished the will of his flame to me, and I knew the dance was coming to an end. I was honored he would give me the ending, and I wasn't going to disappoint.

As we danced and the fires became one, I edged toward the empty bonfire pit. When I was close enough, I took control of both flames and directed them into the sky. The flames completed their merge and soared into the air with giant wings. The bird's long, flowing tail attempted to keep it anchored to my will, but I forced it to move on as I positioned myself in the center of the bonfire pit.

Once there, I made large sweeping arm motions and then pulled the fire down on top of me. Relaxing, I closed my eyes and held my breath as the heat of the phoenix-shaped flame crashed down and consumed me. Staying still for several moments, I finally opened my eyes and looked around.

I was no longer in the bonfire pit. I stood on the outside of the celebration circle hidden behind the shadows of the trees. I watched as people searched for me and I grinned. There were two variations to the dance. One left the final two shamans facing off, and the second, the one I chose, used an illusion to seemingly disappear in fire.

I brushed off small bits of dirt from my clothes and sent a silent prayer of thanks to the gods for the skilled and mysterious earth shaman who helped me. Placing blind faith in someone wasn't something I often did, but I was glad it had worked out in my favor this time.

Slowly, I picked my way back to where I had chosen to sit for the celebration. Only small embers remained in the bonfire pit, and Ne'kall was too busy looking around for me in the dark to think to bring the fire back to life.

Tla'lli, Talon, and Raikidan looked at me with surprise as I sat down next to them. I held my finger to my mouth to make sure they didn't say anything, and they nodded. I watched Ne'kall continue to look around for me and tried hard not to laugh. He obviously had not seen this version of the dance before.

Smirking, I lifted my hand and willed the embers left in the bonfire pit to grow and shape into the phoenix that had seemingly engulfed me. Ne'kall stared at it, eyes wide. The phoenix shape arched its neck and spread its wings as if it were going to take off again, but instead I let go of the flame and it transformed into an ordinary fire.

Ne'kall turned and zeroed in on me. I removed the bear skull and winked. Ne'kall chuckled and shook his head. Bowing graciously, he backed into the crowd and disappeared, ending the dance for good. People clapped and cheered. When the applause died down, music was started back up, keeping the energy for the celebration high.

"Not what I was expecting, but it was pretty interesting," Talon said.

I picked up the rest of my dinner I had yet to finish. "Nothing is ever as you expect." I remarked as

He chuckled. "Touché."

I ate quietly after that. Talon understood my requirement of silence and was more than happy to oblige, choosing to continue conversing with Tla'lli.

It wasn't long before I grew bored. Everyone around me was enjoying themselves, acting normally, while I kept to myself like usual, and didn't look normal. Stifling a sigh, I removed the bear skull from my head and continued eating. My consumption halted when Raikidan lightly tapped my arm. I looked at him as he stood. He jerked his head as if telling me to follow and then walked away. Curious, I put my food down and followed.

No one paid us any mind, much to my relief, as we made our way out of the throng of people and into the darkness of the forest. The farther we moved from the celebration, the darker the forest became. I was curious of Raikidan's intent but also annoyed with his silence. What did he want with me all the way out here?

Suddenly, when the light from the bonfire was no longer able to guide our way, he held up a clenched hand and opened it, revealing one of my fire butterflies. It fluttered its wings but didn't fly off, creating a new light source. I eyed Raikidan but he only passed me a quick glance with a matching grin before continuing on, giving no hint as to his intentions. Determined to find out what he wanted, I pursued.

I didn't have to follow much longer. Once we entered into a small clearing he stopped walking. I glanced around to find nothing spectacular about the clearing. The light of the full moon, unhindered by thick tree cover, lit it up and bathed the ground in silver light.

I looked up from my studying when I noticed Raikidan approaching. He stopped only inches away and held out his hand with the butterfly perched on it. The fire butterfly flapped its wings and fluttered over to my shoulder, where it took a new perch.

"You looked like you could use some space," Raikidan finally said. "I know you don't like crowds much."

I chuckled and gazed up at the stars in the sky. "To be honest I was fine being around all of them. They're my comrades, not random people on the street."

"So you were completely fine?"

I looked at him and nodded. "Yes, but thanks for the thought."

Raikidan nodded and watched me.

"What?"

He sucked in a tight breath. "Do you mind if I ask you a personal question?"

I eyed him suspiciously. "It depends."

Raikidan stepped closer and took my arm into his firm grip. He slid his fingers over my skin, feeling the tiny scars that littered my skin. The action sent a strange sensation through my body.

"You told me these were battle scars," he began. "But how many are really self-inflicted?"

"A better question would be how many are actually battle scars?" Raikidan shifted his gaze to me mine as I pulled my arm away. "I didn't see full battle much. My design as assassin meant I stayed hidden until I found my target and eliminated him. I was good at what I did and was rarely ever caught, let alone hurt. But as good as I was, I also didn't listen well. I didn't like being a pawn and I wanted to make choices for myself. So, I disobeyed orders constantly and as a result ended up hurting myself." My teeth caught my lower lip briefly. "But the pain didn't deter me like it did others. It reminded me I could feel something. It told me I was alive and I lived off of feeling that pain. Sometimes that pain ended up being the only thing that got me through."

Raikidan grabbed a hold of my arm again and rubbed his thumb over the scars.

"My words bother you."

He nodded. "I don't see how someone could live a life like that."

"When it's the only life you know, you see it as normal…"

Raikidan continued to gaze at my arm, before loosening his grip. "What is the worst scar you've given yourself? What scar shows the biggest order you defied?"

I pulled my arm from him again and held it close to my body, thinking over his questions. He wanted to know the worst one. Could I really remember that far back? Of course I could. I remembered that order and my defying action well as if it happened yesterday.

As I thought about that moment in time, my hands reacted and instinctually went for the area I had harmed myself that time. I realized that the moment I touched that area, in my state I would relive that memory. I snapped out of my remembering and pulled my hands back up to where I had held them last, before they could touch their intended destination and show Raikidan.

"Don't make me remember that," I whispered. "Please."

"Sorry," he said quietly. "I didn't mean to upset you."

I set my gaze on the sky. "Don't worry about it."

"Eira…" His trailing off confused me, but before I could look at him, he took my hair clip.

"Raikidan!" I shouted. "Give it back!"

He chuckled and held it out of my reach. "You can reach better than that."

I smacked him hard in the chest. "I'm not playing games. Give it back!"

Raikidan blinked in confusion from my refusal to play along. "What's your problem? You're not normally like this."

"I didn't allow the soldiers to play around with it and I'm not about to let you. I won't risk my hair clip being damaged."

"That's not what I meant. You know I'm going to be careful with it. I know it's important to you. I was just harmlessly playing around. You're usually more carefree and playful with me than most other people."

"Right, like you care about that."

His brow furrowed. "What are you talking about?"

I snorted. "Don't give me that. You acted like you could care less about my existence while your fellow dragonkin were around. Hell, you could care less about my existence when anyone is around to see us together!”

"Eira, you don't understand. It's not like that."

"I don't understand?" I snatched my hair clip from him. "I understand perfectly. You're ashamed to be around me. I understand you're not really here to help. But here's a newsflash. I don't play that game. You can't act all friendly with me and then turn around and pretend I don't matter when someone else is around. I don't put up with two-faced people, or in your case, dragons. So do us both a favor and just leave."

I turned to leave, but Raikidan grabbed me by the arm. "It's not like that."

I yanked my arm free. "Then what is it like, Raikidan? Go on, tell me." Raikidan gulped and hesitated. I shook my head, a mix of disbelief and anger raging inside me. "Like I thought. And here the spirits tried to give me a dream and make me believe you're really just alone and need someone. They tried to tell me someone else was as alone as I was, but they're wrong too! You're not lonely. You're bored. So take your stupid boredom and go home."

Raikidan blinked. "Go home?"

"Yeah, go home!" My lip curled, my frustration taking over. "You've obviously not here to help. You're here because you're bored but you're also too ashamed to be seen near me and I'm not putting up with that, so just go home. I choose to be alone not because I want to, but because it's safer. You, on the other hand, choose it because you feel like it, so you have fun being alone."

I spun on my heels and was almost knock to the ground when I ran into someone.

"Sorry about that," the male voice said. "I shouldn't have came so close."

I looked at him with a glare. I was surprised to see Xaneth's mate but didn't show it.

"What do you want?" I spat.

His brow rose but didn't reply harshly. "I'm here for him."

"He's all yours," I muttered. "Now get out of my way."

I pushed passed him and headed back to the celebration. The more distance I put between Raikidan and me the better, and Xaneth's mate would only help.

"Cheery, isn't she?" Xaneth's mate said.

Raikidan let out a growl and Xaneth's mate replied in the same way. It didn't take a scientist to understand they were no longer speaking common, not like I cared much. I knew this had been a bad idea from the start. *I should have ignored his fake offer and kept going about my business.* I sighed and slowed to a stop. *But if I had done that I wouldn't be here. I'd still be running instead of facing my problem…*

Taking a deep relaxing breath, I continued on, allowing my fire butterfly to guide me back to the celebration. By the time I sat back down next to Talon, no one would have known I had been upset.

"Where's Raikidan?" Talon asked me.

I shrugged and picked up what was left of my food. "Doesn't matter."

Talon eyed me curiously but soon shrugged it off and went back to conversing with others. I ate the rest of my meal in silence and didn't mind this time. Or, I thought I was going to eat the rest of my meal until a little chirp caught my attention. I looked up to Rimu looking at me with curious eyes. I figured he was looking at my food so I placed it down but his gaze never left me.

It took me a moment to realize he was looking at the butterfly perched on my shoulder. Chuckling, I moved the butterfly from me to his head. Rimu tilted his head as if he were trying to get a better look at it, but failed and wound up wandering around aimlessly. His siblings made their way over to him to take a look for themselves, but when I felt they were getting too close, I put extra life into the little butterfly and sent them chasing after it.

They chased the fire butterfly around the bonfire, and even with joint efforts, failed to catch it. Human and elf children watched on. It was obvious they wanted to join in but were afraid of being trampled, and I didn't blame them. Dragon whelps weren't careful or gentle in the slightest.

Feeling bad and understanding their want to play, I focused on the bonfire and pulled more butterflies out of it. The children squealed and ran after them, and even Rimu's siblings tried to take one for themselves. The children's enjoyment entertained the adults and got them to enjoy the celebration even more, if that were possible.

Content with the results of my actions, I went back to eating, though paused when I sensed eyes on me. I shifted my gazed up to see Talon watching me. "What?"

He shook his head. "Nothing."

I snorted and went back to eating once more. I briefly stopped eating again when someone sat down next to me, and I didn't need to look up to know who it was. I wasn't at all pleased that Raikidan had chosen to stay.

He leaned close and whispered into my ear. "You're wrong about why I'm here, and I have no intention of going home."

I grunted. "Whatever."

He sighed and leaned back on his hands, still maintaining a close space between us. Trying to ignore his presence, I reached down on my plate for some food only to realize I had none left to eat.

"Here." Raikidan sat up and handed me his plate he had barely touched.

"Keep it," I muttered.

"I'm not going to eat it so you might as well."

"Wouldn't that confuse your instincts?"

Raikidan hesitated and then looked down at the food he was offering. Snorting, I leaned forward on my bent legs and watched the children play with my creations. I could hear Raikidan growling from time to time but paid him no mind. I didn't care who he was talking to or what about.

My eyes began to wander after several moments and ended up resting on my bag. Compelled for no real reason, I reached for it and pulled it into my lap to dig through. I wasn't sure what I was looking for, but my body did, since I completely ignored almost everything in the bag. My search came to an end when I came across an object wrapped in a violet silk cloth. I unwrapped the object and put my bag aside.

In my hands was my pan flute. I had put it in here when I had been packing, but I didn't have a true reason for doing so. Taking a steady breath, I lifted the flute to my lips and began to play. The chatter around me died as everyone began to listen. My song was soft and serene and was carried into the night by the soft breeze that filled the air. I continued to play, but part of my attention was pulled when Raikidan started growling again.

His growl sounded aggressive, but when I glanced at him he was grinning like mad. Slowly, my eyes scanned the crowd and they rested on Zaith, who sat by a tree across from us. He was glaring our way, and dragons who sat near him whispered amongst themselves, glancing at him from time to time as if they were mocking him.

Doing my best to keep my concentration on my flute playing, I lazily traced his glare to Raikidan, and everything fell together. Whatever this red dragon's problem was, I was really getting sick of it. I didn't see how he had been given leadership of the clan. With the way he acted, it made me doubt he was much older than Raikidan, though I had this strange feeling deep inside that told me I was wrong.

Pushing my questions away, I focused on my flute playing. This issue with Raikidan was no concern of mine anymore. I wasn't going to be a pawn in his little games, and he could deal with his own problems.

Once my song ended, I skillfully transitioned to another, and this song piqued my men's interest the most. The song was low and slow, and it wasn't long before the words of the ancient song were rolling off Talon's tongue. For several moments it was only Talon singing but eventually other soldiers joined in, creating a harmony of ranges.

"I didn't know anyone knew Old Tongue anymore, let alone humans," a dragon commented.

"You don't know much about speech origins, do you?" an elven villager said. "Humans were the first to speak Old Tongue."

"That's just a legend," another dragon objected.

The elf shook his head. "Not a legend, a *Story of Old*. It was the humans who first learned to speak, and it was the humans who taught the other races to communicate with them. It was that first teaching that spurred the diversity of languages today, but it was also that teaching that killed the Old Tongue.

"The fact that these soldiers harness even a piece of Old Tongue on their lips brings this scholar some peace. It is good to know Old Tongue isn't more than just writings in a text in our vast libraries that only exist to collect dust."

I tried not to smile at the old elf's words, in fear of messing up my playing. This song was special to us soldiers. It spurred hope in the weak and healed the broken. It was a song whose title was long forgotten but in the place of the title's absence, placed peace in the souls of the weary.

Tomorrow I'd head back to camp, with news of what I had accomplished, but for now, I played this song, along with many others, just as old as the first, long into the night. This celebration would end with Tales of Old that were not spoken, but felt from even the most dead of hearts.

My eyes snapped open. A metal door clanged and footsteps stomped down the stone hall. Soldiers were coming and I wouldn't doubt it was my turn to be interrogated. I wasn't sure if they were the cause of my awoken state or because of what just happened in my dream, but it didn't matter. Nothing did.

Two soldiers unlocked the door to the cell and headed straight for me. One hauled me to my feet while the other watched everyone in the cell to make sure none of them tried to attack.

I didn't fight the soldier as he dragged me out of the cell and I didn't react when he grabbed me by the hair roughly in hopes of getting a reaction. There was no need to, because I didn't care. I didn't care about anything anymore. I wasn't going to snitch, no, I'd never do that to the others, but I didn't care for life or anything that happened anymore.

I'd be interrogated, brought back, and then I'd sleep and continue to remember…

GLOSSARY CHARACTER

DALATREND

LEADERS
Taric – Former ruler of Dalatrend, nu-human, deceased

Zarda – Ruler of Dalatrend, nu-human

MILITARY
Rick – Nu-human experiment, general, deceased

Verra – Nu-human experiment, general, vendetta against Eira and Amara, deceased

Zo – Nu-human experiment, general, interested in Eira

REBELLION

COUNCIL
Adina (*ah-DEE-nah*) – Oversees Team 7, nu-human experiment, first Dalatrend shapeshifter experiment

Akama (*ah-KAH-mah*) – Oversees Team 5, nu-human experiment, first Dalatrend Seer experiment (not planned), twin to Enrée

Eldenar – Oversees Team 4, nu-human experiment, first Dalatrend war experiment

Elkron – Oversees Team 6, nu-human experiment, first Dalatrend elementalist experiment

Enrée (*EN-ree-ay*) – Oversees Team 2, nu-human experiment,
first Dalatrend Battle Psychic experiment (not planned), twin
to Akama

Genesis – Oversees Team 3, first nu-human, necromantic
abilities

Hanama (*HAH-nah-mah*) – Oversees Team 1, nu-human experiment, first Dalatrend anthropomorphic experiment

TEAM 1
Assassin based

Evynne (*Ev-een*) – Nu-human experiment

TEAM 2
Recruitment based

Dan – Nu-human experiment, former lieutenant to Eira

Innon (*EYE-nin*) – Battle leader, Nu-human experiment, former commander

TEAM 3
Income based, former Brute and foot soldier mostly

Andariel – Nu-human experiment, double ear prototype,
brother to Azriel, former medic, strip club owner: Midnight

Argus – Nu-human experiment, inventor

Aurora – Nu-human experiment, Underground computer tech

Azriel – Nu-human experiment, double ear prototype, brother
to Andariel, former medic, night club owner: Twilight

Blaze – Nu-human experiment

Eira (*AIR-uh*) – Nu-human hybrid experiment, battle leader,
former commander, assassin, fire shaman, mother to Ryder.
Alt names: Laz, Laz'shika (*laz-SHEE-kah*)

Lena – Nu-human, partner to Zenmar

Orchon (*OR-con*) – Nu-human, bouncer at Twilight

Raikidan (*RYE-ki-DAN*) – Black and red dragon, cousin to
Corliss, Guard in training

Rylan (*RYE-lan*) – Nu-human experiment, experimental

shapeshifter: wolf, former captain, artificial mental bond
with Eira, ice elementalist, interested in Ryoko

Ryoko (*Ree-OH-koh*) – Half-wogron experiment, clone of
Peacekeeper Ryoko, Brute, former lieutenant, best friend to
Eira, interested in Rylan

Seda (*SAY-duh*) – Nu-human experiment, psychic: Seer, twin
to Nioush

Xantar (*ZAN-tar*) – Nu-human experiment

Zane – Nu-human experiment, uncle to Eira, brother to Jasmine and Amara, former soldier, mechanic

Zenmar – Nu-human experiment, crippled in a skirmish,
partner to Lena

TEAM 4
Reconnaissance based

TEAM 5
Psychic based

Vek – Nu-human experiment, psychic: Battle Psychic, registered

TEAM 6
Research and development based

TEAM 7
Reconnaissance based

Chameleon – Nu-human experiment, molecular fusion ability,
former assassin

Doppelganger – Nu-human experiment, temporary cloning
ability

Ezhno (*EZ-no*) – Nu-human experiment, Underground computer tech

Mocha – Nu-human experiment, anthropomorphic: cat

Nioush (*NEE-oosh*) – Nu-human experiment, psychic: Battle
Psychic, twin to Seda

Raynn (*rain*) – Nu-human experiment, battle leader, former
general, clone if Peacekeeper Raynn

MOLES
    Ryder – Nu-human experiment, son to Eira and Rylan
    Talon – Nu-human experiment, bone spike ability

MERCENARIES
    Arnia (*ARE-nee-ah*) – Nu-human experiment, twin to Jaybird,
    metal elementalist, former mole
    Jaybird – Nu-human experiment, twin to Arnia, air elemental-
    ist, former mole

SHAMANS

NORTH TRIBE
    Fe'teline (*fey-TELL-een*) – Nu-human, fire shaman
    Ven'lar (*ven-LAR*) – Nu-human, healing shaman

SOUTH TRIBE
    Ir'esh (*EAR-esh*) – Chief, elf, father to Tla'lli, earth shaman
    Ne'kall (*nay-CALL*) – Elf, son to Del'karo and Alena, father
    of four, fire shaman
    Tla'lli (*teh-LAH-lee*) – Elf, daughter to Ir'esh, wind shaman

EAST TRIBE
    Nela – Nu-human, lightning shaman
    Se'lata (*say-LAH-tah*) – Elf, spice merchant, earth shaman

WEST TRIBE
    Alena – Elf, wife to Del'karo, mother figure to Eira, mother
    of Ne'kall and twelve other children, healer
    Daren – Human, Valene's adopted father, inn keeper, former
    partner to Valessa
    Del'karo (*del-CAR-oh*) – Elf, mentor and father figure to Eira,
    husband to Alena, father of Ne'kall and twelve other chil-
    dren, fire shaman
    Ken'ichi (*ken-EE-chee*) – Nu-human, friend to Eira, Guard and
    healer

Maka'shi (*mah-KAH-shee*) – Leader, half-elf, ice shaman, widow
Mel'ka (*mel-KAH*) – Elf, elder, storyteller, earth shaman
Shva'sika (*sh-VAH-see-KAH*) – Elf, sister to Xye, mentor and
    adopted family to Eira, lightning shaman
Valene (*Vah-LEEN*) – Human, daughter to Valessa, Eira's and
    Daren's adopted daughter, plant-based earth shaman
Valessa – Human, mother to Valene, former partner to Daren,
    earth shaman, deceased
Xye (*zeye*) – Half-elf, brother to Shva'sika, attempted to court
    Eira, healer, deceased

DRAGONS

Corliss – Green and black dragon, cousin to Raikidan

VELSARA WILDS CLAN
Anahak (*an-ah-HAWK*) – Black dragon, mate to Xaneth, father
    to Rimu and six other offspring
Rimu – Black and red dragon, son to Anahak and Xaneth
Xaneth (*zan-ETH*) – Red dragon, mate to Anahak, mother to
    Rimu and six other offspring
Zaith – Clan leader, red dragon

GODS

Anila (*ah-NEE-lah*) – Goddess of air
Arcadia (*are-KAY-dee-ah*) – Goddess of spirits
Genesis – Goddess of life, partner to Zoltan
Gina – Goddess of health and healing
Halcyon (*hall-SEE-on*) – Goddess of the sea
Imera (*eye-MEER-ah*) – Goddess of literature and knowledge
Jin – Goddess of refined earth
Kendaria – Goddess of water
Koseba (*koh-SAY-bah*) – God of shapeshifting
Le'carro (*ley-CAR-oh*) – God of lightning

Lunaria – Goddess of the moon
Nazir (*nah-ZEER*) – God of death and corruption
Phyre (*fire*) – God of fire
Raisu (*RAY-sue*) – God of dreams
Rashta (*RAH-sh-tah*) – Goddess of judgement and rebirth
Rasmus – God of love and fertility, partner to Savada
Satria (*sah-TREE-ah*) – Goddess of war
Savada (*sah-VAH-dah*) – Goddess of sex and seduction, partner
   to Rasmus
Sela – Goddess of psychics, sister of Tyro
Solstice – Goddess of ice and winter
Solund – God of the sun
Tarin – God of nature, partner to Valena
Tyro (*TIE-roh*) – God of psychics, brother of Sela
Valena – Goddess of earth, partner to Tarin
Zoltan – God of life, partner to Genesis

MISCELLANEOUS

Rosa (*ROH-sah*) – Succubus, mated to Zaedrix
Voice – Mysterious voice that speaks to Eira inside her head.
   Malevolent
Zaedrix (*ZAY-driks*) – Incubus, mated to Rosa

SPIRITS

Amara (*ah-MAR-ah*) – Nu-human experiment, general, mother
   to Eira, grandmother to Ryder, sister to Jasmine and Zane,
   water elementalist, deceased
Jade – Nu-human experiment, former soldier under Amara,
   deceased
Jasmine – Nu-human experiment, aunt to Eira, sister to Amara
   and Zane, geneticist, deceased
Tannek – Nu-human experiment, former soldier under Amara,
   deceased
Zeek – Nu human, former soldier under Amara, deceased

PEACEKEEPERS

Assar – dwarf, deceased

Pyralis (*PIE-ral-iss*) – Red dragon, former Velsara Wild Clan leader, deceased

Raynn (*rain*) – Human, deceased

Reiki (*Ray-KEY*) – Green dragon, deceased

Ryoko (*Ree-OH-koh*) – Half-wogron, earth shaman, deceased

Varro – Elf, healer, deceased

GLOSSARY LANGUAGE

ELVISH

Elvish is an eloquent language, light on the tongue with an airy sound. Even the usual consonants of common don't hold the same harshness in Elvish. Many elves and other humanoids raised with Elvish as their mother tongue carry this light speech over in their common.

While not the easiest language to learn, Elvish is a favorite among the linguistically gifted. Those who seek to learn this language seek out elves before any other race and are taught by full immersion. Some elves will provide a few words for the humanoid to start with but it's not common to do so. The elves believe this technique is the best way to learn and creates a better understanding of the language for everyday use.

Written Elvish is just as elegant as spoken, usually written in script by native speakers. Non-natives tend to forgo the script, which is accepted by native speakers, though the handwriting is still expected to be neat, and flourished on important documents. Sloppy writing is considered an insult.

DRACONIC

Draconic is a guttural language made up most of grunts and growls with the occasional tongue flick, exhales, or teeth clatter. It's difficult for a non-dragon to learn, as the formation of these words are foreign to most humanoids. Some sounds are impossible for non-dragons to create so other sounds are substituted as an alternative. Even dragons taking a humanoid form must make these changes. Rarely is a humanoid able to perfect the speech, even when raised among dragons.

Those attempting to learn are always taught single words before attempting sentence structures. Draconic sentence structure is similar to Common, but with a possessive edge due to the mindset of dragons. There are no contracted words in Draconic, as such, dragons who don't speak common often, tend to use the same sentence structures of their mother tongue when they do speak common.

It's not common for dragons to write in the current age but there is a basic written form of the language that was used more extensively in the past. This written form is comprised of glyphs easily created with dragon claws and easy to decipher for most dragons no matter the cleanliness of the script. Non-dragons find this writing easier to learn than the spoken language and most of the time will stop learning after they've master it.

Phrases translated to Eira in the series:

> *Ion cuvk* – Our kind
> *Lazmira, sa xruzk* – Lazmira, my child
> *Zity, gyexy, lgunum, ziaeza, lynyvuma, lmnyvwmr, fulkis*
>   – Love, peace, spirit, loyalty, serenity, strength,
>   wisdom

LOST LANGUAGES

Thought the history of Lumaraeon, language has developed and died, but some have left a more notable impact on the races. These forgotten languages hold important information lost during the millennia of turmoil making them important topics for scholars.

OLD TONGUE

Old Tongue, also known as God speech, is the most ancient form of speech that was replaced by the various languages of Lumaraeon, ultimately dying out among the mortal races. Much of the language was lost during the War of End and with no one but the gods around to remember, the language was thought dead. Until a large find of books in the Eternal Library turned up after a new entryway was found, eight hundred years ago.

Scholars have done their best to decipher the old language and have since found new discovery sites all over Lumaraeon to help with their research. But while the tongue is researched, it is not know if the translations are quite right, and no one has thought to ask the gods, not even Imera, the goddess of literature and knowledge.

ABOUT THE AUTHOR

Shannon Pemrick, is a full-time USA Today bestselling author, and fuller-time geek and dragon obsessed. She also has too many novelty mugs, not enough chocolate, and a forbidden love-affair with all things shiny.

Shannon resides in Southern New Hampshire with her overly sarcastic husband and one too many pets who steal all her bed space. When she's not burning her fingers across a keyboard or trying to squeeze into a spot on the couch for movie night, she's rolling dice and getting lost in RPGs or searching for brides for her dragon overlords.

You can learn more about Shannon by visiting her website at:
Shannonpemrick.com